Praise for
UNTAMED

"Addicting and heart pounding—you won't be able to put it down until you've devoured every word."

—Christina Lauren, *New York Times* bestselling author

"Sexy, heartbreaking, and hilarious, UNTAMED is an epic emotional roller coaster. It has all the feels! If you loved Kellan Kyle, hold on tight—Griffin will rock your world! He's cocky, sexy, hilarious, frustrating, and surprisingly tender. My heart pounded for him, broke with him, and ultimately soared. Loved it from beginning to end! UNTAMED is an automatic reread!"

—Emma Chase, *New York Times* bestselling author

"No one writes a sexy rock star better than S. C. Stephens. Griffin will rock your world!"

—Kristen Proby, *New York Times* bestselling author

"S. C. Stephens does it again! Griffin is every delicious book boyfriend fantasy come to life! Stephens takes you on a wild ride of love, lust, and self-discovery that's both passionate and heartbreaking. This book was pure magic!"

—Jennifer Probst, *New York Times* bestselling author

"S. C. Stephens knows how to keep a reader turning the pages. From the first page to the last, every wiseass inch of Griffin unspooled my heart. Dare I say he's trumped Kellan Kyle? I do! Pure deliciousness!"

—Gail McHugh, *New York Times* bestselling author

"A sexy, witty, yet poignant story that will seep inside you and pull at your heartstrings. This book will make you laugh, cry, and everything in-between."

—Kim Karr, *New York Times* bestselling author

Praise for
THOUGHTFUL

"S. C. Stephens at her best! A sigh-worthy romance you will never forget, *Thoughtful* is full of her trademark emotion and toe-curling tension. A brilliant look into the mind of one of our most beloved book boyfriends. I consumed it; it consumed me. I didn't want it to end."

—Katy Evans, *New York Times* bestselling author

"Just when you thought you couldn't love Kellan Kyle more, S. C. Stephens makes you fall in love with him all over again. In typical fashion, S. C. draws you in, makes you feel like you are part of the story, and doesn't let you go until the very last page. Emotional and addictive, it's a story you'll come back to time and again. Superb!"

—K. Bromberg, *New York Times* bestselling author

"*Thoughtful* is an emotional roller coaster ride, and Kellan Kyle is going to make you swoon and sigh in the most delicious ways."

—Lisa Renee Jones, *New York Times* bestselling author

Untamed

Untamed

S. C. STEPHENS

FOREVER

New York Boston

Forever
Hachette Book Group
1290 Avenue of the Americas
New York, NY 10104

www.HachetteBookGroup.com

Printed in the United States of America

RRD-C

First Edition: November 2015

10 9 8 7 6 5 4 3 2 1

Forever is an imprint of Grand Central Publishing.
The Forever name and logo are trademarks of Hachette Book Group, Inc.

The Hachette Speakers Bureau provides a wide range of authors for speaking events. To find out more, go to www.hachettespeakersbureau.com or call (866) 376-6591.

The publisher is not responsible for websites (or their content) that are not owned by the publisher.

Library of Congress Cataloging-in-Publication Data

Stephens, S. C.

Untamed / S. C. Stephens. —First edition.

    pages ; cm.— (A thoughtless novel ; 5)

ISBN 978-1-4555-8884-8 (softcover) — ISBN 978-1-4789-0314-7 (audio download) — ISBN 978-1-4555-8886-2 (ebook) 1. Rock musicians—Fiction. 2. Man-woman relationships—Fiction. I. Title.

PS3619.T476769U58 2015

813'.6—dc23

2015028087

This book goes out to all the Griffin fans who ceaselessly asked for more, more, more! Since his first appearance in *Thoughtless*, you've laughed with him, laughed *at* him, and watched him grow. If you haven't already, I hope you completely fall in love with him after reading *Untamed*. I know I have.

Acknowledgments

Aside from Kellan Kyle, Griffin has to be my favorite D-Bag. Everything he does makes me laugh. But what I really love the most about him is the growth he's had over the course of the series. Finding a way to continue that growth for him was tricky, but I think *Untamed* accomplishes that, and I'm very proud of his journey.

This book would not have been possible without the love and support of my readers. Thank you for being so patient with me! I know my books take a while to get to you, but I hope you find them worth the wait. Each one represents countless hours, numerous doubts and fears, and more than a few tears. Writing is not an easy profession, but seeing the final product and hearing your praise and encouragement makes all the blood, sweat, and carpal tunnel worth it.

I would like to thank all the authors who have supported me. For this being such a competitive business, I've never felt anything but encouraged by my peers. To K. A. Linde—my friend, my sounding board, and my rock—I adore you! To Nicky Charles—the reason I self-published in the first place—I can't thank you enough for showing me the ropes. To Jenn Sterling and Rebecca Donovan—the two of you are bright spots in my day. Thank you so much for your endless sweetness! To Katy Evans—your tweets and retweets always make me smile. Thank you for sharing me with your fans! To K. Bromberg—my release-day buddy! You have such a beautiful soul. Thank you for sharing your day with me in such a kind and generous way. To Sunniva Dee, Danielle Jamie, Alexa Keith, Alex Rose, and more—thank you for sharing your stories, your excitement, and your support! And much love to the authors who move and inspire me—Jillian Dodd, C. J. Roberts, Kristen Proby, Tara Sivec, Nicole Williams, Tarryn Fisher, T. Gephart, Katie Ashley, Karina Halle, Christina Lauren, Colleen Hoover, Abbi Glines, Jamie McGuire, A. L. Jackson, Tammara Webber, Emma Chase, Kyra Davis, Kim Karr, Claire Contreras, Cora Carmack, and so many more!

A huge heartfelt thank-you to the bloggers who have endlessly supported me—*Totally Booked Blog, Flirty and Dirty Book Blog, Fictional Boyfriends, Schmexy Girl Book Blog, Three Chicks and Their Books, The Rock Stars of Romance, Shh Mom's Reading, Kayla the Bibliophile, Maryse's Book Blog, Brandee's Book Endings, Martini Times Romance, The Autumn Review, SubClub Books, Sammie's Book Club, Lori's Book Blog, The Book Enthusiast, Bookish Temptations, Verna Loves Books, The Book Bar, A Literary Perusal, We Like It Big Book Blog, Bare Naked Words, Fictional Men's Page, Love N. Books, Vilma's Book Blog, Southern Belle Book Blog, Kindle Crack Book Reviews, One Click Bliss, Kricket's Chirps, Perusing Princesses, Talkbooks Blog, BJ's Book Blog, Nancy's Romance Reads, The Literary Gossip,* and many, many, many more!

Much love to the tweeters and posters who make going online so entertaining—Janet, Shelley, Christine, Sue, Simmi, SL, Jamie, Bianca, Jane, Jasmin, Tam, Deb, Keisha, Tiffany, Joanne, Katie, Ellen, Denise, Erin, Natalie, Lisa, Charleen, Nicky, LJ, Nic, Sharon, AM, Laayna, Christy, Liis, Glorya, Gerb, Chelcie, Sam, and way too many more to name! Your frequent messages warm my heart, make me laugh, and lift my spirits!

To all the *Thoughtless* support groups and fan pages out there—just knowing these exist is surreal. Thank you for all the time, effort, and passion that you pour into your pages!

I cannot fully express my thanks to my agent, Kristyn Keene of ICM Partners—your help and guidance on this book were invaluable! As were the numerous pep talks and words of encouragement that you shared over the last year. There were times when I sorely needed the boost! Many thanks to my amazing Forever/Grand Central Publishing family—Beth deGuzman, Marissa Sangiacomo, Julie Paulauski, and Jamie Snider. You've all made me feel so loved and welcome! And a special thank-you to Megha Parekh, for your mad editing skills!

And lastly, much love to my friends and family for their endless patience. Especially when a deadline has me scrambling out the door, canceling at the last minute, or locked in my office all night. So sorry!! And to my kids…you have no idea how much I love you…but please stop screaming at the top of your lungs, or coming up to me and saying, "Mom, hey Mom…hi," when I'm trying to finish a scene. Just kidding. I will always make time for you. ♥

Untamed

Chapter 1

There Is No Cure for Awesome

I wasn't one to brag, but I had a good life. Screw that. I *was* one to brag and I was going to do it as often and as loudly as I could, because I had the greatest fucking life in all the history of great lives. Not many people could boast like I could boast. Not many people were in the most successful band in the world. Just me. Oh, and my bandmates. I guess. Whatever.

And in thirteen days, eighteen hours, thirty-two minutes, I was going to be on the road again. The summer tour for the D-Bags' second number-one album was coming up fast, and I was itching to get started. I'd waited in the background long enough, been playing an instrument that had been assigned to me long enough. This tour, everything was going to change. It was my time to play lead guitar, my moment to shine in the spotlight. I was going to rule that fucking stage, and no one was going to stop me.

When I first joined the D-Bags a few years ago, I had been under the completely logical assumption that once my overall awesomeness was known, I would replace my cousin as the lead guitarist; I'd even told the guys as much when we'd officially formed the band. And even though Matt had agreed with me, telling me, "Whatever you say, Griffin," the band had yet to give me a shot at being the musical star. They'd shoved me in the bassist position and then left me there. I belonged front and center—lead guitarist was practically tattooed on my forehead! All the guys knew it, and whenever I brought up the fact that Matt and I should switch instruments, they blew off my request with ridiculous comments like, "Matt has more talent." Whatever. My left nut had more talent than Matt; he wished he was as awesome as me. The guys were all just worried that they'd be forgotten if I was really given a chance to shine. Well, fuck that. I didn't plan on staying in the shadows for long. Nobody put the Hulk in the corner. Nobody.

Thankfully, I had been blessed with panty-dropping good looks, a smoking physique, more sexual know-how than an A-list hooker, and more talent in my pinkie finger than most possessed in their entire bodies. I was a lucky son of a bitch too, and things had a way of working out for me. I guess I had good karma or some shit, because even bad situations ended up being fucktastic. Take my childhood. When my mom found out she was pregnant with me, we lived in Wichita. Yep. I was almost born in fucking Kansas. Kansas! But my dad lost his job and we had to move in with his brother, so I ended up being squeezed out in the Land of Spotlights—Los Angeles. Straight out of the womb, I'd been destined for greatness.

Even at a young age, being a rock star had appealed to me—I dressed up as Gene Simmons for six Halloweens in a row. I think it was the idea of millions of people screaming my name, crying when they saw me, idolizing me. The thought of being put on a pedestal was intoxicating. Who wouldn't want that? Plus, what profession, outside of porn and prostitution, guaranteed you all the sex you could handle? None that I could think of.

But I supposed Matt was the real reason for my career choice. We'd lived together for the first eight years of our lives, then we'd lived on the same street, then we'd moved out together. Even though we drove each other crazy more often than not, we were almost always around each other. There was no one I liked making fun of more than Matt. And for as long as I could remember, Matt had been obsessed with music. Like, unhealthily obsessed. On-the-verge-of-needing-an-intervention obsessed.

When we were preteens, he used to say shit like, "Music is life," and "Everything else is just background noise." I think crap like that was why Matt had been a virgin until he was nineteen. And a half. He'd devoted his entire young life to music, but what he'd failed to realize was that music was just a means to an end. From the beginning of time, music was only designed to do one thing—get people laid. *Sex* was life…literally…and everything *else* was just background noise. After Matt's first time, I think he started to understand that fact. He'd certainly eased off on the "Music fuels the world" comments.

Unlike me, Matt hadn't really planned on being a rock star though. He'd thought it was a pipe dream, but I'd known it was inevitable. All we had to do was wait for the right moment. Wait for fate to find us. And it had.

After high school, I'd kept my options open. It used to drive my parents crazy that I hadn't done anything productive after I graduated—by the skin of my teeth. I'd sort of ambled around for a couple of years like a lost degenerate. That's what my sister said anyway, but I'd known what I was doing. Timing was everything, and I couldn't take the risk of being stuck at some lame-ass job when fate came knocking on my door. It wasn't laziness, it was preparedness. I needed to be free, to be one with the winds of change, or some poetic shit like that. I had to be ready. And it was a good thing I was too, because if I'd had commitments I couldn't get out of, Matt and I never would have been able to form a band with Kellan and Evan.

We met them at a strip club. It wasn't often that I could get my cousin to go out for a little bump and grind with me, but after a few shots at the bar, I could have talked Matt into anything. Fucking lightweight. Matt, as always, was completely uncomfortable being around mostly naked girls. Because I cared about his personal growth, and because it was hilarious to watch him turn bright red, I did what I could to help him with the girls. We were kicked out of the club twenty minutes later. It wasn't my fault though. I mean, how was I supposed to know that bringing a pogo stick up on stage was frowned upon? In my humble opinion, I thought I was improving the show.

Evan and Kellan had been at the club that night and had found us in the parking lot after we were rudely evicted. As usual, Matt was whining when they'd approached us—something about how much of an idiot I was. I don't know, I hadn't really been listening. But after introductions, the conversation had shifted to music, and Matt had finally been in seventh heaven. He was happier discussing music styles with a bunch of dudes than he had been watching silicone jugs jiggling up and down in front of our faces. I'd suspected it for years but had known without a doubt in that moment that Matt was completely out of his mind and would never be right in the head.

The two of us had signed on with Kellan and Evan and—boom!—the D-Bags were born. And I discovered that, as I'd predicted, music was a surefire path to sex. And, oh my God…there was so much sex to be had! Backstage sex. Parking lot sex. Wall sex. Bathroom sex. Whips and chains sex. Cosplay sex. One-night stands. Threesomes. Orgies. *And a partridge in a pear tree.*

It was a never-ending smorgasbord of carnal delight. All I had to say was, "I'm in a band," and whatever chick I was talking to was instantly intrigued. It was so easy it was almost *too* easy. No, not really. It was fucking amazing and I loved every second of it.

The only thing that put a slight damper on the awesomeness of my life was my inferior position in the band. The guys had no idea what a gift they had in me, and even though I told them repeatedly that I deserved a shot on lead guitar, time and time again, they kept holding me back. That was my only real complaint about being in the band. Oh, that and fucking Kellan routinely stealing my pussy! Even when I called dibs! Before he went and got all "domesticated," that used to really piss me off. And then, to make things even worse, the fucking thief wouldn't even share sex stories. *If you're gonna swipe my slit, asshole, at least have the common courtesy to share the deets!*

But no, Kellan would get all weird and tight-lipped. Almost embarrassed. Didn't make sense to me at the time. Still didn't—I sang that shit from the rooftops! But, then again, I was amazing in bed. I was such a good lay, even *I* wanted to sleep with me. Kellan probably sucked at it. He only got the chicks because he had the "lead singer" badge. The girls probably cried afterward it was so horri-ble. Yeah, that made sense. Poor pathetic asshole. Maybe I should cut him some slack? Nah. It was his obligation as the front man to be good at sex. If he couldn't hack it, I'd gladly replace him. I could sing *and* thrust my hips. Easy as nailing an unsatisfied wife after Mother's Day. Yeah…I could totally do it. Fuck being lead guitarist. I could be lead *everything*.

I pictured myself standing in the center of the stage, the fans hollering, jumping up and down, flashing their tits as they screamed my name. Kellan shrank into the background, smaller and smaller, until finally the darkness at the back of the stage swallowed him whole. I could only see shadowy, fingerlike shapes lightly flicking the bass line strings. He was messing up the song, but I let it go…because I was awesome like that. I'd talk to him about it later though, maybe give him extra rehearsals. Ha!

It was hot under the center lights, but I loved it. The heat was like a lover's fingers over my bare skin. If only I were naked, so I could feel the warm vibrations everywhere. The crowd would go crazy for that. They were already clambering to get to me; secu-rity was having a hell of a time keeping them back. By the looks on their faces, I knew that if they did make it up on stage, they would tear me to pieces. Being mauled to death with love, lust, and desire…not a bad way to go.

They started chanting my name, over and over. "Griffin! Griffin! Griffin!" I held up my hand to appease them…

"Griffin…do you have a question?"

My vision of writhing fans evaporated as a pair of emerald-green eyes came into focus. Anna. My gorgeous, sensual goddess of a wife. "No…I wasn't listening. Can you start over?" The full lips below the penetrating eyes frowned, but I knew she wasn't really all that upset. My mind often wandered; she was used to it.

It still surprised me some that I had taken the plunge, cut my-self off from the pack, picked just one type of cereal to eat. Forever. But when the cereal in question was chocolate-coated chocolate flakes dipped in fudge and covered with chocolate sprinkles, it really wasn't that much of a sacrifice.

Anna and I had met several years ago, before the D-Bags were big. She'd thought I was the shit, even back then, when the pool I'd been floating in wasn't all that deep. I dug her even more for that. I'd dug her, but that hadn't stopped me from banging babes after we hooked up. Not even after we'd repeatedly hooked up. Her either. Anna and I'd had a whenever-works-for-you-works-for-me relationship, and I had continued reveling in eager-to-please groupies for a long time. But then, somehow—and I'm still not sure how—everything had started to change. After being with Anna, every other girl had left me wanting. The two of us together were explosive. No, mind-blowing. No…life-altering. I supposed that was why no one else could compare. Anna just got me, and fully satisfied me like nobody else.

Other girls…well, it was like drinking from the ocean with them. Sure, the momentary ache was gone, but I felt worse afterward. Thirstier. I'd just wanted Anna, all the fucking time, and nobody else would do. Admitting I was whipped was the hardest fucking thing I'd ever done, but denying it was getting me nowhere. Anna was enough for me. No, she was *it* for me. So I fucking married her before anybody else could.

Anna sighed, making her lips part in such an erotic way that I almost got distracted with another vision. *God, her mouth on me right now would be fantastic. I wonder if what she has to say could be said naked?* I didn't see why not. She was already halfway there. I was sitting on a large, rectangular ottoman in our walk-in closet while she picked out something to wear for the day. All she'd picked out so far was a black bra with matching black underwear, and even though they were stretchy, supportive maternity underwear, they were hot. I wanted them in my teeth.

"The tour…I decided to come with you. Gibson and I both. Plus Newbie. We're all three coming with you." She placed her hands on the sides of her stomach, outlining the shape of the baby in her belly. Our second kid. According to the doctors, it was another girl, but since those fuckers had told us Gibson was a boy right up until the day *she* was born, we weren't holding our breath on this one. We'd know what the baby was when Anna popped him/her out.

I shrugged. "Okay, sounds awesome." Made no difference to me. In fact, it would make my life a little easier if she did come. I wouldn't have to jack off so much. Although I might have to right now if she bent over again. *Sweet Jesus, my wife is a fucking master-piece.*

Anna turned back to the rod holding hundreds of outfits. I swear she had more clothes than most department stores. This wasn't even our only closet. There was one off the master bathroom too, and another one in an unused guest room that she used. It was almost ridiculous, but she looked so fucking good in everything she owned, I never complained about it. Even still, as good as she looked all decked out, she looked even better naked.

She already had her shoes picked out for the day; she was holding them in her hand while she flipped through her fashion choices. They were black high heels that would make her legs look a mile long. I was getting hard just thinking of her wearing them. Why the hell hadn't she put them on yet? She was teasing me...

Twisting her head to me, her long brown hair seductively curling around her shoulder, she said, "Kiera and Ryder are going too, so Gibson will have someone to play with...not that Ryder does much yet. He's only nine months old. Still, at least she'll have someone to keep her entertained besides us, you know?"

I nodded so she would think I was paying attention, but I really wasn't. She'd mentioned Kellan's kid and his super-rigid wife, but that was about all I got. I was too busy picturing what Anna's ass would look like when she put those shoes on. Uncomfortable things were starting to rub together, and I adjusted how I was sitting while she continued.

"There are two buses for the bands, plus Kellan and Kiera's private bus. Matt is sharing a bus with Avoiding Redemption, but I think Evan is riding with Holeshot and that new band...Staring at the Wall. Kiera said we could stay on her bus if we want, instead of riding with the rest of the guys." She looked back at me with a smirk on her lips. "Well, actually, what she said was Gibson and I could ride with her and Kellan...and if you *had* to, you could ride with us...for a leg or two. So long as they were short legs."

That got my attention, and I glanced up from her outstanding ass to look at her amused face. "Fuck that. I'm riding you the entire time. Fuck whoever tries to get me off you." She raised an eyebrow in question and I automatically shook my head. "You heard me right. I'm riding *you*." I waggled my eyebrows to make it even more suggestive, in case she'd missed it. She hadn't though. My wife had a mind nearly as dirty as mine.

Anna shrugged as she refocused her attention on her clothes. Pulling out a sunshine-yellow dress, she said, "Kiera will be thrilled… but I'd rather ride you too, so she'll just have to deal."

Twisting around, she placed the dress against her body like she was modeling it for me. I tilted my head, like I was really deciding if I liked it. I wasn't. Anything she wore was awesome, so I didn't care what it was. I had another, far more interesting reason to act like I cared though, one that could pay off big for me. Before she even asked my opinion on the dress, I gave her one. "I'm not sure…I need to see the shoes first."

She set the shoes down and started to slip the dress on but I stopped her. "No, no…just the shoes." I kept my voice intentionally low and husky. Anna lifted her eyes to mine, and a playful lust flickered to life in her eyes. With a sexuality that rivaled only my own, she removed the dress and slipped on her heels. She struck a swimsuit-model pose when she was done and my cock stiffened to full readiness.

Goddamn, she was so hot. Even eighty million months pregnant, she was the sexiest thing around. I wanted her to rip her underwear off and straddle me. She could leave the shoes on. *Fuck yeah.*

"I want you to strip and ride my cock," I bluntly told her. "But leave the heels," I added. One of the greatest things about being in a relationship with Anna was the fact that I didn't have to sugarcoat anything. If I wanted her to suck me off, all I had to do was ask. She might not do it, if she wasn't in the mood, but she never freaked out about me asking her shit like that. Even if we were in the checkout line at Walmart, she was cool about it.

With an intrigued half smile on her lips, she sauntered toward me. She played with a long dark curl while she walked, and the throbbing in my pants got so bad, I had to give myself a good rub to make it simmer down.

"We're late, baby," she murmured, as she stepped in front of me.

"Fuck if I care," I said, leaning back onto my elbows on the ottoman. *Yes, do it. I want you.*

Leaning over me, she placed her hands on my thighs to support herself, giving me an outstanding view of her cleavage. I bet the view of her backside right now was equally spectacular. *Fuck.* Why the hell weren't there any mirrors in here? I needed to rectify that immediately.

"Matt will have your head if you're late to rehearsal again," she said. Then she licked her bottom lip and bit it. The soft skin shone in the lights, calling to me. I needed those lips on me. Everywhere.

"I don't give a shit about what Matt does to my head. You, on the other hand..." I thrust my hips up a little, just in case she'd missed that innuendo too. Again, she hadn't. My girl was a hell of a lot smarter than me.

With a smile that even Angelina Jolie would be jealous of, Anna started lowering her head. My eyes widened as her lips approached my zipper. She placed a soft kiss on the ridge of my cock straining against my jeans. She might as well have touched me with a cattle prod. The jolt sent a delicious sizzle throughout my body, and I felt a faint wetness coat the tip of my dick. I was so ready for her. I was about to start begging if she didn't do more than just kiss me. No, not *about* to beg. I *would* beg; I was man enough.

"Please, baby. I want that gorgeous mouth over me, tracing me, teasing me. Then I want that beautiful body on top of me, so I can slide inside you. I want to feel your wet pussy tighten all around me, while we start to move..." I lifted my hand over my lap, then made a rocking motion, like I was holding on to her hips, guiding her, moving her faster and faster... "Oh yeah, just like that, baby."

I was doing such a good job of mimicking the movement that I could almost feel the buildup starting. Damn, could I come without even touching her? Maybe, but that wouldn't be nearly as satisfying.

Anna let out a throaty chuckle as her hands slid up to my zipper. "You say the hottest things, Griffin," she said in a low voice. I stilled my hips as her fingers pulled back the metal holding my beast in place. Damn thing was about to destroy the town if she didn't tame it soon.

Once I was free, I lay back on the ottoman and let my head hit the cushion. I was growing out my chin-length hair, and I'd put it into a low ponytail. That was pretty uncomfortable to lie on, so I yanked the band out while Anna adjusted my underwear and released me. I hissed in a breath as her fingers touched the throbbing, sensitive skin. "Fuck, yeah…"

I closed my eyes so the haphazard pile of clothes scattered around the room wouldn't distract me. With my sight out of the picture, my other senses sharpened. I could feel the cooler air on my cock, feel Anna's fingernails lightly scratching my abdomen, and hear the mixture of my light groans and Anna's seductive purrs. "Ready, baby?" she whispered.

"Yes," I groaned, reaching down to grab her hair. *Now…*

A jolt went through me when her tongue touched my cock, then a groan escaped me. "Fuck, that feels so good…" She lightly ran up the shaft, then flicked the piercing at the top. I groaned again. I wanted this so bad, all of my senses were amplified. The tiniest touch felt like a lightning strike of sensation. "More… please…"

And that was when my heightened senses heard something terrible. Awful. Ill-timed.

In the next room, a baby monitor was resting on Anna's nightstand. It had been on this entire time, but I hadn't been paying attention to it. Anna either. But now, it was sort of impossible to ignore. A high-pitched, metallic-sounding squeal was blaring from it. "Mommmmmmmmmmmmmma! Want out!"

The sound of Gibson's voice put Anna instantly on parental alert. I looked at her right as she looked at me, and I knew the raging cock between us had been all but forgotten. "Gibby's up from her nap. I gotta get her."

Sitting up, I grabbed her hand as she straightened. Bringing her fingers to my protesting member, I pleaded, "Five minutes won't hurt her."

Anna giggled but pulled away. "Sorry, babe. I don't like leaving her up there. And besides, she'll scream the entire time, and you know that will throw you off."

I pursed my lips, wanting to argue with her but knowing I couldn't. There were times when just hearing Gibson cooing through the monitor made it impossible for me to come. I had to shut the damn thing off, and Anna hated it when I did that. And she was right anyway. Gibson had a set of lungs on her, and if we didn't come set her free from her bedroom prison, she'd just get louder and louder; turning off the monitor wouldn't make a lick of difference.

I fell back on the ottoman, and my forgotten love stick started drooping. Such a waste of a perfectly good erection. "Fine." I'd just been cock-blocked by my own daughter. What. The. Hell.

Anna slipped on the lemon-colored dress; it clung to her curves, making my cock reconsider rising. Gibson screamed again though, and it plummeted back to earth. Once she was dressed, Anna gave my cheek a quick kiss. "You should get dressed. We've gotta go."

I raised my hand in a gesture of irritation and agreement. Whatever. It was all downhill from here. Anna watched me for a second, then leaned down and placed her lips against my ear. "As soon as Gibson goes down for the night, we'll come back here and I'll finish what I started." She licked the inside of my ear and a huge smile broke over my lips. Today was the best day ever.

Once Anna was gone, I rubbed my forlorn semi. "Sorry, Hulkster. Gotta put you away for later."

Peeking down at myself, I could have sworn I heard my dick answer me. *But you promised I'd get to play!* Frowning, I tucked myself back into my pants. "I'm not stupid enough to make promises. To anybody. Or any*thing*," I amended, since I *was* talking to my junk. That was something I'd learned early on. If you never swore your life to anything, you couldn't get bitten in the ass by it later. It was human nature to go back on your word; that was why I never gave it.

Even my wedding vows had had all the pertinent pledges removed. Anna and I had tied the knot in some city hall back East…somewhere. I don't remember where. Our ceremony had been just us and the judge, and it had been about as simple as it could be. Basically, it had gone something like this—*Anna, do you take this douche to be your husband? Yeah, I do. Griffin, do you take this knockout to be your wife? Sure, why not.* And that was all the promise we'd given each other. It was all that was needed.

When Anna came back into the room, I was my usual self—just a half chub was trying to poke through my jeans. But even that faded when I saw the little miracle in my wife's arms. "Daddy!" Gibson tossed her hands my way and leaned so hard in my direction that Anna had to struggle to hold on to her. Gibson's little face scrunched with annoyed concentration while she fought against her mom. Then, with a pout that only a little kid could make adorable, she turned and scowled at Anna. "Want Daddy." She said it as a command, not a request. Gibson was only around a year and a half, but she already knew what she wanted, and she fully expected to get her way. She was so much like me, it was scary.

Anna rolled her eyes but stepped closer so Gibson could reach me. When her little hands touched my skin, they suddenly became razor-like talons. Like an eagle securing a fish from the sea, Gibson clamped onto my forearm with a surprising amount of freakish strength. "Ow, shit! Relax, Gibs. I'm right here."

Grunting, I pulled her into my side and examined what was left of my arm. I half expected to see a mutilated flap of skin hanging off the bone. Instead, all I saw were bright red streaks where she'd raked me. Anna winced. "Guess I need to cut her nails. Sorry."

I shrugged. "The day isn't truly awesome until a gorgeous girl has scratched me up. I wear my war wounds with pride." Looking at the design she'd left behind, I added, "I might actually get this one tattooed on me. How cool would permanent shred marks be?"

Anna smiled, then shook her head. "No, if you want claw marks to tattoo, I'll give you some good ones. Then every time you look at them, you can remember how you got them."

"Damn…yeah, that's a much better plan. Fuck, you have the best ideas."

Gibson grabbed my nose and pulled my attention her way, where she liked it. Girl had a jealous streak a mile wide. Looking at her was like looking at a miniature version of me, if I were a girl. She had the same light blue eyes, same blond hair, although hers was a pristine platinum color while mine was a little dirtier. As it should be. She gave me a smile full of shiny white teeth, then spouted, "Fuck."

Anna crossed her arms over her chest, but her expression was more amused than annoyed. "I think we're at the point where we need to start watching our language."

I looked past Gibson to Anna. "Watch my language? You might as well ask me to hop on one foot while reciting the alphabet backwards. I can't police myself like that twenty-four/seven. I'm exhausted just thinking about it."

Anna swished her hands at Gibson. "Well, she's starting to copy you, and if we don't put a stop to it now, she's going to start calling people cocksuckers soon."

I started laughing. "That…would be so awesome."

Anna put her hands on her hips; true irritation was starting to edge out her amusement now. "No, it wouldn't be." She smiled. "Well, yeah, it kind of would be, but as parents, we have to put a stop to that kind of stuff." She sighed. "Well, we should try anyway."

Looking back at Gibson, I frowned. "I suppose I could try." Even though I was sure she didn't have a clue what we were talking about, Gibson laid her head on my shoulder, wrapped her arms around my neck, and patted my back like she was encouraging me. Yeah, if it would help Gibson, I would try to control my mouth. There wasn't much I wouldn't do for that little girl.

The three of us started heading toward the bedroom. Anna grabbed her purse off the bed; the covers were rumpled and falling off, but neither one of us had bothered to fix it. Why put it together if we were just going to mess it up again? That was my philosophy anyway, and Anna seemed to agree with it. We had a tendency to think alike, which really freaked me the fuck out.

As Anna slipped the strap of her mammoth bag onto her shoulder, she looked over at me. I'd shifted Gibson onto my back and I was bouncing her up and down…like a pogo stick. Mmmm, I loved pogo sticks.

"Before I forget, your dad called." She frowned after she said it, and I wondered if Pops had done or said something to piss her off. It wouldn't surprise me. Dad had no filter. Mom said it ran in the family. Whatever.

"Yeah? And what did that fucker want?"

Anna sighed, indicating Gibson with her hand. I scratched my head as I thought of a more kid-friendly way to put it. Minding my tongue was a pain in the ass. "Uh, what did that…feller…want?"

Anna laughed at my cheesy fill-in word, then frowned again. Rubbing her stomach, she said, "They want to come up for the birth. All of them. And they want to stay here."

Well of course they did. My place was fucking fantastic, much nicer than the shitholes my family called home. Once the money from our second album had started pouring in, I'd done what anybody in my position would have done. I'd contacted a real estate agent and told her to find me the most expensive house in Seattle. Sadly, we hadn't ended up buying that one, but the one Anna and I had settled on was definitely in the top ten. This place was outrageous, outlandish, and way too big for just three people, or four, or ten. I loved it.

I wasn't the only D-Bag who had invested in real estate. Kellan and Kiera had a huge secluded place north of Seattle, in the middle of BFE, and Matt and Rachel had a swanky condo downtown, with an amazing view of the pier and the Ferris wheel. Both of those spreads had required a ton of dough, although neither was as pricey as my place. Evan was the only one who'd bought a modest home. He'd actually purchased his old loft. Well, his loft and the auto body shop beneath it. He'd converted the business into extra living space and an art studio for Jenny. It was cool. I guess. Kellan

hadn't liked the fact that Evan had done that though. That particular auto body shop had been the only place Kellan had trusted to
look after his car. Pansy. It was a car, get over it already. And he
had, eventually. Although he'd hired the chick mechanic to be his
personal car person. Hmmm, I needed a girl in my garage, wearing
a bikini, covered in grease, looking over my hot rods. Ha-ha! Hot
rod…

"Griffin…? Did you hear what I said?"

Shaking my head, I snapped out of my dirty-girl fantasy. "Uh,
yeah, Mom and Pops are coming for a visit. Sounds cool."

Anna sighed. "They're *all* coming, Griffin. Your mom, dad,
brother, sister, nieces, aunts, uncles, cousins. It's going to be chaos,
and that's the last thing I need when I'm sleep deprived."

I gave her a sympathetic smile, even though it didn't sound like
a big deal to me. "It will be fine. This place is huge; you'll barely see
them. They'll probably spend most of the time at the pool anyway."
The house had an indoor Olympic-sized pool with a ten-person
hot tub right next to it. A selling point for me.

Anna didn't look moved by my argument, so I added, "And you
won't be sleep deprived…you just listed off about a dozen babysitters. We could go on vacation if we wanted."

"I'm not leaving my newborn infant with your family. Not even
for a month in Cabo." Her expression told me that she really meant
it. So did her next words. "You need to call him back and tell him
they can visit for a weekend, but that's it."

"A weekend? Babe, they'd barely get to see the newest Hancock.
How about a month?"

Anna turned to face me with her arms crossed; she had her
game face on. I knew what that meant. *Negotiation time.* "The
offer on the table is five days after the baby is born. What's your
counter?"

I thought for a second. "Twenty days." Anna cringed but didn't
object. That was the rule for negotiations—Person A had to accept
Person B's offer without complaint, and vice versa.

"Okay," she muttered. "Game room."

Spinning on her heel, she sauntered out of the room. With an eager laugh, I followed her. Anna and I had come up with a completely fair way to solve disagreements. Fair, and fun. Personally, I thought we were geniuses for thinking of it, and every married couple should follow our example. Maybe Anna and I should market the idea and sell it. Yeah...we could be marriage counselors. We were awesome at this shit.

We walked down a hallway filled with gaudy works of art. The more ridiculous something was, the more I liked it. There were statues of pissing kids, dog-faced fish, and flying monkeys. My home was filled with portraits of gigantic asses, which Anna swore were pumpkins; a Monty Python–like rendition of God in the sky, who kind of looked like me with a beard; and my favorite piece—a dog dropping a deuce in the crapper. Anna made me tuck that one away in my office. I thought it would be more appropriate in the bathroom. I mean, come on! A dog *on* the toilet *above* the toilet? What could be more awesome than that? I'd lost that negotiation though, and once a winner was declared, there was no getting out of it. Negotiation results were set in stone. Literally. I had them written down on a boulder in the yard.

The "game room" was on the other end of the house, and it took a few minutes to get there. I almost reminded Anna that we were running late for rehearsal, but I didn't. I loved this game. Sometimes I disagreed with Anna about stuff just so we could play. The game room was kid paradise. We had a movie theater–style popcorn machine, so the room permanently smelled amazing. We had a half dozen old-school arcades, Frogger included. We had a ball pit for Gibson, which is where we usually found her when she disappeared on us. We even had an indoor batting cage and a boxing bag. But what Anna and I used to settle disputes was in the center of the room: the Ping-Pong table.

Anna started setting up while I set Gibson down by the ball pit. She squealed and made a beeline for the colorful plastic balls. With a mighty jump, she belly flopped on top of them and started swishing her arms and legs like she was making a snow angel. I almost wished the pit were bigger so I could join her.

When I headed to the "negotiation" table, Anna already had

ten cups set up on her side, forming a pyramid, and was working on setting up the ten cups for my side. Anna's cups were filled with seltzer water, since she was preggers and couldn't drink. It took some of the fun out of the game, but it couldn't be helped. Baby Hancock would have to wait at least fifteen years to play the real beer pong. Anna had won that negotiation too.

I helped Anna fill up my cups with a tasty chocolate stout; it was more like dessert than alcohol, but I had a massive sweet tooth. Once everything was set up, we flipped a coin to see who went first. "Heads," I told her with a smile. If given a choice, I always chose head, although tail wasn't bad either.

Anna tossed the coin up, caught it, then smacked it on the back of her hand. When she lifted her fingers, we both leaned in to see who would be first. Predictably, it was tails. "Me first," she said with a grin.

"Not a problem. I prefer going second anyway." I pinched her butt. "Ladies should always come first."

Anna laughed in that low seductive way that made my dick twitch. Then she grabbed her ball and lined up her shot. "Here's to a short visit," she said, before she let her ball fly.

It expertly splashed into one of my cups, and I nodded in approval. My girl had skills; it kept the game interesting. "Game on, babe. Game on."

Chapter 2

The Day Awesome Died

It was official. My family was staying for twenty days. Anna had accepted the outcome of our game, but she wasn't happy about it. A deep frown was fixed on her face as we packed Gibson into our "family" car—a bright yellow Hummer; I wanted people to see us coming a mile away. For safety reasons, of course.

Anna glared at me as she buckled Gibson into her car seat. "I can't believe you made that last shot," she murmured.

Still feeling buzzed from the game, and my admittedly lucky toss that had won me the argument, I huffed on my knuckles, then rubbed them against my shirt. "Never doubt the master, babe."

She rolled her eyes but smiled. "Well, when I'm too tired and irritated to put out anymore, remember that *you* wanted it that way."

The smile fell off my face. "What do you mean? You always put out…that's what makes us work so well. It's the glue that holds us together." I made my fingers interlock, then pushed them together and apart a few times, simulating the act we were both so very good at.

Anna gave my body a once-over before she answered. "I'm not saying I won't *want* to jump your bones, but the odds of it happening will diminish with each day your family stays here. Just warning you now."

"Well, that sucks." I tossed Gibson's bag of crap into the back more harshly than necessary. It fell on its side and some of her diapers spilled out. Guess I should have thought that one through a little more before I'd fought for it. Too late now. Maintaining the sanctity of the negotiation outcome was the closest to keeping a promise that I got.

With a sniff, I told Anna, "I'm not worried. I bet I can change your mind." Grabbling myself, I jostled the boys in an age-old gesture of *I know you want this* seduction. "A few days without the Hulk, and you'll be climbing up the walls. You'll be begging for a little action."

Shaking her head with an amused smile, Anna replied with "Only time will tell."

A slow smile spread over my lips. "Oh yeah, that's what I thought."

She frowned as she got into the driver's seat. "That wasn't a yes."

My grin grew wider as I stepped into the passenger's side. "It wasn't a no either. Your ass is mine, Milfums."

She started the car. "Whatever…Dilfums." By her expression, she didn't believe me. But I knew, from the bottom of my loins, that as soon as she was cleared for takeoff, she'd want to take a ride on the Griffin Express again. Past experience told me so.

The drive to Kellan's place took forever. I honestly had no idea why he insisted on living in the middle of nowhere. Or why we kept having rehearsals at his place. Evan's place was fine. Even better than ever now, since he had more room than before. And it was close too. It didn't take three thousand hours to get there. Sure, Kellan had a soundproof room all set up with recording equipment, and yes, he lived far enough away from the world that we weren't bothered by anything but the occasional raccoon or grizzly bear, but honestly, the isolation wasn't worth the sores on my ass.

By the time the Gate of Mordor was finally in front of us, my buzz was completely gone. And just when I could have used it too. Gibson was watching her favorite TV show on the overhead DVD player. It was the third episode on the disc, and my patience was wearing thin. If one more of those little half-wit bastards asked me some stupid shit like what color the sky was one more time, I was going to punch something.

Kellan's "fortress of solitude" was circled by a six-foot-tall wood-and-metal fence. It screamed, *Leave us the hell alone!* They hadn't built the moat yet, but I was positive one was coming soon. In front of the imposing nine-foot-tall metal gate, there was an intercom box. Since the gate was closed—as always—Anna rolled down her window and pressed the call button. After a half minute, a thin, reedy voice sounded from the speaker. "Please state your full name and the nature of your business."

Even though he was trying to disguise it, I instantly recognized Kellan's voice. Leaning over my wife, I shouted into the speaker box, "My name is Griffin Suck-My Hancock, and I'm here to punch Kellan Kyle in the nuts. Now let me the fuck in, antisocial fucker."

Kellan sounded more like himself when he responded. "Wow. Do you kiss your kid with that mouth?"

Cameras were everywhere around the entrance. There was one on the intercom, and one on each side of the gate. Getting in this way unnoticed wasn't possible. Stretching over Anna so Kellan would get a clear shot of my face, I replied, "Yeah, I also lick my wife like an ice cream cone." I waggled my tongue, just to gross him out. Or Kiera, if she was watching too. With a smile, I added, "In fact, I'll do it right now while I'm waiting for the gate to open. You can watch."

I dropped my head into the slim space between Anna's stomach and the steering wheel. She laughed and started threading her fingers through my hair while a disgusted noise came from the intercom box. It didn't take long for the gate to start squealing open. "God…just get in here before I change my mind and have the gate permanently sealed…along with my eyes."

Gibson giggled as I lifted my head from Anna's lap. "I-cream, Daddy! I-cream!" Anna snorted as she looked back at her daughter, then she quickly drove us through the gate. Kellan might actually lock us out if we took too long.

Kellan's driveway was about sixty thousand miles long. There were a couple of decently sized potholes too. Kellan should really be a better homeowner and fix that shit. After the third bump, Anna put a hand on her belly. "I have to pee so bad," she said through clenched teeth. I wasn't surprised; she had to pee every five minutes. When the three-story estate came into view, Matt and Evan's cars were already parked in the driveway. Anna stopped beside Matt's rig, threw the Hummer in park, then dashed out the door without even turning the car off. As I watched her perfect ass bounding away from me, I wondered if she'd just pick a bush outside and squat. I wouldn't blame her if she did. Kellan's house was on a hill, and there were at least a hundred steps leading to the front door. Maybe more. It was annoying. Before he put in the moat, he should really consider an escalator. Or a boom lift. That would be awesome.

Turning around in my seat, I faced Gibson. "Looks like it's just you and me, kiddo."

Gibson gave me a toothy grin. "I-cream."

Laughing at her one-track mind, I unbuckled my seat belt. "Okay, we'll see if Auntie Kiera has any." Gibson clapped her hands while I shut the car off.

After slinging Gibson's bag over my shoulder, I freed her from her car seat and scooped her into my arms. She yawned, making me do the same. "Yeah, I know. Uncle Kellan practically lives in another country. We'd already be done with rehearsals if we were still at Uncle Evan's place, but nooooo, we've all got to suffer so Kellan can have his 'privacy.'" Giving her a serious look, I added, "Sometimes family sucks. Not always…but sometimes."

Gibson tilted her head like she was considering my statement, then she closed her eyes and started falling asleep. Patting her back, I laughed. Then I turned to look at the five thousand steps in my way and groaned. "Goddammit," I muttered, then began the hours-long trek.

I was hot and sweaty by the time I reached the top. Then there were five more damn steps to get up the front porch. I was freaking done with stairs by the time I got to the brick-red door. I knocked on it with my boot, then yanked it open with my free hand before anyone could respond.

Kellan and Matt were in the entryway, along with Matt's girl-friend, Rachel. Rachel was glued to Matt's side, like she'd float into space if she wasn't holding on to him. Kellan and my cousin were discussing something about the band's schedule. Looking at Matt was like peering into a hazed, cracked mirror. Sure, we looked alike, but my hotness was crisp and clear while his was muted, a sepia-toned replica that didn't hold a candle to my brilliance. Kellan was...well, a lot of girls seemed to think he was the be-all and end-all of male perfection. No, sorry, girls. He's not. That strong jaw, deep blue eyes, and just-fucked hair was nothing special. And sure he was ripped, but...his body was just so-so next to mine. My body art made my skin much more interesting than his bor-ing, chiseled lines. Whatever. His abs were airbrushed on anyway. I'd read that somewhere, and I totally believed it. Kell didn't work out enough to have definition like that.

Matt was in the middle of a sentence, but I interrupted him as soon as I stepped into the room. "What the hell is up with all those steps, Kell?" Readjusting Gibson, I snarked, "You know, maybe you should have put the driveway on top of the hill *with* the house, instead of at the bottom of the hill. Then you wouldn't have to climb freaking Mount Everest every time you got out of the car."

Kellan frowned. "I didn't design the house, Griff."

I shrugged off Gibson's bag and it hit the ground with a thud. "Yeah, but you can redesign it, can't you? It's not like you're the lead singer of the most successful band in the world, with more cash coming out your ass each morning than most people make in their entire lifetime." I paused a minute, then finished with "Oh wait, yeah you are. Fix this shit."

The click of Anna's heels echoed on the tile as she stepped into the room. "I agree with him on this one, Kellan. That climb sucks, especially when you have a bowling ball pressing on your bladder. I almost had to water your roses."

She lifted a brow at him and Kellan flashed her his trademark million-dollar grin. "I'm glad you didn't. How are you feeling, Anna?"

I knew Kellan was all gung ho about his wife, but sometimes his niceness toward mine irked me. Maybe it was because of how we'd hooked up. Me and Anna, not me and Kellan. She'd been visiting her sister, Kiera, and had been goo-goo-eyed for Kellan for all of five seconds, until she'd gotten a whiff of me. After that, Kellan hadn't had a chance with her. I think he still resented me for that. Anna was the one who got away. *Well, sorry, Kell, but she's all mine. From those luscious lips to that five-star ass...mine.*

Anna sighed as she walked toward me. Patting her stomach, she answered him with "Like I wish it was September already."

Kellan's eyes got that sympathetic softness that I had seen girls swoon over time and time again. Whatever. I could make that silly-ass I-care-about-you face too. "You sure you want to go on this tour, Anna? It pretty much knocks on your due date."

Anna yawned and nodded at the same time as she stepped to my side. Since Gibson was half-asleep on my shoulder, I figured my two girls would be napping during rehearsal. I wished I could join them. "Yeah," she told Kellan. "It beats hanging around the house, bored out of my mind, while you guys are out having all the fun." With a grin, she looked up at me. "Besides, being on the road during the last part of my pregnancy is good luck for the baby. Just look at how gorgeous this one turned out." She gave Gibson's shoulder a soft kiss.

She was right about that. Gibson was perfect. We'd been somewhere back East, on tour with the hotness that was Sienna Sexton, when Anna had spit Gibson out. I'd missed the show that night to be there at the hospital, but that hadn't mattered to me. Still didn't. I'd miss every show in the world to be there when my kid was being born.

With another yawn, Anna took Gibson from my arms. Gibs let out a sigh and stretched, but that was the only move she made. Anna squeezed her tight, then looked over at Kellan. "She didn't sleep well last night. I'm gonna go lay her down. Where's Kiera?"

Kellan pointed upstairs. "She's putting Ryder down."

Anna nodded, then sighed when she looked at yet more stairs. Turning to me, she leaned in for a kiss. "I'll see you after rehearsal."

Seeing an opportunity to make out with a hot girl, I cupped her cheek and drew her lips to mine. Our mouths moved together, and I pushed my tongue inside her. She let out a low noise that instantly ignited me, and I grabbed her face with my other hand. *Yeah, game on...*

We were just getting hot and heavy when someone cleared their throat. I looked up to see Matt grimacing at us. "Dude, get a room."

Pulling away from Anna, I smirked. "We're in a house, jackass. That's like one giant room."

Anna giggled, then she rubbed my arm, said goodbye, and walked that sweet ass away from me. I watched her swaying figure until she was completely gone. Once she was out of view, I adjusted my junk and turned to Kellan. He was eyeing me with a mixture of disgust and amusement. When I stepped up to him, he took a step back; his hands drifted down to cover his privates. I was confused at first, until I remembered what I'd stated as my "business" earlier at the gate.

"Relax, sunshine. I won't damage your family jewels. Anna wants another cousin for Gibson and Newbie." Tapping my jaw, I reconsidered. "Maybe I should though. It might help you hit the high notes."

Kellan took another step back. "I can hit the ones I need to hit just fine, thanks."

I cracked my knuckles. "Okay, but the offer stands if you ever change your mind."

"Noted," he muttered with a laugh.

"Evan here?" I asked. His truck was here, but he could have gone for a walk or something. Although I had no idea why he'd want to. He'd probably get run down by wolves or chased by Sasquatch. God, I missed civilization.

Kellan pointed out back, where the soundproof room we used for practice was. "He's working on something with Jenny."

Instantly, the picture of Evan bending his fiancée over his drum set entered my head. I mimicked with my hips what Evan was most likely doing. "Yeah, I bet he's working on something."

Rachel made a noise and I shifted my attention her way. She

shut her mouth and her cheeks flushed bright red. Rachel was shyer than Kiera, which was saying a lot. The girl so rarely talked that I often forgot she was there. And when she did speak, her voice was usually soft and polite. Just once I wanted to see her lose her ever-loving mind. There was a freak buried under the calm, I just knew it.

Rachel's eyes searched the floor for a moment before lifting to Matt's. "I'm going to grab Jenny and start working on her website."

Matt nodded, then cringed. "I still think she should reconsider the name of her gallery."

Rachel shrugged. "She has her heart set on it."

Confusion washed over me like dirty seawater. *What the hell are they talking about?* "What's she naming what? What gallery? Like an art thingamabobber?" An idea struck me and I immediately offered it up, because I was thoughtful like that. "Does she need a subject to paint?" Sticking my tongue out, I cupped myself. "'Cause I've been told my *subject* is a work of art."

Matt's expression turned bland while Rachel turned even redder; the tips of her ears were almost purple. After Rachel hurried away like her hair was on fire, Matt frowned at me. I was used to his thin lips turned into a perturbed scowl, so it didn't faze me. In his typical sarcastic voice, Matt droned, "No, I think what you were told was that *you're* a piece of work. While similar sounding, there is a distinct difference between the two. I can draw you a diagram, if you don't get it."

While I flipped him off, Kellan answered my question. "Jenny is opening an art gallery downtown. She's calling it Bagettes. It's opening the day before the tour stars, and we're all playing at the opening." Kellan looked at me expectantly, but all this was news to me. Seeing my blank expression, he scrunched his brows and said, "We've been talking about this for the last three rehearsals, Griff. You don't remember that?"

I shrugged. They talked about a lot of shit that I didn't pay any attention to. I was usually too busy planning my moment of awesomeness. A moment that I was going to bring up today. It was

time. As soon as we were all together, I was going to demand the
spotlight I deserved.

With closed eyes, Kellan shook his head. He opened his mouth
like he was going to say something, then he shut it again like he'd
changed his mind. Whatever. I didn't need another lecture anyway.

Kellan led the way to the studio, and Matt and I followed him.
Matt smacked my back as we walked through the living room. He
was smiling, so I figured I'd amused him somehow. That was how
we worked. Snarky, rude, belittling comments mixed with a touch
of humor. We pissed on each other then laughed about it later. It
was our thing. I clapped him on the back as well. *No harm, no foul.*

Kellan opened the slider to the backyard and waved us through
like he was our butler. The image of Kellan waiting on me hand
and foot, always at the ready with a tray of beer-a-ritas and pork
rinds, snapped into my head. Ha! That would be fucking awesome.
I snorted as I walked by him, but he didn't ask what was funny. He
knew better than to ask.

The studio was on the far side of the pool. The cool water
looked refreshing, and I considered shoving Matt in as we walked
past it. I didn't though, which made me appreciate myself even
more. The guys should really give me more credit for all the shit I
didn't do. If they only knew how many awesome ideas I passed on,
they'd be truly impressed by my self-control.

Jenny and Rachel were exiting the studio as we approached it.
Rachel had her laptop under her arm, and Jenny was beaming,
pleased as punch about something. Evan's fiancée had been a staple
at our favorite bar since almost the beginning. I knew her as well as
I knew the bar menu. Speaking of…Pete should really update his
menu. He didn't even have tongue tacos on there. What respectable
bar doesn't serve tongue? If it were my bar, I'd serve tongue with
everything. My tongue. To chicks.

"Hey, Jenny. Bagettes, huh?" I said as she walked by me.

The perky blonde turned to point her breasts in my direction.
"Yeah…I was going to call it D-Bagettes, but I thought that might
turn some customers away, so I shortened it." She tilted her head,
like a confused puppy. "I'm surprised you remembered."

Giving her a wicked smile, I tapped my skull. "I remember everything. My mind is a steel trap—nothing gets out."

Matt elbowed me in the ribs. "Nothing gets in either."

I gave him a glare. His ass might get shoved into the pool by the end of the day anyway, and he'd only have himself to blame. I could only be good for so long, after all. "You're lucky you look like me," I told him. "Otherwise I'd have to wipe the floor with you." Matt looked horrified that I'd just pointed out our similarities. While his face morphed through various stages of disgust, I matter-of-factly stated, "I have too much respect for the genes to kick your ass."

Kellan and Jenny laughed at my comment. Rachel frowned, and for a minute she looked just like my cousin. As disbelief washed over his face, Matt held up a finger. "Wait a minute…let me get this straight. The reason you haven't 'kicked my ass' yet…is… 'respect'?" He made air quotes with his fingers as he said it.

With a smile, I nodded. "Yep."

"It has nothing to do with the fact that you couldn't fight your way out of a wet paper bag? No…a wet newspaper. A lying-on-the-ground, completely flat newspaper," he said with an *I'm so clever* smirk on his lips.

A guffaw escaped me. "What are you talking about? I'm a badass. Remember that time I whooped that guy in L.A.?"

"He was blind."

I lifted my finger in defense. "I didn't know that at the time. And honestly, he was talking shit. Shit-talking overrides the handicap home base, so he was fair game."

Matt's mouth dropped open. "Handicap home base?" Still looking stunned, he shook his head. "Every day, it still surprises me that we're related." He looked over at Rachel. "I don't think I'll ever truly accept my reality."

Smacking his chest, I laughed. "Yeah, I know. It's hard to be related to a godlike creature such as myself. I'd feel the same if I were you…but thank God—otherwise known as me—I'm not you."

Matt looked about to speak, but Rachel beat him to it. "We're going to work in the house, babe."

Looking grateful for the distraction, Matt turned his full attention to her. "Okay. I'll come find you afterwards."

Matt gave her a chaste kiss on the cheek while Kellan opened the door to the studio. It had been silent before, but now the sound of drums filtered out to us. Evan was working on a beat for one of Kellan's new songs. I wasn't sure how Kellan kept dreaming up stuff, but he was always approaching us with new lyrics. And Matt and Evan went gaga for anything he showed them. But whenever *I* showed them anything, they turned their noses up. *We can't sing about belching, Griffin… The chorus can't be about telling people to buy extra copies of our album… You can't put your actual phone number in a song, dumbass.* Prissy bitches. Their sense of awesome was skewed.

I waved at Evan once I made my way to the "pit," where the instruments were. He spun a stick in his hand and nodded his head up in greeting. With tattooed sleeves on both arms, Evan had the most body art of all of us. He won the most piercings title too, with a brow bar, gauges, and both nipples done. He didn't have a penis piercing though. I was the only D-Bag with the balls to claim that prize.

While I opened the cooler for a tasty beverage, I heard Matt say, "I'm starting to feel sick, guys."

Finding a beer amid the pop, I straightened up. "Right before tour? That sucks. Hopefully you're done blowing chunks before we head out."

Matt shook his head. "Not sick-sick, nervous sick."

I felt lost at sea again. I knew Matt didn't like being center stage, but we'd done this a gazillion times. He shouldn't be freaking out about it. "Why the hell are you nervous? We've been doing this shit for years."

Matt gave me a dumbfounded look, like I was missing something obvious. I hated that look. It made me feel stupid, and I wasn't. I had smarts. Smarts, skills, *and* looks. I was the whole package—a triple threat of awesomeness.

"Because of Rachel…" he slowly said. "And that thing I'm going to ask her before we go on tour. You know what I'm talking about?"

Nope. No clue. "You're going to ask her to…join the band? I don't know, man, I like Rachel and all, but I don't think she can handle the limelight. I think she'd run off the stage screaming… which would actually be kind of entertaining, so, yeah, let's ask her."

I looked around, all smiles, but nobody was smiling with me. Did they object to Rachel being a part of the band? *Wow… harsh.*

Matt sighed. "No, dumbass, I'm going to ask her to marry me." He held his stomach. "I'm gonna throw up."

With a laugh, Kellan patted his shoulder. "You'll be fine. It's easy. Four little words, that's it."

I started counting them on my fingers, then stopped when Kellan shifted his grin to me. Disbelieving that my cousin was willingly going to jump into the marriage pool when he really didn't need to, I did the nicest thing possible. I attempted to talk him out of it. "Why on earth would you do that? Stay boyfriend and girlfriend. It works the same, and it's super-easy to end it if things go south. You just never call her again."

All three guys stared at me with looks I knew well—someone was going to start scolding me. What did I say? Temperamental assholes. I held my hands up to deflect the verbal blows I felt coming. "No offense or anything. I mean, Rachel is superhot, so I totally get why you'd want to nail her for life, but why go through all that marriage crap if you don't have to? You've already got the best part." I chugged my beer, then crushed the can and tossed it into the garbage. *Swish. And the crowd goes wild!*

Matt opened his mouth, shut it, then opened it again. After another second of silence, he turned to Kellan. "Once again, I have no clue how to respond to that."

Kellan shrugged, then turned to me. "If you object to marriage so much, why did you get married?"

So no other fucker would try to take what was mine. I shrugged. "I knocked her up. It was the right thing to do." I snapped my head to Matt. "Holy shit! Is Rachel pregnant? Is that why you're all super-eager to walk down the aisle? When's she due?"

Matt let out a sigh of losing-his-patience irritation. "She's not pregnant. That's not why I want to marry her."

Seeing an opportunity to mess with him, I curled my lips into an impossibly sexy devil-grin. "You sure about that? I did lean over her the other day when she was working on our website. And...it's a well-documented fact that I'm incredibly virile. I may have accidentally impregnated her. If I did, you have my deepest apologies."

Matt's eyes widened in fear. "Do *not* even joke about that." He shuddered, like he'd just witnessed his worst nightmare come to life right before his eyes.

I felt the laughter coming, but I held it in. I wasn't done tormenting him yet. "Yeah, sad thing is, we look so much alike...how will you ever *really* know the kid isn't mine?"

Matt's face turned a rosy shade of pink that kind of reminded me of the sun setting. How beautiful. His words weren't nearly as pretty. "I really fucking hate you."

The laugh I'd been holding in finally escaped me. Smacking his arm, I shook my head. "You've been saying that for years. I don't believe you anymore."

Matt sighed again, shook his head, then walked away to grab his instrument. Kellan jabbed me in the shoulder while Evan shook his head. *What?* It was funny. And true. And Matt would get over it. He'd make some jab about me that was ten times worse, but would he get reproachful glares for it? No, he would get laughs. It was totally cool to smack me down, but if I did the same thing, whoa...everybody got their panties in a wad. Whatever.

Kellan and Matt took their places and I trudged over to mine. God, we knew these songs backward and forward. Was practicing them still necessary? It's not like we were going to forget them if we took the next couple of weeks off. As I picked up my bass, I tried explaining my thought to the guys. "Yo, dudes, why are we still doing this? We're going to be playing the same shit every night for weeks on end. Can't we take a break? A calm before the storm, so to speak?"

Matt scoffed at me. Was he still hacked off? He usually bounced back quicker. "One day you're going to have to take this job seriously, Griffin. It's not all fun and games; you have to put in a little effort."

I turned to face him across from me. "I put in effort. I showed up, didn't I?"

Obviously still mad, Matt dropped his guitar back onto its stand. "It's not just about showing up and playing the songs we hand you, jackass. You're the only member of the group who doesn't contribute to the process. You don't help with new songs, you don't help with the schedule, you don't help with marketing." He threw his hands up into the air. "For the life of me, I can't think of one thing that you actually *do* for the band. Besides run your mouth, of course."

The entire room went so silent I could hear everyone's breaths. *Well.* Make one remark about impregnating his girlfriend and Matt got all kinds of bent out of shape. Guess she was off-limits. Fine. Tell me that to my face, don't body-slam me to the floor in front of everybody.

Kellan walked over to Matt. He put a hand on his shoulder and murmured something I couldn't hear. Matt seemed to calm down after hearing it though. I glanced back at Evan, but he was studying a speck of dirt on his drumstick like it was suddenly the most important thing on earth.

Since no one was stepping up to defend me against Matt's outrageous accusations, I decided to defend myself. "That's not true, cuz. I contribute. Or I try to, at least, but you guys shoot down every idea I come up with. Kind of makes me not want to share my ideas, since I know you're just gonna say no. Sometimes before you even hear me out." I lifted my guitar like it was a gun and fired a couple of shots into the air, destroying my thought-children before they even had a chance to grow and flourish. Dream killers.

Matt and Kellan exchanged a look, then glanced back at Evan. He shrugged, then nodded. Still looking like he was struggling to rein in his bad mood, Matt locked eyes with me. "Okay...you may have a point." He pressed his lips together like just admitting that caused him pain. "So…do you have an idea you'd like to share? We're all ears." He cringed, but closed his mouth.

My heart started thudding harder as I looked around the room. This was it; I had their complete and total attention, and there was no way they could say no this time. They couldn't deny me anymore, not after I'd just pointed out that they never listen to me. I deserved this, and unlike all the times I'd asked them for a shot before, this time, they were going to give me the opportunity I'd wanted since day one. I could feel it. Today was my day.

Trying to look like it didn't matter much to me, I casually tossed out, "Yeah, I think I should take the lead on 'Stalker' on the tour. It's time you guys threw me a bone." That song had a killer solo in the middle. Matt got screams for days after he shredded it, not that he noticed. He rarely looked up from his instrument to see the frenzy going on around him. Damn waste.

Matt considered my request for exactly point five seconds. "No."

Heat rushed up my spine, encircled my head, and pounded on my brain. I knew they wouldn't hear me out. Well, fuck that. I deserved a chance. "Okay, how about a different song then? You can pick it."

Matt crossed his arms over his chest. "No."

My cheeks felt like someone was holding a flame over them. "No? Just no. You still won't even fucking consider it? Why the fuck not? We both started playing guitar as leads, Matt, and you know I'm great at it. The only reason I've been stuck on bass is because I somehow drew the short straw when the band formed. I got fucked, but it was never supposed to be permanent and you know that." Matt narrowed his eyes but didn't respond to my valid points, so I looked over at Evan and Kellan for support. "You guys got an opinion about this? Or is Matt the sole leader of the band now? Should we rename ourselves Matt-Bags? Or how about Door Matts?"

Kellan appeared to not know what to say. He looked over at Evan with *What should we do?* written all over his face. Evan cleared his throat, then pointed at Matt with his drumstick. "It's his instrument, man. It's his call. If he says no…that's his right."

"And what about my rights? I've wanted lead guitar from the first day we all hooked up, but I was outnumbered then and I'm outnumbered now. You jackasses won't ever give me a chance!" My voice was loud and gruff, powerful and pissed.

Matt's voice, however, was calm when he answered me. "You don't respect the art form, Griffin. You don't take this seriously enough; you never have. I can't give you that much responsibility when I know you can't handle it. You'll drop the ball, and this band means too much to me to let that happen." After a moment of silence he added, "I'm sorry. I know how much you want it, but you are *never* going to play lead, understand? My answer will *always* be no. You should just accept that and let it go so we can move past this."

The sound of my heart pounding reverberated through my ears. I couldn't believe the fuckers were saying no again...and for good this time. Never? They would never let me play the one instrument I'd always wanted? What the hell? "One song? You won't even trust me with one fucking song? Have I ever dropped the ball on bass? No. I kill it every single night, and every single rehearsal. I may joke around, but I get the fucking job done, and you know it."

Matt's lips pressed into a firm line and his cheeks turned a deeper shade of red, but he shook his head. "My answer is still no. It's not ever gonna happen. Sorry. I wish I could tell you in a gentler way, but I feel like, at this point, it's best to be blunt...so you'll stop asking. We have a system that works; we're not going to change it just so you can live out your look-at-me fantasy. It's time for you to grow up, Griffin."

Grow up? Fuck that. If anything, it was time for me to act like an immature asshole, since that was what they were doing. Opening my palm, I let my guitar fall to the floor. It fell with a thud, and I swear, something cracked. "Thanks for the fucking bone...fucker. If your answer is always gonna be no, then there's no point in me being here, pretending to be a part of this band. Clearly, I'm not actually a member."

Not able to stand his face for another second, I stormed from the room. From behind me I heard Matt yell, "I have to think of the band first, Griffin. It's not personal!"

Muttering, "Neither is that, asshole," I flipped him off as I walked out the door. I heard someone call out for me to wait before the door slammed shut and all sound cut off, but I ignored whoever had shouted it. I was done.

Stomping past the pool, I paused to throw a chair in. The splash was satisfying, so I tossed in another chair. And a table. Fish that out, fucker. Indulging in my temper tantrum gave Kellan time to catch up to me. Emerging from the rehearsal room, he spotted me and strode over. Just when I was about to reach for another chair to throw in his pool, he grabbed my arm. Irritated, I jerked away from him. "Let go, Kell. I got nothing to say to you."

His brows bunched together until they were almost one fuzzy line of concern—*One brow to rule them all…* "What was all that about? And what did you mean at the end there? You are a part of this band, Griffin. You always have been, and you always will be."

Pushing him back a step, I snapped, "It's a little late for the pep talk, bro. If you think I'm so *valuable*, you could have stood up for me in there." I lifted my arms for emphasis. "It gave me the warm and fuzzies how you let him walk all over me."

Kellan sighed. "It's complicated, Griff. Matt's a genius on guitar…he's…it's his instrument, the one he's born to play. But us saying that isn't an insult to you. You're amazing on bass, gifted even. It's just…we each have our part, you know? And we have to do them the best we can." He put a hand on my shoulder. "For the sake of the band, I'm asking you to let this go and just…forget about lead. Please?"

I could only stare at him. I felt numb inside. Was this what giving up your dream felt like? For as long as I could remember, I'd wanted all eyes on me—I'd wanted to be the center of attention. Matt had never wanted that. But he was given the instrument that shone while I was given the one that everyone forgot about. My part was designed to blend, designed to go unnoticed. It was everything I wasn't, and I was sick of being stuck with it. I wanted more, but they wouldn't give me more.

Without answering him, I turned and walked away, toward the house. What could I say to that anyway? Matt had just permanently rejected my chances at ever being lead guitar. Forgetting was the only thing left that I could do. Forget, or stew, and right now, I wanted to stew.

When I got back to the living room, Jenny and Rachel were there working. "Need something, Griffin?" Jenny asked, her pale eyes practically sparkling with happiness.

Ignoring both her good mood and her question, I called out for Anna. "She's upstairs with Kiera," Rachel quietly replied.

Harrumphing some sort of thank-you, I began plodding my way to the stairs. Fucking stairs. I stomped up them, cursing my bandmates with each step. I imagined that the carpet treads under my feet were their squishy faces. I felt a little better by the time I reached the top. "Yo, Anna! Where are you?"

Both Anna and Kiera instantly appeared in a bedroom doorframe. Simultaneously, they both put fingers to their lips. "Shhhhhhh," they both scolded.

I was tired of being reprimanded today, so I didn't lower my voice. "Wake up Gibson. We're leaving."

Anna instantly edged around Kiera to step into the hallway. "What's wrong?" she asked me, while Kiera stepped out of the room behind her. The two sisters were pretty similar, but Anna definitely had a lot more curves than her slimmer and straighter sister. Generally I appreciated those curves, but at the moment, I just wanted to shove them into the car and get out of here.

"There's no point being here right now, so we're leaving. Actually, there's no point in ever coming back here, so we're leaving." I opened the door closest to me, hoping I'd find my sleeping daughter behind it. Nope. Empty.

I moved to try another door, but Anna stepped in front of me. "Let's go outside, get some fresh air."

Dramatically tossing my hands in the air, I gave up. "Fine." What did it matter, since nothing was working for me today anyway?

I headed back to those goddamn stairs while Anna told Kiera

she'd be right back. Not waiting for my very pregnant wife, I sped down the steps and out the door. The fresh air on my face helped calm me down a little, but I was still riled up. I paced the front porch while I waited for Anna. Those sanctimonious assholes.

"Griff?" A soft touch on my shoulder spooked me, and I jumped. Turning, I saw Anna behind me, her green eyes worried. "What's going on?" She indicated the front step, and I grudgingly sat down.

Once I was seated, my mood dropped. I'd started the day so positively, knowing without a shadow of a doubt that this tour was going to be *the one*. But not anymore. It was going to be the same old crap. Dropping my head, I slumped over. Anna sat beside me, and her fingers lightly caressed my back in a soothing pattern. It helped my residual anger, but not my rising disappointment.

"One song. I asked for one fucking song…and they said no." I studied my fingers in my lap while my dreams dissolved in my hands. "Matt just told me that he's not ever going to give me a chance to play lead, and the rest of the guys agreed with him. I'm done…forever stuck on bass…forever in the shadows. I just wanted one song, one moment in the spotlight." With a sigh, I looked up at her. "Four minutes? Is that so much?"

Anna's eyes were heavy with sympathy. Reaching up, she threaded her fingers through my hair. "No…that's not much at all."

I nodded and dropped my vision to my lap again. "Yeah, I didn't think so either. But they won't even give that to me." The anger resurfaced, wrapping disappointment around it like a blanket. "Between me and you, babe, sometimes…I really don't like those guys."

Anna kissed the back of my neck and wrapped an arm around my shoulder in sympathy. "I'm sorry, Griffin."

Closing my eyes, I let her comfort wash over me. At least there was one person on earth who gave a shit about me.

Chapter 3

No Rest for the Awesome

Anna talked me into staying for rehearsal. She said I could play with her lady parts when we got home if I sucked it up and stayed. I think she was hoping we'd all get over the argument before we called it quits for the day, and then we'd all be best buds again. Her plan might have worked too, except I purposefully stoked the chip on my shoulder and goofed off the entire practice. Matt yelled at me three times to pay attention, but I didn't care. They'd already said I didn't respect the art form and they were never going to give me an opportunity to change their minds, so I might as well live up to their expectations. Or lack of expectations.

By the time we parted ways, everybody was frazzled and irritated. Good. I shouldn't be the only one. Matt scampered out of the room the second we were done, Evan following closely on his heels. When I was alone with Kellan, he let out a long sigh. "Was that you letting it go, Griffin? Because you seemed to be doing everything you could to piss Matt off. You were even more obnoxious than usual, which is really saying something."

I shook my head at him. "I never said I was going to let this go. And besides, Matt's the one with the stick up his ass. Maybe the band should pool together and have it surgically removed."

Kellan let out another weary exhale. "He's under a lot of stress right now. Maybe you could see things through his eyes for once, and cut him some slack."

Scoffing, I tossed out, "Because of the proposal thing? If just the idea of taking the plunge is turning him into such a douche, then maybe he shouldn't propose to Rachel. Not everyone is meant for married life."

"What?"

A soft, squeaky voice to our left drew Kellan's and my attention that way. Rachel was standing there, holding her laptop to her chest and looking like she might pass out. Her eyes were wide as she stared at us, shocked. Great. "Fuck," I muttered while Kellan gave Rachel a nervous smile.

"Hey, Rach…didn't see you there," Kellan said, running a hand through his famous hair.

Rachel stepped forward with just one foot, like she was afraid to get any closer. "Matt is going to propose?" she asked, her eyes sparkling with hope. It was clear, even to me, that she was going to say yes when he did ask her.

Still irritated about today's events, I told her, "He *was* going to, but then he realized he couldn't handle being tied down to just one girl, so he changed his mind." *There, Matt. How does having a dream snatched away from you feel?*

Kellan snapped his eyes to mine, and I glanced at him with a *What?* expression. *Matt asked for this.*

Rachel sniffed, and I looked back at her. Her eyes were filling with tears. Damn it. If she talked to Kiera or Jenny, and they talked to Anna, Anna was gonna kill me for saying that. Trying to save myself from getting my ass handed to me, I quickly amended with "But hey, if you don't say anything to *anyone*, maybe he'll change his mind again. He's a wishy-washy asshole like that."

Twin tears rolled off her cheeks and she looked down to hide her face. "I better…get Matt his stuff. He left it behind." She grabbed a jacket and a set of keys on a nearby table.

Elbowing his way around me, Kellan started saying, "Rachel, wait…" but the chick was fast. She was out the door before he could finish.

Looking back at me, he shook his head. "What did you just do?" he muttered, his voice disbelieving.

Pursing my lips, I shrugged. *Got Matt back. Kind of.* "What? At least now it will still be a surprise when he asks her."

Kellan's lips twisted in annoyance. "Yeah, if she doesn't break up with him first." I shrugged again. Wasn't my problem. That was something for the *lead* guitarist to worry about, and that was clearly never going to be me. Kellan scrubbed his eyes. "I have a headache…"

While I was pissed off at Matt, I was all right with Kellan; at least he'd tried to make peace with me. In thanks, I gave him a helpful hint for his migraines. "You should have more sex. Works for me, I never get headaches."

He frowned at my suggestion. "I'm going to go find Rachel and attempt to fix this. Stay here, and try not to piss off anyone else."

With a mocking salute, I barked, "Aye, aye, Captain." He rolled his eyes before he left. I waited a minute and a half, then I left to go find my wife and daughter so we could go home. Kellan had never said exactly how *long* I needed to stay there, and ninety seconds seemed more than adequate. Besides, he was perfectly capable of smoothing things out with Rachel. He was on the job. He'd work his Kellan Kyle magic on her, and she'd forget everything I'd just said, and all would be right in the world. Except she'd still be marrying Matt…the prick who was holding me back.

The next morning I was still fuming, but I decided to take Kellan's suggestion and let it go. Whatever. Matt was just being Matt. I could rise above. I'd been doing it my whole life. Besides, never didn't always mean never. I'd just have to be more creative if I wanted to shine. And if I was anything, it was creative. Just ask my wife.

Rachel didn't show up to the next few rehearsals. Matt said she was busy helping Jenny with her grand opening, but Kellan pulled me aside and told me that she was ticked about what I'd said and didn't want to see me for a while. Whatever. Like a typical girl, she was totally overreacting.

"She knows he's going to ask, but she doesn't know when, so

don't say anything, okay? Maybe we can still keep part of this a surprise." Kellan pinched the bridge of his nose like he had another headache. Guess he still wasn't getting laid enough then.

Shrugging, I told him, "Not a problem. I don't know when he's gonna ask her either." And I didn't really care. Why should I invest in Matt's life if he wasn't going to invest in mine?

Dropping his hand, Kellan gave me a blank stare. "The gallery opening. Remember? We've discussed this so many times…" Holding his hand up, he stopped talking. "Never mind. Just try not to say anything to anyone for the next week or so, okay?"

I zipped my mouth shut with my fingers and nodded. I could be quiet when I needed to be, and not talking to the guys right now was fine with me.

The week before tour, Matt was all nervous and shit, so he canceled rehearsals. I almost told him it didn't matter, that Rachel already knew the proposal was coming and I was pretty sure she was going to say yes when he finally got the balls to ask her. He didn't need to stress out about any of it. But then I remembered the look on Kellan's face when he'd asked me to stay quiet. It was a look that clearly said, *I know asking this is pointless, since you're just going to find a way to mess it up, but here goes…* It was an expression I had seen on him one too many times, on all the guys. None of them had any faith in me. Fuckers. Well I would show them. I wouldn't spoil anything. All I would do was thoroughly enjoy every minute of my newfound free time.

And there was nothing I liked better than killing time with Gibson and Anna. Especially Anna. She was randy as all get-out lately, constantly touching me, massaging me, whispering dirty things in my ear. Keeping her satisfied was almost a full-time job. A fucking fantastic full-time job.

"Yeah baby…play with yourself, just like that…"

Anna was straddling me on the bed, teasing me by rubbing my cock against her soaking wet pussy. The look on her face was needy, like she was going to explode if I didn't sink inside her soon. I felt the same way. She was riling us both up by only giving me a brief taste of what I wanted. I fucking loved it. "Yeah, just like that…"

She circled the tip of my cock around her clit, then dipped me inside her, just a fraction. It took all my willpower not to grab her hips and force her on top of me. I couldn't though; she was the one in control right now, I was just along for the ride.

Grabbing her hips, I squirmed beneath her. "Yes…do it…ride me…"

She let out a passionate growl that made my cock twitch in her hands. She squeezed me harder in response. "You like that, baby?" she said, leaning down as far as her stomach would allow. It brought her beautiful breasts within my reach, and I leaned up to suck a nipple into my mouth.

She was so sensitive that just a light swirl of my tongue made her cry out. "Oh God, yes…"

She let more of me slip inside her and I moaned around her tit in my mouth; my hands clenched and unclenched her hip, urging her forward. *Fucking take me…*

I switched to her other breast, and another inch slipped inside her. *Yes…fuck, she felt good.* She swiveled her hips, sending a throbbing ache right through me. *Fuck.* I needed to thrust, I needed to come. I needed her, now. Releasing her breast, I dropped my head to the pillow and arched my back. "Baby, I can't… More…fuck, I need more…"

"Me too," she groaned, and then she tilted her hips so I sank all the way inside her. *Fuck me…Yes…* "Like this, baby?" she said, sitting back so I had a perfect view of her body. It was almost too much, too intense. I was gonna come and we hadn't even moved yet. *Fuck that.* My body would come when I fucking said it could, and no sooner.

Mentally adjusting myself, I stroked her hips. "Fuck, you're gorgeous…and you feel so good. Ride me, baby."

With her hands gently pressing on my stomach, she began to rock her hips. The ache throbbed harder and harder with each shift of her body, but I ignored it and focused on her—her face, alive with pleasure, her breasts, full and firm, her nipples, peaked with need. She wasn't just gorgeous, she was perfection.

Her hips moved faster and faster, in rhythm with the moans escaping her mouth. I started shaking as I staved off the moment my body was dying for. *Come for me, so I can come for you.* Just when I thought all the willpower in the world couldn't stop my release, Anna dropped her head back and let out a long, euphoric cry. I felt her walls closing around me and I knew I could finally let go. *Thank you.*

"Fuck, yeah, come for me…" I thrust into her hard a couple of times, building up the biggest bang I could. When it exploded from me, I gasped. *Fuck…so…fucking…good.* Then I cried out. "Oh God, Anna. Fuck, yes…" Then I groaned, grunted, and made every satisfied noise under the rainbow. *Fuck…I loved coming.*

With a contented purr, Anna leaned down and kissed me. I whimpered some response; it was all I could do. Damn, even while pregnant, my wife had moves that could make grown men cry. I was one lucky-ass fuck. She carefully extracted herself, grabbed a couple of towels, then curled into my side. I just lay there, recovering from another mind-blowing release. I couldn't wait to do that again in twenty minutes.

"So, tonight's the big night…" she murmured, her breath still unnaturally fast.

"Hmmm?" I really didn't care about anything outside of my cock right now.

Anna sat up on an elbow and stared down at me. "The gallery opening? Matt's proposal?"

"Oh, yeah…that," I said, closing my eyes. Matt, the douche holding my reins, proposing to a girl who hated me was pretty much about the last thing I wanted to talk about. I tried shifting topics. "What's the first position you want to do again once the baby is born? Horny Bull? Petal Pusher? Lotus and the Stingray?"

Didn't work. Anna's mind was firmly focused on my cousin's nuptials. Why chicks dug weddings so much, I would never understand. And Rachel seemed like the type who would want fountains, ice sculptures, doves, and butterflies, but who really needed any of that crap? Personally, I think everyone should do what Anna and I did. *No muss, no fuss, no coconuts.* Just straight to the point, you're married. Boom.

"I wonder how he's going to do it," Anna mused. "Jenny knows, but she's not talking."

"Don't know, don't care," I yawned, flopping an arm over my eyes. I really didn't give a shit about anything Matt did anymore. Fuck him. "Whatever he does, I'm sure it's going to be needlessly complicated. All he's got to do is say, *Hey, wanna get hitched?* How hard is that?"

Anna poked me in the ribs. "You're so romantic, it's almost embarrassing."

Lifting my arm, I peeked up at her. "Do you really want to know what's embarrassing about me?"

Looking intrigued, Anna leaned toward me. "What?"

"Nothing," I said, squeezing her nipple. "Nothing about me is embarrassing."

Anna squeaked in surprise, then smiled in a way that I knew meant she was ready for round two. *Thank you, pregnancy hormones.*

Just as I was reaching out to give her breast a proper fondle, a mood-stopping sound filled the air. "Mommmmmmmmmmmmmm-mma! Want out!"

With a groan, I covered my face with my arm again. "Shouldn't she be able to climb out of the crib by now? My mom said I could climb out when I was nine months old."

Holding her stomach, Anna sat up. "Yeah, well, thankfully, Gibson isn't quite as fearless as you, and she's not big on heights. She's getting bolder every day though," she said with a sigh.

"Good," I answered. "She's a Hancock. She shouldn't be afraid of anything. Matt could learn a thing or two from her. Chickenshit." I bet that was the real reason he'd told me no. He was scared, scared I'd blow him out of the water and forever take his precious position from him. Well, that was one thing he actually should be scared about. He should conquer his fear though, goddammit.

Anna let out a low laugh that riled me up and made me forget all about Matt's fears about me. "You may want to cover that before I bring your daughter downstairs."

I removed my arm from my eyes to gaze at her. "You may want

to ride that before you go get her?" Anna smirked and I shrugged. "Just sayin'. Missed opportunity." Shaking her head, Anna kissed my shoulder, then left me. "Your loss!" I yelled out. And mine. Damn hard-on.

Eventually, we had to get dressed for the gallery opening. It was a formal event, which was annoying. I mean, I didn't mind wearing a suit every once in a while—I looked amazing in a tie—but performing while wearing this getup was going to be odd and uncomfortable. We were a rock band, not a fucking jazz quartet.

Anna fixed my tie with a soft smile on her lips. I'd chosen red, of course. Power color. My jacket and pants were red too. Why stop with just one piece of power? More was…well, more. "You look amazing," she told me.

"I know," I said, eyeing her deep turquoise wrap dress. There was an alluring tie in the front that undid the entire thing. I wanted to pull it. I mean, I *really* wanted to pull it. "You look pretty amazing too," I told her, pride in my voice. My wife was so fucking hot.

"I know," she replied with a playful smirk. Her lips were painted a rosy shade of pink. I thought the color wouldn't look too bad on me if I sucked it off her. Yeah, that was happening before the night was through.

The doorbell rang and Anna looked past me to the hallway outside our bedroom. "Babysitter is here. I should go let her in."

Nodding, I let her walk past me. After she was gone, I looked over my reflection in the full-length mirror. Damn. The red on red on red was totally working for me. Even my hair was pulled back into a low ponytail with a red elastic band. My wife was a very lucky woman; I was fucking hot. Adjusting my tie, I winked at myself, then gave myself a kiss in the air. *Yeah, I still got it.*

Grabbing a full flask off my dresser, because I was sure I was going to need the help to get through this, I stuffed it in my back pocket and headed after my wife. I felt strange leaving my daughter's life in someone else's hands. But we'd used this girl a few times before, and so far nothing serious had happened. It better stay that way. I liked Jennifer, but I'd haunt her for the rest of her natural fucking life if she so much as let a hair on Gibson's head fall to harm.

Anna and Jennifer were talking in the entryway when I got there. Jennifer was holding Gibson, who was playing with her mess of curly hair. It wasn't long before Gibson's fingers were completely tangled in the ringlets. "So, we're probably going to be late," Anna was saying. "I'm not sure how long the opening is scheduled for, but it's a big night for everyone, so we'll probably celebrate afterwards."

"No problem, Mrs. H. It's cool, stay out as long as you need to." Jennifer was seventeen, but sometimes she sounded thirteen. It freaked me out. I'd feel better if a sixty-year-old grandma who'd successfully raised a dozen kids was watching our girl, but Anna was fine with Jennifer's age. She often told me, "Relax, Jennifer routinely babysits for a handful of local celebrities. She can handle watching just one child for a few hours." I guess. But I'd still feel better if someone more mature was watching my baby girl.

Jennifer's eyes swung over to me when she noticed my entrance. Her gaze was approving; she liked my outfit. She always looked at me that way though. No surprise there, most women did. "Oh, hey, Mr. H. How's it hanging?"

Normally I'd say something witty like, "A little to the left," but her words instantly reminded me how young she was. With a frown, I crossed my arms over my chest. "You have our number? And the gallery's number? And the rest of the band's numbers?" You could never be too cautious about some things, and Gibson was one of those things.

With a patient smile, Jennifer nodded. "Yep. I have everyone's digits."

Digits? My lips compressed into a thin line, but I let it go. It would be fine, and Gibson loved her. "Okay, well, no company, no boys, no phone calls, no booze." Suddenly feeling like I was just as lame as Matt, I shook my head. I needed to stop being so douchey. "You can totally raid the fridge though, and once Gibson is down for the count, feel free to use the pool."

Jennifer's smile brightened. "Will do!"

I wanted to lay down some more laws for her, or maybe add some more emergency numbers to her phone, but Anna wrapped her hands around my bicep. "We should go, babe."

I knew she was right, but I still had to resist the urge to fire Jennifer and take Gibson with us. Wasn't the *woman* supposed to be the one stressing over the sitter? I may have been in head-to-toe red, but I suddenly felt a lot less powerful. Luckily, I had a cure for that in my back pocket. Best get this goodbye over with so I could start drinking. "Yeah, okay. Bye, baby girl," I said, giving Gibson a one-armed squeeze and a kiss.

"Bye, Daddy," Gibson said in the sweetest, most adorable voice on earth. God, my kid was cute. Spinning on my heel, I stalked away, nearly dragging Anna with me. *I will not tear up, I will not tear up. It's fine to leave her with an underage stranger.* Damn it. When did I become such a pussy? I might have to turn in my man card soon.

I felt better once I was in my Hummer, cruising across I-90 toward downtown Seattle. But then I remembered that I hadn't reminded Jennifer about Gibson's habit of putting everything in her mouth. We kept the floors pretty clean, and our fun stuff was locked up, but it was amazing what else that kid could find. "Shit," I muttered, wondering where I could turn around on a bridge. "I forgot to tell Jennifer something. We need to go back."

Anna gave me a funny look from the passenger's seat, then dug through her purse and showed me her cell phone. "We can call her if we need to, but it's fine. I already mentioned the mouth thing, ear thing, *and* the nose thing. Jennifer is well-prepared. God, that kid is obsessed with openings. The day she finds her woo-ha is the day I'll need therapy."

Normally, I would have laughed, but I just wasn't in the mood at the moment. "Oh... okay, so long as she's aware... I guess."

Anna placed her hand on my knee. "She'll be fine, Griff." Laying her head against my shoulder she quietly said, "You know, if Kiera, Jenny, and the others saw more of this side of you, they might like you better."

Surprise washed over me. I thought I was cool with those two. "Kiera and Jenny don't like me?"

Retreating back to her side of the car, Anna laughed. "I said they'd like you *better*. At the moment, they think you're...okay."

That made me frown. I wasn't an "okay" person. I was awesome wrapped in awesome smothered in more awesome. They should be squealing to their neighbors that they know me, not that they merely tolerate me, like Anna had implied.

Tossing a playful grin Anna's way, I murmured, "No, what they need is to see the side of me that you see. The intimate side, if you know what I mean. Then they wouldn't think I was just 'okay.' They'd be clamoring around my door every night, like stray cats trying to get a decent meal." I winked at her. "I'll keep myself to myself though, save everyone the grief."

Rolling her eyes, Anna laughed. "How very noble of you."

A wide smile broke over my face as I returned my attention to the sea of taillights in front of me. Noble was practically my middle name.

We arrived at the gallery about an hour late, which was right on time in my book. Matt was flustered when he spotted us outside, talking to the fans. Thanks to us and our awesome diehards, Jenny's gallery was already on the map. It had probably been tagged about three million times tonight already. We were so cool.

"There you guys are. What took you so long?" Matt was dressed to the nines in a full-on tuxedo, and his short blond hair was gelled into rigid, unyielding little spikes. How appropriate. Clearly nervous, he seemed more tightly wound than usual; it looked like he was having muscle spasms he was moving around so much.

Since humor was the best cure for nerves that I knew of, and since fondling myself in front of him was too good of an opportunity to pass up, I cupped myself and said, "What do you think we were doing?"

The fans around me tittered, but Matt's scowl deepened. "We're on in thirty minutes. Try to not be late for *that*, okay?"

I saluted the fucker, but he was already turning to leave. The fans who had been trying to get his attention asked me, "What's up with him?" Disappointment was clear in their voices. Douche hadn't even said hello.

Shrugging, I told them, "Same thing that's always up with him." I mimed putting my finger where the sun didn't shine, and a couple of the girls laughed. "That and he's proposing to his girl tonight. His nerves are basically fucked."

The crowd gasped and squealed. Anna elbowed me, then held her hands out. "You weren't supposed to say anything."

I pointed to the sign above the door loudly proclaiming BAGETTES! "I'm not supposed to say anything to Rachel. These guys don't count." I turned back to the crowd. "You guys won't tell Matt's girlfriend, right?"

More giggling and shrieking. I took that as a yes, and gave Anna a look of triumph. *See, they don't count.* Amused, Anna patted my shoulder. "I'm going to go inside and find a seat. Come find me when you're done."

Watching her waddle away from me, I murmured, "You bet your sweet little ass I will."

Jenny's gallery was exactly what I was expecting it to be—a boring building with a bunch of bland, artistic, nonsensical crap hung on the walls and a few odd-shaped statues blocking the flow of traffic in the hallways. No nude art anywhere. I was instantly disappointed, and I kind of felt cheated as I looked over Jenny's creations.

People were walking around looking all hoity-toity with fluted glasses of champagne, so I found a waiter and grabbed me a couple. It was my obligation to drink for Anna, since she wasn't able to enjoy it. The burden of being a husband.

On the far side of the main room, I spotted my wife hanging out with Kiera, Jenny, and Rachel. I was just about to rush up and goose her sexy ass when Rachel turned and gave me a wicked glare. Jesus. Was she still mad at me for saying that Matt didn't want to be tied down to just one girl? She needed to move on. Obviously, since he was still proposing to her, I'd been joking. Hopefully after this, the ice in her veins would melt.

Not wanting to get an earful about how much of an ass I was, I avoided the girls and looked around for where we were supposed to play. There were a surprising number of people here. Most I didn't know, but a few familiar faces stood out. A couple of Pete's waitresses were here, including Kate, the uppity one who never let me grab her ass. She was standing with Justin, the lead singer of Avoiding Redemption, one of the bands we were leaving on tour with tomorrow. Justin and Kate had been bumping uglies for a while now, but I didn't think they were heading to the altar anytime soon. At least, they shouldn't. They didn't even live in the same city. How the heck was that supposed to work out? Exactly. It wouldn't.

When Justin spotted me, I raised my glass in a toast to him. He nodded his head in greeting, then turned his attention back to Kate. The other members of Justin's band were drifting around the room. There were around six thousand of them, I swear. Okay, maybe not, but however many there really were, it was too many. Bands should be small and simple.

Other bands were here too. The three members of Holeshot, and most of the members of Poetic Bliss, the chick band that had replaced us at Pete's Bar. The drummer, Meadow, was hanging out by a purple-and-pink painting with her girlfriend, Cheye… something. I don't know. I couldn't remember. All I knew about her was she used to dig Kiera. Maybe she still did? Yeah, wouldn't surprise me if she was lusting over Kellan's wife. Maybe they made out from time to time? Mmmm, that was a pleasant thought.

Realigning the stiffy growing in my pants, I turned around to find something else to focus on. Denny and his wife were standing right in front of me. Denny's dark eyes were wide as he took in my outfit. "Interesting suit. Very…red," he said. His voice had a light Australian accent to it that girls went crazy for. I practiced it as often as I could, so I had it down; I practically sounded like I was from there.

"Yeah? Thanks, mate. That means a ton coming from a bloke like you." *Nailed it.* I should apply for dual citizenship, since I was nearly a native.

Denny frowned while his wife, Abby, laughed. "Please stop try-ing to sound like me," he said. "It's embarrassing."

With a wink, I told him, "For you, maybe, but the sheilas go crazy for this crap. Practically tear my clothes off when they hear how awesome my voice is."

Abby laughed a little harder while Denny cringed. "I can guar-antee you they don't think it's awesome."

"Please. You're just upset that we were almost brothers, until you lost your woman to Light-Socket Hair over there." I jerked my thumb over to where Kellan was standing with Hailey, who was his half sister, or some shit like that. Denny and Kiera used to date un-til Kiera dumped Denny for Kellan. I think that's how it went. The details were fuzzy. If the drama didn't have to do with me, I didn't pay much attention. With a smile, I told Denny, "I'd be upset over missing out on being related to me too. I'm pretty amazing."

"So I've heard," Denny said, his jaw tight. Then he smiled and added, "Actually, that's the one thing I'm thankful to Kellan for. I think I would wither and die in your shadow." He let out a sad sigh. "I'm not man enough to be your brother. I'll just have to settle for being your manager."

His lips quirked like he was joking, but I thought he made an excellent point. I raised my glass to him as he started pulling Abby away; she was still laughing. "You make a valid argument, sir," I said in my regular, non-accented voice. "Cheers." I downed the rest of my champagne.

I was just wondering how much the D-Bags paid Denny and Abby to manage the band when I felt someone tugging on my arm; a little of the champagne in my second glass splashed onto the floor. "Watch it," I said, snapping my head around.

Matt was standing there, beads of perspiration on his forehead. He seriously looked ill. "We're on," he choked out.

Feeling a little sorry for the pathetic specimen of a man in front of me, I handed him my drink. "Here, drink this." Without hesi-tation, he gulped it down, then handed me back the empty glass. Wow, he really looked like shit. If he was this torn up, maybe he really shouldn't go through with it. "Dude...you gonna hurl?"

Matt frowned. "I'll be fine. I just want to get this over with."

Nodding, I suddenly realized there was one positive thing that I could look forward to from this unnecessary spectacle. "So... where we going for the bachelor party? Vegas? New York? Bangkok?" I couldn't even say that last one without sniggering. Bangkok...

Matt gave me the evil eye. "Let's just get through tonight, okay?"

Shrugging, I followed him when he started weaving through the crowd. We had plenty of time to plan a killer party. And as family, it was my duty to make sure his bachelor party was unforgettable. The night wouldn't end until I had thoroughly embarrassed his scrawny ass. I'd need llamas, licorice, and lasers. This was going to be fun.

When we got to the section of the gallery that was clearly set up as a stage, I frowned. "Ummm...far be it from me to tell you how to do your job, but aren't we missing some stuff? Like...almost everything?" The instruments were there, but none of the speakers, amps, and microphones. Nothing electronic at all actually.

Matt put his hands on his hips. "We talked about this. A couple times. I swear you never listen to a word we say, which is yet another reason why..." He stopped talking, like he didn't want to get into it here. I kind of wanted him to continue. Just where the fuck was he going with that? Matt let out an annoyed huff, and instead said, "We're in an art gallery, so we can't do a normal set. We're going acoustic."

I frowned as I looked over at my sad, quiet acoustic bass. "Well, that's lame. If we can't play loud, what's the point of playing at all? We can just play the freaking CD on low...then we'd have more time to drink." I pulled out my flask and took a long gulp. It burned going down, then warmed me, head to foot. *So good.*

Matt looked about to curse me out—shocker—but a pair of arms wrapped around his chest. "Oh my gosh! I'm so excited! It's going so well, don't you think?"

Jenny pulled back to stare up at Matt. Her blue eyes were sparkling, her pearly whites were gleaming, her pale hair was glowing, and hope and goodwill for all mankind was radiating out of every pore. The word "perky" was too small an adjective for Jenny. Especially now…when she was a little tipsy. She loved everybody at the moment, probably even me.

While Matt tried to smile through his nerves, Evan unwrapped his fiancée from him. "Babe, remember what I said about tackling the guests? We want them to come back after tonight." Evan's grin was just as big as Jenny's.

Jenny nodded, then shifted to squeeze Evan. "Right. Sorry, honey. I'm just so excited! This is a dream come true for me." Her eyes glistened and she sniffed, like she was going to start crying. *Oh God, please don't.* I hated it when women cried. Kiera patted Jenny's shoulder, but I knew that wasn't going to stop the tears. Jenny needed a distraction.

After Evan left her side to set up his drums, I walked over to her. "Hey, Jenny, if you really want to make your dreams come true tonight, we could go to the back room and I could…" Leaning down, I whispered in her ear everything I could do to her. I was very explicit.

She slugged me in the arm. "Griffin! Ewwwwww! No, no, and hell no! Ugh…I need to go rinse my ears out now. Maybe scrub my brain…"

Laughing, I shrugged as I started walking to my guitar. "Your loss." *Mission accomplished.* She no longer looked like she was going to start bawling.

Once Matt, Evan, and I were settled behind our instruments, Kellan whistled to get everyone's attention, and the crowd gathered around us. Jenny narrowed her eyes at me before turning to smile at Kellan. Rachel gave Matt an encouraging grin, since he still looked like he was about to throw up, and Kiera beamed up at Kellan like he was the most amazing male specimen to ever walk across the face of the planet. Whatever. Anna was standing beside Kiera. She gave Kellan a cursory glance, then shifted her eyes to me. Ha! *Take that, Dreamy McDreamerson.* My girl likes me better.

"Hey, we're the D-Bags, and we're all so excited to be here, playing at the grand opening of Jenny's gallery. She's worked so hard for this, and we're all very proud." Kellan tilted his head as he smiled down at Jenny. Her eyes filled to capacity again and I sighed. *Good job, Kellan. I'd cured her, and you just made her cry again. You can proposition her this time.*

"This one's for Jenny, and her baby: Bagettes," Kellan finished.

Evan began tapping his sticks together in a countdown rhythm that even I understood. I had no idea what song was first in the lineup though. Maybe I *should* pay more attention in rehearsals. Nah, fuck that. If they were never going to give me a shot, what was the point?

I kept waiting for Matt to propose as we played. After each song, I thought, *Okay, now he's going to do it,* but he never did. He looked sicker and sicker as the night wore on, but he never did or said anything to Rachel. It was weird, and kind of a wasted moment. I mean, if he was trying to be all dramatic and shit, how could he top proposing to her during a D-Bags concert? Couldn't be done. By the end of our set, I was convinced that he had changed his mind about asking her to marry him. Poor Rachel. She'd need to be comforted. I could be her shoulder to lean on, so long as she didn't cry too much…and she let me cop a feel in the process.

Thinking of Rachel's breasts naturally made me think of my wife's. She had an amazing rack, even more so now that she was so close to popping. Her jugs were kegs, and I wanted to tap them. Just the thought was giving me an erection, which felt kind of awesome against the vibrations of the bass. Oh yeah…my wife and I were finding a quiet spot after this. Maybe that gigantic curtain decorating the wall behind the stage. Yeah, that sounded like a great place for a blow job.

I was practically bursting at the seams by the time the damn set was done. Fuck, was it necessary to play five thousand songs at this damn thing? Some of us had shit to do. As soon as Kellan thanked the crowed, I set down my bass and sought my wife. *Finally.*

"Thanks for listening. Don't go anywhere, because we've got a special encore for you in fifteen minutes." The crowd clapped and I swore under my breath. *Encore? Are you fucking kidding me?*

Spotting Anna at the edge of the crowd in that damn sexy turquoise-blue wrap dress, I grabbed her elbow. "I need a hand," I whispered in her ear. "Or a mouth," I added, not wanting to limit my options.

I led her palm to my rock-hard cock and her eyes widened. "Oh…yeah, you do." She twirled a lock of her hair around her finger, a coy expression on her face. "Did I do that?"

Discreetly rubbing her hand against me, I told her, "You always do that." Looking around to see if anyone was watching, I pulled her toward the curtain. Everyone was too busy chitchatting with the band to pay us any mind. We slipped behind the thick purple fabric completely unnoticed. The material draped against the floor, so even our feet wouldn't be discovered. It was the perfect hiding place, and really erotic, because we could still hear everyone on the other side of the curtain. Doing it here would almost be like doing it in public, and that was something I'd always wanted to try.

While Anna watched me with hooded eyes, I unfastened the belt around my waist. "You are the sexiest thing here," I whispered. "I could barely concentrate, thinking about you…your legs wrapped around me, your nipple between my teeth, your clit against my tongue."

Anna's mouth dropped open, and she ran a hand over her breast, then squeezed her own nipple. I got even harder. Fucking sexy-ass woman. "Jesus, I need you…"

Undoing my pants, I shoved them and my underwear down my legs. Then I grabbed her hand and pulled her toward me. Our mouths collided in a frenzy of passion. It was all the more exciting because we were purposely being as silent as possible. If only the fuddy-duddies knew what was going down on the other side of this curtain…well, Jenny's gallery would be a hell of a lot more interesting.

While my hands explored my wife's body, her hand stroked my cock. *Fuck, yes.* Could she get down on her knees in her condition? God, I hoped so. I could put my jacket down on the floor so she'd be more comfortable.

Her thumb played with the top of my piercing, and I had to reach out and clench the curtain before I fell over. *Fuck that felt good.*

"Don't do that," she whispered. "You'll pull the whole thing down."

With a great deal of willpower, I released my hold on the curtain. There was a slit in the center of it that let me see out into the gallery. Dozens of people were still out there, talking, milling about. Watching them while Anna rocked my socks off was stimulating, and a low groan escaped me. Jesus, I was going to come all over her hand if she kept touching me like that.

"I don't think I can get down there, baby," Anna murmured, "But...I brought something, just in case..."

She reached into her purse, then pulled out one of our sex toys. It was a fake pussy that we sometimes used when hers wasn't up to the task. She had it with her? Fuck, my wife was awesome. I couldn't even coherently thank her. All I could say was, "Oh my God, oh my God, oh my God..."

Tilting her head, she smiled up at me. "I'll take that as a yes, please."

She used her finger to moisten the inside of the rubber tube, then she pushed it over the top of me. It wasn't the same as being inside of her, but fuck, it was pretty awesome. I clenched her shoulder as she started working it over my body. Staring out the curtain slit, I saw Jenny giving Evan a kiss, Kiera cuddling up into Kellan's side, and Matt staring at Rachel; he finally didn't look all that ill. Everything was right in the world.

Containing my grunts and groans was difficult, especially as the throbbing intensified, and the buildup started approaching. Knowing my body, Anna sped up her hand. I was so close, almost there. "Don't stop," I begged her.

With a throaty laugh, she purred, "Baby, nothing could make me stop right now. You're so fucking sexy when you come. I want to see it...show me..."

Fuck, yes. "I'm almost..."

Out of the corner of my eye, I saw something weird. I didn't want to pay attention, since I was on the verge of an incredible release, but I noticed anyway. People were stepping toward the curtain. Jenny and Evan were coming up to either side of it, and Jenny was telling the crowd, "Before the D-Bags' final song, there is one last piece of art that I'd like to show everyone. It's my finest work, and I'm so very, very proud. I can't wait for you all to witness this…"

Jenny and Evan stepped in front of the curtain, and that's when it dawned on me that there was a very large painting on the wall on the other side of us. And Jenny wanted to show it to everyone. And I was about five seconds away from coming. *Fuck. Me.*

Stilling Anna's hand, I wrenched the sex toy away from her. "Step back, now!" I warned her. Anna was confused, naturally, but she did as I asked and stepped into the recess of the curtain, on the far side of the painting. I wasn't able to move yet, and I didn't have time anyway. The curtain opened, the crowd gasped, and me fondling my junk with a bright purple sex toy was the first thing everyone in the gallery saw. Needless to say, I instantly lost my climax. I couldn't come right now if I was paid to.

Jenny's eyes widened before she spun on her heel and looked away. Evan's cheeks went bright red. "Griffin? What the hell?" With the fake pussy still securely around my cock, I reached down for my pants, but not before I noticed cell phones being whipped out and pointed in my direction. Awesome.

Matt had pulled Rachel front and center for the unveiling, and they were both staring at me like I was some mutation from another planet, then Rachel's eyes glanced up behind me. She gasped and covered her mouth with her hands.

Hoping I didn't see what I thought I might see, I turned to look at the painting. Yep. That was what I was afraid of. The piece that Jenny had been hiding, saving for last, was one gigantic question artistically splashed onto canvas. *Rachel, will you marry me? Matt.*

I had just fucked up his proposal. Again. He was going to kill me. Jenny too. She was crying again, but not happy tears this time. Evan glared at me as he took her into his arms. Great. He was pissed too. Perfect.

Chapter 4

Will the Real Mr. Awesome Please Stand Up

Everyone decided to call it a night after that. I tried apologizing, but no one would give me the time of day. Matt was too furious to even look at me. Evan just shook his head. Kellan was the only one who wasn't completely angry, but he left with Matt. To calm him down, I guess.

I wasn't too worried about it. Once we were on the road, everything that had happened tonight would be forgotten. Water under the bridge. Besides, Rachel said yes to the proposal, so what did it really matter. At least, I was assuming she said yes. There wasn't a whole lot of talking after the incident. Just yelling. Mainly at me. Rachel dug Matt though; there was no way she'd say no to him.

Jennifer was surprised to see us back home so early. I didn't feel like explaining what had happened, so I just told her, "It was boring so we bailed."

She accepted that and started going on about her uneventful evening with Gibson. I was glad her night with my kid was nowhere near as dramatic as my night had been. And I was really glad I hadn't caught her doing something sordid. If I had, it would have been the last time she watched Gibson. Some part of my mind tried to tell me how hypocritical it was for me to think that, but I ignored my stupid brain. Where Gibson was concerned, nothing I said or did could be used as a moral compass. She was on an entirely different level than me.

After I paid Jennifer and she left, Anna hopped on the nearest computer. It was a little early for leaks, but it wouldn't surprise me if my schlong was all over the Internet by the morning. Oh well. At least it was an attractive schlong.

Anna let out a relieved sigh when she didn't find anything. "Maybe it won't get out. I mean, it *was* mostly friends and family there, right?"

"And the local paper." I instantly remembered Kellan telling me to be on my best behavior for the press. Oops.

Anna cringed then bit her lip. With a shrug, I told her, "It doesn't matter. The guys will get over it, Rachel will marry Matt, Jenny's gallery will be a hit, and I'll be headline news for a little while. It's kind of a win-win." I smiled, but Anna still didn't look convinced that everything was okay. "Don't even stress. This is nothing. It will blow over before you know it. I mean, that wasn't the first time I've been caught in an awkward position, and I'm sure it won't be the last. After a while, people will just expect me to do crazy shit like that."

Finally, a slow smile spread over her lips. "Well, maybe next time I can share the awkwardness with you. I feel kind of bad that everyone's blaming just you for this. It was my fault too."

With a mischievous grin, I nodded. "Okay, next time we have sex in public, I'll let you get caught too. Deal?" I held my pinkie out. Giggling, she clasped it with hers.

"Deal."

A limo arrived early the next morning to take us all to the airport; Anna had to elbow me three times in the ribs to get me out of bed. I was not a morning person. Anything before ten was way too fucking early for me. We had a flight to catch though, so I made myself get up and get moving.

The tour was starting in Los Angeles and ending in Seattle. I had no clue where we were going to be along the middle of the tour, but I didn't need to know. Someone would tell me where I was before I hopped onstage.

We were taking a private plane down to L.A., which I was thankful for; riding commercial sucked ass. The limo dropped us off right next to the jet. Anna and I were the last to arrive, but everyone else was still outside, killing time before the flight. Matt spotted me stepping out of the limo, and immediately started heading for the plane. Whatever. I was content to let him sulk, since I was still sort of sulking about him treating me like a subpar member of this band. Anna didn't want to let it linger though. Grabbing my elbow, she told me, "Go talk to him. Please."

I rolled my eyes, but I couldn't refuse her; she'd won the negotiation last night before we'd hit the sack. According to our rules, I had to at least attempt to make it up to Matt.

He was quickly speeding away from me, but I got to him when he was on the first step of the stairs leading up to the plane. "Hey, man," I said, grabbing his elbow. "Wait up."

With an irritated scowl, he looked back at me. "I think it's best if we just avoid each other for a while, okay?"

I let out an annoyed grunt. "Dude, it's not like I did that on purpose. How was I supposed to know the proposal was going to go down like that, huh? Maybe if you'd shared your little painting plan with the class…"

Matt's pale eyes narrowed to cold slits. "I did," he seethed through clenched teeth. "More than once."

Thinking back through all the conversations Matt and I had had recently, I shook my head. "No, you didn't. I would remember." Probably. Maybe.

Stepping off the stairs, Matt made a lunge for me. I managed to back away in time, but his arms were extended like a zombie hunting his prey, and his fingers curled and uncurled like he was mentally choking the life from me. It was kind of creepy. Before Matt could actually throttle me, Kellan stepped between us with his arms outstretched.

"Whoa! Let's not do anything stupid here," he said, looking between Matt and me.

Matt shifted his angry eyes to Kellan. "He ruined my engage-
ment, Kell. Let me choke him. Just until he passes out. We'll all be
thankful for the quiet flight, trust me."

Kellan sighed while I raised my chin in indignation. *Asshole.*
Damn Anna for making this such a big deal. Why the hell couldn't
Matt and I just ignore each other for a while? A long while. Self-
righteous fucker was still on my shit list.

"He didn't ruin anything, Matt," Kellan calmly replied. "Rachel
said yes, and that's really all that matters, right?"

Matt rolled his eyes but grudgingly nodded. "Yeah. I guess."

Kellan patted his shoulder. "Good. Then how about we let this
go so we can get through this tour in one piece?" That made me
scoff. *Letting it go* was Kellan's answer to everything. *Well some of
us aren't as saintly as you, Kyle. Some of us have grudges that aren't
so easily released.*

Matt glared at me once more, murmured, "Fine," then disappeared into the plane.

Kellan let Matt disappear, but when I started to follow him, he
put a hand on my chest. "Maybe you should give him a minute."

Crossing my arms over my chest, I locked eyes with Kellan.
"Why is everyone so bent out of shape about this? It's not like I
embarrassed anyone but myself last night, and I really don't care if
people saw my junk."

Kellan frowned as he shook his head. "That's what you don't get.
What you do affects more than just you. It touches everyone you're
connected to. Try and remember that, okay?"

He patted my shoulder and walked over to Kiera and Ryder.
With a scowl on my face, I watched him leave. I was aware of other
people. Even though everyone treated me like I was a complete
moron, I wasn't. Last night was an honest mistake, a mistake that
any one of them could have made. It wasn't like I was intentionally trying to hurt the band. Not like they were by keeping me tied
down. Jerkwads.

Kellan and Kiera were helping Anna with Gibson, so I hopped
onto the plane to sulk in peace. Matt was in the very back, staring
out the window. Ignoring him, I took a spot by the front. Kellan

was probably right about space, but I was the one who wanted it. Fuckers were always picking on me, holding me to a standard that was almost impossible to maintain. Couldn't they just accept me for the person I was, instead of trying to force me to be someone they wanted me to be? Isn't that what friends were supposed to do?

The plane was a ten-seater, with more than enough space for everyone. It was swanky too, with leather captain's chairs, tables, a kitchen area, and an almost full-sized bathroom. Anna and Gibson sat at a table across from me, while Kiera and Ryder sat at the next table with Kellan and Evan. Matt remained alone in the back. That guy could sulk even better than I could. Maybe it was in our genes.

Evan ignored me for the first third of the flight, then he finally started talking to me. Or *at* me. "Jenny is really upset over what happened at the gallery, and frankly...I am too. What were you thinking?" he asked, his eyes dark and soulful.

Tired of talking about last night, I shook my head. "I was horny. I didn't know the curtain was coming down. I fucked up, and I'm sorry. Okay?"

Evan thought about it for a minute, then nodded and shrugged. "Yeah, okay."

His acceptance made me smile. If only Matt would snap out of it as quickly. But I'd ruined his plans, and Matt hated ruined plans. I'd just have to wait out his pissiness. Easier said than done. He was always getting riled up over something.

It took two weeks, but Matt eventually got over it. He never actually said he forgave me, but he stopped glaring and started joking. I knew we were back on track when he started insulting me. That was how I gauged our relationship—if he was giving me shit, then he wasn't mad at me.

I think it helped that images from that night started popping up everywhere, and some clever asshole had started calling me Hand Solo. It stuck, and the name was everywhere in a heartbeat. Matt thought that was hysterical, and he'd taken up the nickname too. Whatever. Didn't matter. That night had been one of the hottest moments I'd ever had with Anna. It was a fond memory for me, one that reminded me just how amazing, sexy, and up for anything my wife really was, and reminiscing about it made me giddier than a thirteen-year-old with a hidden *Playboy* magazine stashed under his mattress. I wasn't sorry it had happened. All I was sorry about was that I hadn't had a chance to finish.

As things with Matt returned to normal, my thoughts returned to showcasing myself this tour. There had to be a way to do it. If Matt wouldn't give me a chance to play lead guitar, then maybe Kellan would let me be front man. Not for all the songs, but maybe one. Or two. One of the crappier ones that no one cared about.

Since we rode on the same bus together, I had plenty of time to talk to him about it. "Come on, Kell, I know the songs better than you do, and my voice is spectacular. The crowd will love it!"

He looked up from playing with Ryder on his lap. Ryder had a few teeth coming in, and the front of his blue D-Bags romper was soaked in saliva. He was all smiles though; my nephew was rarely unhappy. While Ryder grabbed for a set of plastic keys in Kellan's hand, Kellan shook his head. "No, Griffin. I already said that."

Irritation spread up my spine as the oft-repeated answer to my every question burned in my ears. I was so tired of people telling me no. "Yeah…I heard you. I just don't think it's right."

Kellan's attention had drifted down to his son yanking on the keys in his hand, but he lifted his eyes again after my comment. "You don't think it's right that I sing the songs? That I wrote? I'm the lead singer, Griffin. It's my job."

I rolled my eyes. "You guys are so hung up on labels. *I'm the lead singer. I'm the lead guitarist.* Wah, wah, wah. Would it kill any of you to step outside of the box?"

"We've got a good thing going, Griffin. Now isn't the time to shake things up."

I leaned forward in my seat. "Now is the perfect time, Kellan. Fans don't want us to stay stagnant and predictable. They want fresh, they want new, they want to be knocked off their feet. Frankly…they want me."

Kellan cracked a smile as I relaxed back in my chair again. "They want you? Really?"

Nodding, I jerked my thumb toward the back of the bus, where Anna and Gibson were taking a nap. "That little gallery fiasco went viral, and the fans ate it up. They want more shit like that. They want more *me*. I'm telling you, if you gave me just a little bit of freedom during the show, you wouldn't regret it."

Kellan sighed and looked over at Kiera. She had an expression of horror on her face, but she shrugged, like she didn't have an answer for him. Jesus. It wasn't like I was asking to raise their kid for them. It was one fucking song. Kellan looked back at me, his expression serious. "Maybe we can find something fun for you to do. Maybe a skit or... something."

A skit? Well, acting wasn't exactly what I wanted, but I suppose it was a start. "Sure. Great. Can we start tonight?"

A strange look passed over Kellan's face before he answered. "I have to talk to Matt and Evan first, see what they say. I'll let you know."

"Awesome!" I bolted out of my seat so I could go tell Anna the good news—they were finally giving me a chance. Maybe not in my preferred form, but I'd take any opportunity to strut my stuff. I wondered what I should do for my skit as I opened the door to the back bedroom where my wife was resting. Maybe I could re-create the moment from the gallery. *Hand Solo here. I'm here to rescue... well, myself. I'll be with you in a minute.* Ha! Maybe I should do stand-up instead.

"Guess what, Anna!"

Her curled form stirred a little, and a vague moan escaped her, but that was it. She had Gibson nestled in her arms, and my baby girl looked like an angel lying there with her golden hair fanned out around her. So far she was having a blast on tour. She loved meeting people, and there was always someone new to see. The only part she wasn't crazy about was the long bus rides between gigs. The back and forth rocking of the bus made her carsick. Anna too. She said it was like being on a boat, and she could still feel the swaying motion even when she wasn't on the bus. I wished there was something I could do to help Anna feel better, but other than get her drunk, which wasn't an option at the moment, I was clueless.

When Anna didn't wake up, I sat on the edge of the mattress and debated if I should disturb her or let her sleep. She *did* look wiped. My excitement won out though, and I rocked her shoulder to wake her up. "Guess what, babe?"

"We're there?" she croaked. Turning her head, she peeked up at me. "Are we stopping soon?" She was a little green, and her face was creased from where she'd been resting. There was even some dried drool in the corner of her mouth. She was still superhot though.

"I don't know where the hell we are... but Kellan is going to give me the stage tonight! I'm going to do a skit, or some shit like that."

Anna slowly sat up on her elbow. She studied my face with an eyebrow raised. "A skit? During a concert? That's... interesting."

I shrugged, then laughed. The adrenaline was making me goofy. "Yeah, it's not exactly what I was hoping for, but it's something, and something is better than nothing."

Anna nodded, then held a hand to her stomach, like she was about to be sick. "Sounds good. Wake me when we're there."

She fell back to the bed and my eyes devoured her curves. I was way too jacked up to just go sit down with Kellan and Kiera, twiddling my thumbs. I needed action, something to keep me entertained. And Anna was the best form of entertainment that I knew of. I knew she felt like shit at the moment, but maybe a little fun time would make us both feel better? It had worked a time or two before. "Hey... think you and me can go to the bathroom and make a little magic? I'm too stoked. I need to burn off some energy."

"Can't. Trying not to be sick," she murmured.

"Ah, come on. We'll be in the bathroom, so if you do upchuck, you'll be right there... and remember that one time when you were drunk and you thought you were gonna throw up, but we fucked and you felt so much better afterwards. I might just be the cure you need, babe."

Her eyes flashed open; they were a fiery shade of deep green that seemed to glow with heat, and not the good kind. Before she could pierce me with the laser beams she was charging, I held my hands up. "How about I go, and you stay here and sleep."

The heat dissipated and her eyes fluttered closed. "M'kay." *Whew. That was close.*

I ended up pacing the bus for an hour. By the look on Kiera's face, she wasn't thrilled about my constant movement. Needing something to do, I grabbed Ryder from her and told her I'd keep him occupied so she could have some alone time with Kellan. She seemed uncertain about letting me babysit until Kellan convinced her that I wouldn't break their baby. As if. I rocked with kids.

While his parents presumably got freaky, I bounced the little bundle of energy up and down the aisle, all the while telling him stories that Gibson often requested from me—stories of knights and dragons, and princesses who kicked ass. Ryder yawned, and his bright blue eyes eventually drooped closed; he was asleep five seconds later. *See, Kiera, nothing to worry about. Mini-Bag loves me.*

When we got to the venue, Kellan disappeared to go chat with the other guys about tonight, I assumed. I wanted to go with him, to plead my case and maybe throw around some ideas, but Gibson was being all needy and clingy, probably because I'd spent so much time with Ryder and she hated me paying attention to another kid. She was in for quite a shock when her baby brother or sister was born. But it was clear she needed me, so I stayed on the bus with her and Anna.

"So, what do you think you'll do tonight?" Anna asked me. She looked a lot better now that the bus had stopped moving.

"I don't know…what do you think I should do?" I'd been running over ideas in my head, but all I could come up with was penis puppetry, and I had a feeling the guys wouldn't be cool with that.

Anna shrugged. "Show off your talent." Thinking about what I'd been debating doing onstage made me snort. With an amused smile, Anna amended with "Your nonsexual talent."

Nodding, I thought about what my talents were. Besides being devilishly handsome and a stallion in the bedroom, I was, in my humble opinion, a master rapper. In fact, I knew every lyric to every Vanilla Ice song. And not just his megahits, the B-side stuff too. Nobody could do Mr. Ice better than me. "That's it. That's what I'll do!"

Anna blinked. "What's it?"

Kissing her forehead, I handed Gibson to her. "I gotta find the guys before the show starts. I'm gonna need background music."

"For what? What's your plan?" she asked again.

"You'll see," I said, crooking a smile.

Anna rose to her feet. Gibson reached for me, but I couldn't take her again. There was too much to do! "Wait," Anna said, placing her hand on my arm. "Let's take a moment and talk about your idea. You know, make sure you've got something really great so the guys will be blown away. While I was resting, I was thinking of some things that might—"

Grinning ear to ear, I cut her off with a kiss to her cheek. "I'm sure your ideas are cool, but what *I've* got planned will blow their skulls into a thousand freakin' pieces!" Anna said my name again, but I was too excited to stop and explain it all to her now. I'd tell her when it was a done deal.

There were people everywhere when I hopped off the bus—security, people who worked for the venue, and members of the other bands. I didn't see any D-Bags though. Fans behind a chain-link fence cheered when they spotted me. A few of them screamed, "I love you, Kellan!" I almost stopped and told them I wasn't Kellan, but I didn't have time. The show was starting in a couple of hours.

Justin was the first person I spotted when I stepped inside the building. He was talking to the lead singer of Holeshot, Deacon. They were talking about Kate, from what I could tell. They were midconversation, but I smoothly interjected with "Hey, you seen Kellan?"

Justin turned my way, his lips in a frown. He had a tattoo across his collarbone that I thought was cool, but the script was so elaborate, I could never read it. Knowing Justin, it was something lyrical and poetic. If it were me, it would say something like *Sit Here*, with arrows pointing up. Oh man...I should totally do that.

"Nah, I haven't see him, but the meet and greet is starting soon, so he's probably talking to the radio people."

That made sense. The local radio stations always had contests that allowed people backstage access, where they were free to talk to us and take pictures. It used to be all formal and shit when Sienna Sexton was running the show, but now people just kind of meandered backstage like they were checking out some weird zoo for rock stars. *And over there on your left is the mythical one-eyed beast of Cockistan. Legend has it, the creature only comes out when properly aroused. Let's see if we can awaken it, shall we?*

"Oh, okay." I patted Justin on the shoulder and started to leave, but he stopped me with a question.

"Hey, you're friends with Kate, right?"

I shrugged. "Kind of. Why?"

Like a red stage light was being directed toward him, Justin's face started shifting colors. "Uh, well, we've been together awhile now, and I was thinking of stepping things up. Maybe asking her to move in with me."

Raising an eyebrow, I told him, "You want to ask her to move to L.A.? Don't bother, she won't. Her life is in Seattle, dude." Giving him a sympathetic smile, I told him the hard news that as a friend I had no choice but to deliver. "You're better off dumping her and scoring someone who lives in your town." I snapped my fingers as an idea came to me. "Brooklyn Pierce, that chick with big knockers from that futuristic space show. She's gotta live somewhere around there and she's fucking hot. Dump Kate and date her. Problem solved."

Justin looked dumbfounded as I smacked his arm and walked away. It might take him a minute, but eventually he'd see that I was right. Him and Kate weren't meant to be, but him and Brooklyn... damn, she was smokin'. I couldn't wait to double date with them. Lucky bastard.

When I found Kellan, he was waist-deep in contest winners. They were all around him, and Kellan was smiling as he shook hands, signed autographs, and answered questions. The fans were squealing, giggling, and in some cases, crying. Girls. Such a strange species.

Knowing they wouldn't mind me manhandling them, I started

elbowing my way through the crowd. Surprisingly though, they gave me dirty looks, like they didn't know who I was or why I was intruding on their place in line. Weird. I'd expected to get groped along the way. Oh well.

"Let me through, I need to talk to Kellan," I said, pushing past a trio of girls.

"Wait your turn, dude," one of them replied. She was wearing a KELLAN KYLE IS MY ROCK GOD T-shirt, so I figured she was blind to the rest of us "rock gods."

Narrowing my eyes, I told her, "I'm in the band, and I need to speak to Kellan…my *bandmate*." Just saying it irritated me. Kellan fan or not, this chick should know me on sight.

She scoffed, like she thought I was blowing smoke out my ass. I was about to set her straight, about several things, when someone in front of her said, "No, no, he is in the band. Drummer, right?" she asked. The pigtails in her hair made her look four. Maybe that was why she didn't know my instrument. She was still learning what all the different pieces were.

"Bass," I muttered, shoving my way around them.

Kellan finally noticed the commotion and swung his head my way. It took some jostling, but I eventually worked my way through the obsessed K. K. crew to get to him. He didn't seem happy to see me. "Oh, hey, Griff. Here for the meet and greet? I thought I saw a couple girls wearing Griffin shirts heading down the hall. I bet you can catch up to them if you hurry."

I was getting battered from behind by his overeager fans, but I ignored them and his comment. "What did the guys say about tonight? 'Cause I had this awesome idea—"

"Yeah, about that…" Kellan grabbed a pen from a fan and started signing a CD case. "I talked to the guys and they feel…well, we feel that tonight isn't a good night. We need to sit down and plan something first…work it into the lineup. We've already got a set plan, you know?" He handed the case back to the fan, then looked up at me. Giving me a dismissive pat on the shoulder, he added, "Maybe tomorrow night, okay? We'll talk later, when it's not so crazy." Grabbing another pen, he started signing something else.

My jaw dropped, and I lost my place in line as the Kellan fans pushed me back. Within minutes, I was on the outside of the circle looking in. *Tomorrow?* That sounded like a million hours from now. Why the hell couldn't we just *try* something tonight? Why the hell couldn't we wing it? Made no sense to me.

Just as I was debating it, a girl beside me handed me a Sharpie. "You're with the band, right?"

Frowning, I grabbed the pen. "I *am* the band," I told her. Looking confused, she glanced between Kellan and me. Sighing, I grabbed the glossy photo she had in her hand. It was of Kellan, but I signed it anyway—right across his face. The fan looked at the signature like she didn't recognize it. She thanked me, but her look of confusion didn't lessen. She had no clue who I was. What the fuck?

Behind me, a couple of girls started giggling. I turned around and they smiled at me with crimson faces. "Oh my God, it's you. Hand Solo!"

I gave them a sly grin. Finally, someone who recognized me. "At your service," I said, faking jacking off. I even ended the gesture with an explosion. They squealed and covered their eyes.

After they recovered, one of them stepped forward. She was tall and thin, and the D-Bags shirt she was wearing looked like it had been molded right onto her it was so tight. "You've got to sign my shirt," she stated.

"Gladly." Taking her pen, I scrawled my name across her chest. She laughed the entire time.

Evan and Matt wandered through the area and, leaving the girls to daydream about me, I cornered my bandmates and asked them about me performing tonight. Like they'd rehearsed it, they gave me the same answer as Kellan—*Not tonight, maybe tomorrow.* Between this denial and Matt's absolute refusal to let me play lead, I was fuming by the time we went onstage. I supposed it wouldn't hurt to wait a couple of days, but still, I was ready for my moment—a moment that had been denied me for far too long already.

For the first time in a long time, I really paid attention during the show. Kellan made the introductions, Kellan started the songs,

Kellan spoke to the crowd between the songs. Every once in a while, he would throw a remark our way, but he was in control of the *entire* performance, and most of his attention was directed toward the fans, not his bandmates. He'd chat with them, ask them how they were doing, run down the aisle to say hello to the ones in the back. Every question he aimed their way was met with a resounding shriek of approval that made me roll my eyes in annoyance.

Nothing he was doing was all that special. *I* could ask the crowd if they were having fun. *I* could run up the aisleway to high-five strangers. *I* could sing the songs, gyrate my hips, and point at hot girls in the pit. Kellan wasn't the be-all and end-all of this band. He was just *one* member. As I looked around the stadium, I began to wonder if the fans knew that. All the posters I could see were for him. I LOVE KELLAN. MARRY ME, KELLAN. WE ADORE YOU, KELLAN. KELLAN IS THE MAN. HAVE MY BABY, KELLAN. *Kellan, Kellan, Kellan.* I was sick of his name long before the concert ended.

And every night for the next two weeks was a lot like that night. All I heard from the guys when I asked them if I could have a piece of the performance pie was, *Not tonight, maybe tomorrow.* If we had an off day, they all avoided me like the plague. They claimed they were sightseeing or catching up on sleep, but I didn't buy it. I knew when I was being blown off. All I could do was sit, stew, and complain to anyone who would listen to me.

"Don't you think that's ridiculous? I'm not asking for much, just ten minutes on the mic. Or five. I would be happy with five. A moment in the spotlight, that's all I want."

The girls I was talking to looked between themselves. Then they started simultaneously busting out questions that had nothing to do with what I had been talking about. "So, Griffin, you're sharing a bus with Kellan? What's it like? What's he like? Is he tidy or messy? What does he do during his downtime? Is he really married, or was that just another rumor? I just can't tell what's real or not anymore."

I stared at them in complete shock and disbelief. "Did any of you listen to a word I said? He's an ass. They're all asses!"

One of them put her hands over her heart. She was wearing a KELLAN FOREVER T-shirt. Go figure. Where did they keep finding these fucking T-shirts? "But he's sooooooo hot. And sexy. And talented. I just want to lick him all over."

"You're all brainwashed," I murmured.

One of the girls had a wide face framed with equally wide glasses. She must have heard my comment, 'cause she frowned and looked at me like I'd just told her that her kid was ugly. "You know, you keep talking about how they screwed you over, but you should just be happy that you're a part of the team."

The girl beside her had so many freckles, her face looked like one of those dot paintings that Jenny did sometimes. "Yeah, I mean, so you're not the lead singer or the lead guitarist, you're still the…"

Her voice trailed off and her eyes widened, and I knew she had no idea what instrument I played. "Bassist," I said, annoyed.

Her expression softened with relief. "Right, yeah, the bassist… and that's… super cool."

Wanting away from them, and everyone, I jerked my thumb down the hall. "I'm going to go find a beer now, but if you're looking for a good time, Kellan's that way. Just tell his assistant with the baby that you're there to suck his dick. She'll scoot you to the front of the line."

The freckled girl looked mortified. "We'd never… I mean, we don't know him, and he might be married, and…" She glanced at her two friends. "Let's go," she whispered. The three of them darted down the hall, giggling.

"Kiera is going to kick your ass for that one," an amused voice said behind me.

Turning around, I saw Anna and Gibson standing there. Anna was holding Gibson's fingers in one hand and an open beer bottle in the other. Goddamn, I loved the fact that my wife could often anticipate my needs. It was sometimes eerie, like she was in my head. Oddly, the thought of her residing in my brain didn't scare me at all. There wasn't anyone else I'd want in that mudhole with me.

Gibson immediately reached out for me when they got close enough. "Up!" she demanded, while Anna handed me my beer. Finally, a pair of people who wanted me more than Kellan.

Picking up my daughter with one arm so I could still drink my beer, I gave Anna an appreciative smile. *You're the best.* Then, remembering my encounters lately, I frowned. "I just realized something...besides the fact that my bandmates are lying, chickenshit assholes."

"Assholes," Gibson mimicked with a cheesy grin.

Laughing, I gave her a high five. "Damn straight, kiddo."

Anna compressed her lips as she shook her head. "So much for curbing the swearing..."

She was rubbing her stomach, like the baby was kicking her in the same spot. It had been doing that lately. Wanting to help her out, I snapped my fingers and hailed a roadie who was walking by. "Hey you, go find a chair for my wife." The guy, who looked about twelve, started to turn away, and I grabbed his shoulder. "And a pillow for her back." He turned again and I grabbed him again. "And something for her to snack on." The guy hesitated, seeing if I needed anything else. "Now!" I snapped, shooing him off.

Anna frowned as she watched the guy hurry away. "Thank you for that, I really would like to sit, and I am kind of hungry...but maybe next time you could say please when you're demanding something?"

I took a long swig of my beer. It was my favorite microbrew, one that we'd discovered while barhopping last year. Awesome. "The day I say please to a roadie is the day I stop touring. Being on the D-Bags crew is bragging rights for those guys, and if I don't continually knock them down, they'll get big heads. It's my duty to be a jerk," I said, completely serious.

Anna's mouth twisted into a wry smile. "Well, continue on then. We wouldn't want any big heads around here..." Leaning forward, she kissed my cheek; she smelled like cotton candy. Delicious. Pulling away from me, she returned our conversation to its original course. "So...what did you realize?" She started massaging my neck and some of the tension instantly started leaving me. Fuck, I loved it when she did that.

With my beer, I gestured to the fans loitering around backstage. "These fans...none of them really give a shit about me. Sure, they usually recognize me as being in the band, but they don't know what I play, what I do. And sometimes they don't even know my freaking name. How the fuck is that even possible? All they care about is Kellan. Kellan this, Kellan that, it's all I hear anymore, and it's bullshit. If they love the band, then they should love all of us. Equally. It *is* a group effort after all."

Anna tilted her head as she considered. "I'm sure it's not personal. Kellan is just…larger than life, and so are his fans. But you have your dedicated groupies too. Remember the group that snuck onto the bus a couple of nights ago. That was for you, not Kellan."

I did remember that group, how could I not? They were all armed with green dildos that they'd wanted me to sign. But even they had asked about Kellan. *Where does he sleep? Can we steal a T-shirt? Does he really fart rainbows and moonbeams, 'cause he's so super awesome like that.* Ugh. I was getting sick of it. "Well, if they are going to call themselves D-Bag fans, then they should do a better job of learning about the *entire* band. We're more than just Kellan, and the rest of us deserve some sort of acknowledgment too."

Seeing through my statement to the heart of what was really bugging me, Anna cupped my cheek. "You'll get the praise you deserve, Griffin. I promise. You're too big a star to stay under the radar forever. Your time is coming, you just have to wait it out and be patient."

At first, her words sent a zing of pride through me. *My wife thinks I'm awesome.* But the lift to my spirits was quickly darkened by a confusing mixture of frustration and hope. *When will everyone else think that?* I sucked at patience, especially now that I was getting so close to what I wanted. And so far too. "I don't know how much longer I can wait, Anna. They're holding me underwater and I'm drowning. Something's gotta change. And soon."

An expression passed over Anna's face that I hadn't ever seen before. It vanished into blandness so quickly I almost thought I'd imagined it, but deep down I knew I hadn't. I wasn't completely sure what it was, but it had almost looked like…fear. Or worse than fear. That didn't make sense though. My girl wasn't afraid of anything. Maybe I was just misinterpreting things. But just that one tiny spark of anxiety on her face made a weird churning feeling rip through my stomach. I settled the feeling by remembering her earlier words. She had my back, she believed in me. That belief was what kept me going. Anna was the fuel to my awesome-train.

Not wanting to see that expression on her again, I said something that I thought would appease her. "Nah, don't listen to me. I'm just talking shit again. All I need is to finish my beer, then everything will be right as rain."

A glorious smile lit up her face, and any worry that may or may not have passed over her was gone. "Well then, drink up."

I held the bottle up to her in a salute, then started downing it. Yeah, a beer would solve everything. For now.

Chapter 5

Meet the Awesomes

They say that all good things come to those who wait. Well fuck whoever said that, because I had waited as patiently as a person could be expected to wait, and nothing fucking changed. The entire tour went by and all I heard was the same old line—*Not tonight, maybe tomorrow*. I heard it so often I was considering getting it tattooed on my forehead.

My mood was foul when I got back home to my same old boring-ass routine. Anna was a week or so from bursting, so she was in a foul mood too. Between the two of us, it had been bitch central at the house lately. It was an odd vibe for us, since we were usually so laid back. Or Anna was, at least. It took a lot to ruffle her.

"Not tonight, maybe tomorrow," I said in a high-pitched, mocking voice. I was in our pool, floating in an inflatable chair, a beer in each cup holder and a third one in my hand. Smacking my fist against the water, I muttered, "They can kiss my ass tomorrow, is what they can do. All I've ever wanted, since this fucking band formed, was one tiny second in the spotlight, but none of those assholes will give me a chance. Fame whores."

Anna sighed from the lounge chair she was resting on; she'd heard this rant before. Several times. I was sure she was getting tired of hearing it, but she was my sounding board; I needed her to listen. "I can't bend over anymore," she said in a whine. "And the only shoes that fit my feet are slippers." She looked over at me with pouted lips. "I seriously want this baby out. It better come early. I don't think I can survive six more days of this crap."

Examining her looking all swollen and uncomfortable, yet still the sexiest thing on earth in her two-piece, I sympathized; her feet *did* look like overdone sausages about to split open. I was kind of scared to touch them for fear they would explode on me. "At least your hell will be over soon. Mine is perpetual. So long as Kellan and Matt are running the show, I'm fucked." Taking a swig of my drink, I flicked the water with my forefinger. I wished it was Kellan's face. Or Matt's. I'd even accept Evan's, since he wasn't exactly campaigning for me. Kellan and Matt had him firmly under their thumbs. Conformist.

A couple of droplets landed on Anna and she frowned at me as she rubbed them off her thigh. "You just need to keep trying. If you want this, don't give up. Show them you're serious, and they'll change their minds and give you a chance."

Because I was in a shitty mood, I scowled at her, but I supposed she did have a point. If I could prove to the guys that I wouldn't embarrass them, maybe they'd cave on their ridiculous stance that I couldn't be trusted with anything more important than mixing their drinks. I was so much more than a bartender, and it was time those fuckers realized it.

Anna cocked an eyebrow at me. "Speaking of serious... when are you going to call Matt back? He's left four messages on the machine."

Yeah, and even more were on my cell phone. I fully expected him to show up at my door any moment. But I was irritated and didn't want to deal with him yet. Besides, what he wanted to do was preposterous. "Did you listen to the message? He wants to start working on the third album. We *just* finished the last one. How about we let our brains rest for a sec before we cram more stuff in there? Just saying."

She looked about to comment on that suggestion, but the doorbell rang. Anna grimaced as the loud gong vibrated the walls.

"I'm pretty sure that just woke Gibson up," she muttered before painstakingly rising from her chair. I thought about climbing out to help her, but by the time I was finished thinking it, she was already standing.

As Anna left the pool room to see who was here, I cringed too. Had Matt finally taken the initiative to come collect me, since I clearly wasn't in any hurry to contact him? Only one way to find out. Finishing my beer, I tucked the can by my hip and, using my fingers as paddles, I pushed myself over to the edge.

Grabbing the cool tile, I pulled myself out. I started to walk away, but then I remembered how much Anna hated it when I left wet footprints all over the house, and I dried myself off with a nearby towel. *Awesome husband, party of one.*

Strutting through the house, letting it all hang loose, I headed for the front door to see who was here. When I got to the door, it was wide open, revealing an assortment of people I hadn't expected to see. Anna was standing in front of them, still dressed in her bikini. Hearing my approach, she looked back at me. The smile on her face was clearly forced; so was her cheery voice. "Griffin… your family is here. Isn't that…great?" Her eyes widened on the word "great," and I could tell what she really meant was, *What the hell are they doing here?*

Moving to stand beside Anna, I waved at my dad and my brother, Liam. Both of them were loaded down with bags. Behind them I could see my mom and my sister, Chelsey, getting even more bags out of a minivan; my sister's twin girls were with them. From the looks of all the crap they were unloading, the gang was moving in for months. "Hey guys, good to see you. Wasn't expecting you yet."

My dad gestured at my lack of clothing. "We see that."

Liam dropped his bags and covered his eyes like he'd just been splashed with acid. Falling to his knees, he began dramatically moaning and groaning. "My eyes, my eyes!" he screamed, sounding like the dying witch in *Wizard of Oz*. Liam fancied himself as an actor. I flipped him off while Anna excused herself to grab me something to wear. And probably to curse me out behind closed doors. We'd planned on calling my parents when she went into labor, so they could arrive right *after* the baby was born.

Dad looked down at Liam still writhing on the ground, then ignored him and turned back to me. "I'm probably going to regret asking this, but why are you naked?"

Shrugging, I told him, "I was in the pool."

"Naked?" He bunched his brows. They had been blond like mine when he was younger, but Dad was mostly gray now. He said that was because of us kids, but I called bullshit on that remark. If there was any reason Dad was gray, it was because of Mom. She rode him hard then put him away wet every time she could. More than once I'd joked that he should have *Property of Marsha Hancock* tattooed across his backside. He never laughed when I said that.

I nodded at his question and repeated my answer. "In a pool." When he still didn't seem any less confused, I clarified. "It's basically a gigantic bathtub, and I don't know anyone who uses their suit in the bathtub…that's just weird."

Dad blinked; I swear even his eyes had shifted from blue to gray. "I…guess that makes sense."

Liam, his act apparently over, finally stood up. "Hey, bro," he said, giving me a chin nod. "Nice place you got here. You leasing it?" Liam refused to believe that I was actually more successful than he was. Before the D-Bags got big, he'd constantly rub it in my face how much money he made. But now that I was in the world's biggest band, he may as well have picked his meager income from my ass crack. He was having a hard time adjusting to this new reality.

"Nah," I said, crossing my arms over my chest. It made my package more predominant, but I didn't care. My package was worth the view. "I bought it outright." I hadn't, I still owed a shitload on this place, probably more than it was worth, since I was pretty sure I'd overpaid in my eagerness to live here, but Liam didn't need to know any of that.

He frowned and sniffed in a haughty way that I hated. Liam liked to compare his looks to Brad Pitt, but I thought he looked more like the Sarlacc pit. Okay, maybe not that monstrous. He was a Hancock after all, and he did have our charm, trademark blond hair, and striking blue eyes, but even with all that, he was no A-list movie star.

"Oh," he muttered. Trying to sound wise, he said, "You probably shouldn't have sunk all your money into real estate. Diversification is the key to long-term wealth. Big mistake, bro. Big mistake."

Looking him straight in the eye, I told him exactly what I felt about his opinion on my wealth. "Bite me."

Just as Anna came back with some shorts for me, I heard my mom bellow from the van—"Gregory! Liam! These bags aren't going to move themselves! Set your shit down and get your asses back here for the rest of the luggage!"

I smiled as I slipped the Superman shorts on. *Good old Mom.* As Dad and Liam scurried away to do her bidding, I turned to Anna. "I better help too. Mom can get nasty when she doesn't get her way."

Anna raised an eyebrow. "So can I. Why are they here so soon?"

I shrugged. "I don't know. It's cool though, huh? Now we have help for Gibson. You can rest more…" Sounded good to me. Ever since we'd come back from the tour she'd been complaining about being tired. I think she was still suffering from motion sickness, even though it had been a few days since we'd last been on a bus.

Her green eyes flashed in the sunlight as she thought about that small positive. Accepting the situation, since it was too late to change it, she let out a long sigh. "Oh well. At least it's only twenty days. Too bad for them though, they're missing out on time with Baby Hancock. They should have waited so they had more time with he/she."

Smiling, I lifted a finger. "Actually, that wasn't part of our negotiations." Knowing this wasn't going to go well, I started wading through the bags that Dad and Liam had left on the doorstep to go help Mom with the rest of their stuff.

From behind me, Anna snapped, "What? What are you talking about?" I looked back at her. She was still just in a bikini, but that wasn't stopping her from following me to the driveway. Anna was about as self-conscious about her body as I was. I totally dug that about her.

"The deal was twenty days. Period," she said. Her voice was firm, unyielding. Technically she was right, but there was one small flaw in the pact, and I fully planned on exploiting it.

I raised a finger at her. "No, the deal was that they could stay twenty days *after* the baby was born. That was what you put on the table. We never talked about how long they could stay *before* the baby was born, so these days leading up to it don't count."

Her jaw dropped and I hurried away from her. "You're an ass," she murmured, right on my heels. She could move quickly when she needed to.

She thwacked me across the backside right as we got to the car. I let out a tiny cry of pain just as Mom handed me a bag. Anna hadn't held back, and my ass was probably bruised now. Mom loaded me up with three more bags, then patted my shoulder. "Good to see you, baby. Why don't you put Chelsey's bags in a room for her, then come back for Dawn and Della's stuff." From the way she said it, it was clear that helping my sister and her kids get settled wasn't an option.

"Yeah, okay, Mom." I turned to give one of the bags to Anna and Mom thumped me across the head. I rubbed the knot with a scowl on my face.

"Your pregnant wife does not need to be schlepping bags around. All she should be doing is resting." Mom gently took Anna by the arm and Anna finally smiled. "Now come on, dear, let's get you on the couch." She glanced down at Anna's nearly bare body and her lips pressed into a thin line. "Maybe dressed too."

My sister was wrangling her kids when Mom walked off with Anna, but she paused in chasing them to smirk at me. "Nice shorts. Thanks for putting them on before the girls noticed."

Annoyance twisted my features. "They're four. They don't know enough to care." Both of my nieces had their hair in matching French braids; they looked like they could be the spokeschildren for Swiss Miss with their fair skin, pale eyes, and platinum hair.

Chelsey's husband was a burly, muscular dark-haired guy that I had affectionately nicknamed the Italian Stallion, or I.S. for short, since he reminded me of Rocky. The girls looked nothing like him. The Hancock genes were just too strong for Rock.

"Where's I.S.?" I asked her, looking around for the mountain of a man. Was he still in the car? You'd think the bulging muscles would be easy to spot.

Chelsey gave me a sigh I was all too familiar with from people. It was a *Why don't you know this?* sound that really got under my skin. "Dustin shipped out three weeks ago, Griffin. He's on deployment for at least a year. I know I mentioned that a couple times recently."

I nodded, like I'd known that all along. And now that she mentioned it, it did seem like I'd heard that somewhere before.

Chelsey smiled at me, then turned and barked, "Girls! To me, right now!" Dawn and Della instantly responded. Stopping in front of Chelsey, they stood tall and straight, at attention for their commander. Chelsey had a tendency to talk to her kids like she was a drill sergeant and they were new recruits, and they usually responded to it right away. I'd have to remember that with Gibson and Newbie, although I didn't think Anna would be cool with me shouting at our kids.

Once Chelsey had the girls following her like ducklings, we headed toward the house. Out of the three of us siblings, I was the youngest. Liam was the oldest. Chelsey was pretty close in age to me, just a year older. She was also the coolest sibling, besides me, of course, and the most attractive. Also, aside from me. Good looks ran deep in my family, but they ran a little deeper in Chelsey. She just had that California girl thing working for her, which meant I'd spent a lot of time when we were younger kicking losers' asses who'd thought they had a shot with her. Dreamers.

The pair of us had been pretty tight when we were younger, and we still got along really well. Chelsey was a dancer, the regular kind, not the exotic kind. Before she'd had kids, she'd belonged to a ballet troupe in L.A. I'd been forced to go to so many of her recitals as I kid that I'd refused to go as an adult. I felt kind of bad about that now, since her career was essentially over. With Dustin gone so often, she was practically a single mother.

Dawn and Della ambled inside after us, and I shut the heavy door behind them. Dad and Liam had come into the house with Mom, and I could hear them upstairs claiming rooms. I could also hear Gibson talking to Anna in the living room. Guess all the commotion really had woken her up.

Chelsey let out a low whistle as she looked around. "I'm sure I've said this before, but this really is a nice place you've got here, Griffin. You know, in case none of us have ever mentioned it before, we're all very proud of you. Our little brother, the rock star... it's pretty amazing what you've accomplished."

The praise made me instantly uncomfortable. It wasn't that I didn't like praise. I loved that shit! But pride from a family member, that was just... weird. That was taking awesomeness and applying emotion to it, and I didn't do emotion. I'd rather just skip over all that mumbo jumbo and stick to cold hard facts, like nobody could shred it like me. *That* I'd be totally cool with hearing.

"Uh, thanks," I mumbled. "Want to go pick your room, before Dad and Liam nab all the best ones? I think the pink taco room is still open," I added with a laugh.

Chelsey rolled her eyes again, but laughed. "You're so gross, I don't know how Anna puts up with you."

Sometimes I didn't either. Instead of admitting that, I told her, "Puts up with me? She's just as bad as me, maybe worse." Thinking about my crazy, sexy wife made me smile. Anna was perfect. Fucking perfect.

Chelsey laughed at the look on my face. "Never thought I'd see the day a girl made you look like that."

Gibson came trouncing into the room then. She must have heard me and wriggled away from Anna and Grandma to get to me. She did that a lot. It really pissed Anna off. Releasing the bags about to pull my arms out of my sockets, I scooped her up. She kissed my nose and I laughed as I rubbed her back.

"Yeah," I told Chelsey, "Now I have two girls who knock me to the floor. I'm not the man I used to be." I said it with a forlorn sigh, meant to generate sympathy and compassion, but Chelsey nodded with enthusiasm.

"No, you're not." Just as I was about to get offended, she added, "You're about a thousand times better than the man you used to be."

Again, that uncomfortable feeling settled around me. When did Chelsey get all soft and girly? Aside from ballet, she'd been the toughest chick in the neighborhood growing up, doing all the tomboy stuff that the prim and proper girls hated—skateboarding with me and Matt, throwing out curses and insults that would get us whooped if our parents heard us, and snaring every rodent, reptile, or arachnid we could find. Aside from the budding boobs and pointe shoes, she'd practically been a guy. In fact, I think she still held the record for farthest loogey launched.

Guess marriage and kids had softened her some. Oh well, she was still my favorite sibling, and I hated the thought of stuff being hard for her while Dustin was gone being a hero. She didn't have to be alone. "Hey, just to let you know, my place is plenty big enough for you and the girls. Stay as long as you like." Anna was going to kill me for weaseling out of our negotiation, but surely she more meant my parents and my brother. Chelsey was different, and Anna would be cool with it once she got to know her.

With a soft smile, Chelsey nodded. "Thanks, Griffin. That means a lot to me." After she said it, she walked over and knuckle punched me in the arm. It stung like a bitch, but I laughed as I flipped her off. Guess she hadn't softened as much as I'd thought.

After a couple of hours, everyone was all settled in and Mom was making dinner. Anna was still smiling, so I had to believe she was pleased with having my family around. So far, at least. Dawn and Della were keeping Gibson entertained while Mom worked on her to-die-for spaghetti sauce. My stomach was already growling, and I knew it wouldn't be done for another couple of hours. Can't rush perfection.

Anna was trying to help Mom, but Mom just made her sit

down whenever she tried. Mom's hair was still the perfect shade of blonde, and she kept it in a short, sensible style that required little fuss or muss. If we were at home, Mom would have a cigarette in her mouth while she worked, but she was being respectful of our house and keeping her vice to brief visits outside. Smoking was the one thing Mom had been an absolute hypocrite about growing up; she'd constantly forbid us to pick up the "nasty habit," as she called it. When I was eleven, she'd caught me with one of hers. Instead of grounding me, or giving me a slap on the wrist or something, she'd made me smoke it, plus the rest of the pack, and then another pack after that. I'd never been so sick in all my life. Even now, cigarettes made me nauseated.

I was having a beer with Dad and Liam, and Liam was filling us in on a commercial audition that he was sure he'd nailed for a high-end watch company. He really wanted to get the job; he'd heard that he'd get to make out with a model in it.

In my distracted state of homelife bliss, I did something out of habit that I'd been purposely avoiding doing for a while: I answered the phone when it rang. "Griffin? You *are* alive. Where have you been? I've been trying to get a hold of you."

Hearing Matt's voice on the other end made me clench my jaw. I wasn't ready to talk to him yet, but it was too late now. With a shrug he couldn't see, I told him, "My family is in town. I've been busy with them." It was only a partial lie. True, they'd just gotten here a few hours ago, but I *was* busy with them.

Matt's voice instantly changed. "Oh, okay. Well, tell them hi for me, and we'll catch up soon."

Great. He was going to want to come over now. "Yep. Will do. Thanks for calling."

I was about to hang up, but Matt quickly said, "Wait! I wanted to talk to you about rehearsals. We want to get together as soon as possible and start on the next album."

Now I knew I should have been all gung ho about work to impress both Matt and Kellan, but we'd just fucking gotten home. I needed a few weeks off. And fuck them if they didn't understand that. When I responded to Matt, my voice came out in a whine. Maybe it wasn't the best way to deal with him, but I couldn't help the reaction. "We *just* finished one. Let's take a break. Relax."

The firm, no-nonsense Matt answered me. "We can't, Griffin. This business is competitive, we have to continuously release new stuff to stay relevant. We need to keep pushing the envelope."

Irritation ripped up my spine so fast, the hair stood up on my arms. Push the envelope, stay fresh? That was the same shit I'd been saying on tour, when I'd tried to get them to give me five seconds in the sun. Hadn't meant a damn to them then, so why should it now? "You were fine sticking to the same ole on tour. What's it matter now?"

My voice echoed my mood, and Matt let out that damn impatient sigh that everyone around me seemed to have mastered. "Griffin…" Just the condescending way he said my name set me off. I wasn't three, and he wasn't my dad.

"Don't 'Griffin' me, I have a point and you know it. You guys blew me off, even before the tour, when you flat-out told me no, I couldn't advance my position. So why should I give you the time of day? What's in it for me to be a part of this band?"

Silence fell around my home, and I could feel everyone's eyes on me. Maybe I should have taken this into the other room. Matt was silent a moment before he answered me. "What's in it for you is what's always been in it for you—fame, money, and women. That's all you care about, all you've *ever* cared about, so don't act like we're screwing you over by making sure you get exactly what you love. Rehearsal is tomorrow at three. I'll see you then."

He hung up the phone before I could respond, and all I could do was stare at the damn thing and wait for my fluctuating mood to even out. *Fame, money, and women?* Yeah, maybe that had been my goal in the beginning…and maybe it still was now, but… something was missing. I had a hole in me that wasn't being filled properly, and FMW just wasn't enough anymore.

Dad was giving me concerned eyes when I put the phone away. "Everything okay?"

Trying not to sound too disgruntled, I told him, "Yeah. Matt was just being a douche is all, like normal. He says hi, by the way, and wants to hang out while you're in town."

Dad's worry faded away as he smiled. My parents both loved Matt to pieces. Matt used to joke that they wished he was their son and not me, but I knew that wasn't true. Well, I was pretty sure that wasn't true. I was the coolest person my parents knew. They had bragging rights for being able to say they'd encoded my DNA. They couldn't say the same about Matt. He was Uncle Billy's kid through and through. They even had the same stick poking out their assholes.

I considered bailing on rehearsal, but Matt would just hound me until I showed up, and Mom and Dad wanted to go "watch the show." I told them a few times there wouldn't be much of one, since the "show" was mainly going to consist of Matt, Kellan, and Evan huddling around a piece of paper covered with lyrics that, to be brutally honest, didn't make any sense at all.

They insisted on coming though, along with Liam, Chelsey, and the girls, so the whole damn family was packing up to head out to the countryside. Oh well. At least Dawn and Della would get a kick out of running around Kellan's farm. Okay, he technically didn't have a farm since the only animals on the property were a couple of stray cats, but it had that rural, rustic, there-are-pigs-in-the-shed feel to it.

I sighed as I took one last look at my backyard. It butted up against Lake Washington, and there was a private dock, with a few feet of shoreline that created a shallow area for Gibson to play. But the favorite part of my backyard...there was no grass to mow. The entire space was one gargantuan tennis court. I didn't even own a mower. Neither Anna nor I could play tennis for shit, but just the fact that my "grass" was artificial was amazing. You couldn't find crap like that in the countryside. Kellan was missing out.

When we finally got to Kellan's ostentatious security system, I let Kellan know that my family was with me. Maybe I should have asked if they could come, but asking permission wasn't my style.

After ringing the *Let me the fuck in* buzzer, I said into the intercom box, "Hey, Kell...Anna and I are here, and uh...we've got two cars…'cause, you know, I have family visiting and they want to see your spread." Leaning over the steering wheel, I added, "And just so you're aware, if my dad has a heart attack climbing up your forty thousand steps, I'm totally suing you."

"Always a pleasure, Griffin," Kellan's tinny voice responded.

I smiled up at the camera while the gate squeaked open, then I made an exaggerated waving motion with my hand so Dad would know to follow me. Our caravan wound its way up Kellan's driveway. When we pulled to a stop at the bottom of the steep slope where Kellan's palatial home rested, Liam oohed and aahed. You'd think he hadn't been to my house at all by the way he acted. I mean, come on, my pool was indoors!

"Damn," he muttered. "So this is what being the biggest rock star in the world gets you," he muttered.

Removing my seat belt, I twisted in my seat to toss him a glare. "Second biggest, or equally big to me. We're the same size, I mean."

Liam's lips curled up as an indecent thought snapped into his brain. "I'm sure you are," he told me, amusement all over his face. "But did you measure, just to be sure?"

"Ha. Ha. Go for the penis joke, how original."

Anna let out a soft laugh, and I turned my attention her way. She shook her head as her jade eyes locked on mine. "Nowhere near the same size. Kellan wishes," she added with a wink.

"Damn straight," I said, leaning in for a kiss. Her lips were so soft against mine it made me a little delirious. And she was sweet like strawberries and smelled like orange Creamsicle suntan lotion. It was a heady combination, and I considered handing Gibson to Liam and staying in the car with Anna so we could spend a little quality time together. It had been too long, nearly three whole days, and with her due date right around the corner, I knew it might be three more until she was comfortable enough to get horny. This last week and a half were going to be long for me as well as for her, just for different reasons.

As our kiss deepened, I heard Liam make a disgusted noise and open the car door. Gibson whined about wanting to see Ryder, so I sadly disengaged from my wife to take care of my daughter.

Anna was breathing a little heavier when we separated, and I reconsidered my earlier assessment of her libido. I knew the gleam in her eye fairly well, and I was certain we'd be busting out the toys tonight. Maybe something pink, with a lovely hint of vibration to give my girl that oh-so-special release that she deserved. She was about to deliver my second child, after all.

"Ready?" she asked. My hands flew to my jeans and I started unfastening them. Shit, if she wanted to do it now, I was all in for that. Surely someone would remove Gibson for us. Laughing, Anna stopped my fumbling fingers. "No." She nodded outside, to where my family was gathering and staring. "Ready to see the guys again?"

I sighed, remembering the last words I'd spoken to Kellan when we'd parted ways. *Thanks for being a complete and total tool and yanking me around for the past few weeks. That was awesome. We should do it again sometime. Or never. We could try that.*

Kellan had given me a *Try to understand* face. *It wasn't intentional. We just didn't have time to properly plan anything. Next tour, okay?*

I'd walked away without even dignifying that comment with a response. Next tour sounded an awfully lot like *Tomorrow, Griffin, tomorrow.* But the problem with tomorrow was that it never actually came to pass. There was always another one, waiting.

Shaking off my malaise, I gave Anna a bright smile. "I'm always ready. For anything." Stepping out of the car, I walked to the back to unleash my child. Once she was wrapped around me tight, like a python crushing the life out of its prey, we headed up the numerous steps to Kellan's front door.

Mom was huffing and puffing long before we reached the top. Maybe this would convince her to ease back on the cigs. "Wow… he needs an elevator," she murmured. Having had the same thought more than once, I agreed with her.

When we got to the top, we were all grateful that the trek was over with. At least the trip back to the car wasn't so bad. I set Gibson down while Mom rang the doorbell. I told Mom to just go inside, but she ignored me. Guess she figured she couldn't be as informal as me, since she hadn't met Kellan yet.

With a charming smile, Kellan opened the door and welcomed

us all inside. I could tell right off the bat that Mom and Chelsey were a bit taken with Kellan's looks. Their gazes flicked over his jaw, his hair, his "smoldering" eyes, and their smiles grew with each feature they studied. Whatever. He couldn't rock a pair of shorts like I could. Dude had chicken legs. No one ever mentioned that about him, but it was true. His feet were tiny too, but that was to be expected since, well... everyone knew the answer to that.

Feeling pretty good in my size thirteen shoes—*in your face, Kellan!*—I sauntered through the door after the women. Kiera had wandered into the entryway, and extended her hand to my mom in greeting. "Hello, Mrs. Hancock. I'm Kiera, this is Kellan. It's so nice to finally meet you."

Mom looked back at me as she shook Kiera's hand. "Yes, I don't know how we missed so many opportunities to meet while you were visiting Los Angeles. It's almost like it was orchestrated..."

I shrugged at her implication. "We were busy."

Mom rolled her eyes then looked back at Kiera. "You have a lovely home... but way too many steps."

"We get that a lot," Kellan said with a laugh. I swear Chelsey let out a wistful sigh beside me. That better be because she missed her husband. If she turned into a simpering, starstruck Kellan fanatic, I was going to smack her. Repeatedly, if necessary.

I indicated her once Mom was done with Kellan. "This is my sister, Chelsey. These are her kids, Dawn and Della." They were running around the group of us in one big looping circle, chasing Gibson, so I merely pointed in their general direction.

Kiera's eyes turned sympathetic as she took Chelsey's hand. "Sister, huh? You have my condolences."

Kellan laughed again, and I swear my sister muttered, "Damn." More loudly, she said to Kiera, "Thanks. There have been times when I've needed them."

With a guffawing noise of disbelief, I raised an eyebrow at Chelsey. She may get smacked just for fun if she kept it up. "The only sympathy you've ever needed was over the fact that you could never be as awesome as me. You've come close a time or two, but you're still so far..."

Chelsey smiled at my joke. She was one of the rare human beings who saw the humor behind the things I said, and she usually didn't get too irritated at me. Usually.

Dad and Liam were finally in the house, so I introduced them too. "This is my dad, Gregory, and my brother, Liam."

Liam immediately reached out for Kiera's hand. When she extended it to him, he daintily kissed her knuckles, like we were suddenly back in the fifteenth century or something. I nearly expected him to tell her that her beauty hath no rival, or something equally flowery, but all he said was, "Nice to meet you." *You wasted your moment, dumbass.*

Matt and Evan joined the group, and Kellan shut the front door once we were all inside. As Matt hugged my mom, Chelsey grabbed my arm. Voice intent, she hissed, "Why didn't you warn me?"

I blinked at her, completely lost. "About…?"

She slyly indicated Kellan. "That he is so much hotter in person. I mean, I thought I was prepared for his looks, but clearly, I was wrong." She chewed on her lip. "Dustin wouldn't be comfortable with me being here."

She looked so worried about it, I almost laughed. "Why? Are you going to jump him?"

That remark instantly earned me a glare. "No, of course not. I love my husband."

I shrugged. "Then what does it matter what he looks like. It's the same with me and Anna. I'm constantly surrounded by chicks, but I don't do anything with them because I've got her." Peeking over at my wife talking to her sister, I smiled. *I can't wait to suck on her tits tonight.* "Your husband is enough for you, and my wife is enough for me, so the Kellan Kyles of the world don't matter."

When I looked back at my sister, she was staring at me open-mouthed. "Who the hell are you, and what have you done with my brother?"

I shoved her shoulder away from me. "Asshat."

Chapter 6

And Then There Was More Awesome

After everybody was introduced to everybody, the core group of us moved to the rehearsal room. Mom, Dad, Liam, and Chelsey came with, while Anna and Kiera stayed behind to watch the kids. When I asked Matt and Evan where their gal pals were, they glanced at each other before looking back at me and replying, "Work," almost simultaneously. I took that to mean they were truly working, or they were still irritated about the gallery thing. I was going to assume they were just busy, like the guys said. Not even chicks could hold on to a grudge that long.

Since my family was watching, and also because I wanted the guys to take me more seriously, as Anna suggested, I manned up, let my irritation over the tour go, and tried to take a more proactive approach to the part of being in a band that was a struggle for me—the creative process. I just didn't have lyrics constantly running through my head like Kellan, or rhythms constantly pounding on my skull like Evan. But that didn't mean I didn't have ideas. I did. And I was going to share them with the guys, even if they did moan and groan after hearing each one.

"So, wait, you want us to bring in a didgeridoo on our next album?" Matt asked. By his face, you'd think I'd just told him we should wear kilts...which was actually an awesome idea. Kellan would probably veto it though. Wouldn't want his chicken legs exposed.

"Yeah, I think they sound cool, and do you know anybody who uses them? We'd be totally unique." I looked over at Mom and gave her a chin raise. *See how smart your little boy is? You did good, Mom. Real good.*

Matt sighed as he glanced between my parents. He almost looked like he was unsure if he should respond in front of them. I didn't care. *Go ahead, they can know how much of a genius I am. I don't mind.* "It's not that they don't have a great sound, it just doesn't mix with ours. We're a rock band, so we should stick to the traditional rock instruments."

I gaped at him, surprised. "I thought you said you wanted to be cutting edge? Fresh? Sticking to what works, playing it safe…that's how we go stale. We should surprise people on this next album."

"Yes, surprise people, not turn them away. We want to grow our fan base, not completely replace it."

Crossing my arms, I shook my head. "I think you're being too technical about it. We won't lose fans by trying new things. They'll respect us for attempting to grow."

Sighing, Matt looked over at Kellan and Evan. "Anyone miss the days when he just sat around and played video games while we worked?"

Evan gave him a humoring smile, while Kellan turned to me and said, "We appreciate the input, Griffin, and I actually do think you have a point, it's just not quite the right fit. Keep thinking on it, okay?"

Irritation ran up my spine and the words *Not tonight, maybe tomorrow* rang through my head, quickly followed by *You are never going to play lead.* Guess I hadn't let that go as much as I'd thought. Holding on to Anna's pep talk of not giving up, I gave Kellan a tight smile in response. At least they hadn't flat-out said no this time.

After the guys worked on lyrics that I cared nothing about, and rhythms that were good but all too familiar, we played a couple of our older songs that we'd played five million times before. I knew the guys wanted to show off to my family, so I didn't object to playing "Callous Heart" and "Sucker Punch," since those were two of our better songs, but I thought Matt could have offered to give me the lead, just for today, just so my parents could hear me jam. They all clapped and applauded once we were through though, even Liam, although his was more of a polite golf clap. Chelsey made up for it though with an impressive ear-piercing whistle.

We were just about to pack it up for the day when I walked over and grabbed Matt's arm. "Hey, I know it's your instrument, but can we do another one with me on lead…for my mom and dad?"

Matt hesitated as he looked over at them animatedly chatting between themselves. They looked genuinely proud of me, and I wanted to bolster that image of my greatness in their minds. When Matt looked back at me, I knew my parents had managed to do what I hadn't—they'd swayed him. Looked like I would have to have them around for every rehearsal, since it might be the only time Matt let me play.

"Fine," he said. "We'll do 'Killer.' It's not that difficult…you should be able to play it well enough."

I bounced up and down on my toes. I was so excited. I might have Chelsey film the song, then leak it so the fans could get a taste of what a real D-Bags show should sound like. Matt handed me his guitar and I fumbled a little as I looped it around me. My fingers were shaking I was so giddy. I'd need to calm down, or else I wouldn't be able to play. As I handed Matt my instrument, I tried to remember the song. I knew it backward and forward on bass, but it was far more complicated on lead. I was sure it would kick in once we started though.

My family looked confused, since they'd thought we were done, and I let them know the show was just beginning. "We're gonna play one more, but Matt and I are switching so you can hear me on lead." I looked over at Kellan and Evan. They had their eyebrows raised, but they seemed fine about letting me do this. "'Killer,'" I told them, so they'd know what song to play.

Evan nodded, then started tapping out the intro. I flexed my hands, letting the blood recirculate, since it felt like they'd gummed up at the wrists. Evan's pounding drums started in, busting out a heavy beat for us all to follow. Matt and Evan looked at me expectantly, like they were waiting for me to do something. I couldn't remember how Matt's part began though, which was weird. I'd heard it so many goddamn times, it should be second nature, but now that it was time to play it, my mind was a blank wasteland.

With a shake of his head, Matt started in on the bass line. That's when everything fell into place for me. Letting out a small "oh yeah," I started in on guitar.

It took me a minute to get the hang of playing it, and even then I hit a few wrong chords. Taking a peek, I couldn't tell if anyone noticed. I didn't think so. Kellan joined in when his part began. It sounded weird to me, and I couldn't figure out why, until I realized I was trying to play the bass line during a spot when Matt was typically silent. Oops. Cursing, I stilled my fingers, and waited for the guitar's reentry. Was it after the second line or the third? Fuck, I wasn't sure. It was so much easier to pretend to play the song than to actually play it. I made a guess that it was after the second line, and hoped for the best. Kellan and Matt both shot me irritated looks. Oops, guess the guitar came back in on the third line. Well, what the fuck? Who composed this shit? The guitar should be blaring full force the entire song. Kellan should have to shout to be heard above it.

As I glanced up at my family, I saw Liam grimacing, Chelsey flinching, and both Mom and Dad wearing strained smiles on their faces. Heat blossomed on my cheeks, and I nearly stopped playing so I could chill my face with an ice-cold beer bottle. I could do that on bass, but not on lead. I had to keep going through the discomfort.

There were a few more notes that sounded wrong to my ears, and I cursed my bandmates with each twang. If they'd let me play more often, it wouldn't sound so awkward now. I'd be fluent, effortless. Once again, they were holding me back.

Just as I was about to toss the instrument away in disgust, the door opened, and outside sounds filtered into the room. Kellan, Matt, and Evan kept playing and singing, but the new, odd element to the room distracted me, and I stopped playing. Matt groaned and tossed his hands into the air. Evan frowned and Kellan shook his head.

"Griffin, you have to keep going through the distractions. It's called the *lead* for a reason."

I looked over at Matt, but I didn't have a response suitable enough for the strange feeling ripping through my body. It was almost…shame or embarrassment, but that was ridiculous. *I* didn't feel those things, so I settled on anger instead. If the guys weren't such jackasses, I'd be better at this. Just when I was about to tell Matt as much, Kiera strode onto the "stage."

"I'm sorry to interrupt," she said, a little breathless. Her eyes, a slightly browner shade of green than Anna's, locked on mine. "But I'm pretty sure Anna is in labor. Real labor. I think the baby is coming today."

Unstrapping the guitar, a different sort of emotion flooded through me—excitement and anxiety. A new baby! Today! Shit! We were in the middle of nowhere, we needed to get back to civilization…now!

I set the guitar back on the rack, but I lined it up wrong and it fell off. Goddammit, I didn't have time for this shit right now! Managing to catch the guitar before it smacked against the floor, I tried putting it back on the rack. Matt came over and helped me. I offered him a thanks before hurrying away, or at least I tried to scurry off; he had grabbed my wrist and was holding me there. I was so riled up I almost shoved him away from me, but I managed to control myself enough to say, "Back off, dude, I've gotta go." Kiera was leaving the room with my family, and I needed to go with them. Anna was probably in a good dose of pain. She needed me.

"What was that?" he asked, clearly perturbed by my playing. Kellan and Evan stepped closer and I nearly groaned at all of them. Couldn't this wait?

"What? I was a little rusty, that's all." I tried to move past him, but he put his hand on my chest to stop me.

"You said you knew the songs as well as me, but you were clueless, Griffin. You had no idea what you were playing."

Familiar irritation pushed back the rush of endorphins I'd been
feeling. "I've seen you play them enough times that I feel like I—"

Matt cut me off. "You've *seen* me play? But you don't actually
know the songs... And you thought that would be enough to take
over for me? See... that's just another reason why it won't ever happen, Griffin. You don't get that this isn't a game."

I was just on the verge of telling him that all I needed was practice, but his holier-than-thou tone pissed me off. And even worse,
Kellan and Evan were nodding, like they agreed with him. "Fuck
all of you. I've got a baby to deliver."

Assholes. If they had ever given me the chance I'd repeatedly
asked for, I'd be better. It was entirely their fault that I wasn't.
I elbowed my way past the Judgey McJudgersons, then raced to
the house. My anger and disappointment shifted to concern the
closer I got to Anna. As if it were yesterday, I remembered how
much pain she'd been in with Gibson. I'd never seen someone in so
much agony. I could only compare it to getting my junk pierced.
That... had sucked.

"Anna! Anna, where are you?" I spun in circles in the living
room, wondering which way to go first. Where the hell was my
wife?

"In here, Griffin!" Anna's voice sounded from the kitchen, so
I headed that way. When I got there, I saw a sight that I didn't
quite understand. Anna was calmly making Gibson, Ryder, and the
twins a snack. Ryder had a big grin on his face as he sat in his
high chair, digging into a container of applesauce with a tiny plastic spoon.

"Anna?" I asked, confused. "I thought you were going into labor?"

Nodding, Anna glanced at the time on the microwave. "I am.
Every five to ten minutes. Gibson said she was hungry, so I thought
I would make the kids something to eat before we headed out."

Grabbing her hand, I stopped her from slicing pieces off the
block of cheese. "Kiera can handle that. In fact, we should probably
leave Gibson here with her. Dawn and Della too. But we need to go.
It's a long drive, and you don't want to give birth in the Hummer,
do you?"

Anna's eyes widened as she thought about that possibility. "No...definitely no. Okay, let's go."

"Okay then." Looking around, I tossed my hands in the air. "Where the hell is everyone?" Kiera had come back into the house with Mom, Dad, Chelsey, and Liam, but Anna was in here all alone. That didn't sit right with me.

Anna let out an annoyed huff, then straightened and rubbed her back with both hands. "Your mom and dad are starting the car, and Kiera and Liam went to go get the buggy, so I don't have to walk down the steps." She raised an eyebrow. "Like I can't walk down steps or something."

Closing her eyes, she inhaled a deep breath, then let it out slowly. She was having a contraction right now. I glanced at the clock, making note of the time. I had no idea what she meant about a buggy, but I didn't care. Anna needed to get out of here. "Come on," I said, walking to her side. "We need to get you to a hospital in a city where the doctors don't work on animals in their spare time."

"I don't think that happens here..." She stopped talking, then shook her head. "We have to wait for Chelsey to come back. She can watch the kids..."

I was just about to ask where she was when Chelsey dashed into the room holding a skinny, rectangular pillow covered in little purple flowers. "I looked where Kiera said, but this was all I could find. It smells right though," she said, sniffing it.

I had no clue what they were talking about, but Anna nodded and pointed to the microwave. "It will do. Heat it up."

When Chelsey put it inside and turned it on for five minutes, I finally understood what it was—a hot pack. Waiting the five minutes for it to heat up felt like we were waiting for five years. Kiera came back just as the timer dinged. "Your ride awaits," she said in a bright voice.

Anna's contraction was over by now, so she gave Kiera a scornful look. "I can walk down stairs. I'm not an invalid."

Kiera sighed. "Just get in the buggy, Anna. Don't be difficult." Her features were so similar to Anna's that it was distracting at times—high cheekbones, wide eyes, full lips. At the moment, they were more irritating than appealing though. I just wanted to scoop up my wife and leave already.

"Let's just go. Chelsey, can you hang here with the kids?" I asked. My sister frowned, like she wanted to go with us, but then she nodded.

Giving Gibson a quick kiss, I told her, "Daddy will be back soon for you. You be good for Aunt Chelsey, okay?" Her blue eyes were wide with concern as I scuffed her blond hair; she wasn't sure about this, but she liked my sister well enough to not be too upset. "That's my girl. As soon as your new brother or sister arrives, I'll come get you so you can meet 'em." Her pale lips turned down into an adorable pout. She definitely wasn't sure about the idea of sharing us with somebody, even a new potential playmate.

Kellan, Evan, and Matt entered the kitchen right as we were leaving out the dining room door. "Meet you there," I tossed out. I heard them say something along the lines of "okay," and then we were outside and I was staring at the treasure Kellan and Kiera had apparently been hiding from me.

"You have a fucking dune buggy!" I exclaimed. "How in the hell did I not know about this?"

Kiera pursed her lips then shrugged. "Never came up, I guess."

"You just made my shit list, Mrs. Kyle," I deadpanned.

Kiera laughed while Anna groaned and held the lavender-scented hot pack pillow to her back. Her contractions were starting again. "Can we go," she whispered. "I'm not really feeling so hot."

As I helped Anna into the buggy, I noticed that Liam was waiting in the driver's seat with the engine idling, ready to go. "Hell, no," I told him. "I'm driving."

Scoffing at me, he gripped the wheel a bit tighter. "Not a chance," he stated.

I was about to rip his head off, but Anna clenched my arm. "Don't fight, just get me out of here."

With a sigh and a vow to kick his ass later, I sat with her in the backseat. Kiera hopped in the front with Liam, and he immediately took off; Kiera clenched the side so hard her entire hands turned bone white. I looked over at Anna as the buggy bounced along.

She looked more uncomfortable than scared. The jarring jolt as the tires met the earth wasn't helping the pain any.

When Anna sucked in a tight breath, I screeched at my brother to slow down. He was flying down the steep hill beside the house, nearly hitting small trees and boulders that would surely flip us. Over the noise of the engine, Liam tossed out, "Just trying to get you there fast, bro."

"I'm more concerned about getting there in one piece!" I shouted back. Kiera turned to look at me with wide eyes. She seemed shocked that I would say something like that. I wanted to assure her that it was just Anna's safety I was concerned about, but the words wouldn't come out.

When we got to the driveway at the bottom of the hill, Liam spun out a bit on the rocks, and I saw a couple of large pieces hit the side of my Hummer. "If you dinged the paint, fucker, I'm taking it out of your hide."

Liam rolled his eyes as he shut the buggy off. Ignoring Kiera's comments that that was the scariest ride she'd ever taken and she should have just walked down, I unstrapped Anna and helped her climb out of the contraption. It took some finagling; dune buggies weren't exactly pregnancy friendly.

Once Anna was on solid ground, I hurried her over to the Hummer; it was running, along with Mom and Dad's minivan. "My bag," she murmured as she stepped up to her open car door. "My stuff."

I let out an annoyed grunt. We weren't the prepared type, so we didn't have a hospital bag packed and ready to go in the car. "I'll get everything later, after I get Gibson."

She nodded, then settled herself into the car. She didn't seem to be in as much pain, so her contraction must be over. Hell if I knew for sure though. A chick's body was a mystery to me. Well, the inside at least, the outside, I was an expert at, which is how Anna had wound up this way in the first place.

We'd considered waiting between kids, but me and my siblings were close together, and I loved that. It made us tight. Kind of. If Liam wasn't such a selfish asshole, we'd be closer. Chelsey and me were tight though. Man, I hoped she did all right with Gibson.

Peeling out of the driveway, I hauled ass to the hospital. Kellan better already have the gate open, or I was going to plow right through it. I had no idea who was following me, and I didn't much care. Gibson was accounted for and Anna was with me. That was my world right now.

The next several hours were a blur of pain, blood, gore, screaming, and name-calling, and at one point, a plastic tray of vomit was tossed across the room. Not by me. The day was seared into my memory, even the parts I wished I could forget. But in the end, when I was handed a warm, tiny person swaddled in a pastel pink blanket, it was all worth it.

"Another girl," I whispered, in awe of the miniature version of Anna and me. "Guess the doctor was right."

Finding out the sex was another one of those moments that was forever seared into my memory. I was happy about this one though. "Congratulations Mr. and Mrs. Hancock...it's a girl."

"No fucking way!" had been my immediate response. I'd been so sure the doctor would be wrong again and I was going to have a little man to mold into another me. Oh well. I still wanted a boy, but girls were awesome too, and now Gibson had a sister to do girly things with—dress-up, tea parties. Whatever the hell girls did.

Anna was tired but ecstatic to be over with the uncomfortable part. Physically, at least. The exhaustion part was still coming. "I'm just glad she's finally here...and no longer pressing against my sciatic nerve."

Reaching over, she brushed a finger across our daughter's forehead. Her eyes were wide open; the deep gray studied me like I was the strangest thing she'd ever seen. Lifting up her crocheted cap, Anna peeked at our little girl's head of dark, dark hair. "I think she's gonna look like me," she said as a tired smile brightened her face.

Looking down at my wife's deep mahogany hair, I nodded. "Yeah, I think so too. Lucky girl," I added with a playful wink.

Anna giggled, then her eyes drifted down to the baby in my arms. Her face took on a nearly reverent glow. "We're so happy to finally meet you, Onnika."

My smile matched Anna's as I watched Onnika's tiny features twist into a yawn. "You're about to find out how incredibly awesome your mom and dad are. I'm kind of jealous of you."

Anna laughed again, then held her arms open in invitation. "Gimme. I want to smell her."

Reluctantly, I handed her back to her mother. We'd have plenty of cuddle time later. Pride stretched across my chest as I watched my wife and daughter bonding. All the women in my life were so gorgeous. I always knew I would create attractive kids. I mean, how could I not? But scoring someone as hot as Anna for my partner was what really sealed the genetic deal. My kids were fucking lucky. Ah, who was I kidding, *I* was the lucky fucker.

After a few more minutes of one-on-one time, family started knocking on the door and stealing into the room to get a peek. We'd made them wait outside during the event. Mom hadn't been too happy about that, but Anna had been adamant on it only being her and me. I think Mom had planned on staying anyway, maybe hiding somewhere in the back, but the aforementioned tray of vomit smashing into the wall above her head had changed her mind. When Anna didn't like something, she let you know it. I dug that about her too.

I thought Mom and Dad would be the first ones to enter, but surprising me, it was Kiera and Kellan. Kiera looked over at her sister with an expression of *Don't hit me*. "Can we come in? We waited as long as we could…"

Anna was in a much calmer mood now that the painful part was over. Tears in her eyes, she nodded. "Yes, yes. Come meet your niece. She held Onnika up a little bit. "Onnika, this is your aunt Kiera and uncle Kellan. Guys…this is Onnika."

Kiera's eyes instantly filled with moisture that dropped onto her cheeks. Why did girls always cry around babies? Geez. "Oh my God, Anna, she's beautiful."

A mocking laugh escaped me. "Of course she is. She's a Hancock. Did you expect anything less than perfection?" Kellan laughed at my comment, but Kiera ignored me. I was used to that. She often couldn't handle my unique brand of awesomeness.

After washing her hands, Kiera walked over to Anna's side of the bed. She instantly put her hands out for the baby, and a familiar reluctance washed over Anna's face. There was just something about Onnika that made you want to hold on tight and not let go. Maybe she had superpowers. Wouldn't surprise me. Someone in our family tree was going to develop them one day, that was just a given. And, in a way, you could say I already had them. Sexual prowess was an ability that I possessed in spades.

When Kiera had Onnika, she firmly held her to her body. "Oh God, she's so tiny. Remember when Ryder was this tiny?" From the way Kiera looked up at Kellan, I thought another baby was soon to be in their future. There was nothing like holding a newborn to ramp up a woman's sex drive. I'd bet all the money I had that Kellan was getting laid tonight. Interesting. Not even a day old yet, and Onnika already had *two* superpowers. *That's my girl.*

While Kellan smiled and nodded at Kiera, she turned her attention back to Anna and me. "How did you come up with the name?"

Puffing up my chest, I jabbed myself with my thumb. "It was my idea."

Anna made a scoffing sound. "No it wasn't. You wanted to go with Myrtle again."

Remembering that lost negotiation, I frowned. "It's a family name. I don't know why you have such a problem with it." Anna's face scrunched into the look of disgust she always got when we mentioned my grandma's name. Not wanting to argue about it again, I added, "And I was right, Onnika was my idea. You just supplied the spelling." I gave her a grin and a wink to ease the sting in my words, if there was one. Sometimes it was hard to know what would piss chicks off.

Anna didn't look upset when she turned back to her sister. She had a high tolerance for my crap. "He wanted to spell it A-N-N-I-K-A, but I thought that was too close to my name, so we switched it to O-N-N."

Kiera nodded, then went back to cooing and cuddling Onnika. I didn't think she had any plans to give Kellan a turn. Not willingly at least. Eventually she had to share though, because after a while everyone else walked into the room. And just like that, our place was party central. There were so many people in it, I felt like we should start charging admission.

Aside from Kellan and Kiera, Mom, Dad, Liam, Matt, Rachel, Evan, and Jenny were there. There were also nurses loitering outside the door, and a few people visiting other patients too, from what I could tell. Guess news of a rock star's wife having a baby had already circulated around the hospital. I'd probably have to beat them back to get out of here.

Everyone was all smiles as they passed Onnika around, and whatever tension had been between us suddenly melted away. Rachel and Jenny were fine with me, the guys were fine with me, and I was fine with them. I could barely even remember why I'd been irritated earlier. Another one of Onnika's superpowers. This kid was truly amazing. Again, not a big surprise. She was genetically engineered to be cool.

While Kiera impatiently waited for another turn with Onnika, she told Anna, "I called Mom and Dad. They're heading out tomorrow or Monday. Mom's mad that you couldn't hold out until your due date."

Anna snorted. "She'll get over it. She did the last time."

I expected my wife's happy buzz of newborn bliss to fade, but she looked relaxed and sleepy as she lay there, watching everyone lose their shit over her daughter. It seemed like nothing could faze her at the moment, a fact that was confirmed when she told the room, "I'm so glad you're all here for this, and Mom, Dad, I want you to stay as long as you want! My home is your home! Invite everyone, the more the merrier!"

My eyes widened. Did she really just say that to my parents? I couldn't help but wonder if whatever was dripping into her IV was making her loopy or if she was riding a natural high. Either way, she'd just opened the floodgates, and there was no taking it back. I could see it in my mother's eyes. She'd been given permission to crash for as long as she saw fit, and nothing Anna said or did now would matter. Our negotiation was null and void, but at least *I* hadn't torn up the contract. No, Anna had screwed this one up all on her own.

Chapter 7

Oh Holy Awesome

Thanks to Anna giving my family the green light to stay as long as they wanted, two months later, my home was *still* full of visitors. Every single room was being used up by various relatives who'd decided to "visit" and refused to leave.

Anna's parents were staying with Kiera and Kellan. Kiera said that was because our house was too crowded, but Anna let it slip that the real reason they were staying over there was because they preferred Kellan over me.

She didn't say it quite like that. She'd merely said they "had a few issues with my personality." What? I had an awesome personality, so that couldn't really be it. They were just wrapped up in the Kellan Kyle fantasy, like everybody else.

That really irritated me. I was the coolest person I knew, and certainly Martin and Caroline would come to know that if they spent a little more time with me. I didn't see what problem they could possibly have with me anyway. I'd married their daughter, given her an awesome home to live in, and impregnated her with two of my very best seeds. What more could they ask of a husband? I should be on their Most Awesome Person in the World list.

Anna had deep bags under her eyes as she bounced Onnika in her arms. "Griffin, I've had about as much of this as I can take. When are they leaving?"

We were in our room, where Onnika slept in a bassinet by the bed. We were eventually going to move her upstairs in a room next to Gibson, but Anna wasn't ready to be that far away from her yet. Me either, although I was looking forward to having sex in my bed again. When Anna had felt ready to resume the horizontal mambo, we'd moved over to the closet to complete the act. I just couldn't have sex in the same room as my kid, no matter the age. I never would have thought I'd have a sexual Achilles' heel, but I guess I did.

I knew what Anna meant by her statement. Even with our bedroom door closed, I could hear people talking, laughing, shouting, running, watching TV, stomping, eating, playing, and somewhere, someone was crying. I needed a bigger house.

Shrugging, I told her, "I don't know when they're leaving. You kind of told them they could stay as long as they wanted. I think some of them are planning on moving in." A few of my cousins had jokingly said that when they'd noticed the pool and tennis court. At least, I was pretty sure they were joking. I might have to deal with squatters in the near future.

Anna gave me a look born from exhaustion, a look that said she was frying my manhood in her mind. "I do not remember saying that. Or anything even close to that. I think you told them it was fine to stay longer, which goes against our negotiations. So, according to the rules, I have one free win to use at my discretion."

Crossing my arms over my chest, I raised an eyebrow. "I didn't say shit to anybody." Except my sister, Chelsey, but I didn't mention that. "You were the one feeling all lovey-dovey in the hospital."

"I was doped up on baby juice. That doesn't count."

She closed her eyes, and I saw the tears forming. She was so tired. I'd told her in the beginning that she'd be less tired with everyone around, but that just wasn't the case. Anna felt the need to entertain them, and while they did help with Onnika and Gibson during the day, Anna was still the one getting up all night long with Onnika. I'd tried to talk her into napping whenever she could, but she said it was too loud, she couldn't sleep. I wished there was something I could do to help her, but I was stuck. She'd opened the hospitality doors, and I couldn't shut them. Not on family.

Pulling Onnika from Anna's arms, I gently placed her in the bassinet. She was such a beautiful baby—thick dark hair that curled at the ends, eyes that were turning greener every day, and pink chubby cheeks that must have been kissed fourteen million times by now. It was difficult to put her aside, but my wife was having a panic attack. I needed to soothe her.

Onnika was a pretty mellow baby, so she didn't object too much when I put her down. Anna slumped over, like she had nothing left. I pulled her into my arms, and she loosely wrapped herself around me. "I can't do this, Griffin," she muttered while I stroked her back.

"Sure you can," I told her. "You're one of the toughest chicks I know, Anna. You deal with my shit, you handled being pregnant all on your own when you found out the first time, you started moving into management at Hooters until I started raking in the dough and you didn't need to work. You're an amazing mom to Gibson and a pretty fucktastic wife. There's nothing you can't do, babe."

When I pulled back to look at her, she was smiling. "Yeah?"

Nodding, I leaned down to kiss her. "Yeah." Our lips moved together for a few moments. When we pulled apart, I ran my mouth to her ear. "I want to take you in the closet, run my hands all over you, sink myself inside your wet pussy, and stroke you until you fall apart. Then I want you to take a nap, while I handle the girls."

I peeked over to her eyes, and they were glossier than before. She gave me a hard nod, like she really, really wanted what I'd just offered. I wasn't sure which part she wanted most—the sex or the nap—but I didn't care. The curves of her body were pressed against mine, and all I could think of was her nipple in my mouth, her hand around my cock. Fuck, I wanted her so bad.

We both looked over at Onnika in her bassinet. She was watching a mobile dangling above it. Anna turned it on so it would twirl and play music, then we headed over to the closet. Mom and Chelsey were entertaining Gibson, so I wasn't worried about her needing anything as I closed the closet door. For once, Anna and I might be able to have sex during daylight hours without an interruption. Just the thought made me throb. God, I couldn't wait to touch her.

There was a chaise lounge in our closet now. Or sex couch, as Liam called it. He was totally right too. It *was* a sex couch, and whenever I passed by it, my dick twitched. Anna yawned as she ran her hand over the back of the couch. For a brief moment, I wondered if I'd be a better husband if I left her alone so she could take a nap in here, but I wasn't *that* awesome. I wanted sex.

She shimmied out of her yoga pants, then pulled her long-sleeved shirt over her head. She was wearing a lacy red bra and matching underwear, and I instantly stopped worrying about just letting her sleep. No one who didn't want to be nailed wore under-clothes like that. "Fuck, baby, you look amazing."

"Yeah?" A tired smile brightened her face as she ran her hands over her curves. She wasn't back to her pre-baby body yet, but I didn't fucking care. What she was showing me right now was hotter than the rest of the female population. If I didn't get inside her soon, I might need surgery to correct the internal damage going on.

Unzipping my pants, I showed her my raging hard-on. "Yeah. Lie down…relax."

With another small yawn, she removed the remaining pieces of clothes and then did as I asked. Only, she didn't casually lie on the couch, like I thought she would. No, she straddled it, then lay back with her feet resting on the floor and her legs wide open. Holy fuck. The Promised Land was right in front of me, and I gave myself a few long strokes as I stared in awe at what was being offered. Un-fucking-believable.

Anna yawned again as she stretched out, and I knew that I might lose her to sleep if I didn't get moving. Stopping my own self-exploration, I ripped off my clothes and tossed them aside. Her eyes were closed, but she smiled when I finally touched her. "Mmmmmm." A satisfied groan left her as my hands traveled up her warm, supple body. I straddled one of her legs, mainly to stop myself from nestling between them and thrusting into her. I wanted this to be about her, about relaxing her, about bringing her body so much pleasure that she'd be too exhausted to open her eyes afterward.

My lips placed soft kisses along her skin, almost ghostly soft on her erogenous zones. Her satisfied noise turned to a lusty one, and she squirmed on the couch. Her fingers threaded into my hair when I reached her nipple. I didn't go for it right away. No, I kissed around the area, then skipped over it, then kissed around it again. She hissed in frustration. Only when I swear I could hear her silent plea did my lips wrap around it, and when my tongue flicked it, she gasped. Oh, yeah, my girl was ready.

I played the same game with her pussy. Holding my fingers just out of reach from where she really wanted them. She was panting in no time, and her eyes were open, awake, and looking at me with such heat that my skin felt ten times hotter than usual.

When I finally ran my fingers between her legs, she shuddered, cried out, squirmed, and then she finally begged. Grabbing my backside with both hands, she murmured, "I want you. Now. Please...now."

I was so ready for her my cock was nearly purple, and I prayed I lasted long enough to satisfy her. Adjusting my position, I shoved into her. She arched her back, and her claws dug into my skin. *Fuck, yes.* "More," she breathed, moving her hips against me.

God, yes, I wanted to come. Our hips started moving together with unrestrained purpose. We both wanted this release so much; we needed it. This connection, this reminder of who we were together. Perfect.

Since everything, everywhere was so loud anyway, we didn't hold back. We moaned, groaned, and fully enjoyed the impending explosion. Anna cried out so loud when she came, my ears rang. Then I felt her constrict around me and I couldn't hold back anymore. "Fuck, God, yes, Anna. Fuck, fuck, fuck..."

The world evaporated as the best high in the world coursed through me. *Jesus, I loved this...*

Once we were both spent, Anna started breathing in a low, soft way that I knew meant she'd be snoring soon. Guess she really was tired. Without jostling her too much, I removed myself. Then I put down a little towel, just in case my awesome juice was too much for her. Finding a blanket, I laid it over her so she wouldn't be cold. She smiled but didn't stir. *Good night, babe. I'll wake you when it's time to go.*

I never thought it would take three hours to get a two-month-old ready, but it did. Of course, my mother and I were interrupted by every person who came across us. They all wanted to hold Onnika, play peekaboo with her, and ask her to repeat stuff. Shit like that. It was really annoying considering the fact that we were on a schedule. I felt like Matt whenever I asked someone to give her back so we could get her ready. I needed a nap by the time she was.

Mom told me to get used to it. "Little girls take time. Older girls take even more." I already knew that though. Anna took forever to get ready for anything. It was always worth the wait though. She looked like a fucking supermodel when she was finished.

After we were done with Onnika, we had to deal with Gibson, who needed almost as much time as her sister, since I couldn't let her leave the house without perfectly symmetrical ponytails. When both girls were finally ready, it was well past the time we needed to go. Like a commander ordering troops into battle, I hustled people to their vehicles.

The church Anna had picked out for the ceremony was in Tacoma. Why the hell she had to pick one so far away, when Seattle had a bunch of perfectly decent churches around, was something I would never understand. She claimed she liked the architecture. Whatever.

Anna was browsing the Internet on her phone as I drove us. I was just about to ask her what the score on the football game was when she started laughing to herself. "What?" I asked. "Find something about me?" The Hand Solo incident had died down, but it still popped up sometimes.

"Well, yeah, kind of." She flipped the screen to me, but I couldn't read it while I was driving. "Some fans have started a petition. They want us to change Onnika's name."

I was floored that of all the things to vote on in my life, *that* was what was circulating. "What? I love the name Onnika. What do they think would be better?"

Anna pursed her lips, and I could tell she didn't want to tell me. "What?" I asked, feeling annoyance starting to build already.

"Uh…they want us to name her Kellan…but with a *Y* instead of an *A*. Funny, huh?"

Funny? No, it wasn't fucking funny. It was fucking annoying.

I was so ticked, I almost slammed the brakes and stopped in the middle of the freeway. "They want us to do *what*? Why the fuck would I name my daughter after one of the band members? And Kellyn? Are they fucking kidding me? Goddamn fucking Kellan Kyle lovers!"

Gibson started giggling. Then she proudly stated, "Goddamn!"

Anna lifted an eyebrow at me. "If she says that during church, you get to explain where she heard it."

I shook my head at her. "No one will even question where she heard it…" Anna laughed, but I was really starting to get irritated. "Can you believe there is a petition to get us to rename our child? After Kellan?" I asked, disbelieving and furious at the same time.

Anna didn't seem as flustered as I was. No, she was still all calm and relaxed from the sex in the closet. I kind of wanted her riled up with me right now. I should be more careful with *my* superpowers. Sometimes I didn't know my own strength. "It's not a big deal, Griffin," she said, with a *Please calm down* sigh. "There's probably one for all the others too. Maybe Mattlyn or Evanlyn. Actually, Evanlyn is kind of pretty…"

With a groan of frustration, I stepped on the gas. Joke or not, there shouldn't be a petition of *any* kind to rename my kid. Unless it's Griffilyn. That, I could understand.

I was in a bad mood when we got to the church. Fans wanting to rename my daughter had set me off, but it went deeper than that. Like he was the fucking moon in the sky, the tides came and went with Kellan Kyle, and I was sick of it.

The spirals of the church were dark and ominous against the gray clouds hovering low in the sky. They matched my mood. I hoped it rained. Or hailed. Then my prickliness would be properly portrayed. The parking lot was roped off when we pulled up, and Sam was standing there, looking all scary and imposing in his suit and dark glasses. He used to be the bouncer at Pete's Bar, but now he was Kellan and Kiera's personal bodyguard. He took his job very seriously and was keeping an eagle eye on the lot, ceaselessly on guard to keep the riffraff out. I expected him to open the makeshift gate the second he saw my Hummer, but he only stood there, bulky arms crossed over his chest, his face expressionless.

Pulling up beside him, I rolled down my window. Before I could speak, he held up a hand. "I'm sorry, this is a private service today. You'll have to come back next Sunday."

My eyes narrowed. "I know that, douchebag. It's *my* ceremony."

Removing his unnecessary sunglasses, he looked over my face. "No, sorry. The service is for a two-month-old girl. You don't match the description. You'll have to leave."

I was about to reach over and rip the grin off his face, but Anna beat me to it. "Hey, Sam. Today's probably not the best day. He's having a moment."

Sam looked over at her, nodded, then sighed. "Fine. Take all my fun away."

He turned to open the gate and I flipped him off. "Asshole!" I shouted.

Anna laid a comforting hand on my thigh. It soothed me. Some. A blow job would be better. "He's just playing, Griffin. Relax, babe." I tried to, but my mood was sour, and nothing short of another orgasm would fix it.

The parking lot was a large one, but nothing was open near the front door. Muttering a curse, I parked in the back. The rest of my entourage pulled up beside me, and Anna grabbed Onnika while I scooped up Gibson. I'd dressed her in a plaid skirt, white leggings, and a white sweater with a giant red heart on it. Fucking adorable. I could dress kids professionally, if that wasn't really creepy sounding.

My family got out of their vehicles, and the swarm of us headed toward the dark stone church. Once my daughters were spotted, they were both stolen from me. I wasn't even sure who grabbed them, they were just gone. Clumps of oohing and aahing people pinpointed where they were though, and I caught glimpses of Gibson's skirt as she twirled in a circle. She finally had a group of people paying attention to just her; Gibby's adjustment period to the new baby wasn't going as smoothly as Anna or I had thought it would. We'd assumed Gibson would see Onnika as a doll to play with twenty-four/seven, but so far, all Gibson had seen was a rival. One she wanted to get rid of. She was in hog heaven now that the spotlight was back on her, for a little while at least.

Matt and Evan were standing together near the doors. As I headed their way I saw Matt shake his head and hand Evan a ten-dollar bill. With a sigh, Matt told Evan, "Wow, I really thought I had that."

Wondering what Matt had thought he'd *had*, I asked him, "What was that for?"

Matt smiled. "I bet him that you'd be incinerated the instant you set foot on holy soil, but, here you are…not burning."

"Funny," I muttered, not in the mood.

Looking around, I spotted Kiera talking to Abby; Abby looked like she was only half listening to her client as she cooed at Onnika in her arms. Denny and Abby represented Kiera in her writing career, as well as the D-Bags. The two of us were their only clients though. For now. I was sure they'd expand one day, once they got tired of their day jobs at some swanky advertising agency.

Beyond them Anna was talking with her father, while her mother fussed over Gibson dancing at her feet. As I turned to head inside the church, I heard Matt say to Evan, "Hey, double or nothing he combusts when he steps inside the church?"

Out of the corner of my eye, I saw Evan shrug. "Sure, why not?"

Twisting my head, I glared at each of them. "You guys are ass-holes."

Evan frowned and looked over at Matt. "I think I'm gonna lose this one."

I stepped inside the church and instantly heard Matt groan. Looking back, I saw him muttering something as he handed Evan more money. Just to further emphasize his loss, I stood in the church's doorway and, using my feet to hold the heavy doors open, I flipped him off with both hands. *Incinerate that, asshole.*

That was when I noticed Anna's dad watching me. Dropping my hands, I gave him a feeble chin nod. Trying to be the polite, dutiful son-in-law that Kellan was, I asked him, "How's it hangin', Mr. Allen?" *See, I'm just as cool and friendly as Kyle.* Instead of answering me, Martin rolled his eyes and gave his daughter a look that clearly said, *Why did you do this to me?*

Turning around, I ignored him and continued on into the church. I'd tried, but the odds of that man ever warming to me were slim to none. Oh well, his loss. The doors boomed shut behind me, and the people inside the quiet space twisted to look. While I gave the group of women closest to me finger guns, I spotted a few more friends and family. Denny and Kellan were talking near the front, Liam was a few rows away from where they were standing, clearly eavesdropping.

Liam's face was alight when I walked up to him; I hadn't seen him this excited in a while. Maybe he'd just found out that he'd gotten that new gig after all. If so, I didn't have time to hear about it. He opened his mouth, and I could tell he was going to start spouting about his newfound opportunity. I held up my hands to stop him. "Later. We gotta get this ball moving."

Sweeping past Liam, I spotted the pastor who was performing the ceremony today and made a beeline for him. Time to ring the bell, or bang the gong, or rev up the organ. Whatever they did to announce the beginning of service. The older man smiled when he noticed me approaching. Anna and I had met him a few times in preparation for today. He was cool. Preachy at times, but cool.

"Good afternoon, Griffin," he said, smoothing a purple stole around his neck.

"Yo, Pops, or Father, or…whatever. We good to start?"

He looked about to correct me, or chide me, or start in on a four-hour speech about the errors of my ways, but instead, he closed his mouth, smiled, and nodded. "Yes, we're all set to begin. I'll go tell everyone to come inside."

As I watched him saunter off toward the doors, my gaze came

across Denny and Kellan. Kellan had a strange expression on his face—broody, like he was contemplating all the hardships in his life. I was sure whatever he was beating himself up about wasn't really that big of an issue. *Oh no! Women obsess over me, the media loves me, and everything I say and do is praised by all.* Yeah, tough life you got there, Kell.

Ignoring them, I found a hard pew in front and sat down. God, I was tired. Today had been a superlong, exhausting day, and I didn't even feel like I'd done anything. Anna may be right about the chaos of our house. Maybe it was too much. A little peace sounded fabulous. And so did a nap. Surely no one would mind if I dozed off during this.

I closed my eyes, just to rest them, and heard people entering the church and finding places to sit. I recognized Anna's perfume as she sat beside me. Kiera must have been with her, because I heard her saying, "It still shocks me that you have your kids baptized."

Anna let out a throaty laugh. "It shouldn't. You've met their father, they need all the help they can get."

Cracking my eye open, I shot Anna a glare, but then I shrugged. She had a point. Onnika was with her again, and she was staring at me with an intense expression, like she was trying to communicate how utterly awesome it was to be my spawn. Either that or she was trying to poop. Kellan sat down beside Kiera. Oddly enough, he had the same look on his face. If he was trying to drop a load, I would suggest he wait until after the ceremony. If the crowd was going to smell anyone's excrement, it should be my daughter's.

Kiera reached over to grab his hand, and he gave her a brief smile. While I watched them, Matt sat behind me. Leaning over the pew, he murmured, "Hey, we're all getting together to work on the album after this. It's almost halfway done, and if we keep plugging away at it, we could finish it next month. Then we can start on promotion."

That made me groan. I didn't want to work on it today. I had a house full of people, a tired wife, a daughter who was probably plotting the demise of her sister, and a newborn who needed me.

I was beat, and I didn't have it in me to jam on songs that I'd had zero input on. Irritated, I snapped at the last comment he'd made. "Why do we have to do promotional shit? Isn't that what we pay Denny half our money for?"

Matt snorted and made some comment that we didn't pay him quite that much, but Denny happened to walk in front of me to sit on the other side of Kellan, so I blocked out Matt's explanation of just what Denny did for us.

Denny had an odd look on his face that matched Kellan's. Giving Kellan a sympathetic squeeze on the shoulder, he told him, "You should think about it some more. I know it's a hard move, but I think it could benefit everyone in the long run."

That got my attention. I'd already packed up all my crap and moved once because of Kellan. I wasn't thrilled about doing it again, not without a really, really, really good reason. Leaning forward, I peered past Anna, Kiera, and Kellan to ask Denny a question. "Kellan's moving?" I shifted my gaze to him. "Where are you going?"

The church had started quieting as everyone found seats. I vaguely noticed the pastor take center stage and start his introduction speech, but I tuned him out. If Kellan was disrupting our unit, I needed to know. Rehearsals would be a bitch if I had to fly somewhere else to do them. And knowing Kellan, he was probably taking his family and moving somewhere even more remote. One of the Dakotas, or something.

Kellan shook his head and shushed me. I didn't want to be shushed, so I asked him again, "Where you going? What's going on?"

Kellan sighed, which ticked me off even more. It was a *You wouldn't understand so I'm not going to bother explaining* sigh. I got those a lot. "Later," he whispered.

Someone nudged me in the ribs, and I looked over to see Liam sitting on the other side of me. He was grinning so wide I thought his cheeks were going to crack. "I know where he's going."

"Where?" I said, doubting Liam knew anything.

I heard Denny and Kellan both say something like, "Wait, we can explain," but before they got it out, Liam calmly told me, "Kellan just got offered a solo gig. You're no longer needed, bro." His smug smile set me off. Or maybe it was how exhausted I was or how tired I was of getting passed over by the guys, by the fans, by fucking everyone. And now they were just going to cut me out? *I don't think so.*

Just as I heard the pastor ask everyone to bow their heads in prayer, I snapped my attention back to Kellan and Denny. "What the fuck, Kellan!"

Chapter 8

You Wish You Were as Awesome as Me

Anna somehow managed to calm me down enough that we finished the ceremony. I was steaming mad the entire time though. Who the fuck did Kellan think he was that he could just shuck us off whenever it suited him. We were the D-Bags, not the Kellan Kyle–Bags.

The second the service was over, I grabbed Kellan by the elbow and dragged him outside. This could get ugly, and the pastor was already giving me evil eyes for swearing in his church. A crowd followed us to the parking lot, but I didn't care. I had nothing to hide here. Kellan was the one deceiving everyone by accepting one-sided deals that excluded the foundation he'd been built upon. He'd be nothing without us, and he knew it.

Dropping his arm, I poked him in the chest. I hoped he appreciated my self-control, since I really wanted to slug him in the face. "What the fuck is going on, Kellan? You ditchin' us? Think you're all high and mighty now, huh? Well, who the fuck do you think got you this far!" I poked him in the chest again for emphasis.

Kellan's face clouded as he batted my hand away. "It's not what you think, so calm down."

"I'm perfectly fucking calm!" I shouted.

Denny and the guys had joined us by this time. Evan and Matt looked confused; Denny looked like he was a schoolteacher and we were all his unruly children. His dark eyes locked on mine. "If you stop screaming, I can explain to you just what the deal on the table was. A deal that Kellan rejected, by the way."

His words pierced my veil of anger. "Rejected?" I asked Denny.

He nodded, then looked around at the crowd of friends and family members watching the commotion with unabashed interest. "Maybe we could take this somewhere more private?" Denny suggested.

Glancing at the crowd watching, I met eyes with Anna. She had that same panicked expression that she'd had the last time I'd truly vented my frustrations with the band. She didn't want us fighting. I didn't either, but goddammit, enough was enough. Looking back at Denny and Kellan, I nodded toward my car. "Step into my office."

Denny and Kellan exchanged a look, then Kellan motioned for Evan and Matt. Might as well talk to us all together, since his betrayal involved them too. As we moved toward my Hummer, the crowd shifted to follow us. Kellan looked around until he spotted his bodyguard. "Sam, we need a minute alone."

The big man nodded and instantly went into bouncer mode. "Everybody stays here," he barked, moving around in front of the crowd. Crossing his arms over his chest, he added, "Don't think I won't bust your head just because you're related." One of my cousins sniggered and took a step forward. Sam's eyes immediately locked onto him. "I'll start with you, asswipe. Stay where you are."

While Sam corralled my relatives, I stormed off with the guys. Once we were all sitting inside my car, I started in on Kellan. He put his hands up and interrupted me before I could say much more than "What the hell?"

"I didn't ask for anything, I was simply approached with an offer." Kellan was sitting in the center of the backseat, with Matt and Evan on either side of him. Glancing at the two of them, he repeated, "They approached me, and I said no."

Matt's brows furrowed. "Who approached you? With what?"

Kellan looked up at Denny in the front seat, with an expression that clearly said, *Help me.* Denny responded in that *I'm the boss* tone of voice that I assumed he used at his day job, since he wasn't in any way the boss of us. "The producers of the movie franchise Battle Robots approached Kellan about recording a song for their upcoming soundtrack."

For a second, my only thought was, *Holy crap! Another Battle Robots movie? Awesome! I love that shit.* But then Denny kept speaking, and my entire view of the movie series changed.

"They only wanted Kellan though," Denny said in a solemn voice. "It was a one-time, one-song deal that would have put the D-Bags in the spotlight next summer...if Kellan had said yes. But, like I said, he rejected the offer."

With the look Denny gave Kellan, it was clear he thought Kellan was an idiot for saying no. A small part of me agreed, but the majority of me felt too slighted to let that tiny rational thought slip through. "Why the fuck didn't they want all of us? Why just Kellan?"

Denny looked uncomfortable and wouldn't look directly at me. Then, with a sigh, he made eye contact. "They said...Kellan was the talent. Obviously, that's just an opinion, you're all valuable to the band."

Matt and Evan seemed irked, but I was clearly the only one who was truly outraged. "Fuck. That. Shit. Kellan's just one part of the band. He wouldn't be king of the universe without *us*. In fact, if he did try to do a solo project, it would probably suck because we weren't a part of it. We're the Bags to his Douche."

As one, they all turned to stare at me, wide-eyed. "What?" I asked, still steamed.

Matt shook his head, like he was clearing an Etch-A-Sketch. Evan turned away while Denny looked like he was plotting his next speech. Kellan was the one who responded to me. "I'm not king of the universe. I know this is a team effort, Griff, that's why I said no."

His expression turned hard as he stared me down. "I've done things for this band that I'm not proud of, just for the sake of the *team*, so don't you dare try to turn me into the bad guy here. I said no. I'm not doing it. End of story." Looking pissed, he glanced between Evan and Matt. "Someone let me the fuck out of this car. I'm done talking to this idiot."

Matt and Evan opened their doors simultaneously and stepped out. Kellan followed out Evan's door and then dramatically slammed it shut behind him. He stormed off and Evan chased after him. Still looking like he was processing everything that had been said, Matt shut his door and walked away.

Once the guys were out of sight, Denny let out a long exhale. "What?" I muttered, sitting back in my seat.

"Has anyone ever talked to you about diplomacy before?" he asked.

"No. I'm not a fucking politician."

He sighed again. "I'm just saying there are ways to talk to people that will get you better results than insults, swears, and be-littling." He put a hand on my shoulder. "You might try using your big words one day," he said, his voice condescending.

Brushing off his hand, I slowly extended my middle finger. "That big enough for you? If not, I've got a bigger one." I grabbed my junk and gave myself a good squeeze.

Denny shook his head, then opened his car door. "Nice chatting with you, Griffin. It's a treat, as always."

"Yeah, I know," I said as he closed the door.

Now alone with my thoughts, I started simmering in my anger. Fucking Kellan. Fucking Denny. Fucking D-Bags. I was quickly getting tired of all of them.

Anna joined me while I was still fuming in the car. "You okay?" she asked. "Things with you and Kellan seemed kind of…tense." Her brows were bunched with concern, and she was searching my face like she was looking for injuries, like I'd been duking it out with the guys or something.

Looking at her worried expression brought the weight of the recent argument crashing down around me; I could feel it com-pressing against my chest like a ton of bricks. Not liking the dark path my thoughts were taking, I asked Anna, "Where are the girls?"

"My mom has them. I thought you might want to talk about what happened. Will you tell me what's going on?" She put a hand on my thigh and started squeezing me like a cat kneading its claws. I was sure she had meant the touch to be supportive, but it just seemed nervous to me, like she was sure I was about to crack her world apart. I was pretty sure I wasn't going to. I just needed to be ticked for a while.

With a frown, I told her, "It's just…once again, Kellan is hogging all the glory and I'm being shoved into the background. He is the talent, my ass. You know, babe, between Kellan's selfishness, Matt's dickheadedness, and Evan's indifference…I don't know what the fuck I'm still doing with them." I was a little surprised that I'd said it out loud, that I'd finally admitted it to her so bluntly, but the longer it lingered in the air, the more right it felt.

Anna clearly didn't agree. Her face shifted into an alarming shade of white, and her hand tightened around my thigh so hard I could almost feel the bruise forming. "What are you saying, Griff?" Her voice was shaky, like she was on the verge of losing her composure.

She looked stressed by this conversation, and with everything on her plate right now, what with my family and the new baby, I kind of felt like a selfish dick for adding to her hardships. I knew she thought of the band as family, and she wanted me to suck it up so we could all be happy. But we weren't. Not really. Matt, Evan, and Kellan were happy, but I was stuck. There was nothing I could do about it though. Nothing but bitch, and that wasn't getting me anywhere.

The look in her eyes was making my stomach twist into a knot, and I felt like Sam had me in a stranglehold, but…being stuck in a rut that I couldn't get out of felt worse. Would she stay with me if I jumped this track? I didn't know for sure, and that scared the shit out of me. Wanting to be honest, I quietly told her, "I don't know, Anna. I just don't know."

Anna started patting my knee and nodding, almost obsessively. "It's okay. We'll come up with something together. Just don't… don't do anything rash. Not without talking to me first, okay?"

Since there was nothing I could do at the moment anyway, I nodded. Anna's face immediately brightened, which actually made me feel a little better. At least one of us was happy. And that would have to be enough. But even as I thought it, I knew her happiness wouldn't be enough to tide me over forever. Something needed to change.

I skipped meeting up with the guys that night. Screw 'em. I was expecting an angry phone call, but I never got one. No calls at all. Guess we all needed a break from each other.

Anna needed a reprieve from the chaos of the house, so she'd organized a night out with some ex-coworkers from Hooters. She'd been on track to being on the chain's management team until we'd financially sealed ourselves together. But with what I made, the paycheck there just wasn't worth the time and effort. It made more sense for her to stay home with the kids. I think she missed it sometimes. The independence of having her own income, the adult interaction, the men ogling her, although I ogled her enough, so that shouldn't really be a problem.

She was hesitant to leave me though, knowing I was in a mood. "I can reschedule if you want me to stay home tonight and talk some more. It's no big deal."

I knew that wasn't 100 percent true. Anna had been going stir-crazy at the house, especially with my family here. She wanted a break. She deserved a break. And...I really didn't want to talk. "Nah, I'm fine, everything's fine. Go have fun, you need it."

With a smile sexy enough to be on every billboard in town, she kissed my cheek. "You're the best. I won't be gone long, I promise." A few minutes later, she left, and oddly enough, without her presence near me, my mood darkened like the sun had just set.

My family wanted to chitchat, but I ignored them all and went to my room to sulk. Grabbing a tennis ball, I sat on the floor at the foot of the bed and played a game I liked to call Whack Imaginary Kellan in the Nose.

Repetitiously tossing the ball against the wall, watching it bounce on the floor, then catching it was soothing, and after a while, I stopped picturing Kellan's face—a face that for some reason drove girls crazy—and zoned out. My mood evened as my mind dulled, and when I heard a light knock on the door, I automatically said, "Come in."

When the door creaked open, I expected to see someone holding one of my girls with an exasperated look that said, *Please take them.* But instead, it was Chelsey at the door. She gave me a small wave while I resumed my peaceful habit.

Sliding onto the floor beside me, she slowly said, "So…today was interesting. What was that about with Kellan?"

Thinking about Denny's comment—that the producers thought Kellan was the only one with talent—made my stomach roil again. When I caught the ball, I squeezed it so hard I thought it might split a seam. "Same old, same old. Everyone thinks he shits gold and the rest of us are just his backup dancers. Just once, I'd like people to notice me, ya know? Just once, I want to shine. I want…" I sighed. "I just want a chance…"

Chelsey put a hand on my shoulder. "You'll get it. And if you don't…does it really matter? Isn't being the backup dancer for the biggest band on earth better than being the star of a band no one knows about? Being in a band was all you ever wanted as a kid."

I looked her square in the eye for several longs seconds before answering. "No, it's not enough to be second fiddle in a great band. I want both—to be the biggest star in the biggest band. I want it all."

Chelsey looked sad as she shrugged. "Do you know the fable about the dog with a steak?"

I hated fables. They were all incomprehensible, childish rubbish. "No, but I'm positive it doesn't apply to my life."

"I wouldn't be so sure. The dog in the fable has everything going for him, but he loses it all because he wants more. You might want to read it."

With an irritated huff, I resumed throwing the ball against the wall. "Like I said, it doesn't apply to me. I don't want more, I just want what I deserve to have, what I should already have…" A chance to shine, a moment in the spotlight unclouded by the rest of the guys. That was it. And that wasn't much.

Chelsey sighed, patted my shoulder again, then stood up. "Be mindful of that steak, Griffin. It's rarer than you realize."

Snatching the ball, I looked up at her. "I have no fucking clue what you're talking about."

She sighed, and she looked about ten years older as she tucked her hair behind her ears. "I know. And I'm scared for you, because I feel like…when you do figure it out, it's going to be too late."

I was agitated when Chelsey left the room, and no amount of ball thwacking could restore my serenity. Things just weren't turning out like I thought they would. I thought I'd have my name alone in lights by now, but more often than not, people didn't know who I was, not like they did Kellan. People just had to look at his hair and they recognized him. Me? I practically had to spell it out for them before they understood who I was—*Oh yeah, that bassist guy who got caught jacking off*. Didn't sit right with me. I should be just as big as Kellan.

The sting of fans wanting me to rename my child crawled up my spine, followed closely by that stupid producer's stupid words—*He is the talent*. While that sentence still sizzled my skin, the praises that Kellan's numerous fans bombarded me with shuffled through my brain, leaving whiplike scars across my skull. *He's so amazing, so sexy, so good onstage, he has such a good voice and such a great body, and he seems like such an amazing husband, father, lover, person…*

And you…you're good too.

Fuck that. I was so much better than *good*, it was ridiculous. Sure, I might have blown it when Matt had given me a chance on lead, but that was nerves and lack of practice. They never let me play, so how could they expect me to rock it at a moment's notice. But if they gave me all the chances that they gave Matt, I'd be prolific in no time. I mean, I'm a savant, how could I not be awesome? Which brought to my greatest beef with the band—Matt proclaiming that I'd never do anything but play bass. *You will never play lead*. Those words still pissed me off. I didn't see one good reason why we couldn't share the spotlight.

The guys needed to accept my greatness instead of trying to bury it even further. Yeah, since the very beginning of the band, they'd been too busy holding me back to truly appreciate me. And now I'd bumped into the proverbial ceiling with the D-Bags, and I had nowhere left to go.

Fuck. I needed to be drunk, not hiding in my room overthinking shit I couldn't change.

Tossing the ball into the closet, I stood up and grabbed my keys off my nightstand. Anna would probably be pissed when she got home and found out that I'd left our kids with my family, but at the moment, I didn't care. She could bitch at me all she wanted, I was leaving.

Stepping into the living room, I could hear shrieks and howls from people in the pool. There was always somebody in the pool now. I never got a chance to use it in my preferred way anymore, buck naked. Damn shame, and pretty annoying. Swim shorts were for pussies.

Since the frantic energy in the house was about to make me lose my mind, I held my hands up and shouted, "Whoever the fuck has my kids, please tell them I'll be back in a few hours." I turned to leave as everyone stopped moving to stare at me. Rethinking my statement, I rotated back around and added, "Please watch Gibson with small objects, she still likes to taste…everything. And don't let her bully you into staying up late or having ice cream for dinner, and make her brush her teeth, and watch her around Onnika. And…give her a kiss for me…Onnika too."

My mom appeared at the top of the stairs, Onnika in her hands. She nodded at me, and I knew my kids would be well looked after. I immediately spun around and left. I needed beer. Obscene amounts of beer.

Maybe because I wanted a taste of the old days, when everyone knew me, loved me, and worshipped me, or maybe because I just didn't know where else to go, I ended up going to Pete's. The guys and I still stopped in on occasion, but it was usually for some promotional type thing. The bar was different now, which kind of irritated me. Different waitresses, different band…even a different sign. Where it used to only say PETE'S BAR in modestly sized neon, now it proudly proclaimed: PETE'S BAR, HOME OF THE D-BAGS. That second line was nearly as large as the first.

On a night when I wasn't wishing to reminiscence about the old days, that would have been fine, but tonight, I felt like going back in time. Back when Kellan and I were equals, and I still thought I had a chance to stand out. I'd still had hope back then. Here, at this bar, I had been a god.

There was one thing about Pete's that hadn't changed since the good old days though. The bartender. Ragtag Rita still called the shots here, and she nearly dropped a full glass of beer when she saw me. "Holy shit! Do my eyes deceive me, or is the D-Bag of all D-Bags before me?"

Smiling, I sidled up to the bar and sat on a stool. "It is so fucking good to see you, Reets." *And thank you for not mentioning Kellan.*

With a sultry grin that promised a good time if I asked nicely, she set the beer she'd just poured in front of me. Rita was older, like, probably my mom's age, but I'd still do her, or I would have, before Anna. She had that *I'm desperate to reclaim my youth* vibe about her.

Leaning over the bar, giving me a glorious view of her cleavage, she murmured, "So, hot stuff, you here alone, or are the rest coming in with you?" By the gleam in her eye as she watched the front doors, I knew she was waiting for Kellan to walk through them.

I couldn't escape him no matter where I went.

I started chugging the beer and didn't stop until it was finished. With a mighty belch, I slammed the glass down on the bar and wiped my mouth. *Fuck yes.* That was exactly what I'd needed. "Left the fuckers at home, where they belong. Keep the beers comin'. I want to walk out of here barely able to hold my guts in."

She raised a painted-on eyebrow. "Trouble in paradise?"

"Get me drunk enough and I'll tell you all about it."

Shaking her head, she turned behind her to grab a bottle of Pendleton. "You need something a bit stronger than beer, babe." She grabbed a glass, put a few chunks of ice in it, then poured the whiskey on top, well over the halfway point of the glass.

Yes, she was right, I did need more. And that was why I loved coming here. The people got me. "Thanks, Reets. You're the best thing about this place, you know?"

She gave me a wink as I tilted the glass back. "Oh, honey, I've known that for years."

As I took a large gulp of whiskey, I looked around the bar. Being Sunday, it was fairly empty. Just a few regulars who—I swear to God—came in every night, rain or shine. When they lifted their gazes from their drinks and saw me leaning back against the bar, they started approaching me. Then it was excited thumps on the back and shots all around. God, it was good to be home. I had no idea why I didn't come back here more often.

While I caught up with old friends at a table near the stage, a group of sorority girls came in. I was buzzing my ass off by this point, and the familiar attraction hit me hard. Things were different now, but not different enough that I didn't notice them and want to make them notice me. I was feeling a little invisible, and I needed some feminine encouragement to shake off that feeling. Nothing that Anna would get ticked about, just a bit of... worshipping was all I wanted.

I shifted my chair toward the girls' table. "Hey, ladies!" I yelled. When they all twisted to look at me, I grabbed my cock and put on a smug smile. "See anything you like?"

They all gave me the look I loved to get from women. It was an expression of horror, disgust, and intrigue. If I was that brazen with my clothes on, what would I do with them off? That curiosity alone had scored me more chicks than I could count. But then their expressions changed. One by one, they glanced from me to the D-Bags shrine, then back to me. Once it clicked who I was, they started shrieking loud enough for every person in the bar to look at them.

"Oh my God! You're in the band! You're one of the D-Bags!"

They rushed over to me, faces aglow with earnest interest. Slinking back in my chair, I casually raised a hand. "Yeah, I'm with the band." The band of merry dream-killing assholes. I didn't mention that though.

The girls circled around me like vultures settling in on their prey. Some kneeled to get down to my level, one made herself at home on my lap. The alcohol brimming through my veins really liked that.

While I soaked in the feminine attention, the girls started asking me questions. When what they were saying sank in, I found their presence less pleasant. "So, you're around Kellan Kyle all the time…what is he like? Is he really that good looking? Does he ever…play around with other girls beside his wife? Could we get his phone number? Could you give him ours?" The girl on my lap dramatically let her head fall backward. "God that man is gorgeous. I would let him do absolutely anything he wanted to me…" She started running her hands over her breasts, and that was when I had enough. I shoved her off my lap, and she hit the floor with a thud.

All of her friends let out startled gasps, while the guys around me chuckled. The chick I'd dumped glared at me with eyes that were certainly channeling every evil spirit on earth. "What the fuck? Asshole!"

Not in the mood, I held up a hand. "Save your outrage for someone who gives a shit."

Standing up, she brushed off her short skirt. Her friends swarmed around her, like they were forming a shield. A shield of indignation. "You may be famous and all, but you're just an asshole jerk, like every other guy out there."

"Except Kellan, right? You still want me to give him your number?" She hesitated, like she actually thought I was going to do it for her.

Not wanting anything more from these Kellan-worshipping girls, I turned away with a hard laugh. "Don't worry. I'll get your number off the stall door," I sniggered. "You can go."

Something heavy hit me in the back of the head, and twisting around, I saw the girl clutching her purse to her chest as she shook in rage. She hit me with her purse? That was a new one. "You're a fucking asshole, and I'm going to let the whole world know it."

I shrugged, then turned around and ignored her. She could try, but nobody really knew me anyway. Even my short stint as Hand Solo was all but gone. I'd disappeared back into Kellan's gargantuan shadow, where I was forever destined to stay. Fuck my life.

Numerous regulars went home, but I stayed. I was closing the place down tonight; hadn't done that in a long time. And I was sloppy drunk too. As the night wore on, my phone buzzed more and more often, but I ignored it. I didn't want to deal with obligations right now, I just wanted to get fucked up.

Hours later, I was alone at my table, teetering on the edge of vomiting or passing out, when a guy I didn't know sat across from me. He was wearing a suit, complete with a tie, and looked really out of place here. I tried to tell him to fuck off, but all that came out of my mouth was a weird grunting sound. Maybe if I chucked on his shoes he'd get the message.

With a smile that was way too bright for this late at night, he stretched his hand across the table. "Hi, my name is Harold Berk. You're Griffin Hancock, correct?"

I stared at his fingers but didn't touch him. When he realized I wasn't the handshaking type, he pulled his arm back. "Yeah, that's me. Who wants to know?"

His brows drew together in concentration, and I knew my speech was coming out so slurred it was like I was speaking another language. I didn't repeat myself though. Let him figure it out. "Um, like I said, my name is Harold Berk. I represent Iris Production Studios."

I didn't know what this guy was talking about, but the instant the word "production" hit my ears, Kellan's solo offer flashed through my mind. Pointing at the guy, I snarled, "You tell those lamebrain fuckers that you work for that they are…lame…and they don't know what they're missing. Kellan has the talent…ha! Kellan has the herpes, that's what he has! Well, the odds are good anyway…Dude's a whore." Wiping some spittle off my lips, I finished with "Battle Robots suck anyway. Thirty-foot-tall robots fighting monsters in the streets…fucking awesome." I shook my head, making the world dance. "I mean…fucking ridiculous."

Whatever his name was across from me looked even more confused by my ramblings. "Battle Robots? No, no I'm not talking about that. Or Kellan. I'm here to talk to you."

Curiosity reached through my hazy brain to flip on a light switch of intrigue. "Who are you again?"

The man sighed. "My name is Harold Berk, for the third time, and I represent Iris Production Studios. I'm here to proposition you."

I immediately held both of my hands up, accidently hitting my glass and spilling some whiskey on the table. "I don't do dudes, so you can save the proposition."

The guy...Arnold or something...closed his eyes. "I'm not... that's not..." With a strained expression, he reopened his eyes. "Iris Studios is currently producing a pilot for a TV show. It's about an up-and-coming rock star, struggling to navigate the dark and seedy side of show business as he attempts to make a name for himself. Think *Sopranos* meets *The Partridge Family*. Naturally, we need a musically gifted actor to play the lead. We've searched the world over, Mr. Hancock, auditioned dozens of musicians, but no one else will do, because no one else is you..."

By the way he said it, it was clear he was expecting some sort of response from me. I had no idea what he was droning on about though.

"What?" I said to Arnold Berkanator. "I'm sorry, I wasn't listening. Could you repeat that?"

He looked at my glass, then back up to my face. "Maybe we should talk later, when you're sober."

He handed me a business card, but I swished my hand at him instead of taking it. "Nah, now is good. I remember crap better when I'm plastered. Ask the guys. I learned all our songs shit-faced."

Arnold brought his hands to his head and started rubbing circles into his skull. Ah, he must suffer from the not-enough-sex headaches that Kellan has. I'd sympathize, but I never had that problem. "Like I said, we want you to film a TV show about an up-and-coming musician. You would be the focal point of the show—the star."

The fuzziness in my head instantly evaporated at his magic words—*You would be...the star. The rock star, star.* I slapped my hand down on the table. "I'm in! Where do I sign up?"

Arnold didn't look any less confused by my pronouncement. "Do you want to hear any more details about the show, about your role in it, about our vision, about the steps we'll need to go through to get the show on the air?"

I took a long gulp of my whiskey. It went down as smooth as apple juice now. "Nope. Don't care. You had me at star."

Shaking his head, Arnold said, "Well, all right...I'm glad to hear you're on board. If you give me your number, I'll call you tomorrow with details about the pilot." I instantly reached into my pocket and handed him my phone. He stared at it, blinking, then he finally picked it up. "Getting a show on the air these days is a complicated process, and even great shows sometimes fail. Because of the riskiness involved, I'm obligated to tell you that we're only filming the pilot right now. There is no guarantee the series will be picked up, or that it will remain on the air if it does get picked up. The market is very competitive, but with your high-profile status, I have no doubt that the show will be a smashing success."

Finishing my whiskey, I banged the glass against the table. "Dude, that shit's practically guaranteed to be gold now that you've got me. Just tell me when and where, and I'll be there." For a split second, my foggy brain started wondering if I should talk to the guys first, or Denny. As our manager, he might have an opinion about this. I immediately shook that thought out of my mind. Those fuckers had abandoned me a long time ago, left me to rot in the shadows. They couldn't blame me for trying to find some sunlight. And if it turned into something bigger one day...well, then they would only have themselves to blame for not appreciating what they'd had.

Arnold called himself from my phone to get the number, then handed it back to me and stood up. Extending his hand again, he formally stated, "It was very nice to meet you, Mr. Hancock, and I'm looking forward to our future project."

Instead of taking his hand, I saluted him. "Likewise."

He left the table still looking baffled, and a slow, simmering excitement started to bubble through my insides as I watched him walk away. *You would be the star.* Damn straight I would be.

Chapter 9

To Be or Not to Be…Awesome

I woke up with a pounding in my skull and little or no memory of what had happened last night. Anna screaming at me didn't help any. "You left them with your family! Then you didn't come home until four in the morning! Where the fuck were you?"

Fuck if I knew. I'd woken up outside of Pete's by the Dumpster. I had some vague recollection of Rita patting my leg and telling me to sleep it off…but that could have been a dream. A really weird, fucked-up dream. "I told you, I went to Pete's to blow off some steam, and I passed out somewhere. But I made it home in one piece, and that's really all that matters."

Her eyes narrowed to dark and dangerous slits. It was hot. "Yes, it's much easier for me to kill you when you're alive. I told you I didn't want your family as babysitters. You should have called Jennifer. And why did you need to blow off steam? You told me you were fine."

"And I am, kind of. I just…with everything the guys have done to me recently…I needed…" Stopping myself, I let out an annoyed huff. I was so tired of thinking and talking about the guys. When would *my* life ever revolve around *me*? A dull buzz started humming in my brain. It was different than the whiskey headache beating against my skull. It was almost like the throbbing was trying to tap out a message in Morse code. Something had happened last night that was important, that I should remember…my mind was completely blank though.

Anna got that anxious look that unsettled my stomach. I think she was scared I was just going to up and quit or something. But where would I go? Even I wasn't stupid enough to throw away everything for nothing. *See, Chelsey, I'm not the dog with the steak. The story doesn't apply to me.*

"Are you freaked out that I didn't come home? Because I woke up alone, with all my clothes still on, so you don't need to worry about that." I vaguely remembered a group of girls at the bar, but I also recalled pushing them away from me. Anna had nothing to worry about. My cock was permanently drawn to her pussy. No one else even came close to her perfection.

She pursed her full lips at me, then crossed her arms over her chest. Her breasts were still larger than they usually were, thanks to feeding Onnika, and the movement lifted them even higher; she was practically shoving them in my face. "I should hope I have nothing to worry about. We both decided to end that crap when we got married. Give the children a good example and all that. Plus…I'd be super pissed if you were dick-sticking other people behind my back. We work because we're honest. Brutally honest."

A surprising amount of disgust roiled my stomach. Like I'd ever dick-stick someone else. It didn't even sound appealing anymore. She was all I wanted, all I needed. Surveying my kingdom, I let my eyes linger over the pajama shorts Anna was wearing; they barely covered all of her backside. I wanted to touch the skin that was peeking out. A different kind of throbbing took me over, and amazingly enough, my headache completely vanished. Sex. It really was the tried-and-true cure for all sorts of aches and pains.

Crawling across the bed to where she was standing on the other side of it, I ran my hand up her leg. In a low, sultry voice, I told her, "I don't want anyone but you. Why would I settle for less when I have the perfect woman at home?"

As my hand dipped into her short shorts, her lips shifted into a sexy, annoyed pout. "Stop that. I'm angry at you."

My finger wandered into her underwear, and I tested the waters to see how she really felt. Like I thought it would be, my finger was wet when I pulled it back. Her mouth popped open with a low, erotic gasp, and I gave her a smug smirk. "No, you're not."

I shifted my hand so I could cup her backside. Fuck, she had an amazing ass. I was hard as a rock, ready to go, and for once, we could have sex in our bed. Mom had taken Onnika upstairs with her, and she was still up there. Another bonus...Anna was probably fully rested after a night of uninterrupted sleep.

"Yes, I am," she stubbornly insisted. The anger was gone from her eyes though, so I didn't believe her. "You left the girls with your parents. Onnika is still upstairs with your mom. How do we know if she fed her? Maybe the milk ran out? Maybe your mom is a heavy sleeper? Maybe she...oh God..."

Sometime during her speech, I'd sidled close to her, swept aside her shorts and underwear, and ran my tongue across her pussy. Fuck, she tasted good. Her hand instantly went to my head, holding me in place. "Fuck, that feels so good...don't stop..."

I didn't. I kept teasing her with my mouth until she was soaking, until she was panting, and until she was squirming for more. And just when she got to the point where I knew she'd explode if I continued...I stopped.

With a smile, I lay back on the bed. I was still wearing my clothes from last night, and my cock was straining against the denim of my jeans. It was almost painful, but I knew Anna would help me out, once she recovered.

Her head had dropped back while I'd been servicing her, and now that I had stopped, she snapped her gaze to mine. There was a feral look in her eyes, and for a moment, I thought she was going to hiss at me and order me to keep sucking her clit. Fuck, that would be so hot if she did. Just the thought made me adjust my erection. Damn it, I really needed her to release me soon.

With a casual shrug, I looked around the room. "So, we're kid-free, in our bed...no one around...what should we do?" Innocence in my eyes, I returned my gaze to her. It was chilly in the early morning air, and Anna's nipples were almost bursting through her light tank top. I was going to suck on those next.

Like she could read my mind, Anna ripped off her tank top. "We're going to fuck." With a throaty growl, she shucked off the rest of her clothes, then started in on my jeans. *Thank you, God.*

Anna and I ended up staying in bed most of the day, having sex over and over, like on the first night we'd gotten together. Whenever she left the room to go pump milk for Onnika, she'd start to work on pumping me when she got back. Guess the luxury of multiple babysitters and an empty bedroom had finally gotten to her. I knew the family needed to leave soon, for the sake of our sanities, but I was going to enjoy the freedom today.

We were on our fourth or fifth time, with Anna riding me, her glorious tits jiggling directly above my face. The expression on hers was euphoric, and as she squeezed my pecs, I knew she was close to losing it again. I lost myself in the sensation of her warm wetness moving up and down my cock in an endless rhythm of perfection. I groaned as the throbbing built to something nearly painful.

Anna cried out, "Oh God, Griffin, yes…yes…fuck yes…" then her sounds became animalistic noises that drove me over the edge. Clutching her ass and pulling her into me, I stretched out my body and let the wall of restraint crash down. Pure bliss exploded from my cock and spread throughout my body. The sounds I made weren't coherent words, but they made Anna moan my name. "Yes…come for me, baby…" she moaned.

When we were spent, she sagged against me. "You're so hot when you come," she murmured against my skin.

I ran my hand up and down her back. "I know." And I did. I'd filmed myself jacking off once, just to see what I looked like, and I had to say, it was pretty amazing. Anna was one lucky woman.

We lay together for a while, me still inside her, then Anna whispered, "Griffin…is everything with you and the band cool?"

I adjusted my head so I could look at her better. She was concerned at the least, scared at the most. I wasn't sure how to answer her, so I went with what I thought she wanted to hear. "Yeah… sure. Why? Would you be upset if it wasn't?" Narrowing my eyes, I studied her reaction.

Her expression turned thoughtful as she tilted her head and considered that for a moment. "Not upset. Just worried. Our life…it wouldn't be the same without the band, you know? Plus… Kellan and Kiera, Matt and Rachel, Evan and Jenny…they're family." She gave me a small smile.

I supposed they were, but sometimes being around your family all the time wasn't healthy. Take the situation currently happening at our house, for instance. Remembering our day of freedom made my dick start to stiffen back up. Anna felt the difference, and her eyes widened. "Again? Already?"

Happy to change the subject, I crooked a smile and shrugged. "You've unleashed the beast, there's no putting it back."

She frowned. "I don't know if I can…" She stopped talking as I started moving inside her, gently, slowly, just rubbing our fun parts together with no real purpose other than making us feel nice. "Oh…wow…that feels really good…"

She started moving with me, just as gently, just as slowly. It was hot, and she was right, it did feel good…like getting a backrub in all the tight spots all at once. Her eyes fluttered closed and her breathing picked up as we moved together. It was intoxicating to watch her, and for once, I didn't care if I came or not, I just wanted to watch her do it. "Oh, Griff…I think I can…don't go any faster though…I need…slow…"

I hadn't planned on changing my pace, so I just kept on doing what I was doing. She slowly went from calm and content to squirming with unfulfilled desire. I could tell she wanted to go faster, harder, pound herself onto my cock, but she was taking her time, teasing herself. Fuck, it was hot to watch the erotic torture. I might come after all.

My phone buzzed on the nightstand. I had no idea who it was or why they were calling me, and I didn't care. Voicemail could get it. But then I thought…I've never had sex while on the phone before…this could be really erotic. Knowing Anna would be cool with whatever kinky thing I wanted to try, I told her, "I'm going to answer this, but don't stop. I want you to come while I'm on the phone, baby."

She grunted some sort of acknowledgment, and I smiled as I picked up my cell. I almost answered with "Guess what I'm doing?" but I used the standard "Yeah?" instead.

Anna groaned right on cue, and I had to bite my lip. Fuck, it was just as erotic as I thought it might be. The person on the other end hesitated, then said, "Mr. Hancock? This is Harold Berk. We met last night?"

"Mmmmm, did we?" I had no clue who this Harold guy was or how he'd gotten my cell phone number, but my wife was grinding on me, and he was unintentionally witnessing it, and it was fucking awesome.

"Um, yeah, we talked about the TV pilot. Remember?" Anna sucked in a breath and groaned again, and Harold slowly said, "Is this a bad time? I could call back later?"

Looking at the expression on my wife's face, I shook my head. "No, your timing couldn't have been more perfect."

"Um, okay. Well, I wanted to go over more details about the project you signed on for."

Anna's face grew frustrated, and I knew the speed was too slow for her, I thrust my hips harder, helping her out. *Come for me, baby. Let this guy hear it.* Her reaction was spectacular. "Oh God, yes…there…right there…don't stop…"

I held on to her hip with my free hand and let her have it. Her cries grew more intense, and knowing what's-his-name could hear without really knowing what was going on was about to make me come. Fuck yes.

"Mr. Hancock, maybe I should call back later?"

"No, no, I'm listening. All ears. Tell me about this TV thing. Now. Do it now…" I was talking to Harold, but speaking to Anna. She started panting, then stiffened, and let out an exceptionally awesome cry of release. Unexpectedly, I came right after her. Damn, I hadn't thought I could. I should have known better.

As we lay there panting, the person on the other line quietly said, "Is everything…okay?"

"Fuck, yes." He'd been talking in my ear the entire time I'd been coming, but I honestly had no idea what he'd been saying. I could barely remember his name. Harry? Larry? Fuck if I knew. "Could you repeat all that, I wasn't listening. Start from the beginning."

Anna rolled off me. Lying on her back, she laughed as she shook her head. Some girls might have a problem with what I'd just done, but not Anna. She just found it hot. She was so fucking awesome.

A long sigh from the phone met my ear. "My name is Harold Berk. We met last night at the bar. I told you about the TV pilot, the drama about a rock star? You claimed to be interested in being the star of the show. Do you remember any of this? You were kind of…under the weather."

What I'd been was drunk, but flashes of the conversation were coming back to me, especially after he said star. *You would be the focal point…the star.* But something seemed off. "Wait…I thought your name was Arnold?"

"No, sir. It's Harold." Definite irritation was in his voice now.

"Oh…so that whole thing was real? I didn't dream it?"

He sighed, like he was put out with me. He shouldn't be. I'd just let him listen to a hot girl have an orgasm. He should be thanking me. "It was real, and the offer is real. I can have papers in your in-box this afternoon. Unless you've changed your mind…if that's the case, I suppose I will have to contact another musician on my list. Maybe one of your bandmates?"

I immediately bristled at the thought of another D-Bag stealing this opportunity from me as well; they'd already taken way too much from me. Words rippled through my mind—*You are never going to play lead. Not tonight, maybe tomorrow. He is the talent.* The frustrated phrases settled into the pit of my stomach, where they mixed with the knot of discontent that I always carried around with me. When the answer to Harold's question bubbled out of my mouth, it was laced with power. "No, no way. I'm still in."

Anna was giving me a questioning look, and I wondered what to tell her. If this series took off, and with me as the lead, it would definitely take off, I might have to part ways with the band one day, or at least scale down. She wouldn't be happy about me taking a break from our "family." But I wouldn't be doing it for nothing, I'd be doing it to be a successful actor. It was a lateral move. No, it was a step up. I'd be the lead. For once, I'd be the star...like I should be.

Smiling, I told him, "I'm in one hundred and ten percent."

"Excellent!" he exclaimed. He asked for my email address and I happily gave it: hornyhulk@dbags.com. "The pilot starts filming next month. Can you get down to L.A.?"

Giving Anna sidelong glances, I sniffed and said, "Sure, not a problem." How I was going to do that without everyone going ballistic, I had no idea.

When I disconnected the phone, Anna was staring at me with expectant eyes. I knew what her question was even before she asked it. "Who was that?"

Shrugging, I tried to play it off with vagueness. "Just this guy who wants me to do a little side gig with him. Nothing major." *Yet.*

Her brows drew together as she turned onto her stomach. Nope. Vagueness wasn't going to cut it this time. "What did you agree to, Griffin? I thought you said you wouldn't do anything rash without talking to me first?"

Running my hand over her back, I shook my head. Oddly, my fingers were trembling. I wanted this to happen, I didn't want her to tell me no. "I said yes because it's nothing. Just a one-time acting thing."

Sitting up on her elbow, her expression was precariously balanced somewhere between curious and furious, and I knew I had to be very careful about how I answered her next question. "Like a commercial?"

My heart started racing as I debated what to say to her. She'd just said we worked because we were honest, brutally honest, but if I told her the truth now, she'd never let me go to L.A. She'd tell me I was being foolish, then she'd drag the guys into the decision...she'd hold me back. And I really couldn't handle the idea of Anna holding me back. I needed her support, even if she didn't realize just what she was supporting.

Feeling my headache returning, along with a surge of nausea, I said, "Yeah, something like that. And...they're filming it next month, so I'm going to have to fly to L.A. Just for a couple days though, I won't be gone long."

Fuck, fuck, fuck. *Did I really just say that to her?* Yes, I had. I'd just told a major-ass lie to my wife, one I couldn't hide forever, and when she did find out the truth, she was going to fucking kill me. But I had no choice. She'd shoot down my plan if she knew all the details, and I was dying in the D-Bags' shadow, I needed to break free. She'd see that once the show erupted. She'd support me then, I just knew it. I'd be totally honest with her…when the time was right.

Anna studied me a second longer, and I prayed my poker face stayed in place. Fuck, was I sweating? Just when I thought she was going to call bullshit, a huge smile broke her tepid expression. "Ah, babe, that's great! A commercial was kind of something I'd been tossing around in my mind. It will let you stand out, but it won't interfere with the band. It's a win-win!" Leaning over, she gave me a heartfelt kiss. "See, I told you your talent would be recognized and appreciated soon."

She leaned over to kiss me again, and I had to swallow the lump of shame in my throat; it was the first time the emotion had ever truly touched me, and I didn't like it. At all. I probably shouldn't have done that. But it was too late now…I'd already spun the web, and all I could do was follow it through. But fuck…on the other side of my deceit was the Promised Land—a TV show, where I was the star! Fuck, yes! This was going to be amazing.

The next few weeks were filled with endlessly meeting the guys and working on the new album. I kept quiet on my "side gig," which was a really hard thing for me to do. It made me appreciate myself even more. I mean, if the guys understood the restraint I was using on a daily basis around them, they'd be seriously impressed.

Arnold, Harold, or whatever the hell his name was sent me the lengthy electronic contract right away. Since it all seemed legit to me, I signed it without reading it all the way through. Two weeks after I signed the contract, he shipped me the script for the pilot episode. Luckily, I intercepted the package before Anna saw it, and immediately hid the script away in my office. My lie to my wife would be completely exposed if she saw the thick manuscript I'd been sent—no commercial had that many lines—and if I slipped up now, my dream would never come true. To keep my hope alive, I had to keep Anna in the dark, so I only read through the script when I was alone.

It felt strangely horrible to not include her in my excitement. I was so used to telling her everything, no matter how small, and this was huge for me. Holding back from her made me feel incomplete, like I was constantly forgetting something. But I knew what would happen if I told Anna the truth, and because I wanted this so badly, I maintained the lie. It was temporary anyway. Once the show got picked up, I would have to come clean to her and the guys. Even if I was ordered to keep quiet, I wouldn't be able to hold that shit in.

I was anxious to start filming, and I often practiced my acting technique in the bathroom. But memorizing the script was harder than I thought. I hoped they let me cheat while filming, have someone saying the lines in my ear or holding up cue cards that I could glance at. Something.

By the first part of December, the D-Bags were putting the finishing touches on our third album. Matt was stoked about it, said it was our best one yet. Considering the fact that they'd shot down every single one of my ideas, I wasn't so sure it was anything more than mediocre. It saddened me that the guys refused to listen to me, refused to let me guide our band to epicness. For all of Matt and Kellan's pretty words about pushing the envelope, they were sticking with the status quo. It was disappointing, to say the least. But I had bigger and better things on my horizon, so for once, I wasn't worried about it.

I wasn't worried about the album, but I *was* a little concerned about what I was going to tell the guys when it was time to fly to L.A. to film the pilot. I'd have to explain my absence somehow, and I had no idea what to say. "I'm blowing you guys off for a while" probably wouldn't go over too well. It was a Saturday afternoon in mid-December when I finally got the call from Harold that I'd been waiting for.

"Mr. Hancock, I hope you're having a great afternoon. All ready for Christmas?"

Even though he couldn't see me, I shrugged. "Yeah, guess so." Anna had been shopping for the girls almost nonstop. I swear our house had enough pink and purple presents in it to fill about six Toys for Tots trucks. She claimed most of them were small items, but I didn't care. Kids should be spoiled, no harm in that.

My gift to Anna was better than anything she'd picked up for the girls though. Not long after Onnika's baptism, I'd gotten one-way plane tickets for all of my relatives and sent them packing. Our house was blissfully quiet again. My parents were already trying to plan a return trip for the holidays, but I told them they'd have to wait until the next baby. God, I hoped Anna didn't get knocked up again too soon. She'd kill me.

"That's great!" Harold exclaimed. His tone never truly changed much, even when I was doing my best to either annoy him or embarrass him. It was like he was always in a great mood, no matter what was happening. I think I could have told him I was contemplating ending it all over the holidays and he would have answered me the same way. He reminded me of Jenny, but in an unrealistic way, like he silently cursed me the second he hung up the phone. Whatever. So long as he made me famous, I didn't care what he thought about me.

"Good news, Mr. Hancock, everything is ready and we're all set to film the pilot episode on Monday. Pack your bags, it's time to come to L.A."

"Great...I'll be there." Somehow.

"Perfect!" He gave me some pointers on where to go and how to get there, and then said, "Everything about this show is top-notch. I can't wait for you to see the set. See you Monday, Mr. Hancock."

"Yep, see you then." Frowning, I tucked my hair behind my ears. It was nearly to my shoulders now, and I could easily pull it back into a ponytail if I wanted. I loved having it loose and free though. What should I tell the guys? Would they be fine with the same thing I'd told Anna? Probably not, they'd bitch that they weren't included. I ignored the annoying section of my brain that was shouting that I would bitch too if I were them and focused instead on my storytelling skills. Fuck, I was a horrible liar. Hmm, it had to be somewhat realistic to be believable. I'd just say I was visiting family for a while. Yeah, that would totally work.

I let the guys know I was leaving when we met up that night at Kellan's recording studio. "Hey, so…I'm gonna be heading out of town for a while…I'm leaving tomorrow night actually." Matt, Evan, and Kellan all twisted to look at me. We'd just finished the final pass on the last song, and everyone was putting away their instruments. I was still playing with mine, while a strange emotion ripped my belly apart. Fear? Nerves? Guilt? Nah, couldn't be that. I wasn't doing anything wrong. I deserved this.

Matt furrowed his brow. "We just finished the album. We've got to get it to the label so they can start production. We'll have interviews starting soon, promotional tours, late-night TV gigs…you can't disappear right now, Griffin. We've got work to do."

I held up my hand to stop his rambling. "I know. Chill…I was just thinking of visiting my parents for a few days. Maybe check up on Chelsey. Her husband is still overseas, and she's raising those girls alone, you know?"

Mentioning my sister softened Matt. "Oh, well, yeah, that's fine. Just…don't vanish or anything."

A small smile played across my lips. Vanishing was the last thing I intended on doing.

Chapter 10

Awesometopia

The following night, I was on my way to Los Angeles to film the pilot for my sure-to-be-a-hit TV show. Anna had offered to come with me to keep me company and to check out the set of the commercial she thought I was filming. Having her there would bust apart my lie though, so I'd had no choice but to weave another half truth, something that would make her want to stay home. "It's just a few days, babe, and I'm gonna stay with my family while I'm there. Mom wants to do a late Thanksgiving/early Christmas mega-holiday, so everyone is going to be there. It's gonna be crazy loud."

For a minute, I thought I'd miscalculated Anna's desire to join in the festivities, but once I mentioned that it would be loud, she grimaced. "Yeah, okay. If it's just a few days, I guess I'll stay here. I *am* sad that I won't get to see the set though...which reminds me, what is the commercial for anyway? You never did tell me..."

She tilted her head as she stared at me, like she was just now realizing it was odd that I'd never gone into detail about it. And it *was* odd. And hard. Resisting the urge to tell her every aspect of the show was slowly giving me an ulcer. Keeping secrets sucked. The truth would come out soon enough though, and hopefully when it did, she wouldn't be too steamed at me to listen—I was dying to tell her.

"Oh, well it's..." I looked around the bedroom for inspiration. What would I be good at selling to the world? Condoms? After-shave? Baby-making juice? Seeing something delicious on my dresser, I told her, "Whiskey. It's a commercial for whiskey." Even as a jolt of guilt knotted my stomach, I couldn't contain my smile. That had been a well-crafted lie. Me being a whiskey spokesman was totally believable. And actually, that would be pretty awesome. If this opportunity led to that one, it would complete the circle of my epicness.

Anna gave me a bright grin that made my dick throb. If she hadn't been holding Onnika, I would have tossed her down on the bed and given her some of my superspecial baby-making juice be-fore I left. "That is perfect for you, babe. You're gonna nail this! I can't wait to tell everyone."

Knowing she couldn't do that yet, I firmly reminded her of something I'd said right after I told her I took the job. "Remember our plan, Anna. I need to be the one to break it to the guys, or else they're gonna be whiny little prisses about me doing something outside of the band. They'd probably try and compare it to Kellan almost taking that solo gig last month, but it's nothing like that. For one, this is acting, not music, so it doesn't count... but those asses won't see it that way, so until it's said and done, I need you to re-spect the sacred pact of husband and wife, the *My secrets die with you* bond, and not say a word. Not even to Kiera." I'd said that with a stern finger raised to her face. I couldn't risk her sisterly bond trumping our marriage bond. I needed her to support me on this, even if she didn't understand why.

Anna had rolled her eyes at me, but agreed. "Whatever, Griffin. I don't see how they'd be upset with you doing a commercial, but if you really don't want me to say anything, then I won't." Then she'd given me a fond smile and kissed my nose. "Have a safe flight and a great trip... and say hi to your parents for me."

A tidal wave of remorse had washed over me after she'd sweetly wished me well. I'd almost told her right then and there that I was a crap-filled lying douche, and filming a commercial wasn't really why I was flying to L.A. But I was so close to getting what I wanted;

I just had to be strong for a little while longer. The look on her face had actually helped me contain the truth. She was so wonderful, so trusting. I couldn't stomach breaking that trust by confessing what I was really doing. The words just wouldn't come out. I knew I'd have to tell her one day, but today wasn't that day. I'd deal with the consequences of my actions later, once the action had paid off for me. For us.

I'd rented a limo for my stay in Los Angeles, and the driver was waiting for me at the airport when I touched down. I had him take me to a five-star hotel near the studios, where I had a room waiting. I could have stayed with my parents like I'd told Anna, but it was too risky. My family would talk to Matt's family, who would in turn talk to Matt, and if he found out what I was *really* doing here, I'd never hear the end of it.

My driver rang me early the next morning to take me to the set. *Really* early the next morning. My eyeballs stung as the air hit them, and I nearly told the fucker to come back at a decent hour. But then I remembered what was happening today and I sprang to my feet. Today was the day I became a TV star.

I practically skipped to the car I was so excited, and even though it was a ridiculously early hour, I texted Anna once we started moving. *Almost showtime.*

Her response was fast; she was probably up early with Onnika. *It's not even eight in the morning yet... you must be dying.*

Yeah, kind of. I was so excited though that I didn't care how early it was. I responded to her text with a winky face. She could interpret that any way she wanted to.

When we got to the gate of the studio, my heart started pounding with excitement; this was so fucking awesome. It would have been even better if Anna was here to share it with me, but there would be another time for her to come check it out, I was positive of that. The driver had my credentials, and we easily passed through the gate. Harold was waiting in the parking lot with a golf cart when we pulled up. He smiled as he waited for the driver to open my door. Once I was out of the car, he extended a hand to me. "Mr. Hancock, it is so good to see you again. How was your flight?"

"Groovy," I said, looking around as I shook his hand. "So... where do we go first?"

"Glad you asked. I'll give you a brief tour of the set, then it will be on to hair and makeup. After that, I'll introduce you to the rest of the cast and we'll do a read-through. If all goes well, filming will start tomorrow."

As we got in the cart, Harold gave me a sidelong glance. "Did you get a chance to memorize the script?"

I scoffed as I leaned back in the stiff seat. "Of course, dude." Mostly.

As we drove along, we passed warehouses with various costumed people shuffling about. I saw Roman soldiers talking with zombies, rough and tough cowboy types sipping coffee with a man in a dog costume, and more cheerleaders than I could count. I'd just entered awesometopia.

After what felt like five hours, we finally made it to the warehouse we'd be using; it was in the very back corner of the lot. Harold parked the cart, then we climbed out. "Now, we're sharing this warehouse with a few other productions, so it's going to feel a little cramped at first." He gave me a bright, cheesy grin. "But as soon as we get picked up and we're a hit, all that changes. Only the best for you." He patted me on the back.

Smiling, I draped an arm around his shoulders. *Only the best for me...* now we're talkin'.

I followed Harold through the massive building holding various sets, and when we finally got to my show, tentatively titled *Acing It*, my heart started beating faster. This was it! My chance at glory.

The first set we walked through was a typical bar with a stage set up for a band. It was so eerily similar to Pete's, I almost wondered if Harold had taken notes during his visit and given them to the set designers. It just made my job that much easier; I already felt like I was home. As Harold walked us through the bar set, he said, "First, we'll get you to wardrobe. They've got your outfits pretty much done, but they'll want to test them. Then we'll get you into rehearsal. Once the first episode is in the can, I'll start shopping it around to networks."

Harold looked back at me; he was still wearing a big shit-eatin' grin on his face. "But don't you worry about that part, Mr. Hancock. This is going to be an easy sell. Cult classic is written all over this thing." I nodded in agreement. I'd already known that.

After checking out the bar set, we went through a living room and bedroom set. As I gazed at the thin mattress where my character—Ace Gunner—presumably slept, I wondered if he'd be gettin' lucky on the show. With a name as fucking cool as that, he really should. Plus, he was a rock star, and I knew from experience that being a rock star meant sex, sex, and more sex. I wondered if Anna would be cool with sex scenes, then decided she would be. It's not like I'd be penetrating anybody or anything.

I was damn near giddy when we finally got to wardrobe. Dressing up reminded me of doing music videos with the guys. It was strange to not have them here with me...but cool too. No one could hog my spotlight if it was only shining on me.

Ace's outfit mainly consisted of weathered jeans with a studded belt, a V-neck T-shirt, and a dark brown leather jacket. As I examined myself in the full-length mirror, I got a little turned on; I was bad-assed hotness. Anna better get out her boxing gloves, 'cause chicks were gonna go nuts for me.

Damn. This was gonna be so amazing.

Once wardrobe had a bunch of pictures of me in my ovary-blowing outfit, Harold herded me off to hair and makeup. They were experimenting with Ace's look today. Making him even hotter, if possible. "We need to lose the blond," the makeup girl said after inspecting me for all of five seconds.

"Excuse me?" I told her. Surely I'd misheard that. Girls dug blonds just as much as dudes.

"No blond," she bluntly stated. "Your character is dark, your hair needs to be dark." She tilted her head. "Not black...but deep brown."

I looked at myself in the mirror and tried to picture me with brown hair. I couldn't get there. "Umm, I don't think so," I told her.

She shrugged. "Your opinion doesn't really matter. You signed away the rights to your looks in the contract you signed. I could give you a pink Mohawk if I wanted. But I don't, so you should be grateful. That hairstyle does have to go though…" She made a face like she was pained just looking at me.

"Fuck that!" I exclaimed, pulling my hair into a neat ponytail. It had taken me forever to get it to the length I liked.

Pushing her glasses up her nose, she let out a long exhale. "I'll sedate you if I have to, but I *am* cutting that mop. Something fun and shaggy…Kellan Kyle–ish. He's got great hair."

Narrowing my eyes, I grabbed a pair of scissors off her counter. "If you give me Kellan's 'do, I'll cut you."

She didn't look too intimidated by my threat. "It probably wouldn't work on you anyway. Not everyone can pull off that style. Now sit." She indicated her chair and I pouted in refusal. Snapping her fingers, she repeated, "Sit!"

I did what she said that time, but I made sure she knew I wasn't happy about it.

Two hours later I had brown fucking hair. She'd chopped it too. It was longer than Matt's, shorter than Kellan's, somewhere in between like…Denny. Fuck. I looked like Denny now. Anna was gonna flip when she saw this.

After my hair was completely fucked, Harold took me to meet the rest of the cast. As I shook hands with the two girls and two guys who would be my bandmates, a sense of rightness flooded through me. The four of them looked at me like I was the most amazing thing they'd ever seen. I already felt like a star, and we hadn't even recorded anything yet.

After a few practice run-throughs, we began filming. It was a lot more difficult than I thought it would be, but with the help of the director and my castmates, I got through it, and a few days later, the pilot was in the can and I was flying back home to my wife.

Even though I told her I would hire a car, she picked me up at the airport. She was a sight to behold when I spotted her in baggage claim, but knowing what I'd done behind her back instantly made a knot form in my stomach. When Anna saw me, she did a double take and her jaw dropped. She was grinning when she walked over to me though. "Oh my God...your hair..."

With a sigh, I told her, "I know...I look like Denny, right?"

Biting her lip, she shook her head. "No...you still look like you...the sexiest man on earth, but it does give you a little... edginess. Like you're a badass."

"I *am* a badass," I told her, my lip curling into a grin. And I truly felt like a badass under her praise, but then the knot in my stomach tightened, sending a jolt of guilt and remorse through me. My smile dropped. *Maybe I should just tell her now and get it over with.* She'd be crushed though, and she was so happy to see me. Later. I'd tell her later.

Misinterpreting my expression, Anna tossed her arms around me. "Aw, babe, don't worry. I like it! In fact, I think you should keep it that way for a while." Grabbing my cheeks, she told me, "I am so proud of you, Griffin." Then she smothered me with kisses. Good thing too, because if she'd stared at me a moment longer, those big, trusting green eyes would have broken me. But she ended up unintentionally distracting me with sex appeal, and I was able to firmly lock away the guilt. It was over and done with anyway, and it was all going to be okay. I was sure of it.

I knew Harold was busy shopping the show around to networks, but waiting for him to call and tell me it was sold was making me antsy. Anna thought my jitters were for the new D-Bag album releasing in the spring, and because I wasn't ready to fess up to her, I let her think that. But the minute Harold gave me the green light, I'd have to break the news to Anna and the guys, and the thought of what I might tell them was chewing up my insides.

Every day, I mulled over things I could potentially say, but none of them sounded all that great. As it was, all I'd told the guys about my jaunt to L.A. was that I'd gotten a bug up my ass to cut and dye my hair. They'd rolled their eyes and made some joke about blondes not having more fun after all. I didn't react to their jibes, because I knew when they found out the truth it was going to be a shitstorm. On both fronts—home and work. While I hated the fact that I'd purposely kept Anna out of the loop, I was glad I'd gone through with it. I was making new dreams for myself, since Matt and the guys had smashed my old ones into the ground.

Before I knew it, it was February, and I still hadn't heard anything from Harold. I didn't know what that meant, and a trace amount of doubt started to dull the shiny hope surrounding my new dream. I couldn't imagine *no one* wanted the pilot though, so there must be a bidding war for it. Yeah, that had to be what was happening. He would call me anytime to tell me the good news, I just had to be patient. Luckily, I had something time-consuming to take my mind off it.

The D-Bags were ready to start promoting the first single off the new album. It was some romantic, fluffy piece of crap that I could have played with my eyes closed. The beat was infectious though, and I had a feeling it would go viral soon. We were debuting it live in Seattle at a local radio station that frequently promoted us. Then we were doing a media blast, hitting every major metropolis in every time zone, all in the span of a few weeks. It was short, fun, and frantic, and just the four of us. The fiancées stayed behind at their jobs, and the wives stayed home with the kids, since they wouldn't handle the frenzy well.

Our last stop on the tour was in New York City. Aside from Seattle and L.A., I think New York was my favorite place on earth. There was just so much going on here. The constant commotion, the hustle and bustle, the always having somewhere to go, no matter the time of day—it was a dream come true for an overactive type like me. I didn't even need coffee in this town. The chaotic surge of life was enough to keep me energized.

As our car took us to our hotel, Matt laid out the plans for the day. "Okay, we've got two radio gigs today, then *Live with Johnny* tonight." I puffed out an irritated breath at hearing that last one and Matt tossed me a glare. "Get over it, Griffin. It's a big show with a big audience, and we need to be on it."

"Dude's an asshole. I don't see why we need to do anything for him," I muttered.

Matt ran a hand through his short hair. I swear he had less of it now. The stress of running the band and planning his wedding was getting to him. I might have felt sorry, but he was the one who'd had Denny line up this gig, so I didn't. I hoped all his hair fell out. He should have known better than to go back to Johnny's. The guy was famous for being an ass to his "guests." He was like the evil love child of Ricky Gervais and Simon Cowell. Nobody who went on that show came out unscathed, but we were all supposed to be okay with being insulted. It was "part of the act" as Denny frequently told me. Whatever. Guy was a douche; the last time we'd gone on the show, he'd basically ignored the rest of the guys and ragged on me the entire time, insulting me in odd ways that I wasn't even sure were insults, but I was sure I didn't like it. Smart-ass, pansy-loving jerkwad.

"I know he's not the nicest host…but we're not doing the show for *him*, we're doing it for *us*. He has a very loyal, almost cultlike following, and if he says, 'Buy their album,' then that's what they'll do."

Rolling my eyes, I countered with "And if he says, 'These guys are tools, don't give them the time of day,' *that's* what they'll do. We should just ignore him. There are plenty of other late-night talk shows out there."

Matt leaned back in his seat. "You don't have to talk to him. Just sit back and let us do the work. You're good at that." The last part was really quiet, but I still heard it. Matt was starting to sound just like Johnny. Assholes.

After a brief rest at the hotel, we headed out for radio gigs. Like always, Kellan stole the show. All the questions were directed at him, and all the answers came from him. Occasionally, I would try to interject something, but more often than not, I was ignored. Or given a polite, dismissive laugh that clearly said, *Cute, but please be quiet and let us talk to the real star.* After the second gig, I was sick of interviews. Interviews about Kellan, that was. I was more than ready to talk about me and my still-secret upcoming project. Nobody asked though, and I couldn't volunteer the information yet. God, I hoped Harold had good news soon.

Anna called me that night while we were driving to Johnny's studio. "So, how's it going?"

"Same old, same old," I said. "All Kellan, all the time…" Kellan was talking on the phone too, probably to Kiera, so he didn't hear me. He was smiling, laughing, and looking genuinely pleased with every aspect of his life. Maybe he got a high from keeping me under his thumb.

Anna sighed. She hated it when I said stuff like that. "You're a star too, babe. The brightest in my sky." She sighed again. "Hurry home. The girls and I miss you."

The thought of my three girls at home, all missing me, made a brightness flare up inside me. Even if Kellan stole the show at work, I was the center of *their* world, and that was really comforting. "Yeah, I miss you guys too. Make sure you all watch Johnny's show tonight, especially Gibson. I want her to see her dad rock the house."

Anna laughed. "We wouldn't miss it. But if he spends the entire interview slamming you again, I might have to reach through the TV and strangle him."

My wife was so fucking awesome. "Please do. I hate that cocksucker." After Anna agreed with my sentiment, I told her to give the girls a kiss for me. She said she would, then we hung up. With Anna having my back, I felt a little better about this upcoming performance and interview. *Let that fucker try and make me look stupid.* I dared him to.

When we got to the studio, we were led in through the back and politely hidden away from the world by a girl with headphones and a clipboard. She stared at Kellan the entire time she explained what amenities were available for us.

She gave Kellan a bright smile and didn't leave until he thanked her. It made me roll my eyes. *There are four of us, chica.* Maybe *we* needed something. Looking around, I asked the guys, "Want to bail and go check out the nightlife around here? It's been a while since I've kicked your guys' asses at Find-a-Skank."

They all shook their heads; Evan even yawned.

"Fine," I muttered. When did our band become such sticklers for the rules? We used to be rebels. We used to be rock stars. We used to shun responsibility and laugh in the face of order. Chaos ruled our lives. I missed those days.

What felt like hours later, Kellan's starry-eyed PA came in to tell us a commercial break was happening soon and we needed to get ready. We followed her to the stage, waited for the light to change to signal that a commercial was in progress, then stepped out from behind the curtain to take up our instruments.

The crowd watching the recording went nuts when they saw us. Johnny threw up both of his hands and snapped, "Save it for the camera, people!" They shushed a little, but the occasional "I love you, Kellan!" rang through the space between us and them.

Tossing on a fake smile, Johnny, the man too awesome to have a last name, strode our way. I clenched my jaw as he approached us. Douche was plastered in heavy makeup, giving him the appearance of a tan that he didn't really have. "Boys! So good to have you back. Kellan, you're our number one requested artist." He stretched out his hand to Kellan, and Kellan, being the ambassador of goodwill that he was, shook it.

"Thank you for having us. It's an honor to be on the show."

I snorted after hearing Kellan's words. Honor, my ass. It was an obligation, nothing more. My derisive noise got Johnny's attention. His pudgy face swiveled my way, and his cordial smile twisted to smugness. "New member?" he asked. Extending his hand to me, he said, "You must be thrilled to be a part of the band. I'm Johnny, welcome to my show."

I didn't take the fucker's hand. Brown hair or not, he knew full well that I was an original member of the band. "Bite me, cornhole." Matt elbowed me in the ribs, but I didn't care. My comment had finally wiped the smile from Johnny's face.

"Articulate as always," he said, then that damn smile came back. "See you boys after your set."

Matt grabbed my elbow. "Don't make a scene," he hissed. "Just do your job."

I shoved him away from me. "I'm nothing but professional...so step off, ass munch."

Matt scrubbed his face with his hands, then stopped and took a deep cleansing breath. "It's going to be fine," he muttered to himself before turning to his instrument.

"Of course it is," I stated as I picked up my bass. "I'm here, aren't I?"

None of the guys responded to my encouraging comment, but they didn't really have time to anyway. The commercial break was ending. A crew member off-screen was giving Johnny a countdown, and his face split into a cheesy grin when the guy signed zero—*showtime.*

"Welcome back. Without further ado, ladies and gentlemen, I give you…the D-Bags!" He swished his hands our way and the cameras directly in front of us turned on. The well-trained crowd screamed louder than when they saw us the first time.

Evan tapped out a rhythm to start us off, then we took off. We played our new single, the song we'd been promoting nonstop for the past couple of weeks. I was glad this was the last time we'd be playing it for a while. I needed a break. Or at least variety. The same song over and over was killing me.

When we finished, I nearly said, "Thank God," but I didn't. Restraint was quickly becoming my new middle name.

Johnny came over and made a big show of greeting us. With a hand on Kellan's shoulder, he led us to a line of four chairs next to his desk.

I tried to take the seat next to Kellan, but Evan beat me to it. Matt took the last seat, the one farthest away from the action, so I sat next to Evan. Matt looked green. As much as he pressed the issue that we needed to do stuff like this, he hated it. I found that weird. I loved the spotlight.

"Congratulations, guys, on your latest single. The album is releasing in March, correct?"

Kellan switched into professional gear and answered all his questions about the album and the direction of our music. I was so bored I almost fell asleep. When were we going to talk about me? My phone buzzed in my pocket, and I pulled it out and glanced at the screen. Matt shot me a horrified look, like he couldn't believe I'd just done that on live TV. I wanted to tell him to relax, the audience wasn't watching me, they were busy listening to the "Kellan and Johnny Show."

I'd just received a text from Harold. As I read it, a smile broke over my face. *I hope you're sitting down when you read this... because you are about to be a star! I just signed a six-episode deal for Acing It. Book your flight, it's time to start working on more episodes! Naturally, we can't do much without our star, but filming is scheduled to start on Monday. Hope to see you there, and congratulations!*

Fuck yes! I texted him back, *I'll be there.*

As if he knew I'd just received kick-ass news, Johnny leaned forward and asked, "Are we keeping you from something more important than debuting your single on live television?"

With a smirk, I shoved my phone back into my pocket. "Sort of, but I handled it."

I'd meant it as a joke, but Johnny clearly wasn't amused. With a tight smile, he said, "You looked like you were about to nod off for a minute there. Too many late nights? I've heard that not everyone can handle the life of a rock star."

His expression and tone were so condescending, I almost told him to go to hell. Instead, I sneered, "Don't worry about me, I got this."

He furrowed his brows, like I'd somehow lost him with my statement. "So, from what I understand, Kellan here handles the lyrics, Matt, aside from being one of the most gifted guitarists I've ever heard, works on managing and promoting the band, and Evan handles the melodies. What is it that you do again?"

I was both pleased to finally be talking about myself and irritated that this guy was insinuating I had no value. His question was also disturbingly close to Matt's complaints about me. Kellan started spouting some bullshit PC answer, but I interrupted him. "I'm the heart and soul of the band. The people person. The crowd-pleaser."

Johnny raised his eyebrows, then nodded. "Oh, I guess that makes sense. In my experience, the person with the least amount of musical talent is generally thrust into the role of spokesman, and you definitely seem like the type who can shoot the breeze for hours. Odd though... why have you been so quiet this whole time? Letting Kellan take the lead?"

Did he just insult me? I couldn't quite follow what he was saying, but it seemed like he'd just praised me *and* put me down. "I was just waiting for a good question," I told him.

A spark of something flared in his eyes, and the crowd got really, really quiet. Matt grabbed my arm and tugged, trying to convey some silent message, but I didn't care. This guy was a jackass.

"Oh, so sorry if you found talking about your career to be on the boring side. Is there something you'd rather be talking about than the work that's pulled you from the depths of obscurity, where I'm sure you would be neck-deep in mediocrity without it?"

Again, I couldn't follow him. If he was going to call me lame, why couldn't he just fucking say it? Kellan asked, "How about we play another song for you?" but both Johnny and I ignored him.

I decided to be blunt, since Johnny couldn't be. "What's your beef with me, dude?"

Johnny steepled his fingers on his desk. "Beef? No beef. Just conducting an interview. It's what I do." He lowered his fingers so they all pointed at me. "I'm just trying to figure out what *you* do, that's all. It might seem to an outside observer that you in no way contribute to the band. It might seem that you are riding the coattails of your bandmates' talents. To someone on the outside looking in, it might seem that you don't belong here. It's my job to give you an opportunity to refute that."

That was when my anger flared and my restraint cracked. Dick couldn't call me worthless without repercussions. Pulling my phone out, I held the screen up to him. "Want to know what this was? A job. I'm going to be the lead actor on what is probably going to be the hottest TV show on the planet. What do you think about my talent now, jerk-off?"

Every single person in the studio turned to stare at me. Oh shit. I probably shouldn't have said that here, but oh well. It was done now. Johnny's mouth dropped open, and it was a full five seconds before he could speak. His eyes were sparkling though, like I'd just created a mega-holiday, just for him—Halloween, Christmas, *and* his birthday all rolled up into one shiny package of talk-show gold.

"TV, huh? Good luck with that. But what about the band? What will you do once you're a 'successful' actor?"

My mind flashed back to the numerous rejections and disappointments I'd had recently. Kellan's voice rang in my ear: *Not tonight, maybe tomorrow.* Matt's condemnation trickled through my mind: *I can't think of one thing that you actually do for the band.* Even Johnny's thoughts echoed through my head: *You don't belong here.*

Just as I was contemplating how to tell the guys I might have to leave them one day if the show got big enough, Matt opened his mouth. "Don't be stupid, Griffin. You can't take an acting job right now. Call them back and tell them no."

Anger ran up my spine, heating my skin and making every hair on my body stand on end. I was so sick and tired of him telling me what to do, holding me back. They all fucking held me back. Well, no more. I was making my own mark on the world, starting today.

Standing up, I ripped the mic off my clothes and dropped it onto the chair. "I quit. I quit this interview, I quit this band, I quit this life. You can all go to hell." And with that, I walked off the set.

Chapter 11

Awesome Does What Awesome Needs to Do

My phone began buzzing before I was ten feet from the stage. I was so ticked, I wanted to ignore it, but I couldn't; when I glanced at the screen, I saw it was Anna. Fucking hell. Even though I was fuming, a knot of dread started growing in my stomach. I should not have just done that on live TV. I should have held it in until I could talk to her first, like I knew she wanted me to. Shit, now I was going to have to tell her I lied. She was going to kill me.

"Hello?"

"What the hell did you just do…on national TV?" Her voice was strained and rough, like a volcano churning with molten lava, waiting to explode. On me. How the hell was I going to explain myself without her flying off the deep end? And how far off the deep end would she go? Fuck. This was supposed to be my moment…I needed her beside me.

Wading past people who were holding their hands up trying to stop me, I tried to deflect the rampage I felt coming with confident nonchalance. *This is no big deal.* "Relax, everything is fine. I don't need this gig. I've got a TV thing in the bag. They want to start filming on Monday, so as soon as I get back, we're grabbing the girls and heading to L.A." Walking to the greenroom, I stepped inside and closed the door. I wanted to be alone when my wife erupted.

"L.A.? Is this another commercial?" she asked, clearly confused. Then she got angry. "Did you just quit the band to sell alcohol on TV?"

Closing my eyes, I decided it was time to tell her everything. She was already mad anyway, how much worse could it get? *Please don't let it get any worse. I need my chill wife right now.* "Well...I actually didn't film a commercial while I was there. It was more like a pilot...for a weekly show...which is great for us. You wouldn't believe how much money hot shows pay their actors. This will make what the D-Bags paid me look like minimum wage." It was only then that I wondered just what my salary was...I couldn't remember what I'd agreed to in the contract. It hadn't seemed important at the time.

"I don't care about the money, Griffin!" she snapped. "The band...they're family. You can't just quit them!"

Her voice was superheated now; the volcano was spewing ash. Well, I had my own storm brewing inside me too. My gaze snapped to the television screen showing the stage. The guys were storming off it, while Johnny was standing at his desk, clearly asking them to stay and talk.

I scowled at the screen and let that dark fury take me over. "Yeah, they're family...family that's been jerking me around, Anna. They don't listen to me, they don't take me seriously, they never give me a chance. All they do is hold me back. Sometimes you have to get out from under your family's wings to really fly." Damn that was good, almost poetic. *And the guys say I can't write lyrics.* Impressed with myself, I added, "Honestly, babe, I've been thinking about quitting the band for a while." Maybe just as a wish, or a fleeting thought that never went anywhere, but yeah, I'd been contemplating it. And now that it was done, I felt great about it.

Anna's breath was shaky, like she was hyperventilating, and I swear I could hear her heart thudding, even over the phone. She was having a panic attack, and there was nothing I could do about it. Except possibly make it worse. "Griff, I don't think this is a good idea. Talk to the guys, tell them you were joking. Then when you get home, we'll sit down and...discuss your options."

Joking? She wanted me to tell them I was joking? Fuck that. This was the most serious I'd ever been in my entire life. And "discuss my options"? In other words, "you're incompetent, so let me map out your life for you." No, thank you. I might have gone about it the wrong way, but I was right about this. I felt it in my bones. "I *need* this, Anna, and I need you on board with it. You're my wife."

She took a long time to answer me, and when she did, there was an unmistakable note of pain in her voice. *Fuck, I'd hurt her.* "You said you filmed a whiskey commercial. You *lied* to me."

Seeing where this was going, I quickly interrupted. "I said it was *sort of* like a commercial, and it is sort of like a commercial. A really long, complicated commercial…and my character *does* order whiskey in the pilot…so that's not really lying." Even I knew I was full of shit, but what else could I say to her? *Yeah, I totally lied to get my way. Sorry.* She was already hurting. If I confessed what I'd really done, she'd change the locks at the house and call a lawyer. A brief wash of ice water filled my veins. God, I hoped she wasn't so upset that she wouldn't let me come home.

Her tone was frostier when she responded to my outlandish excuse. It actually relieved me to hear the anger. Fury was better than pain. "Fine. Then you skated around the truth so you could do what you wanted, regardless of the consequences. I don't like that, and I don't like what you've done. You should have told me the truth about this opportunity so we could have talked about it before you up and quit the band on live TV. Ugh! You fucking suck, Griffin, and I'm so fucking mad at you right now! Why the hell didn't you just tell me about this earlier?" Everything she was saying was completely true, which was exactly why I didn't want to hear it right now. I just wanted her on board, with me 110 percent, no matter what.

The residual ball of anger inside me wanted to tell her that it was my career, and I didn't have to run *anything* by her, but I had enough sense to not say that at the moment. I quit the band on an impulse but I didn't want to quit her. As calmly as I could, I answered her question. And admitting it took a lot of fucking willpower. "I thought you'd say no if I asked, so I didn't. But it's done now, and I need this. Are you with me?"

She let out a loud growl of frustration into the phone, then she barked, "We'll talk about it when you get home!"

She disconnected and I stared at my phone. Anger and guilt were still taking turns battering my insides, but oddly, the thing I felt the most at the moment was relief. I wasn't hiding anything from her anymore and she was allowing me to come home. That was something.

As the door to the greenroom burst open, my temporary relief vanished. "What the fuck was that, Griffin?" Matt's face was so red, he looked sunburned.

Boxing up all the conflicting emotions I'd felt while talking to Anna, I puffed up my chest and focused on my indignation. "*That* was me standing up for myself. Taking charge of my life." Vindication swept through me as I spoke. I had earned this shot at greatness; they couldn't take it away from me this time.

Matt tossed his hands into the air. "Unbelievable." He indicated Kellan standing beside Evan. Both men looked just as upset as Matt, although they hadn't started in on me yet. "So, when you were pitching a fit about Kellan doing a side gig, that was just hypocritical bullshit. Right? The rest of us better put the 'team' before everything else, but you can just do whatever the fuck you want! Right?"

He had a point, but I didn't want to admit it. They'd wronged me too many times; I owed them a little payback. "That's just it. We were never a team! There was you guys and then there was me. You never gave me a chance, so I had to go make one on my own." I pointed at myself with my thumb. "It's *my* time now."

"You're an asshole!" Matt snapped.

"Fuck you!" I retaliated. "You put me in a box and I'm suffocating. You can't blame me for wanting a little air."

"Yeah...we can." Matt's eyes were cold pebbles of steel in his blazing face. I'd never seen him so pissed.

Even though his hand was shaking with rage, Evan placed it on Matt's shoulder in an attempt to soothe him. Kellan shook his head. "Did you even think about what this would do to the band? The media circus you've just created. The album, the tour, the future…Did any of that enter your mind? Or were you too busy thinking about how awesome you were to care?"

I shot Kellan a glare. "It's really easy to be super judgey when you've got the entire world eating out of the palm of your hand. You've never had to be in your shadow, so you have no idea how I feel."

Kellan raised his hands. "Do you think that maybe you could have talked to me about it? Instead of being…well, you?"

"This is pointless." Grabbing my jacket off the couch, I swung it over my shoulder and prepared to leave. "What's done is done."

Evan was blocking the door. Looking up at his stone face, I snipped, "Want to get out of my way?"

He shook his head. "You've been a part of this band since the beginning. You can't just up and leave."

My lips compressed. If they'd wanted me to stay so bad, they shouldn't have treated me like I was an irritant. Something they all just put up with. "I never swore I'd stay."

"You signed a contract," Matt countered.

Glancing at him, I shook my head. "Not the same thing. We both know I can get out of that easily enough. I'm free to come or go as I please, that's how I live my life." I raised my chin, defying him to tell me what to do again.

Matt sniffed, then indicated the door. "Well then, by all means… go and be free."

Looking away from me, Evan stepped aside so I could open the door, and without saying another word, I left the D-Bags behind.

The minute my plane landed in Seattle, I was bombarded by phone calls and voicemails. At least five of them were from Denny. *Call me* was the gist of his message. I didn't plan to. I knew exactly what he'd say—*You're making a mistake, you should have run this by me, you need to publicly take back what you said, blah, blah, blah.* I didn't want to hear any of those things, so I didn't need to see or speak to him.

Denny disagreed.

When I opened the front door of my house, he was standing there in the entryway, waiting for me. "Oh, fuck no. What the hell are *you* doing here?" I asked, tired and annoyed.

Denny indicated Anna beside him; Anna looked as ragged as I felt, worn to the bone, like she hadn't slept a wink. "Your wife let me in. She seemed to think it might be a good idea if you and I talked." Anna had her arms crossed over her chest, and her lips were compressed into firm, flat lines. *Listen to him* was being broadcasted from her so loudly it made my ears ache. That was about the last thing I wanted to do though.

I held up a hand. "No need. I know exactly what I'm doing, and I don't need your advice or opinion."

Denny took a step forward. "I know about the TV show. The guy approached me before he approached you. I said no. It wasn't a good deal, it still isn't."

My jaw dropped open. "You said no? Why the fuck would you do that without consulting us first? We don't pay you half our earnings so you can withhold information from us."

Sighing, Denny shook his head. "For the umpteenth time, you don't pay me fifty percent. But regardless, I *did* mention this. We had a group meeting about it. Don't you remember that conversation?"

I tried to think back to what he was talking about, but I was jet-lagged, frustrated, and mentally depleted. And besides, his meetings were always so boring. I usually tuned him out after the first five minutes. "Can we do this later? I'm wasted." I left the door open so he could exit, but he didn't leave. Instead, he crossed his arms over his chest, in a mirror image of my agitated wife. Stubborn fucker.

"Fine," I sneered. Slamming the door closed, I dropped my bags in the entryway and raised my hands. "Go ahead, I'm listening. Say what you have to say."

Denny glanced at Anna, then back to me. "Anna told me he approached you at Pete's. Don't you think it's weird that he met you in a bar instead of going through your agent?" I furrowed my brows but didn't say anything to that. I guess it was kind of weird. Taking my silence as agreement, Denny continued. "He contacted me about *Kellan* doing it first, and I declined for him. Then he called back for Matt, and then for Evan, and then, eventually, for you. He asked for *all* the guys, and I declined for each of you. We had a group meeting once I realized he was just fishing for a name to sell the show. You pay me to keep your best interest in mind, and that is *exactly* what I did."

His words tickled something dark inside of me. They asked for Kellan and the others *first*? I was last choice? No...that couldn't be true. They wanted me and only me. He'd said so. "You don't know what you're talking about, man. We must be talking about different deals."

Denny sighed, and a look of defeat came over him. "I know you're not going to listen to a thing I say, but I'm begging you...for the sake of your family, if nothing else...this is not something you should get involved with, believe me. It's a step down and a huge risk. There is no guarantee the show is going to go anywhere, and the pay is—"

Lifting my chin, I cut him off. "That's one opinion. Mine is different. I think it's a great opportunity, a chance for me to show my worth." And that's why everyone didn't want me to do it.

Maybe seeing an angle he hadn't tried, Denny latched onto my statement. "Look, I know Kellan's fame can be overpowering, but you're important too. The guys—"

I interrupted before he could finish whatever lame argument he'd cooked up. "No, I'm not important *too*, I'm important *period*. And I'm going to prove it. I'm doing this. You and the guys will just have to accept that and move on."

Holding his hands up, Denny tried one more time to persuade me into seeing things his way. "Fine, do the show...but don't quit the band. Take a sabbatical, see what happens...you don't need to cut all ties and walk away."

But that was just it. I did need to. I'd gone as far as I could with the D-Bags, and if I stayed with them, I knew exactly what would happen—I'd shrink further and further into the shadows. They'd clipped my wings, and I was dying to fly. "No. There is nothing left for me there. I want out of the band, permanently. Make it happen."

Denny closed his eyes and I could almost see him cursing me in his mind. "Okay, I'll have papers drawn up, dissolving your interest in the band." With a forced smile, he held his hand out. "Good luck, Griffin. I think you're making a mistake, but I honestly do hope this works out for you."

With a genuine smile, I took his palm. "It's me. Of course it's going to work out."

He left with a shake of his head, and the entryway echoed with silence after he was gone. Wondering if Anna would dig into me again, I looked back at her. She didn't seem mad though. No, she looked terrified. "Griffin...he's removing you from the band. Legally. This is real, do you understand that? You won't be a D-Bag after this."

Her words tickled something in the back of my brain, something chilly and painful. Not moving forward because of some lame sentiment about my past conflicted with my new dreams though. I had to close a door so I could open another one. Right? "I know that, Anna. I'm cool with...not being a D-Bag anymore." Man, that was weird to say.

Anna inhaled a deep breath, then pressed her hands against her stomach, like she was feeling ill. "Don't be hasty about this, Griffin. Take the sabbatical if you want to try this TV thing, but don't quit the band."

Wishing everyone would stop second-guessing my choices, and a little irritated that Anna had called my future career a "thing," I shook my head. "No. This is the path I'm supposed to be on. I can feel it. The D-Bags were a stepping-stone, but I don't need them anymore." Saying that made me feel like I had a frog in my throat, and I had to swallow three times to remove it. It was true though. I'd given them their chance. They'd blown it.

Anna took a step toward me; her eyes were glistening. "You told me once that ever since you were little you wanted to be a rock star. You made it. You're there. Why would you want to throw away your childhood dream?"

Running a hand down my face, exhaustion seeping through every pore, I let out a long sigh. "I said I wanted to be the *star* of a rock band, not band member number four that nobody knows or cares about." I lifted my hands as I pointed out what should have been obvious to her. "All they care about is Kellan, but the guys won't let me do anything to change that. They never let me do anything. They hold me back. All I wanted was one fucking song—one! And the fuckers wouldn't even give me that. I can't go anywhere with them. I'm stuck." Despair started to creep in as I thought of the boxy cage they'd thrown around me. Truth be told, I'd stay with them...if I thought it would get me anywhere. But it never would, and Anna needed to accept that. If she felt so strongly about me remaining a D-Bag, then she should be having this conversation with them.

Anna put her hands on my chest, imploring me to listen. "Okay, you're right, but quitting isn't the answer. *Talk* to them. *Please.*" I could hear the utter desperation in her voice, and it freaked me the fuck out. I'd never heard anything like it from her before. Anna didn't beg, not like this. But goddammit! This was my only chance to break free. If I didn't take this opportunity, I'd never get another one. I firmly believed that.

"I have, Anna, several times. It doesn't make a difference, and it never will. This is the only way." *Please accept that. Please stand by my side again. I'm not sure I can get through this without your support.*

Her lips compressed in a familiar expression of frustration. "We're supposed to be a team. Why are you suddenly making deals behind my back and deciding everything that happens to this family? Don't I have a say? Don't I have a vote? I mean, can't we at least negotiate about this?" Even though she looked exasperated, her eyes were full of pleading, full of hope that I'd let her earn a chance to win the argument. I couldn't afford to though. Not this time. I was going to have to be a chauvinistic jerk to help her past her unfounded fears, but she'd thank me before this was all said and done. We were going to come out of this even stronger. I knew it.

Knowing I was being a bossy asshole, I shook my head and firmly stated, "We're leaving Seattle, Anna. This is happening. End of discussion." She opened her mouth, but I turned away to go find my daughters. Hopefully they would be excited for me, since nobody else was.

Like Kellan had predicted, a shitstorm sprang to life after I very publicly dropped out of the band. I think every branch of the media called me; it was kind of awesome. I was finally getting a chance to speak, and I told them all the same thing: I'd hit a wall with the D-Bags, and I was branching out to try something new, something where I could be the star.

Some assholes asked me if my rash decision was due to jealousy. I told those guys to suck it. I wasn't jealous, I was tired. Tired of being chained and restrained. It was time for the Hulk to be free.

"So we're going to move to Daddy's hometown. That cool with you?" I was explaining to Gibson that we'd be getting on a plane tomorrow and might not ever be coming back. I wasn't sure how she'd take it.

She tilted her head of blond curls and gave me a look of complete and total trust. I stuck my thumb out in an A-okay gesture and with a big grin, she copied me. "Okay, Daddy." At least someone had my back.

I patted her head, then gave her a kiss and stood up. Anna was holding Onnika while she watched Gibson and me. "We all packed and ready to go?" I asked her. A car was coming in the morning for us and some of our stuff. We'd send for the rest of our crap once we found a permanent place down south.

Anna nodded in answer, but she didn't look happy about doing it. She wasn't one to stress about things, so her reaction to my announcement was wiggin' me out. Once she got over the fact that I'd sort of lied to her...and basically forced her to go along with my plan...I thought she'd be 100 percent on board. Especially after I explained how kick-ass our life was going to be when the show got huge. She didn't seem moved by our upcoming awesomeness though. She seemed moody, pissy, and full of doubts, more like her

sister than herself. Motherhood had sucked some of the carefree-
ness out of her.

I cupped her arms, just above her elbows. "We're gonna be fine.
Better than fine, even. You don't need to worry about anything…
except making sure we all get up on time to make the flight, because you know I'm unreliable as shit when it comes to stuff like
that."

"Shit." Gibson giggled.

Anna sighed as she glanced at our little mockingbird. When her
eyes returned to mine, they were a little lackluster, like she was just
going through the motions. She'd looked like that ever since I'd told
her we were leaving. "Don't worry…I know my job. Just don't be
out late, otherwise nothing I do will wake you up."

Hoping to see the smile I knew and loved, I crooked a grin and
told her, "There's always *one* thing you can do to wake me up…"
I wriggled my eyebrows so she'd know exactly what I was talking
about. She gave me a humoring smile as she shoved me toward the
door, but that was about it. I'd kind of been hoping she would take
me up on my suggestion. My bed had been so frosty last night it
had made the Antarctic seem warm in comparison. It concerned
me some. Anna usually attacked me when I came home from a
trip, but she'd told me she wasn't in the mood and had turned onto
her side when I'd started nibbling on her. She hardly ever turned
me down. And I'll admit, the rejection hurt a little.

Thinking maybe a date night would cheer her up, I asked, "You
sure you don't want to go out with me? We could get a sitter for the
girls?"

Anna looked around our home like she was memorizing it.
"No…I want to be here tonight…"

I really didn't understand the sadness that had been hovering
around her since our argument. I'd expected the burst of anger, but
the lingering melancholy…I just didn't get it. I wanted her to be as
excited about our new life as I was. It worried me that maybe she
wouldn't get over this…but we were L.A.-bound tomorrow, our
new life awaited, and it was going to be epic. *The Griffin Show: all
Griff, all the time.*

Hopping into my Hummer, I left my house for one last hurrah in Seattle. I really was going to miss it here, especially Pete's, which is where I was headed. Even though I'd been raised in L.A., I felt like I'd grown up at the bar...come into my own, if you will. Since I didn't know when I'd be back, I felt like it was the only place I should be tonight. As I pulled into the parking lot, I wished Anna had decided to come out with me. Since we'd met in this bar, it felt wrong to not say our goodbyes together. Pete's was a milestone location for our relationship. She should be here.

Pushing aside that pensive thought, I shoved open the double doors to Pete's like I was breaking them down. I wanted everyone to hear me coming. Since it was Saturday night, the place was packed. Numerous heads swiveled at my grand entrance; my skin sizzled as their eyes devoured me. *Yeah...I loved being the center of attention.*

A cheer went up in the bar when people recognized me. That was one of the best things about Pete's—I was *always* recognized here. By the regulars, if nothing else. As expected, the fans started swarming around me, fondling me and asking questions. Their questions weren't the kind I'd been expecting though, and their touches were more violent than usual. "How could you break up the band! How could you leave! Why are you doing this to us, when we've supported you for so long!"

The heat in their voices surprised me. I'd been expecting nothing but congratulations from the fans. "What the fuck are you going on about? I'm switching one awesomeness for another, that's all."

"You're *changing* the band!" One red-faced girl shouted at me. "You're ruining everything! How do you sleep at night, knowing you destroyed the D-Bags!"

I stared at her, dumbstruck. *Ruining everything?* I was making it better. For me, anyway. And I slept just fine, thank you very much. I was about to tell her that when a voice from the middle of the bar broke through the chatter.

"Yeah, Griffin! How do you sleep, knowing you fucked over the people who gave you the great life you resent so much?"

I looked over the various heads surrounding me until I found the owner of the voice. Matt. I should have known. He was standing near another clump of people, holding a beer and sneering at me like I was committing a sin just by being here. Rachel was with him, and by the way she was supporting him, I figured Matt was plastered. That would explain the outburst. Matt generally didn't like to attract attention to himself.

Shoving some customers out of the way, I strode forward. "You got something to say to me, cuz?"

Matt tapped a finger against his jaw. "I'm not sure...but I think I just said it." He turned to Rachel. "I was speaking out loud, right?"

Rachel sighed, then said something quietly and tugged on his arm. She looked like she didn't want to be here anymore. I kind of agreed, but I was too mad to leave. "Screw you, Matt. I'm only doing this because you left me no other choice."

Matt's face turned an even deeper shade of red, and he started storming toward me; the fans between us quickly got out of the way, and Rita at the bar warned us to be good or she wouldn't hesitate to call the cops on our asses. I glanced over to see her summoning the bar's bouncer. I didn't have time to worry about it though, because Matt had reached me, and he was pissed enough and blitzed enough that he wasn't happy stopping with verbally assaulting me.

With both hands against my chest, he shoved me backward. I stumbled but caught myself. "Dude! Lighten the fuck up," I snapped.

He let out a sardonic laugh. "Lighten up? You fucked the band three weeks before our album dropped. You're the most selfish person I've ever met. I always knew you were a piece of work, but I had no idea what a fucking fucker you were until now. But you know what, it doesn't fucking matter. We'll replace your ass and move on. It will be easy as can be; I know a dozen guys who would love to have what you just threw away."

He was in my face, shouting at me like I'd gone deaf or something. His words were tiny logs being set on my internal fire, stoking me piece by piece. If he didn't shut his piehole soon, I was going to shut it for him. "Cool it, Matt. I'm just about done with you."

His face turned incredulous. "Just about? I thought you were done. Well, I am too. We're no longer family. You're dead to me, asshole. And the D-Bags are better off without you!"

That did it. My body reacted before my mind could process what was happening. My entire arm tensed, my fingers curled into a rigid ball, and then I pulled back the coiled power and released it. My fist connected with Matt's jaw and he spun to the ground. Rachel was instantly by his side.

Once she saw he was okay, she stared up at me with wide, horrified eyes. "Have you lost your mind!" she shouted.

Hovering over Matt, I shook my head. "No. I finally found it. And I'm finally seeing my 'friend's' true colors. So much for blood being thicker than water." I wanted to spit on Matt, but I thought better of it. He wasn't worthy of my saliva.

The bar's bouncer wrapped his fingers around my biceps and pulled me back. Turning my head, I spat out, "Let go of me, asswipe. I'm done pummeling him."

The man, who could have been Sam's twin, gruffed, "You'll be done when you're outside." He manhandled me past the crowd that was booing me. *Booing* me. I almost couldn't comprehend what I was hearing. Were they all drunk? Matt had started that shit; I'd only been defending myself. He was the bully here, not me.

As I was being dragged away, I shouted back at Matt, "Oh, by the way, I'm taking *my* name with me. You can't use D-Bags! That was mine!"

I saw Matt scrambling to his feet. He followed us, spouting, "No, that's not true. Your idea was Douchebags. I'm the one who suggested shortening it. It's *my* name!"

I sneered at him; he had a trail of blood running out of the corner of his mouth from where my aching fist had connected with him. "We'll let the lawyers settle this one."

Matt put a hand on my shoulder. The bouncer told him to back off, but Matt ignored him. "You're already quitting the band... don't kill it too."

With a sneer, I tossed out, "What do you need my name for anyway? Just call yourselves Kellan's Bitches, 'cause that's what you are."

Matt stopped moving with us, and the crowd soon swallowed him up. But not before I heard him mutter, "Enjoy Hollywood, Griff."

"I plan to," I shot back, then Blockhead unceremoniously shoved me out the front doors. I landed on the cement in a painful pile.

"Don't come back," he ordered. "You're officially banned from the premises."

My hands were scraped and bleeding, and my elbow felt on fire, but ignoring my aches, I shot to my feet. "You couldn't pay me to come back to this dump," I sneered.

He only smiled, then walked back into the bar. I waited for the rush of outraged fans to come outside, gushing about how awful I was treated and how they'll never frequent this place again...but no one came out. Not a single human being checked to see how I was doing. I didn't want to admit it, but that stung.

Anna was surprised to see me when I got home, since I hadn't been gone very long. I told her Pete's was dead and she hadn't missed much. I wasn't entirely lying. Pete's *was* dead to me now; I couldn't go back if I wanted to. Not that I wanted to ever go back there. Pete's could suck it. Matt was dead to me too now, but I didn't mention that to her either. No point.

I fell asleep wishing I was away from here already, and ended up waking up an hour before the car taking us to the airport was scheduled to arrive. When Anna finally stirred, I had the mountain of bags we were traveling with stacked by the front door, a pot of coffee brewing, and a vodka Red Bull in my hand. Might as well start the day out right.

"You beat me. I don't think you've woken up before me...well, ever." She yawned and stretched after she said it, and I did the same. I might have woken up before her, but it was still freaking early.

My hip hurt from where that jackass had tossed me on the cement. I inconspicuously rubbed it while I told Anna, "I'm just excited to go. This is going to be so much fun. You'll see." She gave me a small, unconvinced smile before getting up to get ready.

The doorbell chimed just as Anna finished getting dressed. Time to go. Wrangling the kids and all our stuff took a surprising amount of time. Gibson cried and refused to leave her purple room. Onnika needed food, then a diaper change, then another outfit. By the time we finally made it to the airport, I was done with this trip. Couldn't we just be there already?

We needed two carts to hold all our stuff, and even then I was bogged down with bags. When the automatic doors swished open, I spotted something that put me even more on edge. Kellan and Kiera were here. Kellan was dressed in a ball cap and sunglasses, but he still had a group of fans around him. He was smiling, autographing scraps of paper, and posing for a few pictures. Airport security was hovering around the crowd, looking a little uneasy. I figured they'd put a stop to this in about three more seconds.

Readjusting the car seat in my hand, the diaper bag on my back, and the stroller balancing on the cart, I worked my way to Kellan's circle. He looked up when he noticed me, then gave me a wave. Fans in the crowd turned my way, but if they recognized me, they didn't show it.

Anna squealed when she noticed her sister. Clutching our daughters tight, she dashed over to where Kiera was standing off to Kellan's side. They hugged, and Anna's smile was the brightest I'd seen since I'd told her we were leaving.

Kellan politely brushed through his fans to get to me. Wondering if he was going to chew me out like Matt had, I brusquely asked, "You here to bitch me out too?"

Kellan sighed, so I figured he knew about the incident with Matt at the bar. "No. I'm here to say goodbye. Regardless of… recent events…you're family, and I can't let you leave without a send-off."

I didn't want to be moved by the fact that Kellan gave a shit, but I was. He extended his hand to me. I hesitated, but eventually took it. His grin under his ball cap had the lingering fans sighing like he'd just asked them to marry him. "Good luck, Griffin. I mean that."

Nodding, I pumped his hand a few more times, then let go. "Thanks." I felt like I should add some sappy shit about how I appreciated his encouragement, but the words wouldn't come out. All I kept hearing in my mind was *Not tonight, maybe tomorrow*. Well, tomorrow was today.

I had to peel Anna away from Kiera. She had tears in her eyes when she said her final goodbye to her sister. "I'll call you when I land," she told her as their fingers finally separated.

"You better," Kiera said, wiping her eyes.

Even though I didn't get why this moment was getting so unnecessarily dramatic, I found it hard to swallow; it was like my throat was superglued shut. I started herding my wife toward check-in, then stopped and looked back at Kellan. "Hey, Kell," I called out. Even though he was wearing dark sunglasses, I could tell his eyes were locked on mine. "Tell…" *Tell Matt and Evan I'm sorry.* My mouth wouldn't form those words though. "Thanks for seeing us off."

Kellan nodded, then held his hand up in a wave. With nothing more to say, I turned my back on him, and Seattle.

Chapter 12

Let the Awesomeness Begin

Anna was near silent on the plane. Holding Onnika in her lap, she stared out the windows like the endless sea of clouds was some all-encompassing book that she couldn't put down.

I told her that my parents were picking us up from the airport, but all I got was a nod in response. Even the flight attendant didn't get a verbal answer when she asked Anna if she needed anything. Just a shake of her head while she stared out the window. Whatever funk she'd slipped into, it was so unlike her. It scared me some that she wasn't snapping out of this. I missed my spunky, carefree wife who didn't bat an eye at all my outlandish antics. Her ability to accept all my craziness was one of the main reasons we worked so well. If she lost that ability now, I wasn't sure what that might mean for us. God, I hoped my old Anna returned soon. I needed someone to bounce my excitement off of. I needed her to be stoked about this.

When the plane touched down in L.A., I was rearing to go. I was tired of this tiny, cramped cabin. Tired of my tiny, cramped life. I wanted to explode out into the world. See my name forty feet high. See the crowds losing their shit at just a glimpse of me. See the judgey critics speechless, because my awesomeness was impossible to portray in mere words. As the world was soon to find out, nothing in the English language could properly summarize me. I was ready for the solo spotlight. I'd been ready my entire life.

While I watched luggage landing on the rotating belt, I wondered if I could still call myself a D-Bag. I'd been one for so long, it was odd to think of myself as anything else. But Denny was disavowing me, so technically...I was an ex-D-Bag. That thought darkened my mood a bit; it wasn't all that long ago when the band had been everything to me. But they hadn't felt the same, obviously, and now I was a reformed D-Bag. *Nah, I'll always be a douche.*

My inner joke perked my mood back up, and a laugh escaped me. Anna flashed a glance my way; the lingering sadness in her eyes momentarily shifted to prickly anger. Even though I was happy to see any sort of mood change from her, I had to know what had sparked it. "What?" Thinking maybe she wasn't happy about our temporary arrangement, I told her, "Are you ticked we're staying with my parents? It's temporary, babe. Soon as we're settled, we'll start looking for a place. Promise."

She looked away, and the brief spark of angry life left her. Damn it. I really had no idea how to deal with sullen women; I had zero experience. If a chick turned moody, I checked out. But I didn't want to do that with Anna. She was my dream girl.

Once we had our bags, we met my dad outside. He looked haggard when we all piled into the minivan. "Something up, Pops?" I asked.

With a glance at me, he sighed and ran his hand through his hair. "Let's just say, the house is kind of...busy right now. This may be the most peace and quiet I've had in a while. God, I've missed being able to hear myself think."

I looked around the crowded airport, cars coming and going, people shouting, hustling, and scrambling to get somewhere else. This was peaceful? Anna sighed after Dad's comment. Tossing my arm around her shoulder, I gave her as encouraging a statement as I could. "It's my family...how bad could it possibly be?"

Her blank expression clearly told me just how epically awful she was sure it was going to be. It also said that if I ever wanted to get laid again, I should start looking for a place as soon as possible. I started scrolling through the classifieds in the van.

As the airport became indiscernible in the rearview mirror, I thought over the complete and total lack of a fan freak-out there. No one had asked for an autograph, no one had screamed, no one had bitched about me leaving the band. No one had even recognized me. *What the hell?* Wondering if my parents had heard the news about the band, I asked Dad, "So…did you see me on *Live with Johnny?*" That puffed-up cocksucker.

Dad frowned. "No…I must have missed it. What night were you on?"

I rolled my eyes. Typical. Unless I gave them about ten reminders, my parents missed everything I did. Except making children. They flocked to grandkids like flies to a shitpile. "Well, you missed a good one. I quit the band."

Dad snapped his gaze to me; he jerked the wheel along with his head, almost colliding us with a taxi. Maybe I should have driven. "Why the hell would you quit the band?" He gaped at me like I'd just told him I was having a sex change.

Frowning, I indicated the road. Last thing I needed was to damage my face because Dad rear-ended somebody. Especially now, since I had nothing to fall back on. This gorgeous mug was about to be my sole source of income. "I found something better. The TV show? Remember? That's why we're here."

Dad closed his eyes and I almost socked him in the arm. Pay attention, old dude! "Griffin…TV shows are a dime a dozen around here, you know that. And most of them never even get picked up, and if they do, they only last a season at best. You know that too. When you said you were filming one, I just assumed you were doing it for fun, in your downtime. I didn't realize you'd quit…" He groaned, like he couldn't believe he'd raised such an imbecilic child.

My hands clenched into fists. Why was my family always the first to condemn me? "This one is getting picked up, that's already a done deal. And it's going to be huge, so you can quit freaking out." I looked around the car; Anna was in the middle part of the minivan with Gibson and Onnika on either side of her. She still looked dull around the edges, like she was in mourning. "Everyone can quit freaking out…and have a little faith in me." Facing front, I crossed my arms over my chest. This was supposed to be different.

Anna sighed, then rested her hand on my shoulder. "We do, Griff. We do." It was the first words she'd spoken since we'd left Seattle. Smiling, I met eyes with her in the rearview mirror. It looked strained, but she was smiling too. Seeing a positive emotion on her almost made me crumple with relief. Thank God, she was recovering. I wasn't sure what I would have done if she'd never bounced back.

Then Dad said something I wished he hadn't. "What's with your hair?" I still had the short cut and brown dye job that I'd gotten when I'd filmed the pilot, although my blond roots were starting to show through. I'd need a quick fix before we started filming again.

I was about to answer him when Anna's grip on my shoulder tightened. I slowly turned to meet her heated gaze. "He didn't see your hair when you filmed the 'commercial'?" Before I could explain, she answered her own question. "No…of course he didn't see it. Because you didn't really stay with your family while you were here. You lied to keep me away…so I wouldn't find out that what you were filming wasn't really a commercial."

Shaking her head, she leaned back in the seat and turned to stare out the window. Fuck. And just when I'd been getting somewhere with her. Dad looked over at me with a frown. "You were in town and didn't say hello? Marsha is not gonna like that." Great.

When we got to Dad's house, I immediately understood what he meant by "busy." Mom was babysitting the twins for Chelsey, and about a billion of my relatives were visiting; both Mom and Dad came from super-huge families. Somebody was always stopping by. The house was chaos incarnate. Liam was there too, practicing lines for an audition.

Liam blinked in surprise when he saw me. "Wow, you actually did do it. You quit the band. Are you an idiot or just plain stupid?"

I was about to comment, but Anna beat me to it. "Griffin's not an idiot. He made a career change, that's all. He's got a plan…and it's going to work out fine."

She said that last part like she was convincing herself as well as my brother, but I was too impressed that she'd actually defended my decision to really care.

I pulled my gaze away from Anna as Dad started pointing to a room down the hall—my old bedroom. "The four of you are going to have to share a room." He shrugged, like nothing could be done about it. Anna sighed but followed me as I walked down the hall-way to our new, albeit temporary, home.

When we got to my old bedroom, which was still awesomely decorated in KISS and Poison posters, I turned to Anna. "Thanks for that."

"For what?" she murmured, laying Onnika on the ground.

"For having my back with Liam. For saying I wasn't an idiot for doing this."

Anna gave me a small smile then started checking Onnika's di-aper. "I'm still not sold on this, Griffin, and I'm still really pissed that you agreed to this behind my back, that you lied multiple times, and that you ever spouted the words 'end of discussion' like some controlling dickwad asshole…but I didn't like what he was saying." Peeking up at me, her tiny grin slightly widened. "You may be an idiot, but you're my idiot."

Grabbing her hand, I yanked her to her feet. She squeaked as she let go of the elastic on Onnika's diaper, making Onnika smile. Her deep green eyes were a smaller version of her mother's; even though Onnie's dark hair wasn't very long, they were near twins al-ready.

Wrapping my arms around Anna's waist, I pulled her tight to my body. "Come with me tomorrow."

Relaxing, she linked her arms around my neck. "To the set?"

I nodded. "Yeah. Come with me and check it out. Then maybe you'll get excited about this."

She chewed on her lip, and my cock twitched. Damn that was sexy. "Maybe…All right, I'll go with you. Could be fun." She smiled while she held her lip in her teeth, and I saw the familiar playful gleam in her eye spark to life. *There's my girl.*

I was just about to ask Gibson to take her sister into the next room when Mom appeared in my doorway. "Oh good, you're here. You can help me make dinner. And by help, I mean get your ass in the kitchen." Her smile was warm but her words were firm. There was no getting out of kitchen duty once it had been assigned to you.

"Thanks, Mom, be there in a minute." Maybe after a quickie with my wife.

Mom started walking away, then she stopped, walked over to me, and smacked me across the head. "That's for not visiting while you were in town. Nice hair."

She left the room and Anna started laughing. My head hurt, but hearing Anna laugh again was a relief. "Serves you right. That's karma telling you not to lie, especially to your wife." Her eyes grew icy, and I knew that even though she was trying to let it go, she was still pissed about my deception.

Holding her shoulders, I looked her square in the eye. "I'm sorry, okay? And I won't do it again." We were already here, there was no reason to lie again now. This was going to be smooth sailing from here on out.

Resentful fire brightened her eyes. "You better not lie to me again."

Giving her a sheepish smile, I made an X over my heart.

Anna pursed her lips, then slowly nodded. "Okay…why don't you tell me about your show then, so I know what to expect tomorrow."

I was giddy to finally be able to tell her about it. Holding it inside had been killing me, but once the secret was out of the bag, and I could talk about it, she hadn't wanted to listen. Every time I'd tried to tell her about the show the last few days, she'd quietly left the room. "Well, for starters…I'm a rock star." Her eyes widened and I grinned. "Yeah, I know, ironic, huh? And in a way, appropriate. I'm still living out my childhood dream, it's just bigger and badder than ever."

Anna gave me a small smile that was more on the encouraging side than the humoring smile, and my mood lifted even higher. With Anna firmly at my side, there wasn't anything I couldn't do. I was going to own this town, it was just a matter of time.

The next morning, Anna and I made our way to the studio in my dad's minivan. It was embarrassing to drive it, but we hadn't had a chance to get a car yet. I texted Harold when we were there, and he met us in the parking lot in a golf cart, same as before. He said hello to me, then took in my wife with surprised eyes. "Mrs. Hancock...it's a pleasure to meet you. I'm Harold Berk, the executive producer of the show. We're so thrilled to have your husband on board." He extended his hand in greeting.

Anna gave him a polite smile as she shook his hand. She didn't exactly share his opinion on the matter. "Yes, I believe I've heard of you. Briefly." Her irritated eyes flashed a glance my way. Even if she did forgive me, she'd never completely let this go.

Harold laughed at her comment and released her hand. When his gaze got a little too lengthy, I stepped in front of Anna. *Yes, my wife is hot. She's also mine, so go ahead and back that dirty thought up. It'll never happen, bro.*

"Should we get going?" I asked.

Harold returned his eyes to mine. "Yes! Hop in, and I'll take you to your new home away from home." As Anna and I scooted in beside him, he told me, "I should let you know, Mr. Hancock, you're the only cast member here who has their own trailer. You should feel very special."

I gave him a heated glance. "Well of course I should. I'm the star. Remember?" I considered asking him if what Denny had told me was true—that he'd asked every other band member to do this before he approached me—but I decided not to. Denny had it wrong. Thinking of Denny made me think of Matt and our tiff at the bar. Was he still mad at me for that? Yeah, probably. I was still mad at him for his comment—*You're dead to me.* Whatever, fucker.

Harold kept his eyes glued to the street as he answered me. "Yes, yes. The most important star."

Anna had her brows furrowed when I glanced at her, so I gave her an easy breezy grin. This was going to be amazing. I could feel it in my bones.

Walking around the set helped bring Anna out of the funk she'd been stuck in, and for the first time in a long time, I saw genuine excitement on her face. Seeing it helped remove the final remnants of guilt that had been hanging around my gut. Given enough time, she was gonna be cool with this. In fact, just watching her face light up as we walked around reminded me of the old pre-responsibilities Anna. It amped me up to see the playful girl I'd married returning.

Anna squealed when she saw the bar set. "It almost looks exactly like Pete's!" I smiled at her reaction; I'd thought the same thing myself when I'd first looked at it.

Harold seemed uncomfortable with the similarities. "No, no, it's a generic bar...I assure you."

He quickly moved us along to the living quarters sets after that. Anna gave me a crooked grin when she ran her finger along the edge of my bed. Since I'd been away from her on that damn promo tour for weeks, and then cut off by her prickly anger or strange mopey mood for the past few days, it had been forever since I'd had sex. My cock started coming to life and I suddenly wanted to take Anna to a private room more than I wanted to continue this stupid tour.

I had work to do though. I had to get my hair touched up for one thing. Fucking brown hair. I almost growled at the hairdresser when I saw her again. It was her fucking fault that I looked like Denny. And once she was done removing all traces of my glorious blondness, I resembled him even more.

Anna seemed to like it though. When we were alone, she fingered a dark strand with a curious smile on her lips. "You know, this is the one aspect of all this that I actually like. You pull off the dark look really well, babe. Very sexy..."

The look in her eyes told me just how much she enjoyed what she was seeing. Grabbing her hips, I pulled her into me. "Oh yeah? Just how sexy is it? Am I making you wet, baby?"

She ran a hand down her shirt, outlining the succulent curve of her beautiful breasts. "Mmmm, you know you do. All the damn time."

Seeing Anna get more and more into this TV idea was turning me on faster than her body. Her support meant everything to me, and now that I was finally starting to get a little bit of it, I wanted to physically reciprocate. I wanted to worship her body, to thank her for accepting all my shit. It was the least I could do. "You are so gorgeous," I murmured in her ear. "Every girl on this show is going to wish she looked as hot as you."

She let out a soft moan as she tilted her head back, exposing her neck. I placed a soft kiss against her jugular. All thoughts of being responsible on my first day of the job instantly left me. What could they do if I disappeared for an hour or so? I was the star, the reason this show was going to skyrocket. They'd tolerate a slight delay for epic glory, I was sure.

Once we were outside, I pressed Anna's back into the hair and makeup trailer and she groaned as our bodies came together. "What do you want me to do to you, baby?" I asked. Bringing my hand to her chest, I barely touched her nipple with my finger. The light touch drove her crazy, and her eyes were heated when they locked on mine.

She threaded her hands into my new dark 'do. "I want you to take me back to that bedroom set and screw me on your new bed…"

Well, fuck me.

I looked around for our guide, but Harold had disappeared once he'd delivered me to makeup. He'd said he'd be back to take me to rehearsals, but who knew when that might happen. And he never told me to wait here… surely he could find me if I toured the set again with my wife. My hot, horny wife who I hadn't fucked in weeks.

Grabbing her hand, I pulled her away from the trailer and led her back to the bedroom set. It wasn't the most private place in the world, since most of the walls were missing so the cameras had room to record. This particular set was already prepped though, so no one was around when we stumbled across it.

Laughing, I flung myself onto the bed, pulling her with me. She laughed too, then attacked my mouth like we hadn't kissed like this in years. And it felt like years. I was rock hard in under six seconds.

"God, you feel good, baby," she murmured between breaks in our lips.

"You too," I repeated, grabbing her ass and pulling her hips into mine. By the way we were both already panting and groaning, I knew this was going to be a brief but powerful fusion. Good thing too, since someone would eventually come in here for one reason or another.

Thankfully, Anna was wearing a loose skirt, and hiking it up was easy. While she nibbled on my ear, I slipped a finger into her underwear. Fuck, she was so ready. An erotic cry left her mouth as she jerked against my hand. "Yeah, you like that?"

"Yes…fuck, yes. More, Griffin. I need more…"

She rotated her hips, grinding her pussy against me. I just about came it felt so good. "Yeah, baby…I'm ready for you."

Pushing her back a little, I unzipped my jeans and freed myself. I wasn't quite as naked as I wanted to be, but I didn't have time for anything else. I didn't even take Anna's underwear off; I just moved them to the side so I could plunge into her.

She sat up on my lap, dropping her head back and showing off her chest. Fuck…they should really be recording this. It should be the opening scene of the show.

"Oh God, Griffin," she cried, moving against me.

Grabbing her hips, I worked her over me. "Call me Ace," I murmured. My peak was approaching faster than I wanted it to. *Fuck, this was hot.*

Anna slowed her pace and looked down at me, then glanced at where we were and smiled. I wondered if she felt as electrified by the openness of our setting as I did. Any second, someone could walk around the corner and see us. It made every nerve ending in my body come to life. I was sizzling, and I hadn't even come yet.

Closing her eyes, she cried out, "God, Ace…you feel so good. More…I need more. I need you to come. Come with me."

Fuck, yes! My hand ducked under her shirt as we moved together with a furious intensity. Ripping down her bra, I twisted her nipple between my fingers. She instantly clenched around me. "Yes, Ace, now…now," she cried as she climaxed.

"I'm there, baby," I got out, just before I finished.

Oh my God…I loved being an actor.

After our grunting, groaning, and panting calmed down, she

lay on my chest. Giggling, she made a circle over my pec. "I can't believe we just did that...Ace."

Even though my jeans were chaffing me, I didn't care, that was fucking amazing. Squeezing her breast still in my hand, I nodded. "Let's do that before every show, 'kay?"

Anna smacked my chest, then carefully removed herself from me and stood up. I wanted to keep lying there with my spent dick on view for the world to see, but Anna tucked me back into my underwear. She looked around with a secretive smile on her face, like she couldn't believe we'd gotten away with that with no witnesses.

Harold found us just as Anna was straightening the covers on the bed. "Oh good, there you are. I thought I'd lost you. Everything...okay?" He quirked a brow as he took in Anna's actions and the pleasing flush in her cheeks. My girl had had an orgasm for the record books. But I'd totally bend her over and give her another one if she wasn't satisfied yet. She deserved it, after what I'd put her through recently.

Anna giggled in a charmingly seductive way that made me want to sit her on my lap. "Oh yeah...everything is good." Smiling brighter, she turned to me. "Let's go meet your costars."

It gave me no end of delight that she was finally as eager about this as I was. We followed Harold with fucking springs in our step. Everything was turning out exactly as I'd hoped. It just reaffirmed the fact that I was doing the right thing by cutting ties with the D-Bags. It was time.

On the way there, Anna asked Harold about the pilot. "So, who picked up the show? What network?"

Harold started playing with his tie while he walked. "LMF."

Anna and I exchanged a glance. I hadn't heard the name before, and it was clear Anna hadn't either. "LMF? I've never heard of 'em. You sure they're legit?"

Harold nodded. "Yeah, yeah, they're a bit on the new side, but they are a real up-and-coming network. They're going to blow the big boys out of the water soon. And they're the perfect vehicle for this program...they're focusing on real cutting-edge stuff. And they are crazy about you. They are going to promote the hell out of this show. You'll be everywhere!"

Smiling, I hugged Anna tighter. "Everywhere...I like that. So, when's it airing?"

Harold's smile matched mine. "Monday night, prime time."

My smile dropped. "Wait...I'll be competing with *Monday Night Football*?" *Damn, even I might not watch me now.*

Harold swished away my concern with his hand. "With DVRs it doesn't really matter anymore. It will hardly affect us, and who knows, it might even help. This is an incredible deal for us, truly something to celebrate!"

Grinning, I replayed screwing Anna on the set. Damn straight I was celebrating. I was going to rule the airwaves this fall. *Take that, D-Bags.*

When we got to the room where the rest of the cast was waiting, I introduced my wife. "Anna, this is my 'band'—Vicky, Elijah, Cole, and Christine. They play Scarlet, Crash, Stix, and Kiki. Guys, this is my wife, Anna." On the show, Vicky and Christine's characters—Scarlet and Kiki—were blonde, busty babes who totally wanted me...they'd even gotten into a hair-pulling catfight over me in the pilot. It was awesome. I think Cole's character, Stix, wanted me too, but I wasn't entirely sure yet. But all my costars' eyes were on my wife right now. She ruled the room just by being in it. *Yep, I know. Go ahead and be jealous, 'cause that hotness you see before you is all mine.*

"Nice to meet you all. I just saw your set. It's pretty amazing." She winked at me and my dick twitched. Fuck, I'd love to take her on Ace's bed again.

Harold handed me a script though. "Best get started." He introduced me to the guy who'd be directing the episode; it was a different person from last time.

While I flipped through the script, the director dude held his hand up. "Okay, in this episode, the main story line is Scarlet hooks up with Stix to try and forget about Ace."

He pointed at me, and I nudged Anna in the ribs. "Fat chance of that, huh? I bet she cries afterwards. Sorry, dude," I said to Cole. He flipped me off.

While Anna laughed, Harold approached her. "Excuse me, Mrs. Hancock, would you like to watch the completed pilot? It's an amazing piece of work, if I do say so myself. And then I could arrange for a ride home for you. This is going to be a long day, and the actors need to focus."

I bristled at that, I'd wanted Anna here for the whole thing, but Anna seemed content to let me work in peace. "Knock 'em dead, babe. See you tonight." She gave me a kiss on the cheek, then left with Harold.

I clapped my hands together once she was gone. "All right! Let's kill this shit!"

When I got home after rehearsal wrapped up, I felt like my head was going to explode. It was a lot to remember, and I already felt like I remembered too much, what with all the D-Bags lyrics and rhythms spinning in my head. I supposed I could let myself forget those, now that I didn't need them anymore. That thought made my chest hurt, like an elephant was stepping on my sternum. I didn't want to deal with that feeling right now though, so I shoved it to the *I'll worry about that later* section of my brain. It was a full section.

Mom and Dad's place was chaos, with a half dozen relatives visiting for dinner; that happened a lot. Anna greeted me at the door with Onnika in her arms; her smile seemed forced, and I wondered what had happened since this afternoon. She'd been in such a great mood while touring the set with me. Onnie smiled and I reached out to take her. "Hey, baby girl, I missed you."

Just as Anna was handing her to me, Gibson weaseled her way between us and unceremoniously shoved Anna away from me; Anna almost lost her hold on Onnika with the unexpected movement. "Gibson!" she snapped, "I almost dropped the baby. Be careful."

Ignoring her, Gibson tossed her arms around my legs like we'd been separated our entire lives. "Daddy!" she exclaimed.

"Hey, kiddo," I said, putting a hand on her back. "Be nice to your sister...and listen to your mom." Anna's smile turned genuine as she kissed Onnika's head. She always liked it when I backed her up.

Lifting Gibson, I twisted her around so she could ride on my shoulders. Usually when I did this, she grabbed my hair and used it like reins, but I had a lot less hair now. "This is weird. I like your old hair," she told me. She timidly patted my Denny-hair like it was some bizarre animal that might bite her.

"I know," I sighed.

Mom barked an order from the kitchen to help her with dinner, so Gibson and I headed that way. I recited lines to her while I walked. "Kiki, I know we had a thing once, but it's time to move on. The band comes first." I pointed up at Gibson. "Now you say, 'But Ace...besides bass, you're my only love.'"

"Ace bass." She giggled.

I shrugged. "Close enough."

Mom pointed to a bowl of potatoes when I got to the kitchen, so I moved to the counter to help her peel them. Anna stepped close to my side. "So...Harold showed me the pilot. Have you seen it?"

Shaking my head, I told her, "Nah, I was too busy promoting that stupid album." A flash of something painful washed over me— that "stupid album" was releasing soon. Without me. I shook my head harder to shake out the feelings I shouldn't be having. Didn't matter what the D-Bags were doing. Gibson giggled as she wrapped her arms around my head to hold on. "Why? Is it awesome?"

"Um...well..." As I looked over at Anna, she was worrying her lip. I didn't take that as a good sign. "It got picked up for prime time...so it must be good, right? I mean, they wouldn't put a bad show on the air." She said it like she was both trying to convince herself and encourage me. She was failing at both.

With a sniff, I grabbed a peeler and started peeling. "Nope, they wouldn't. And besides, nothing that I'm involved with could ever be considered bad. Just look at us." I flashed her a charming smile, but Anna only gave me a halfhearted grin in return.

Chapter 13

Welcome to Awesometown, Population: Me

It took an entire week, but eventually the four of us did find somewhere to rent. And just to show Anna that everything was going to be fine, I found a place that was even bigger than our home in Seattle. From what the real estate chick told me, one of the Spellings owned it; it was luxurious to the max, and it came with a monthly price tag that was close to what the average person made in a year. It was ridiculous, even I could admit that, but it was a statement I needed to make. We were headed for greatness.

Anna wasn't so sure. "This is too much, Griffin, even for us." She looked around our new foyer with wide eyes—everything was marble. "And we'll have to hire half a dozen people just to maintain this place…"

"Already taken care of," I told her with a smile. "We have three housekeepers, one for each floor, two cooks, a butler…to do whatever butlers do…three yard guys, a pool guy, and two drivers. Oh, and two nannies, one for each girl." I gave her a *You're welcome* wink. She wouldn't have to lift a finger. Once again, I was back at awesome husband status.

She didn't seem as pleased about my lineup as I thought she would be. "We can't afford that many people, Griffin. And I don't mind doing stuff around the house."

"Yes, we can. We're rich, babe. And you shouldn't have to do anything around the house. That's the benefit of being rich."

She took a calming breath. "We did well off the two D-Bag albums, and hopefully the third, but that won't last long if we—"

Swishing my hand, I blurted out, "No, I signed off on the third when Denny gave me the papers. I won't get anything from it."

Anna was stunned; in a heartbeat, her skin seemed to lose all its color. "You...what? But you were a part of creating that album, you deserve a cut. How could you sign it away? And why would they ask you to do that? It's not right."

As Anna wondered how the guys could screw me over like that, indignant anger twisted her features. But she had it wrong. The guys hadn't asked. I had. Denny and Abby hadn't been happy with me when I'd told them I didn't want a dime from the D-Bags, but seeing as how I was giving them more money *and* letting the guys keep the band's name, they shouldn't complain about anything when it came to me. "They didn't ask. I told Denny to add it to the paperwork. I don't want their fucking money...and I don't need it."

I had also signed off on residuals from the first two albums, but I didn't think now was the right time to mention that. Anna might actually have a heart attack. Abby and Denny had spent over an hour trying to talk me out of my decision, but nothing they said could erase what Matt had screamed at me—*You're dead to me.* Maybe it had been a rash decision, but if I was dead, then I shouldn't be paid. Plain and simple. And if I hadn't contributed to the band like they'd all unanimously decided, then I shouldn't be paid. Maybe I was being stubborn and prideful, but their words had left deep gashes in me, gashes that couldn't be filled with money. And besides, I didn't need their pity paychecks; I was about to cash in on a much larger one.

Anna's anger at the band evaporated, and unabashed fear took its place. She looked around our new place with horror in her eyes. "Griffin...how much are you making on the show?"

I wasn't so stupid that I couldn't hear the warning bells ringing in my ears. Anna was trying to be supportive, yes, but her mood had turned pessimistic since she'd watched the pilot. Personally, I didn't see what was wrong with it. I'd watched it and I thought we all looked great. Well, *I* looked great. My castmates were a little dry and the script was cheesier than a 1960s horror movie, but whatever. I would carry the show to success.

"Enough," I told her, being purposely vague. Truth was, I wasn't sure what the hell I was making. I'd seen a few small deposits in my bank account, but they were nothing to write home about. I'd tried reading the contract to figure out what the arrangement was, but it was written in legalese. All I could find was something about all the cast members only getting a base pay salary until the show was picked up for a full season, then the primary leads could renegotiate their contract, if both sides saw fit to do so. LMF had only ordered six episodes…I was pretty certain that wasn't considered a full season. I didn't know how to explain that to Anna though, so I kept quiet. And technically I wasn't lying; whatever we made *would* be enough. It had to be.

Anna seemed to instinctually know I wasn't telling her everything. Eyes wide with panic, she opened her purse and pulled out her cell phone. "Call the band and apologize," she said, holding the phone out to me. "It's time to end this. Think of our future, Griffin. Think of the girls' future."

Dread seeped into me at seeing her support starting to slip away. I wanted her behind my decision, no matter what it was; I didn't want to go back to being the only one stoked about this. For a split second, I almost reached for the phone, but then Matt's words tore through my brain. *We're no longer family.* No. I'd rather be the only one excited about this job than grovel at Matt's feet.

My mind set, I crossed my arms over my chest. "No, I'm following through with this, Anna, and it's gonna be amazing. I'm *going* to be a star, the show is *going* to be a hit, and Matt is *going* to choke on his words." She looked confused by that last part, but I didn't bother explaining. Leaning into her, I hissed, "I'd rather lose everything than go crawling back to that asshole."

Her mouth dropped open. "Griffin…"

Shaking my head, I repeated, "No, I'm doing this, and you need to back me up. We're a team, remember?" I knew I was being bossy, but this was important to me. I needed her on my side.

Her fingers curled around her phone. "I do remember…but do you?" She indicated the ostentatious house around her. "This wasn't a team decision, none of this was. *You* decided all of this for us without even talking to me about it. I didn't want this. I didn't want to leave Seattle, leave my sister, leave my home. I only came with you because we're a *team*…but it's pretty clear to me that if we really are a team, then you're the captain, and the girls and I are just your…cheerleaders." Her tone was icy and bitter. Jade fire was flaring from her eyes, and a red flush stained her cheeks.

I knew I was walking on thin ice, and I knew she had a valid point, but I had one too. This was *my* career, *my* money, so ultimately, what I did with it was *my* choice. "When it comes to my job, then…yeah, I guess I am the captain. But *I'm* the one providing for you and the girls, so I think that gives me the right to the promotion. When it comes to the parenting-type stuff, you can be the captain, okay? But it doesn't matter, because we're all still on the same team. And Team Hancock doesn't need the D-Bags. We don't need anyone. We'll survive on our own. Trust me, Anna…please?" My voice came out strained, pleading. It was weird for me to hear it that way. Outside of sexual favors, I wasn't one to beg.

"I do, Griffin, but…" Stopping herself, she stared into my eyes for several silent seconds. I held her gaze, unwavering. Confident. I wasn't scared about this future, she shouldn't be either. Finally, after a long moment, she nodded. "Okay, Griff, I'll let you take the lead on this, and…trust that it will work out." She looked around the house. "But can we go down to a housekeeper, lawn guy, and driver? Otherwise I'll be bored out of my mind."

Relieved, I leaned down and gave her a long kiss. "If that's what you want, sure."

She nodded once our lips parted, then a soft, wistful sigh escaped her. What she wanted was a thousand miles north of here, but at least she was willing to make due for now. I hoped.

When my parents came over later to check out our spread,

they were clearly impressed by Castle Cock. "Wow, son, you've...
outdone yourself," Dad stated.

"I know," I said, pride swelling my chest. "Isn't it amazing?"

Liam had come with them, and his expression of being unimpressed was clearly forced; his mind was currently being blown. "If
you ask me, I'd say you were overcompensating for something," he
stated in a holier-than-thou voice.

"Good thing no one asked you then," I countered.

Chelsey had come too, and she patted my back in approval. "I
think it's awesome, Griffin. Well done."

My smile expanded so much my cheeks hurt. *Yes, well done
indeed.* And considering how awesome the premise of the show
was, I could probably have three more houses like this in the near
future. I was going to be set for life. I just needed the world to
catch up to how incredible I was, and that would happen soon. Not
nearly soon enough, but soon.

Looking over the group, I said, "This is a long tour. Do you guys
want any refreshments before we begin?"

Dad nodded. "A beer would be fantastic."

I pressed a button on the headset in my ear. "Alfred, can you
please bring six beers into the living room for me and my guests."

His reply in my ear was instant. "Yes, sir."

Liam's jaw dropped. "You have a servant? Named Alfred?"

I shook my head. "No, his name is Carl, but I like calling him
Alfred better." Anna shook her head. She hadn't been thrilled when
I'd kept the butler on, but come on...a freaking butler? Hell yeah,
he was staying.

When we were on our third beer and looking into the fifth
bathroom, Mom apparently decided it was time to have a heart-
to-heart. "So...your uncle Billy came over the other night. He told
me about how you and Matt had a blowout before you left Seattle.
Want to tell me what happened?"

With a sniff, I shook my head. "Not much to tell. I told him I
was quitting, he called me an asshole, said I was dead to him and
that we weren't family anymore." I took a swig of beer. "Oh, and he
told me the band was better off without me." *Prick.*

Mom took a pull off her beer. Everyone was oohing and aahing over the Jacuzzi, but her eyes never left mine. "Was that before or after you slugged him?" she asked.

I looked over at her with a sigh. "Honestly, I don't remember. But either way, the jerk was asking for my fist in his lip."

"I'm sure he was." She let out a long exhale. "Hancock men are proud, self-absorbed creatures. But lovable, once you look beneath that."

Wondering if she was insulting me or complimenting me, I stayed quiet. She smiled as she looked from me to Dad. "Gregory and Billy used to fight like cats and dogs. Worse than cats and dogs. Someone was always coming home with black eyes and statements that they never wanted to see so-and-so again. Then time passed and they got over whatever the fight had been about, and all of a sudden, they'd be best friends again." Her eyes returned to mine. "You and Matt have always mirrored the two of them. You'll get past this and be fine. Don't you worry, honey."

I bristled at her comment. "I wasn't worried. If he wants to miss out on being a part of my life, then it's his loss." A knot of something dark and ugly twisted in my stomach as I thought of our rift being permanent, but I pushed it aside.

Mom gave me a sad smile, then patted my back. "Of course, dear."

Two weeks later, I was still filming the same damn episode. If I thought rehearsing the same songs with the guys over and over was bad, acting out scenes was even worse! We did the same section over and over and over. My brain was frying from the monotony, and I couldn't understand why the camera dude needed a shot of me saying, "Sure, Crash, whatever you say," fifteen thousand times. It was ridiculous.

And the rest of the cast. Don't even get me started on them. There was always something wrong with one of them. Someone was hungover, someone couldn't remember their lines, someone was mad at someone, someone was late. It was one fucking thing after another, and all any of it did was make the day even slower.

And since I was typically the one who'd goofed off in the past, being forced to be the responsible one was a shock to the system.

But as much of an annoyance as the cast was, their squabbles were nothing compared to the chaos going on behind the scenes. Between the writers, the directors, and the studio execs, someone always had a problem with what we were doing. It seemed like every other hour I was handed a revised script. Remembering what I was supposed to remember and what I was supposed to forget gave new meaning to the word "frustration." At this rate, I didn't see how we'd ever finish filming one episode, let alone the six that LMF had ordered.

And if we didn't finish the six episodes, then we'd never get picked up for a full season and I'd never see a decent paycheck. I didn't want to worry about it, because I wasn't one to worry about stuff like that, but it was starting to eat at me. I'd asked Anna to trust me…I needed to deliver on that.

After spending most of the day doing nothing more than being filmed pretending to play a song on the stage, I was drained. While my driver took me home, I pulled out my cell phone and stared at it.

The album was dropping today.

Matt was probably in full-on freak-out mode. Nervous, sweating bullets, anxiously skimming for early reviews. He took it all so seriously, like he was personally being judged. Dude needed to relax before he worked himself into an early grave. Maybe being married would help. I should call and find out when the wedding was. Evan's too. Even though there was crap between us right now, surely I was still on the invite list.

Making a split-second decision, I found Matt's name in my phone and called his cell. It didn't even ring, it just went straight to voicemail. Weird. Maybe his phone was dead. Not wanting to leave a message, I disconnected and called someone else instead. He actually picked up.

"Evan, dude…what's up?"

There was a long pause before he said anything, and when he did, it was just my name. "Griffin." From the way he said it, I couldn't tell if it was a statement or a curse.

"Uh, yeah." Tilting my head, I wondered if he had a problem with me too. Well, if he did, it was reciprocated; he never said goodbye to me. Since it was fresh in my mind, I asked him about it. "Why didn't you see me off at the airport? Kell did."

"I guess Kellan is a bigger man than I am." Evan let out a long exhale, then started in on me. "What the hell are you thinking, Griffin? You quit the band for a *TV show*? One that might or might not actually go anywhere? Are you nuts?" I opened my mouth to answer him, but he plowed right over me before I could. "And what the hell happened between you and Matt? You know the real reason why I didn't show? Matt dropped by after you decked him, and I spent the next three days calming him down."

"Well, he—"

Evan cut me off with more heated words. "And you threatened to take the name. The *band's* name. The name that we've been trying to make mean something for years, and you were just going to hijack it from us? You have some nerve."

Now I was starting to get angry. "I didn't. I let you guys keep it."

"But you still threatened to take it…like you wanted to punish us or something. So tell me, Griff, what the hell did any of us ever do to you?"

Steam was practically coming out of my ears now. Calling him was a mistake. Caring about the band was a mistake. Cutting all ties was best for everyone. *The D-Bags are better off without you*, Matt had told me. I doubted that, but I guess we'd see. I was done.

"You know what, Evan, why don't you, Matt, and Kellan get back up on your high horses and ride off into the fucking sunset together. It's clear to me that none of you get me, and none of you ever will." I hung up the phone before he could further rip into me. My ass was sore enough.

My driver was staring at me in the rearview mirror. Not in the mood, I barked, "What?" His eyes returned to the road, and finally feeling somewhat in control, I told him, "Drive faster. I want to feel like I'm flying." Fuck them all.

When I got home, I was not in the mood to deal with any more crap. I just wanted to grab my wife, take her into the sauna, and mix our sweat together. Along with other fluids. Anna was on the floor playing with Onnika in the living room when I came upon her. Gibson was tossing blocks at Onnika, and Anna was reprimanding her. "Stop it, Gibson! You're going to hit her in the eye."

Gibson didn't look like she cared. But she brightened when she noticed me. Running over, she leaped into my arms with a squeal. Anna turned to smile up at me. "Hey, babe. How was work? Dinner should be done in twenty minutes or so." She batted her feet together as she lay on her stomach. She was wearing short shorts that almost exposed her ass. My dick made its approval known. I needed her. That would make me feel better.

Extending a hand to her, I said, "I need to talk to you."

With furrowed brows, she let me pull her to her feet. "Everything okay?"

Almost on cue, Carl appeared in the living room holding a tray with a bottle of beer on it. He knew what I liked to have as soon as I got home. Except today. Today I needed more. Turning to him, I said, "Alfred, watch the kids for a minute, will ya?"

Gibson crossed her arms over her chest, pouting. "No, Daddy. Stay."

I ruffled her hair. "I just need to talk to Mommy for a minute. We'll be right back."

I had to pry her off me before I could leave the room with Anna. Walking at a brisk pace, we made it to the sauna room in no time. It had a bench that wrapped around the entire room; I wanted to spread Anna out on it.

Pulling her inside, I quickly shut the door. "Griff? What are we doing in here? Can't we talk somewhere less sweaty?" she asked, while I turned up the heat. When it was ready, I added some water to the rocks, releasing a nice, relaxing puff of steam.

"Griff?" Anna asked again. "What's up?"

A bead of moisture appeared on her upper lip and I sucked it off. "Strip. Now." I started pulling at her clothes, baring more and more of her creamy skin. Yes…this would make my day disappear.

She let me pull off her shirt, then unbutton her shorts. Even though she was kissing me back, there was a question on her face.

"Everything...all right?" she asked, when she was just in her bra and panties. Moisture was beading up on her skin, making it an irresistible draw. I couldn't wait until our bodies were sliding together.

I sucked the hot air down in sharp pulls while I got to work on my jeans. "Yes. I just need to fuck you." *Then everything will be perfect.* "Make me come, baby. Make me come all over you."

Her eyes lit up at my suggestive words. She pulled my jeans down as she sank to her knees. "Baby, I'll make you come so hard it will be a week before you can do it again."

I laughed at her remark, then her mouth was on me and every thought in my head vanished. *Yes, take it all. I don't want it.* I explored her body for twenty minutes before I finally drove inside her. The heat and the sweat nearly made me nauseated, but it only amplified the release. Our orgasms echoed around the room, sizzling as loud as the rocks steaming in the center of the space.

Fuck, yes, that's what I needed.

When I was spent, I climbed off her and lay down on the bench. Closing my eyes, I flopped my arm across them. Now I needed a nap. I felt Anna stand and hover over me. "Babe?" I mumbled some incoherent response. I just wanted to stay in the void awhile longer. Anna sighed, and I heard her pick up her clothes. "I'm gonna go rinse off and check on the girls. Gibson is probably picking on Onnika...who is probably freaking out that I'm gone...And dinner is probably done now, so don't be too long, okay?"

I held my thumb up, and she tenderly kissed my forehead before she left the room. I shivered when the sudden chill of the outside air hit me. I should get out, I just didn't want to move yet...*The D-Bags are better off without you.*

And I was better off without them.

When I finally got my lazy, relaxed ass up to join the family for dinner, I noticed that Anna wasn't as refreshed as I was. "What's up?" I asked her, as Alfred set a plate of steak and potatoes down in front of me. Yes. Sex, steak, and starch...every day should end this way.

Anna sighed as a smaller plate was set in front of her. "It's

S. C. Stephens

just…I know we haven't been here long, but…the people here are so fake, it's already driving me crazy. I can't tell who is being nice to me because they like me and who is being nice because they want something from me. And it sucks not having someone around here I can hang out with." She looked over at the girls. "An adult who doesn't pick on her sister every minute of the day or need something from me every five seconds…" She sighed again as she looked over at me. "It just makes me miss home."

She had a frustrated expression on her face, and even I understood the real meaning behind her words. "We *are* home, and we'll make new friends, Anna. Actor friends who are almost as successful as me. They won't use us for anything. It'll be completely legit. Just give it time." *We're not moving back to Seattle.*

Like she heard my silent addition, Anna frowned and let out a small sigh. I wasn't sure if she was purposely trying to hate it here, but she refused to get into L.A. life. I think she would have before we had kids, when she was a little more wild and carefree, but now everything just seemed to annoy her. Even the near-constant sunny weather. More than a few times, I'd heard her sigh and say, "I miss rain." It was weird to me. Who actually missed rain?

"Actors as friends," she muttered. "Yes, I'm sure they'll be completely real, all the time. Nothing fake there…" She looked out the window while I cut up my perfectly cooked steak. Gibson beside me was picking up pieces with her fingers while Onnika was helping herself to some baby oatmeal. Everyone was content but Anna.

Wondering what could perk her up, since the awesome sauna sex hadn't done it, I tossed out, "Well, we could invite some friends down? Maybe…" My voice trailed off as I ran through Anna's list of friends. Not Jenny, she would bring Evan. Not Rachel, she would bring Matt. Not Kiera, she would bring Kellan. Why the fuck did all of Anna's best friends have to be in relationships with my best friends! Well, my ex–best friends. Irritated, I finished with "Troy and Rita?"

Anna snapped her gaze back to me. "Troy and Rita? That's the best you could come up with?"

I shrugged. "Some of your Hooters friends then. I don't care, invite whoever you want. Have a girls' weekend."

Anna turned thoughtful, so I knew she was considering it. Good. Maybe she'd like it better here if she realized it wasn't a life in solitary imprisonment. We had the means to make most anything happen. For now. God, I hoped the full season got picked up soon. Anna would flip if she found out I was making minimum wage, or damn near it.

Right at that moment, Onnika decided playing was more fun than eating. With a mouth full of oatmeal, she blew a raspberry right in my face. The sticky, half-eaten shit went all over me. "Goddammit, Onnie." She laughed while I wiped oatmeal mud off my face. Anna laughed with her. "Hilarious," I told them both.

Handing Anna the spoon, I walked over to the counter to get a towel for my face. And hair. And behind my ear. How the fuck did it get back there? While I worked, Anna said, "Okay, Griff...I'm going to take you up on your offer and have some girls over this weekend. Could you find something to do for a few hours?"

I gave her a thumbs-up. I could handle myself for a night, and besides, I think Anna really needed this.

When I left that Friday night to hang out with the cast at Elijah's, Anna was all smiles. I wasn't sure who she'd gotten to come over on such short notice. Maybe Kate? She'd probably come down just to see Justin.

After saying good night to the kids—reading Gibson a princess story, while we both wore tiaras, of course, and singing a lullaby to Onnika—I gave Anna a long, savory kiss. "I'll be fucking you later," I murmured in her ear, "girlfriends or no girlfriends."

She bit her lip and pulled on the waistband of my jeans, until our hips met. "Yes, you will," she matter-of-factly stated.

Fuck me running. Why couldn't this party be over with already?

Elijah was a crazy alcohol pusher, and I was three sheets to the wind by the time my driver took me home. I was also horny as fuck. I started stripping in the car so I would be ready for Anna. The driver glanced at me in the rearview mirror and cleared his throat, but he didn't say a word. Dude was silent as stone 99 percent of the time. I appreciated that.

By the time he stopped the car in the driveway to let me out, I was in my birthday suit. I grabbed my house keys but left the rest of my crap in the car. I'd have Alfred get it later. The night breeze was cool on my bare skin, but it only made me stiffer. Fuck, I couldn't wait to ravage my wife. I stroked my shaft while I unlocked the front door. I'd be balls-deep inside her in five, four, three...

When I opened the door and stepped inside, my hazy brain instantly remembered that Anna had out-of-town guests with her. Maybe attracted by my noisy, drunken attempts at unlocking the door, one of them was in the entryway. "Oh my God, Griffin!"

She spun around so her back was facing me, but I'd already seen her. And recognized her. "Kiera? What the fuck are you doing here? Is Kellan with you?"

Over her shoulder, she stuttered, "Why are you naked? Did you leave naked?"

Letting go of my cock, I scratched my head. "No...I don't think so..."

"Well, put something on...please."

Even though the lights were off, I knew her cheeks were flushed. Girl blushed over every damn little thing. Grabbing a vase nearby, I dumped the flowers and water on the outside step, then closed the door and covered my junk with it. "There, I'm decent."

Kiera slowly turned around, but she didn't look any more comfortable with my makeshift covering. My cock was still hard as a rock inside the vase, and none of me touched the sides. My piercing was almost touching the bottom though. Fantasizing that the vase was really Anna almost made me come. I bet *that* would really make Kiera blush.

"As I was saying...what the fuck are you doing here?"

She frowned. I was drunk enough that it was easy to see Anna in the gesture. A pale imitation of her, yes, but close enough to make my boner throb. "Nice to see you too, Griffin. I still can't get over your hair. You almost look like..." She tilted her head, and I could see her comparing me to her ex.

I held my hand up; I didn't want to hear it. "I look like me with darker, shorter hair. No biggy. Is Kell with you?" I shifted to look down both hallways, but I didn't see him.

"No, it's just me, Jenny, and Rachel. Anna said she needed a girl-friend weekend, so here we are."

Great, the three women who probably hated me the most were who Anna had invited over. Awesome. "Oh" was all I could get out.

Kiera indicated the door. "I just heard a noise, and wanted to see what it was. I didn't realize..." She sighed and pointed down the hallway where a couple of guest rooms were. "I'm gonna go to bed. I'll see you in the morning. Hopefully with clothes on..."

She darted away after that. Removing the vase from my cock, I waved with it. "Maybe. I might just wear this again!"

I was certain I heard her groaning.

I spent the rest of the weekend ignoring the trio of visitors. Well, pretending like I was ignoring them. I was attentive to their every word, especially when they talked about the D-Bags. It's not like I wanted to know what the guys were up to... but if they were crying and shit over me being gone, well, I wouldn't mind knowing about that.

From where I was sitting, I heard Kiera say, "The third album is doing well, but the guys feel like it's incomplete, you know? I mean, they can't tour, they can't do music videos, they can't really promote it at all. I think it wouldn't have done nearly so well without all the hype around the way Griffin... Well, he made quite an exit."

There was a moment of silence, then Anna asked, "Couldn't they just bring in someone else to tour with? I mean, I hate the idea, but they need to promote. I'm sure Griffin would understand." Sure I understood. They were going to shove someone else in the shadows. I hoped he/she liked it there in the darkness.

"Matt feels like they should just let it go and start fresh. They're having auditions this weekend, to replace... him..."

That was Rachel's voice, from what I could tell. The girls were hanging around the pool in the backyard, splashing their feet in the water. I was in the living room with the doors open. For the fresh air, of course.

Jenny's voice broke the stillness. "This is the second one they've had. So far…no one's been a good fit. That's what Evan says anyway. Personally, I think the guys just aren't ready to move on. They keep hoping…"

Another pause, then Kiera spouted, "Is Griffin really going through with this, Anna?"

I glanced up to where I could just see the tops of their heads over the potted plants around the front of the pool. I wasn't sure how Anna would answer her sister, but I hoped she gave her a resounding yes! I was absolutely going through with this; the guys should just suck it up…and move on. Even as I thought it, a confusing knot of anxiety started forming in my stomach.

Anna's response was so quiet, I had to strain to hear her over Gibson singing along to the TV show she was watching. "Shhh, Gibby," I snapped.

Stopping, she glared at me long enough so that I heard Anna say, "He's excited about his show. He says it's going to be bigger and better than the band, so, yeah…he's really going through with it."

The murmuring got quieter after that, and Gibson got louder, so I didn't hear much more. I'd heard the truly important part anyway—they hadn't found anyone yet.

Anna was in a wistful mood after the girls left Sunday morning. During lunch, she relayed all the pertinent information she'd gathered. "So, Jenny and Evan are starting to talk kids, which means they're starting to talk wedding plans…but she's really busy with the gallery, so they're still in no hurry."

I gave her a brief smile in response, and she took that as, *Please, tell me more!* "Rachel was really quiet about her plans with Matt, but I bet they tie the knot soon. Maybe a winter wedding…that would be fun." She sighed, and I couldn't help but wonder…if Matt and Rachel really did walk down the aisle, would I be invited? *You're dead to me.*

Shaking my head, I redirected my attention to Anna's ramblings. "Kellan and Kiera are actively trying for another baby, so, you know what that means…" She giggled, and her lips curved into a knowing smile. *Yeah, it meant Kellan was coming a lot. I'd rather be doing the same than listening to a rundown of their lives. They don't want anything to do with me.*

Putting down my sandwich, I told her, "Maybe it's time we tried for another baby? Why don't we try out some of those things in the Kama Sutra book you picked up?"

Anna's eyes brightened, and I wasn't sure which idea she liked more—kinky sex or another baby. "Can we go for another marathon session? I think it's time we attempted to break our record."

Standing up, I held my hand out for her. "We should get started then. I'll grab the water…I have a feeling I'm going to need to be well hydrated for this." Over my shoulder, I tossed out, "Alfred, watch the girls for a bit." Anna was laughing as I pulled her away, and I was glad I'd suggested her having a girls' weekend. I might have to put up with occasional visits from the D-Bags' Bitches if it meant keeping my wife happy.

Chapter 14

Awesomesauce. For Best Results, Add Me

In between filming, rehearsing, and rerecording voice crap that hadn't turned out right, I was doing interviews. Everyone was still going nuts over the whole band breakup. I didn't really want to talk about it anymore, but talking about it gave me a chance to talk about my show—and *that* I did want to discuss.

Stretching out in my motorhome-trailer, I enjoyed a moment of peace and quiet while I waited to be called to the set again. There was a lot of standing around and waiting involved in this job. I hadn't expected that. I hadn't expected a lot of things, like pissy directors telling me I couldn't convince an ape I was a human. He'd sent me to my trailer to "cool down," after I'd informed him that his penis was more appropriately sized for a fruit fly than a dude. I'd even given him a friendly tip, that manscaping that shit would make it look bigger, but he hadn't appreciated my thoughtfulness. Whatever. The break was nice anyway. My feet hurt.

I was just considering popping open a beer when the door to my trailer was knocked on. Was it time to return already? Ugh, I couldn't yet. Maybe if I ignored them, whoever it was would go away. No such luck. The knock returned even louder. Damn it.

"Mr. Hancock? Are you in there?"

Recognizing Harold's voice, I smiled and got up to get that beer.

He wouldn't be the one collecting me to go back on set. I had time. "Yeah. Come on in, Harry."

Opening the door, he frowned as he walked inside my trailer. "I wish you wouldn't call me that." Like always, he was wearing a suit, and I couldn't help but wonder what he did all day that required him to wear a tie.

"How's it hangin' on your side of the universe?" I asked him.

Normally he'd roll his eyes when I talked, but today he only gave me a tight smile. "Things are just fine, my friend," he said, taking a spot on the couch. "How is filming going?"

We'd just started filming the second to the last episode earlier this week, and it was already giving me a headache. It seemed like most of my scenes involved me standing in the room while other people talked. It was a waste of my talent, if you asked me. But the writers said my silence made my speeches more impactful. Whatever.

"It's going," I muttered. I popped open a beer, brought it to my lips, then changed my mind and offered the bottle to Harold. He had just called me friend, after all. With a small grimace, he shook his head and turned it down. Then his expression shifted to reluctance. It was subtle, but I saw it. "Something going on?" I asked, sitting on the opposite end of the couch.

"Nothing major, but I feel obligated to tell you…LMF has decided to go a different direction with their fall lineup, but not to worry, *Acing It* is slated for midseason replacement. That's actually good news for us. Some of the greatest shows in history started out as replacements." By the smile on his face, you'd think we'd just won the lottery. I wasn't so sure.

"They're pushing us back? This wouldn't be because of the crap between the writers and shit, would it?"

Harold seemed surprised that I knew about that. His face immediately settled into a carefree expression though. "Oh no, of course not. All television shows have drama behind the scenes. It helps fuel the drama happening in front of the camera. But have no fear, Mr. Hancock, the show is moving forward perfectly. It's just a matter of time before you're on top of the world."

"Okay…good." Even as I said it, I couldn't help but think I'd already been on top of the world with the D-Bags…but not really. I'd been on top, but in the backseat. Now, I was the driver.

Once we were done filming the six episodes LMF had ordered—a feat that I had doubted on more than one occasion would ever actually happen—the really fun stuff began. Parties, parties, and more parties. Say what you will about the entertainment industry, they sure knew how to wine and dine. The fluffy schmooze coming out of people's mouths was as consistent as the alcohol going in. And everyone I met told me how incredible I was and how amazing this show was going to be. I was in heaven.

Anna wasn't enjoying it quite as much as me. "Again? This is the fourth party this week. I'm all for having a good time, but I'd like to spend some evenings with my family too." She was flipping through the clothes in her closet, looking for a party dress that she hadn't worn yet. By the look on her face, I could tell a shopping trip was in her future. Personally, I thought she should just wear what she was wearing now—a black and pink bra with matching boy shorts. Damn, she was smoking. Maybe she was right about sitting this one out…

Shaking those thoughts out of my mind, I told her, "The network wants us to go. It's good for the show…I guess. Fuck if I know why we really need to be there. All I know is it's an open bar."

Sighing, she muttered, "It always is." Turning to look at me over her shoulder, she asked, "Chelsey is going to watch the kids tonight, right? As much as I like Carl…he's not a babysitter."

Our enormous closet was divided down the center by a long row of dressers. As I opened a drawer to pull out some clothes for tonight, I imagined laying Anna on top of them and having some fun with her before we left. Another time maybe. "Yeah, Chelsey should be here soon."

Anna turned back to her clothes. "Good. Remind her to keep Gibson away from Onnika." With a long exhale, she shook her head. "I don't know what her problem is with her sister. I asked the doctor, but he said it was just sibling rivalry." Pulling out a tight, black dress, she turned to me with a pout on her full lips. "It seems like it's more than that though. I mean, just the other day I caught Gibson drawing a picture of our family."

She paused, like that was supposed to mean something to me. "Yeah. And?"

"She crossed out Onnika in every single picture." Raising an eyebrow, she clarified her statement. "She didn't just forget to add her, she made little stick people for all of us, then scribbled Onnika out. Hard. With a marker." She shook her head. "It seems deeper than rivalry to me."

I shrugged. "She'll get over it."

Anna put her hands on her hips...her curvy, luscious hips. "Maybe you could talk to her."

"She's two and a half. She's not gonna understand me."

Anna's arms folded across her chest, the alluring dress between them. "She understands more than you think. She's a smart girl...she takes after Kiera." Her voice grew wistful at saying her sister's name. Anna talked to Kiera as often as she could, but she missed seeing her. Even I knew that. She was probably due for another girls' weekend.

Not wanting to think about Kiera, or Kellan, or any of the others, I shook my head so hard my vision blurred. "Fine. I'll talk to her."

Grabbing my high-end duds, I dressed while Anna put her outfit back on the rack and resumed scanning her wardrobe. When I was done, I studied myself in the mirror. Damn, I was hot.

After giving myself double shooter guns in the mirror, I headed to the bedroom. Onnika was in a contraption that let her sit up, bounce, gnaw on things, and turn around. I wished they made the toy in adult size...and with room for two. I could have a lot of fun in something like that.

I looked to the closet, but Anna was still searching for something to make her look even more incredible than she already did; she'd be looking for a long time, if that was really her criteria. How do you beat perfection?

Kneeling in front of Onnika, I jiggled a toy near her face; the bell on it made a tinkling sound that she seemed to like. She cooed, laughed, and tried to wrap a grubby hand around it. Every day she looked more and more like her mother. She was going to be a knockout when she got older. Fuck. I was going to have to kick so many teenage assholes' asses. A few adults too. My job with these girls would never be over.

I ran a finger over her forehead; her skin was so soft, it boggled my mind that anything could be that silky. It made me want to pick her up and hold her, which made me think, again, that maybe Anna had a point and we should sit this one out.

"Gibby picking on you, Onnie? You probably don't even know what that means yet. Well, one day you'll be old enough that you can take her. You take 'em all, Onnie. Don't let anybody hold you back, not even family." A stupid lump blocked my airway and I had to swallow. God, I'd been hanging around women too long.

Onnika smiled and laughed as I kissed her cheek. "You be good for Chelsey, okay?" I told her, standing up. She blew a raspberry at me. I had no idea if that meant *Will do* or *Fuck you*. Either way was fine with me.

Turning around, I made my way to the living room to find my eldest daughter. She was standing in the center of the room with Carl/Alfred, trying to get him to play horsey. Alfred was just standing there, looking dignified and aloof, and I instantly knew what Anna meant about him not being a good babysitter. Alfred would do anything we asked him to, but if it was a task he thought was below him, you'd know it by the perturbed twist of his lip and the disdainful way he only used his thumb and forefinger to pick things up.

Gibson was holding a jump rope out to him and saying, "Horsey!"

Alfred, trying to remain professional, told her, "I have no idea what you're saying, Miss Hancock, but if you'd like to jump over your rope, I'll gladly walk out to the patio with you."

Undeterred, Gibson lifted the rope higher. "Ride, horsey." Her tone of voice was something akin to *Do what I said right now, damn it!* My girl did not like being told no.

Slapping Alfred on the back, I said, "She wants a ride, A-Man," then I plopped down on my hands and legs and let out a long neigh, complete with a snort and headshake. Gibson giggled at my display, then scrambled onto my back. I helped her loop the rope under my armpits and around my chest. The first time we'd played this game, I'd put the "rein" in my mouth. Big mistake.

Flicking the reins, Gibson shouted, "Yaw!"

I reared up a little, then obligingly took her for a stroll around the room. When we were finished, I plopped her onto the couch. She fell into hysterics and immediately asked for another turn. Squatting at the couch so we were eye to eye, I held up a finger. "In a minute. First, we need to have a chat, little lady. Why are you picking on Onnika?"

She only gave me a blank look, so I tried a different approach. "Do you like your sister?"

That got me a pout. "She's mean."

"Mean? How is she mean? All she does is sleep and shit. Errr, poop." I looked around, but Alfred had left and Anna was still getting ready. Good.

Gibson only frowned and crossed her arms over her chest. I wasn't sure if she was getting me or not, and I really didn't know how to get a toddler to tell me what they were feeling, and I kind of didn't want to. That whole emotional crap...it just made me uncomfortable. Anna should really be handling this.

"I'm sure she's not trying to be mean, honey," I reassured her. There. Parenting done for the night.

"She not share," she stated, unmoved by my encouragement.

Gibson was usually the one stealing crap from Onnika, so I had no idea what she was talking about. "Share what? A toy? Bring it here and show me."

I thought for sure she'd bring me her favorite doll or something, but she didn't. She stuck her finger in *my* chest, and just like that... I got it. She was jealous. "Oh...well..." *Damn it, I really wish Anna was the one doing this.* "That's not really Onnika's fault, she's just little and she needs more one-on-one care, but that doesn't mean we care about you less. We don't. You're our firstborn, and Mommy and Daddy love you to Pluto and back, 'cause that's the farthest planet…or moon, rock, whatever the hell they're calling it now."

Gibson tilted her head, and I knew I'd lost her. Touching my finger to her cheek, I made myself say, "We love you as much as we love Onnika, and you never need to worry about that. There is always enough to go around when it comes to family. Okay?"

She nodded and stretched her arms out for a hug. As I embraced her, I noticed Anna standing on the other side of the room, watching us in a tight blue dress that hugged her curves. She was smiling, so I figured I had done an okay job. Good. I did *not* want to have to be all mushy-gushy again anytime soon.

It took two hours to finish getting ready, prep Chelsey when she arrived with her kids, and say goodbye to Gibson, who suddenly didn't want us to leave and was sobbing as we walked out the door. Anna looked worried in the car, so when Chelsey called me and let me know that Gibson was fine and she was braiding her hair, I relayed the message to her.

"That's good," she murmured, not looking relieved.

"Something up?" I asked, putting my hand on her knee. The smooth skin made mine tingle. Maybe we should skip out on this and go find a hotel. Have a little private party of our own.

"I was just…" She hesitated, then turned to me in the backseat with her. "Why do you never talk to me like that?"

Since I'd been picturing her spread out on a sea of white sheets, I needed a little help connecting the dots. "Like what?"

"Like the way you did with Gibson. I mean, I can't even remember the last time you told me you loved me. It might have only been that one time, before we got married…"

I tried to think through our past conversations, but I couldn't remember either, so I quickly gave up. It didn't matter anyway. It was just a word. "You know I don't like being all plain and predictable. It's overused anyway."

She thought about that, then shrugged. "Yeah, I know, but it would be nice to know what I meant to you every once in a while. Sex is really the only time you're vocal about what you like." She grinned in a cocky, playful half smile.

I ran my hand higher, to her thigh. Maybe we could just do it back here. Wouldn't be the first time. "There's a lot to praise during sex, especially sex with you."

Her smile turned full and wicked, then she frowned. "Well, it would be nice to hear some 'praise' during the off times too."

Shifting my focus to the road, I considered my options. I spoke them while I thought. "Well, I'm not doing the *I love you, you complete me* crap like Kellan does. It's nauseating. But...how about... whenever I say, 'Baby, you're the bee's knees,' you'll know what I really mean."

She raised her eyebrows. "Bee's knees? Are you from the 1920s?"

Looking over at her, I wriggled my eyebrows. "Would you prefer something else? Tiger's titties? Panda's pussy? Beaver's... beaver?"

Shaking her head, she laughed. "You're absolutely ridiculous."

Releasing her thigh, I grabbed her hand and kissed the back of it. "And you're the gorilla's grapes, sexy girl."

By the time we got there, Anna seemed to be in a better mood, much more agreeable to the idea of spending the night out with me. Maybe I'd turned her on with my sweet speech. I should try that more often. They do say you catch more flies with honey. Or was it whiskey? Both were true, if you asked me.

The party was being held at a private residence of some guy in the industry who worked with everybody, so everybody showed up at his parties. From what Harold told me, several celebrities were going to be hanging around the shindig, and the more we mingled with them, the better.

Our driver stopped the car, then rushed around to Anna's door and let us out. It made me smile that we were the only ones to arrive in a bright-ass yellow Hummer; I'd had my almost-tank driven down from Seattle. We could run over all these limos and sedans if we needed to.

I told the driver I'd text him when we were ready to leave, then I escorted Anna down a sidewalk covered with a red carpet. It was so Hollywood, I wanted to throw up a little, but I only rolled my eyes and cleaned the bottoms of my shoes as I walked. Hopefully I'd stepped in dog crap so I could add a little flavor to the cheesy roll of carpet.

When we got to the front door, a butler in a tuxedo was standing there. He had a tray of champagne in his hand, but as I reached to grab a couple, he pulled back and firmly stated, "Tickets, please." Fuck...the tickets...They'd sent them in the mail, and Harold had warned me to grab them. They were printed on paper lined with gold foil...cheesier than the carpet. I had no idea where they were, probably in the garbage.

I was just about to tell the guy that Griffin Hancock didn't need credentials to get into a party when Anna stuck her hand into her purse and pulled them out. She handed them to the butler with a charming smile that made me want to suck on her lip. He glanced down at them, then extended his tray of booze. "Help yourself, there's more inside."

I grabbed four, just because I could. As we were walking through the door, I handed Anna two of them. "Thanks, babe. I thought we were screwed. I'm glad you remember shit like that. I would lose my nutsack if it weren't for you."

Grabbing a fluted glass with each hand, Anna leaned up to kiss my cheek. "I know." My girl didn't meekly back away from a compliment when it was deserved. Yet another thing I dug about her.

Double-fisting it, we walked into the room packed with people. At least half of them I recognized from some TV show or movie. There were way more celebrities here than I'd anticipated, and I suddenly knew I was right where I belonged—with the stars.

Half a dozen drinks later, I was flying high and feeling no pain. Hollywood soirées were fucking awesome! Bring on the party! Cristal for everyone! Anna and I were dancing on the outside terrace, trying to get a picture of me grinding my ass against an actor from one of those crime shows, when Harold tapped me on the shoulder.

"Mr. Hancock, are you having a good time?" he asked. His tie was a colorful pattern of varying shades of purple squares. It was a party...what the fuck did he need a tie for? My shirt was wide open, so my gold pimp chain was exposed. Ah, yeah.

I engulfed him in a huge hug. "Arnold! How the fuck are you?" I screeched, loud enough for several partygoers to narrow their eyes at me.

"It's Harold, remember?" he stated, carefully removing himself from my grasp.

Playfully punching him in the stomach, I snorted, "Yeah, I know. Just giving you shit."

Harold gave me a smile that was clearly forced. "Yes, well, I'm glad to see you're enjoying yourself. Remember to get as many photos with celebrities as you can. The more you're associated with A-listers, the more you'll be noticed."

Anna raised her phone and I pointed at it. "No worries there. We've been all over this place."

Harold's smile turned genuine. "Great." Looking around, he leaned in and motioned toward the house. "If we could go somewhere quieter, I have a proposition that I think you'll find highly intriguing."

Harold always thought all of his ideas were amazing, but I was buzzing something fierce, so I slapped him on the back. "Sure. Let's go, bro."

Grabbing Anna's hand, I followed Harold as he turned and weaved his way through the crowd and back to the house. Glancing over my shoulder, I took in the panoramic view of the city below us. At night, and when I was a little drunk, L.A. was kind of beautiful.

When we got into the house, Harold moved us to an office that nobody was in. Well, I thought it was an office. Either that or it was a shrine to golfing. I picked up a club and practiced my putt while Harold shut the door.

"Thank you for coming to this. I'm sure the constant parties get wearing after a while."

I scoffed at his comment. "Nah, I love this shit. Well, I love getting fucked up with my girl, at least. The schmoozing part I could do without." Harold had asked me to introduce myself to everyone, but all I'd really said was, "Hey, I'm in a show, you're in a show… how about a selfie?"

Harold's smile was sympathetic, like he understood. "Yes, that part can be a bit…tiresome. But anyway, the news I have for you will make all the mingling worth it." Clasping his hands together, he looked between Anna and me with an expectant smile. Since I still didn't know what the big deal was, I paused in my putt to make an irritated *Get on with it* gesture with my hand. "Well, as you know from past experience, the VMAs are soon approaching. I was able to get you an invitation and appearance on the red carpet. The real red carpet," he said, jerking his thumb toward the front of the house.

"The Video Music Awards?" I asked, confused. "What does that have to do with our TV show?"

"Nothing," he admitted. "But you're an up-and-coming celebrity, and the show attracts all sorts of guests, not just the musical ones."

My mind was reeling with alcohol, and his words were slow to process. All I knew was that he was telling me I was going to be on a televised awards show. Sounded like fun. Anna was quicker on the draw though, and she spotted something that I should have seen right away. "The D-Bags will be there."

Her smile was so bright after she said it, I was sure passing planes would see it if we were still outdoors. My expression wasn't quite so joyful. Letting go of the putter, I crossed my arms over my chest. "The D-Bags will be there," I repeated, my eyes only on Harold. He had to have known that when he'd signed us on. I did *not* want to be anywhere *those* guys might be.

Before Harold could respond to my statement, Anna grabbed my elbow. "Griff, don't be like that. Maybe this is a good thing, a way to mend the rift between everybody. I know you miss them, and they miss you too…"

That comment made me scowl. "Those fuckers don't miss me, they don't give a shit about me. They wrote me off. I'm not going anywhere they're gonna be."

"You don't have to see them or make an appearance with them," Harold interjected. "But it will add extra hype to the show if you're at the same ceremony as the D-Bags. Everybody will be talking about it, and the more exposure the better."

The fact that he'd planned this for the hype made me purse my lips. "And if we do meet up, and somebody gets slugged?"

Harold's face broke into a one-sided grin. "The more exposure the better. You want to be a star, don't you? And besides, this could help get you on the air faster."

An irritated huff escaped my lips. I wanted to say yes to his statement and no to his request, but I couldn't really do that. Anna didn't voice her argument again, but she squeezed my arm, silently asking me to say yes. "Ugh, fine. You guys win. I'll go to the stupid awards show."

His smile widened and he patted my shoulder. "Great! Now, keep on pimping your show. Everyone in that room should know who you are and be excited that they know you."

Puffing my chest out, I grabbed Anna's hand. "Yeah, yeah they should."

Harold opened the doors and left. I was about to follow him when Anna pulled on my hand, holding me back. "Babe…quick question."

I looked over at her with a raised eyebrow. "Yeah?"

"I'm a little drunk, so maybe I misunderstood, but…when he said the VMAs could get you on the air faster…what did he mean? Isn't your show airing in September?"

Remembering that I'd purposely not mentioned that conversation with her, I stumbled for something to say that wouldn't piss her off. She'd call me a liar again if she knew that I'd known about the show being pushed back for a while now. "Yeah…that was weird, huh? I'll ask Harold about it next time I see him. Maybe he just meant they'd debut it in August or something." Well, fuck. There went my personal goal to not lie to her again. I needed the out though, and this gave me time to prep her for the bad news.

Like the awesome wife she was, she completely bought the crap I was selling her…which made me feel like shit. *I should fess up, but that would just worry her, and she's having such a good time right now. I'll do it later.* "Oh, okay…well, should we get back out there? Make some waves?"

She said that with a giggle and a shimmy of her hips, and suddenly going back out to that party was the last thing I wanted to do. Holding Anna in place, I looked back at the office door. Harold had left it ajar, but it was closed enough for what I had in mind.

I pushed her back until the tops of her thighs pressed against the massive desk in the room. Hands on either side of her, I pinned her against the about-to-be-well-used furniture. "You are way too hot to stay in that dress."

It took her a second to focus on me, and I knew she was buzzing just as hard as I was. "Oh yeah…what are you going to do about it?" she asked. Her finger ran along the deep V of her neckline, emphasizing the breasts I wanted to suck on.

I turned her around so I could get to her zipper. As I pulled it down, I whispered in her ear, "I'm going to peel it off you, then lay you down on this desk and make you come so hard, everyone at this party will hear you. And when they hear you screaming for more, I'll be a god in their eyes." The zipper went all the way down the dress, and when I got to the bottom, it practically fell off her.

Heat in her eyes, she turned to face me. "You're already a god. That's why just the thought of you in me does this…" She took my hand and shoved it into her underwear. I instantly twisted my hand so I could feel how much she wanted me. She let out an erotic moan as I slid against her.

"Fuck, Anna…you're so wet…" Removing my hand, I grabbed onto her hips. "Lay back…I want to taste you."

She didn't just sit down on the desk. No…she laid herself across it like she was doing a photo shoot for *Maxim* or *Playboy*. She arched her back, let her arms fall above her head, and propped one foot on the desk, highlighting every fucking asset she possessed. "Jesus," I murmured, "you're so goddamn hot."

Anna still had her phone in her hand, so I reached over and grabbed it. This shit needed to be documented. I snapped a few pictures of her sprawled on the desk. She didn't complain or ask me to stop, she just ran her hands over her body, making each shot even more erotic. My cock was throbbing, straining against my clothes. I released it, then took a picture of it. Anna wasn't the only erotic thing in the room.

I pulled her underwear off, snapped a few pics, then tasted her, just like I'd promised. She cried out as she held my head in place, and I switched the phone from still pics to video. That sound she just made needed to be captured. While I sucked on her clit, I moved the camera to get a shot of her face. That was something I didn't typically get to see, and I couldn't wait to play it back later. After that, I tried to get a shot of me licking her. Fuck, I couldn't wait to see that either.

When she was all riled up, ready for me, I filmed my hand giving myself a long stroke. Glancing up at Anna, I panted, "This is so fucking hot, I can't wait for you to see this."

She squirmed on the desk, groaning, "Just do it. I need you in me." Then she moved her hips down the desk so I could stand as I drove into her.

Holy fuck. I hoped I could hold out. This would really suck if I filmed myself doing a three pump. Making sure the camera had a good angle, I eased into her. Sounds from the party were drifting into the room, and I loved that the camera was picking them up. Those faint noises were quickly replaced by Anna's throaty moans though. Fuck yes.

I tried to keep a slow pace so the camera could get the full length of my cock sliding in and out of her...but it felt too good. It wasn't too much longer that I was pounding into her. She had to hold on to the edge of the desk to keep still, but even with that, her back was sliding up and down the wood; she'd never looked hotter, and I was so glad I was forever capturing the moment.

Having sex while filming with a cell phone was tricky, but I held her hip with one hand while holding the phone in the other. Anna's cries intensified, and I knew she was close. Thank God...I wanted to come so bad. She arched her back when she released, and moaned my name—loudly. I was just a second behind her. "Fuck...yes...shit...Anna..." I almost dropped the phone as the burst of pleasure stole my breath, stole my voice. Only incoherent groaning remained. Goddamn I loved having sex with my wife.

When we were spent and I could barely stand anymore, I

turned off the recording. Cheeks flushed, her smile radiant, Anna sat up on her elbows. "Did you record that entire thing?"

Winking, I handed the phone back to her. "Oh yeah."

Anna's eyes were mischievous as she bit her lip. "Let's watch it when we get home."

Removing myself from her, I shook my head. "Fuck that, let's watch it in the car on the *way* home." Anna laughed, and I knew with absolute certainty that we would be watching it in the backseat.

When we finally left that office, hopped up on post-sex endorphins, we strutted back to the party like a king and queen entering court. Anna was charming and seductive as she stuck her hand out and made introductions. Even though I'd rather goof off than be serious, I tried to follow her example.

"Hey, I'm Griffin Hancock, star of *Acing It.*" The celebrity I was looking at still didn't seem to know me, so I added in some backstory for clarification. "I used to be the bass player for the D-Bags."

Her eyes widened as recognition seeped into her. "Oh yeah, the D-Bags, I love them! I thought I recognized you. I saw you on *Live with Johnny* when you quit…pretty gutsy. Your new show must be incredible to leave all that behind."

Leaning in, I grinned at her. "You have no idea."

With a laugh, she started in on what sounded like a resume of her accomplishments—off-Broadway plays, commercials, modeling shoots. When she was finished listing her positives, she pulled her phone out. "We should meet for lunch and talk more about your show. Let's swap numbers…"

It went a lot like that for the rest of the night; I practically doubled the contacts in my phone. Whenever I explained the show, and that I was the member of the D-Bags who'd walked away at the peak of our popularity, people were thrilled to talk to me and eager to see what my new show was all about. They were all excited for my success and wanted a chance to work with me in the future. By the end of the night, I was the most popular guy in the room.

There was no stopping me now.

Chapter 15

When Awesome Attacks

Several weeks later, near the end of August, the moment I'd been dreading was finally here—the fucking VMAs. My entire immediate family was at the house, helping Anna and me get ready, plus a bunch of extended family too. I think they thought they'd get to go if they helped with Anna's hair and makeup. Anna was both grateful for their help and annoyed with their hands-on presence. Stating that there were too many cooks in the kitchen, she sent everyone but Chelsey into the living room.

I was good to go in my snazzy dark gray suit. I even had styling gel in my dark hair; it was all slicked back like Jack Nicholson.

While I waited for Anna, I flipped through a gossip magazine resting on the coffee table. It didn't take me long to find something that absolutely shocked me, and my chest went cold with icy dread. "What the fuck? Is this shit true?"

"Is what true?" Liam asked. Knowing he wouldn't have a clue, I stormed off to find the one person in the house who might be able to clarify the crap I'd just read.

"Anna!" I yelled, bursting through our bedroom door. She was sitting at her vanity, watching Chelsey curl her hair. She looked like a million bucks in her clingy white dress, but I was too enflamed to really care. I did, however, sneak a peek at the ample cleavage she was showing.

"Have you seen this?" I said, thrusting the magazine at her face.

She pulled away so she could focus on it. "See what?" Chelsey stopped curling her hair, and both girls studied the article that had just blown my mind. Anna's mouth fell open while she read. When she was finished, she looked up at me. "Is this true?"

"I was hoping you knew," I told her. "Have you talked to Kiera, Jenny...Rachel?" *Or the guys?* I didn't ask that last part though. I didn't want to say their names, especially if this article *was* true. "What about last month, when Kiera visited? She mention anything about this?" Not wanting to hear any more gossip about the band, I'd spent the entire weekend at my parents' place while Kiera had stayed with Anna.

Anna looked like she was at a loss as she handed the magazine back to me. "No...she didn't mention anything, and we haven't spoken in a week or so. They've all been so busy, and I knew we'd get to catch up tonight...There is just no way this is true," she suddenly decided, her face firm. "One of them would have called me."

She seemed so sure that for a second I believed her. But then Matt's words filtered through my head—*You're dead to me.* "I wouldn't be so sure. Matt could have asked..." Anger flooded my stomach, and I tossed the magazine onto the bed. "That fucking son of a bitch! I can't believe he eloped and didn't invite me!"

The magazine landed on the article in question. It was a two-page spread on Matt's nuptials. No wedding pictures were there, but then there wouldn't be any photos. It said the couple had an impromptu secret wedding, with only close friends and family in attendance. *Close friends and family.* The article then went on to point out the very glaring fact that I hadn't been invited. Or wanted. Or even informed. I'd been snubbed personally and publicly. He really had disowned me. They all had...

Standing, Anna looked over my face, then told Chelsey, "Give us a minute, please."

I paced beside the bed, swearing and fuming. Chelsey gave me a sympathetic pat on the back before she shut the door behind her. I was too riled up to respond though. Pointing at the door where they'd just exited, I yelled, "She should be ticked too! She's family, same as me, and that fucker excluded her too! And you! He left you out of the loop, and even your friends played along with his plan. Aren't you pissed?"

I felt like steam was rising from the top of my head, and my cheeks felt like someone had poured acid on them. Anna was calm as she stepped up to me. Placing both hands on my arms, she stated, "We don't know if this is true."

I balled my hands into fists; I felt like driving them through a wall. "Yes, we do. This is exactly the type of crappy payback thing he would do. He snubbed us, Anna. He snubbed *me*." Something else besides hatred started bubbling up inside me. It was thorny and painful, and I didn't want to touch it or feel it; I wanted to drink it away.

Anna's eyes started watering, which only made the sensation in my gut all the more uncomfortable. "I need alcohol," I muttered, pushing past her.

She grabbed my elbow. "Wait, let's talk about this. We've never really talked about…how you feel about leaving the band. So… how do you feel?" She seemed just as uncomfortable saying it as I did hearing it.

Jerking my elbow away, I raised my chin and pushed away the turmoil trying to boil to life. *I am Griffin Hancock…nothing bothers me. Nothing even touches me.* "I'm fine. Leaving those fuckers was the best decision I ever made, and I haven't looked back once since making it."

Anna pursed her lips. "Griffin…I know that's not true. I know it bothers you that—"

Raising my hands, I cut her off. "The only thing that bothers me is that the alcohol is out there and I'm still in here. But that's something I can easily fix." I turned and left without another word.

The drive to Inglewood took a while, and I was silent the entire ride. I'd rented us a limo so we could show up in style, but I wasn't enjoying it. I wasn't enjoying much of anything, except the minibar.

"You might want to slow down, babe. Throwing up on the red carpet may not be the type of exposure Harold had in mind."

Anna looked amazing with her hair curled and pinned, her makeup emphasizing her plump lips and smoldering eyes. If I were in a better mood, I'd rip off all her clothes and take her right here in the backseat. She'd be pissed that her hair and makeup were ruined, but she'd let me do it, and she'd rock the just-fucked look all the way down the carpet. But my mood wasn't up, so my dick wasn't either. Fuck my life.

Ignoring her statement, I tipped back my Hennessy. My head was nice and fuzzy, but I'd rather be blacked out. Anna sighed and recrossed her legs. She didn't ask me to stop again, and I didn't until we arrived at the venue and the car door opened. "Showtime," I slurred.

The driver helped Anna out, then me. I almost toppled over when I stood all the way up. I'd massively overdone it, but I didn't give a shit. I slung an arm over Anna's shoulders and stumbled my way up the carpet. Anna had to help me walk straight, and she struggled with my weight some, but I was smiling and waving, just like Harold wanted.

Some classy chick in a fancy dress approached me with a microphone. "Well, hello," she started to say. I didn't let her finish though. Ripping the microphone out of her hand, I turned to the cameraman standing behind her. "Griffin Hancock here! What the fuck up, world!"

The woman tried to get the mic back, sputtering, "You can't say that on TV!"

Turning so she couldn't take the microphone away from me, I pointed at the camera. "Keep a lookout for my new show, *Acing It*. It's going to blow your fucking mind!"

She finally got a hand on the microphone and yanked it away from me. "Prick!" she screeched while I laughed. Anna pulled me away with a long sigh.

Once we finally got to the end of the carpet, Anna was huffing and puffing like she'd just run a marathon. I was totally fine, buzzing in all the right places. Looks like I was in the mood after all. As we walked through the doors, I told Anna, "Let's go back-stage somewhere and fuck. Or on the stage. You know I've always wanted to do it on a stage."

Anna elbowed me in the ribs. "I don't think you're in any shape to do anything but pass out. Let's just go find our seats."

"Fine," I muttered, "but I have to pee first."

By the time we found a bathroom, mingled, and schmoozed with people, the show was about to start. Anna herded me to our row, then stopped short when we got there. "Fuck," she said under her breath.

Getting excited, I started unbuttoning my shirt. "Yeah? You want to do it right here? In front of the crowd? Works for me!"

She slapped her hand over mine, stopping me. "Griff…" She tilted her head toward the only two empty seats in the row. I didn't see why she looked worried, until I noticed who was occupying the full seats. All the D-Bags and their bitches.

"Fuck, no." I looked around the auditorium for that slimy pro-ducer who'd set this up. "Where the fuck is Harold? I'm gonna fucking kill him! There's no way I'm fucking sitting here! No fuck-ing way!"

My screaming got the attention of everyone in our area, in-cluding my ex-bandmates. Kellan looked surprised to see me, Evan looked conflicted. Matt just looked pissed. Squeezing Rachel's hand tighter, he narrowed his eyes at me. "What are you doing here? You're not in the band anymore, remember?"

I glanced at his hand holding Rachel's, and sure enough, there was a shiny gold band around it. Fucker really did get married without me. "It's true, isn't it? You really did tie the knot? Thanks for the invite, asswipe."

Matt's face turned a deep red. "It was close friends and family only. You're neither anymore."

That got under my skin, and I took a step forward. "You fucking piece of shit!"

Kellan stood up and put his hands on my shoulders. Even plas-tered, I registered the clicking of camera phones going off. Harold had wanted a show, and here I was giving him one. "Calm down,

Griffin. It wasn't like that. It was…a spur-of-the-moment thing. Let's go into the lobby and we can talk about it."

I shoved him away from me. His kindness was just as grating as Matt's disdain; I didn't need sympathy. "Don't do me any favors, Kell. He's just mad because I don't need him anymore, and he can't control me. I don't need any of you anymore. I've got my own thing, and it's bigger and better than anything I had with you guys. You're all just jealous, and you can all suck it!"

Turning around, I stormed off. "Griffin, wait!" Kellan called.

I could just hear Matt responding with "Save it, Kell, he's not worth chasing after. If he wants to go, fucking let him."

Grabbing Anna's hand, I yanked her up the aisle. Some PA person working on the show tried to get us to sit down. "The lights are flashing, sir, that means you have thirty seconds to find your seats."

Towering over him, I snapped, "Then you have twenty seconds to get the fuck out of my way." I pointed down to the front of the auditorium, where our seats used to be. "I'm not sitting down there. I'm going home." Fuck Harold. I'd made my appearance. That was all that was required of me.

The PA raised his hands. "I can get you different seats. I'm sure someone in the back would be more than happy to swap with you."

I crossed my arms over my chest. "Whatever." I really didn't care if I stayed or if we left anymore. I just wanted this night to be over with.

I tried not to look at the band throughout that stupid awards show, but my new seat was positioned in such a way that if I wanted to look at the stage, I had to look over their heads. And even though I didn't want to, I noticed them: Evan and Jenny laughing over some stupid inside joke; Kellan and Kiera kissing, they were always fucking kissing; Matt and Rachel whispering sweet nothings to each other. Whatever.

And it was really hard to ignore them when they went onstage to present an award. The big one—Video of the Year. Whatever. The audience screamed and hollered for them like they'd never seen them before. I booed. Someone had to. Hearing only positive feedback was what inflated egos, and theirs were inflated enough.

After the show, Anna asked me if I wanted to try talking to the guys again. My blank expression was answer enough for her. Looking torn, she jerked her thumb to where the guys were standing, chatting with the winning band. "I just want to say hi to Kiera and the girls…see how they're doing."

Frowning, I glanced over to where the bitches were clinging to their Bags. "They're having a great time keeping secrets from us, that's how they're doing. It's obvious they don't want us around, so I say fuck 'em."

She sighed. "I'll just be a minute." She turned and walked away without another word.

Well. So much for Team Hancock. Guess I was on my own with this one. Well, fuck if I was going to just stand here and wait around for her. I had better things to do, like pimp my show. Turning, I made my way toward a group of girls. By the way they were tittering, I figured they were fans, not musicians. Perfect.

"Hey, ladies. Griffin Hancock here. I'm about to make all your dreams come true, every week, starting…well whenever a sucky show gets canceled." I looked around to make sure Anna hadn't heard me say that. She still didn't know the show was a midseason replacement.

"Ooooh, Griffin…of the D-Bags, right?"

I contained a groan. One day people would associate me with something else first. Something bigger, better, badder, and bolder, and I couldn't fucking wait.

By the time I was done working the room, Anna and the D-Bags were gone. Hoping she hadn't left for the night with them, I made my way out to the cars. I found Anna out there, waiting for our driver. She looked frosty. The ice in her eyes only grew colder on our drive home. Finally, I couldn't take it anymore.

"What?" I asked.

Turning to me, she unleashed the full fury of her ire. "I thought you would at least try making peace with the band."

I gave her a curious tilt of my head. "What made you think I wanted to try? Did you not see the ring? They fucking snubbed us, Anna. I'm surprised you gave them the time of day."

Her cheeks flushed. "I know…and I'm not happy about that, but this feud has gone on long enough. Someone needs to be the bigger person."

Leaning back in the seat, I turned my head toward the window. "It's not going to be me. I'm happy where I'm at. If they want peace, then they better drag their asses to my house. They can kiss my ass on my front lawn."

She inhaled a deep breath, then the car was silent.

When we got home, she went right to our room and slammed the door shut. Whatever. She could be mad at me over this one, that was fine. I wasn't sucking up my pride to apologize to the guys. I didn't need to. They were in the wrong, not me. They'd used me, abused me, then fucking excluded me. Fuckers could go to hell for all I cared. Bigger and better things awaited me.

Chapter 16

You Heard Right, I Am That Awesome

It took Anna a couple of days to calm down after the VMAs. When she finally started smiling again, I knew she was over it. Or as over it as she could be. She wanted me to make up with my D-Bag family, but that wasn't happening. They'd gone too far. But I supposed I could cut their girls some slack, or at least hide out while they visited. Anna seemed to need their friendship. Whatever. It made her happy whenever I suggested she invite them over, so I told her to give them a call. Even Rachel I'm-Married-to-a-Douchebag Hancock could come over...so long as I wasn't around to hear about her fucking nuptials. Asshole.

While Anna made plans, I went to my office to see if there was any news about the show. Grabbing the phone, I dialed Harold. "Hey, Harry. Do you have good news for me? Have we been picked up for a full season yet? 'Cause I'd love to get paid. Or maybe you've heard about an earlier start? I've kind of had to hide the delay from my wife, so if we could get this going in September or October, you'd be making my life a hell of a lot easier." I listened for Anna, but she was downstairs on her cell phone talking to Kiera, or was last time I saw her.

Harold's voice was crisp and professional. "I'm sorry, Mr. Hancock, unfortunately, I don't think I'll be making your life any easier."

"What do you mean?" I asked, confused.

Harold paused a moment, then said, "First off, I want to thank you for your time and energy with this project. Your enthusiasm and desire to make the show a success was evident in everything you did."

"Um, okay," I said, scratching my head. "Thanks for the kudos, but what's going on? You almost sound like you're saying goodbye. You leaving me, Harold?"

His voice still stiff, he continued on like he was a recording and not an actual person. "Regretfully, LMF and the creator have decided to…part ways. The show is being shelved as all parties involved move on to other projects, and all the cast members are being released from their contracts. I'm very sorry, but the few episodes that were filmed will most likely never be shown."

"What the hell are you talking about, Harold?" I suddenly felt like I was back in school and the teacher was explaining a subject that was so pitifully easy that everyone could do it. Everyone but me. And just like at school, I felt like I was missing something that should be obvious. It only confused me even more.

Harold let out a frustrated grunt, similar to my schoolteachers when they had to "dumb down" something so I could learn it. "*Acing It* has been canceled, Griffin. Thank you for your time and energy, but your services are no longer needed."

Like a massive earthquake had just struck the city, I lost the ability to stand. Luckily for me, a nearby couch was close. I landed on it with a thud. "What?" I whispered, stupefied. "Canceled? It can't be canceled, it hasn't even aired yet. What you're saying doesn't make sense…"

"Yes, well, to put it bluntly, the studio and the creator have decided that it is no longer worth their time and energy, and ultimately, it's their choice."

"But…how can they decide that before it airs? It's going to be huge, they just have to stick it out!" I was screeching into the phone now, but my tone didn't alter Harold's.

"I'm very sorry to have to tell you this. I was…very hopeful about this one." He said it like he did this all the time. I didn't. This show was all I had.

"This is bullshit!" Standing up, I began pacing. "We'll go some-where else, somewhere where the people have more vision."

"We can't, Mr. Hancock."

"Why the fuck can't we?" I yelled into the phone.

Harold sighed. "The show doesn't belong to us, it belongs to the creator, and he's decided that he wants to go in a different direc-tion. And besides…no one else wanted the show. LMF was our only prospect."

I had no clever retort to that. No flash of brilliance to make this all pan out. All I had was a knot of indigestion roiling in my belly, mak-ing me feel like I was going to throw up. "But…I gave up everything for this…" I whispered. What the fuck was I going to tell Anna?

Harold sniffed. "Yes, that is unfortunate, but these things hap-pen. You just have to dust yourself off and try again. I'm sure one day you'll be a huge success. Best of luck, Mr. Hancock."

He disconnected the line before I could respond. I stared at the phone for a second, then dropped it onto the couch. One day I would be a huge success? Those were his parting words of wis-dom for me? But I'd already been successful before him…with the guys…and I'd left the band to do this. Because this was supposed to get me even greater success. But now…it hadn't even really started and it was over, and the band was over, and I had no fuck-ing clue what to do. The knot of tension in my stomach started replicating uncontrollably, and I had to lean over and put my head between my knees. Taking deep breaths, I tried to focus my vision; it kept wavering in and out. I'd bet everything on this gamble, given up my spot in the band, created tension in my otherwise flawless marriage, and all because I hadn't really thought the show was a gamble. It was supposed to be a sure thing. And now it was gone. *Jesus…what the fuck do I do now?*

Three hours later, I was still in my office, staring at the gold records lining the walls, trying to think of a way to keep my dream alive and to keep my marriage from falling apart. If Anna knew it was all for nothing…the crack between us would grow into some-thing truly ugly. I felt numb. I felt hopeless. I felt defeated. *It wasn't supposed to turn out this way.*

A timid knock on the doorframe got my attention. A bare leg swung through the door and wrapped around the frame, and with a bright smile on her lips, Anna rotated her body into the room. She was hugging the doorframe like it was a stripper pole. Any other day the sight would have given me an instant boner, but I was too shell-shocked to be aroused. *My plan had been flawless... what the hell had happened?*

"There you are. I just got off the phone with Kiera. She and the girls are coming up next weekend." Her smile was bright and carefree, then it turned playful. "Were you watching porn in here? Without me?"

She giggled and a brief smile lightened my face. It instantly fell off as the heaviness of reality weighed down on me. Fuck. How did I tell her I was a failure? I'd asked her to trust me. I'd assured her everything would work out. I'd be a loser in her eyes if she knew the truth. I couldn't handle the thought of being anything other than amazing to her. *I'm so proud of you, Griffin.* Goddammit.

Seeing my expression, Anna let go of the doorframe and stepped into the room. "What's going on? Did you hear something about the show? When's it airing? I think it's so weird that they won't tell you. And it's not on the schedule yet... it's only a few weeks away?"

Ice-cold fear froze my limbs, while acid-like doubt gnawed holes in my stomach. *How do I tell her what a fuckup I am?* That I'd given up my plush high-paying job, ripped her from her home, her family, and her friends, lied to her, broken her trust... for nothing. She hadn't wanted to come here, she hadn't wanted me to do this, but she'd gone along with it because we were a team and she believed in me. And I'd just lost the only hope I'd had to prove to her that I could be a star without the guys. If I told her the show was canceled, she'd freak out. She'd be furious about everything I'd thrown away to do this. No, she'd be more than furious, she'd leave... she'd go back to Seattle and leave me here to rot. Or she'd ask me to come with her, but I couldn't go back there. I just couldn't. Not as a failure with my tail between my legs.

It made me feel even sicker, but I couldn't tell her the truth. Not completely. Not yet. I needed to ease her into the truth, give it to her gradually, in pieces, so she didn't panic, so I had time to think of a backup plan. With that in mind, I decided to tell her something I should have told her a while ago. She'd be upset, but not nearly as upset as she should be. "Uh…Harold called…I sort of have bad news." I had to swallow the sudden lump in my throat. Fuck. I'd been so close to having everything I'd ever wanted.

Anna's face fell, and she placed her fingers over her chest, like her heart was pounding and she was trying to calm the organ down. "What? Is there a problem with the show?"

Forcing a smile to my face that I hoped looked realistic, I shook my head. "No, no…it just got pushed back. They're going to use it as a midseason replacement. You know, when one of the other shows fail. Harold said not to worry, that tons of successful shows get their start that way. It doesn't mean anything." But the show being canceled does. Fuck.

Anna didn't seem to know how to process that. She seemed concerned but didn't know if she should be. "Oh…well…are they still paying you the same? Even though the show has been delayed?"

You mean, are they still paying me next to nothing? And have we used up the little that they did pay me by renting this McMansion? Yes. "Oh yeah, we're fine there, babe. No worries." Shit. I was so fucked.

Anna inhaled a deep cleansing breath. After she let it go, she murmured, "It will be fine, it will be fine, it will be fine…" By the way she said it, it was clear this was a chant she repeated often. She left without another word, and a bitter despair washed over me once she was gone. *What the fuck did I do? What the fuck do I do? How do I fix this?*

I didn't have an easy answer for that. In fact, the only answer I could come up with…was to try to get on another show. Anna would flip if I told her I was jobless and auditioning though, and she was already holding on by a thread, I could tell. I'd already fucked up so much for her, and I couldn't admit what a disaster my master plan had been, and the fact that I didn't have a decent backup to that plan. So to save face, and my marriage, I did a really horrible thing. I flat-out, no-way-to-deny-it, deceitfully, horribly, shamefully lied to my wife. I lied to her, to save *us*, because I knew it was all over if I didn't. And I couldn't comprehend us being over. Just the thought of her walking out on me made me feel like I'd inhaled a handful of glass shards; every breath hurt.

The Monday after Kiera left, when Anna was chipper and recharged, I told her the "good news." Grabbing her waist, I pulled her in tight, and prepared myself to do something I didn't think I'd ever have to do again. "Hey, I wanted you to be the first to know…the show got picked up for a full season! I'm going in today to begin filming the rest of the episodes." *Please forgive me for this.*

Anna's jaw dropped in surprise. "Wow, babe, that's great!" The pride on her face made the nausea and remorse return. This show was supposed to be my shot at greatness. Now look at me.

She squeezed me tight, which was a good thing, because I was sure I looked pretty damn guilty at the moment. Pulling back, she asked, "So when is the show going to be on?"

Not able to meet eyes with her, I swished my hand and looked around for my coat. "Uh, January, I think. I don't know yet…I gotta go, babe." I felt sick as I left the house, and I even dry-heaved in the driveway, but I didn't have a choice. I needed time, and now I had until January. Hopefully by then I'd have something better lined up.

Auditioning was tougher than I thought, and after going to a few of them, I had to give my brother Liam props. I had no idea what I was doing, and that was plain as day to the people running the auditions. In fact, I was beginning to wonder if Harold would have given me Ace's part if he'd bothered auditioning me for it. By the way I was being ripped apart on an almost daily basis, I doubted it.

Every day, I was getting more and more frustrated. And every day, I avoided my wife as much as I could. I left for my "job" early in the morning and got back home as late as I could. I even went "in" on the weekends to avoid being at home. I just couldn't handle the feeling in my stomach whenever I was around my family. It was like my gut was lined with razor blades, and every time they looked at me with pride in their eyes, my muscles clenched and those blades sliced me open. I couldn't take it, so I made sure I wasn't around.

Since I didn't actually have a job, and I couldn't fill up all the hours in the day with auditions, I hung out a lot. I went to bars, strip clubs, all-you-can-eat buffets…wherever I could veg for hours at a time. I even drove to Vegas once…or twice. Anything to occupy my day. Sometimes I shopped, and then I'd leave the trinkets for Anna and the girls around the house, for them to find while I was "working." The small gestures helped alleviate my guilt, and Anna always texted me smiles and kisses after she found them, but she didn't like how much I was gone.

"I never see you anymore. I know what you're doing is important…but they *are* going to let you come home every once in a while, aren't they?"

I sighed into the phone as I sipped on my beer. I was such a fucking dick. "Work comes first, babe, you know that. But don't worry…they'll give me time off for the holidays." God, I was beginning to give Matt a run for his money in the douche of the year category.

Anna sighed too. "So in two months, I'll see you?"

"Milfums…it's temporary, you know that."

"I know…Dilfums. Kill it today, okay? Then hurry home to me. I am so bored here without you. Carl can be entertaining at times, but he's not you."

I forced myself to laugh at her comment. "Yeah, I know he's not…no one is. I gotta go, babe, I'm getting called on set." I cringed as Anna said goodbye and hung up the phone. The bartender gave me a raised eyebrow but thankfully didn't comment on my obvious lie. Since I had nowhere to go for another eight hours, I ordered another beer. Damn it. How long could I keep avoiding my life?

Around midnight, I made my way home. I felt like shit when I walked through the door. This sucked. I'd been poised for greatness, and now my life no longer had direction. The only thing in front of me was a looming deadline of the shit hitting the fan, and I'd always sucked with deadlines. I had no clue what to do, and I wasn't used to that feeling.

Since childhood, I'd always known what my destiny was—fame. And once I'd found the D-Bags, I hadn't questioned my life or the road I was on. I'd known I was on a skyrocket to success, and all I'd had to do was stay the course. But then I'd gotten there and realized it wasn't what I'd thought it would be. It was like my path had been parallel to the path I'd wanted, so I'd gotten off it. And now that I was off that path, for the first time ever, I was questioning my choices, and I was beginning to wonder if my view of that original path had been skewed. Maybe it hadn't been so bad after all. Maybe I could still climb back onto it? All I needed was a hand to help me up…

Without allowing a moment to second-guess myself, I headed to the kitchen and picked up the phone to make a call. I dialed a number that I hadn't dialed in ages, and when a familiar voice answered, I had to swallow the knot blocking my throat. Then I wrapped myself in an armor of nonchalance. This was no big deal. *Yes, it was.* "Hey, Matt…good you're up. It's me, Griffin." There was silence on the other end for so long that I almost thought he'd hung up on me. "You still there?"

"Yeah, I'm still here. Although I'm wondering why. I should hang up right now and block your number."

The frostiness in his voice got under my skin, but I did my best to ignore it. "Are you still cross with me for decking you? Is that why you snubbed me at your wedding? Come on, man. That was forever ago."

"Decking me? You think I'm mad about…?" I heard a deep inhale, then a long exhale. "What do you want, Griffin?"

Closing my eyes, I said a quick *Let this work* prayer. "Just wondering if you'd found a bassist yet. I've got some time to kill…so if you need anybody…" *Please take me back.*

Matt scoffed. "Are you kidding me? You've got time to kill, so you want back in…since you've got nothing better going on right now? Unbelievable." He let out a humorless laugh. "What happened to your show? Your shot at stardom, since apparently being in a successful band wasn't stardom enough for you."

The truth was too horrible to say, so I told a creative lie. "They're restructuring, and it may be a while before it goes on air."

"Restructuring? I heard the studio dropped it. That bad, huh?" He let out another unamused laugh. His comment surprised me though. I didn't realize that news was out there. Fuck, if Anna heard about it…

"You checking up on me?" I asked, my fear making me defensive.

"Nope, someone just happened to mention to me that it crashed and burned, and since you're calling me begging for your old job back, I'm guessing that rumor was true. Must have sucked pretty badly if it didn't even make it to the air." His voice was so condescending, a chill of indignation went down my spine. Sanctimonious asshole.

"I wasn't calling for my job back, jerkoff, I was just calling to get some intel on you guys."

"Right. You're just spying on us, to see how we're doing?"

"Exactly. I'm curious about my competition." Even as I said it, I knew this was where my path had been directing me all along. I was born to be on the stage, surrounded by thumping music and glaring lights. Movies and TV weren't my destiny. Being a rock star was. I'd always known that, I'd just forgotten it for a moment or two.

Matt's voice was dubious when he responded. "Competition? *You're* going to put out an album?" He started laughing, and there was humor in it this time. A lot of humor. It only vindicated my decision. Yes, this would fix everything.

"What do you know about putting together an album, Griffin? In fact, what do you know about music at all? You never paid attention to anything we did. Ever! Your entire career with us was based on us doing all the work so you could goof off."

His words were soaked in truth, but they incensed me anyway. "Someone had to lighten the mood. What with all the brooding and melancholy and seriousness…I'm the reason people liked us and liked coming to our shows. Because I'm the only one who knew how to have some fucking fun! And I know plenty about music. You just watch, cuz. Because I'm about to impress the shit out of you."

I hung up the phone before he could give me some lame-ass response. Smiling for the first time in what felt like days, I headed to my office to get started on lyrics. Fuck them. Fuck them all. I would do just what Harold said—dust myself off and keep going. And if I couldn't join those fuckers, then I would beat them.

Chapter 17

Awesome Strikes Back

Having a little purpose while I was "working" during the day made some of my hope and good humor return. While I killed time in bars or diners, I started writing down lyrics. I figured it wouldn't take me too long to have a handful of awesome songs. I mean, Kellan came up with them all the time. A huge part of me wanted to tell Anna my news, wanted to stop the charade of filming *Acing It* every day and start bouncing ideas off her, but I couldn't yet. I couldn't tell her I'd been deceiving her in such a big-ass way that the fib I'd told her about the pilot now seemed like an innocent little white lie. I couldn't tell her anything until I had a contract with a record label under my belt. A killer contract that would ease all of her worries. She'd still be mad at me for breaking her trust again, but maybe then she wouldn't kill me.

Songwriting was more time-consuming than I thought it would be, and I found myself doing it all the time, even on the rare occasions when I was home with Anna and the girls. Like one Saturday afternoon, when I was in my office trying to come up with lines that were intriguing and thought-provoking. What I was writing down though was closer to fifth-grade poetry. Dirty fifth-grade poetry. "Roses are red, violets are blue, let's strip off these clothes so I can do you." Direct and to the point. Sounded good to me. I circled it in red—a keeper.

By the time the afternoon melted into evening, I had enough keepers for an entire song. Ha! Kellan acted like coming up with lyrics was challenging, but this shit wasn't so hard. It flowed out of my mind as easily as beer down my gullet...whatever the fuck a gullet was. Wanting a drink now, I yelled over my shoulder, "Alfred! Beer me!"

"Yes, sir," came his response. I knew he'd been close.

Alfred returned while I was scribbling down more masterpieces. He set the bottle on my desk, and I instantly wrapped my fingers around the cold glass. I couldn't pull it toward me though, because he was still holding on to it. "Dude, if you're expecting a thanks, think again. I don't thank people I pay." I glanced up, but it was Anna standing in front of me, holding my drink hostage.

"I know," she replied. "And I still think you should. Even though you do pay them an obscene amount of money, it's the decent thing to do."

Sitting up in my chair, I told her, "I've never been decent. You know that."

She crooked a small smile, then glanced at my desk. "What have you been doing up here all day?"

I'd been transferring all of my good lyrics onto one page. Wondering what she would think about them, I held the page up to her. "I've been writing a song."

Her face instantly transformed from curious to almost euphoric. "Oh, Griffin, that's great news. Is it for the band? Did you call Kellan or Matt? Did you guys patch things up?"

I froze with the piece of paper still in the air. Shit. I hadn't expected her to leap to that conclusion. Honestly, I hadn't thought about having to give her a reason for writing a song. Wrapped up in my project, I'd forgotten that Anna was in the dark...about a lot of things. So, what should I tell her? The truth? That I was working on getting a record contract of my own? No, she wouldn't understand why, since she thought the show was still going. And without a contract, I couldn't come clean, but...the show *was* about a rock star. Knowing fate had laid the perfect lie in my hands, I told her,

"No...it's for the show. They're letting me write Ace's stuff. Pretty awesome, huh?" *Fuck.*

She pursed her lips, but then smiled. Coming around my desk, she plopped herself onto my lap and wrapped her arms around my neck. She leaned in, squeezing her breasts into my face. "Oh, I was hoping you and the band were getting back together. But this is good too. It's just, it's been so stressful with everyone broken up...like my parents have gotten divorced or something. You don't even come home anymore when Kiera and the girls visit."

I pulled away so I could look up into her face. "I'm not getting back together with them, Anna. Ever. I wrote this song for me. For *my* band." Not wanting her to read too much into that, I amended with "My TV band, anyway."

Her smile fell. "Yeah, your TV band." She shook her head. "Griff, I know you're excited about this show, but why don't you go back to them? Kiera tells me they haven't found a replacement yet, and Matt is itching to start another album since the last one...didn't do as well as expected. I'm sure if you called him and apologized...Maybe you could do both? The show and the band?"

My gut started clenching at her suggestion. *I tried that.* But Matt shot me down, belittled me. No, going back wasn't an option anymore. "Apologize? For what? I didn't do anything wrong. Those assholes shoved me in a box, and when I tried to get out, they tried locking it. That shit doesn't work on me though. I need freedom."

She clamped her mouth together so hard, I could see the muscles in her jaw tighten. I wasn't sure if she'd taken my comment personally or if she was upset that I still wouldn't consider it. I was just about to tell her that I didn't mean her when she shook her head and said, "Okay, so...the show is going to let you write songs? Maybe I can help you?" She looked over at my lyrics again, reading them this time. She frowned. "Please tell me this isn't one of them."

I released the paper, letting it float to the desk. "What's wrong with that song? It's awesome."

Her eyes drifted over the sheet. "I'll make you moisty, you'll be so tasty." She shook her head. "One...that's gross. Two, it doesn't even rhyme. Three...I'm pretty sure they won't play it on TV."

Wishing I could defiantly cross my arms over my chest, I shrugged. "I like the song, if they don't play it, then they're stupid."

Closing her eyes, Anna dropped her head into her hands and started shaking it. "Oh boy," she muttered. "I hope they know what they asked for when they asked you to write lyrics." She opened one eye at me. "How is everything going, by the way? On the show, I mean."

The suspicious look in her eyes made my body stiffen in alert, like I was about to be attacked. Did she know something? No, she'd be a lot angrier if she knew something. "Fine... great."

She opened both eyes and frowned. "Are you sure? Because there are these rumors circulating online that the show was canceled. I haven't put much stock in it, because you've been working so hard, but it keeps popping up. And all I can find when I look for news on the show is bad stuff." She narrowed her eyes and scanned my face like she was searching for the truth in my reaction. Fuck. Goddamn Internet.

My heart was thudding, but I managed to keep my expression as blank as possible. *I know nothing.* "I don't know what to tell you, babe. News is crap. But trust me, the show is still going, we're all working hard, and everything is fine. Just fine." *Or at least it will be, once I have a record deal in place and don't have to lie to you anymore. I really fucking hate lying to you. But I hate letting you down even more.*

She frowned but nodded. "Well, maybe we should think about downsizing... at least until the show airs."

I glanced around at my mansion of all mansions and shook my head. "No, you're a queen, and you should live like one. And besides, I'm going to be huge, so I should act like it. If I go into this timidly, all scared and shit, I'll never amount to anything. No... bigger and better... maybe I'll hire even more people to have around here, to do stupid stuff like... paint all the flowers different shades of green..." The least I could do was keep her surrounded by the finest things in life. She deserved that and so much more.

Anna immediately put her hands on my chest. "Please don't. We're fine just the way we are."

I studied her for a moment, then conceded. Considering that I didn't have a contract yet, that was probably good advice. But once I did, all bets were off. I was spoiling her rotten. "Okay, but the minute I think you're not being lavished enough, I'm hiring someone to dote on you."

With a seductive half smile, she ran a fingernail down my cheek. "But the only person I want doting on me is you...and you're gone so often, that doesn't happen much anymore. I'm lonely."

Recognizing her words as a green light for fun, my cock instantly sprang to life. I pulled her more firmly into my lap, letting her feel it. "I'm here now, baby, and I can dote on you all night long. You just tell me what you want."

"I want you to rip off all my clothes, spread me out over a desk again, and fuck me so hard I can't stand straight." My dick started throbbing at her words. But that was nothing compared to her next ones... "But before you do all that...I want to taste *you* this time." With that, she stood up, shifted my swivel chair, and sank to her knees.

"Fuck, yes," I stated, undoing my jeans as quickly as I possibly could. I probably shouldn't do this, since I was being a lame-ass fuck and keeping so much from her, but damn it, she needed this too. Just like she'd said, she was lonely. Turning her away would only fuck us up even more.

By the time my pants were around my ankles, my cock was straight and proud, the piercing in the top shining in the bright light of the lamp on my desk. Anna made a purring noise as she ran her finger along the metal; every nerve ending in my dick sizzled with pleasure where the piercing rubbed against me.

"So hot," she said in a throaty exhale. "I can't wait to have you inside me." I didn't know if she meant her mouth or her pussy. Either one was fine with me.

Her lips wrapped around me as she took me into her mouth, sucking me deep inside. A panting groan escaped me as she stroked me; she didn't even have to use her hands. She played with my balls instead, and I had to grab the armrests of my chair. The throbbing, tingling, burning ache was so delicious—my entire body felt like I was being jolted with electric bolts of ecstasy. Over and over and over, to the rhythm of her mouth pulling me deeper and deeper.

Letting my head fall back, I reveled in the erotic delight. "Fuck, yes, Anna. Just like that...don't stop."

She moaned, and the vibrations along my skin nearly undid me. I started moving my hips, meeting her lips thrust for thrust. I didn't know if she was going to let me finish, but I hoped so, and I repeated, "Don't stop..." *Let me come.*

She moved against me harder, and I knew she wasn't quitting. I could feel the buildup approaching, and I did nothing to stop the sensation. *Fuck, I wanted this so bad.* Almost like she could feel my rising desire, Anna squeezed my balls at the exact right moment to send me over the edge. "Oh fuck...yes..." I groaned as I came. Both her mouth and her hand turned soothing instead of urging, prolonging my orgasm. *God, damn...*

When she finally pulled away, leaving me spent, gasping and tingling with residual lapping waves of pleasure, her smile was devilish. "My turn, baby," she stated, slipping off her skirt.

She started to pull down her underwear, but I reached up to stop her. "Nuh-uh. You requested that *I* rip your clothes off." Grabbing the scant material at her hips, I pulled them down her lean legs. Seeing what I wanted made my cock start coming to life. I ripped her top off, followed by her bra, then, with a mighty shove, I knocked everything off my desk. After plopping her on top of it, I urged her to lie back, then I propped her legs over my shoulders, and dove in to taste just how much she wanted me.

She grabbed my head, holding me there while an erotic cry echoed around the room. "Oh God, Griffin...yes, yes, fuck yes, that feels so good!" My cock hardened with every moan coming from her, and I was ready for more by the time she was falling apart beneath me. I let her finish, because I was a firm believer in tit for tat, but the minute her orgasm spiked, I pulled my mouth away so I could thrust into her.

She gasped as I entered her. "Yes, I'm still...oh, fuck, yes... fuck me!"

Her orgasm lasted a fucking eternity, and when it finally ended, mine erupted again. I slumped over her, well and truly satisfied. She held my head to her chest, our bodies still connected. While our breaths returned to normal, I noticed the spilled beer on the floor. Damn, and I could really use a drink right about now. I was thirsty as hell. Curious, I shouted out, "Alfred! I need another beer!"

His response was instant, and it came from right outside the open door. "Yes, sir."

Anna laughed, then poked me in the ribs. Guessing what she wanted, I shouted, "Make that two, Alfred. The misses is parched too."

"As you wish, sir," was his calm reply.

I laughed as I resettled myself on Anna's chest. I fucking loved having a butler. But having Alfred was nothing compared to making my wife happy. I just hoped I could keep her that way and prayed with everything inside me that I got a deal soon.

Once I had a song that was worthy of being a G. Hancock original, I needed to record a demo of it so I could start shopping myself around to record labels. Because I didn't know where else to go, I visited my old recording studio, where the first D-Bags album was recorded. The fee to use the place for just an hour was fucking ridiculous, but I paid it and scheduled a time to come in. Money was no object when fame was on the line.

All the original guys were still working there when I showed up—what's his name, and that guy. The dude mixing the sound was different though, since the studio had brought in some exclusive talent for our first album, but the guy on staff helped me figure out what to do, which I appreciated.

When it was my turn to go up, I recorded the song that Anna had turned her nose up at. I had to. It was awesome coated in awesome, and the best thing I'd come up with. I didn't have any sort of beat though, so I just made my own noises—beatbox style. It totally worked with the song though. In fact, it was so cool, I decided I might use it on the final album.

Once I got some copies in my hands, I started mailing them to record labels. I didn't even call to ask if they wanted them. I just found their address online and mailed them a copy. Then I sat back and waited for the offers to roll in.

Since I was feeling great about my options, I Express-mailed Denny a copy to give him the first crack at representing me. With it, I sent a note that said, "I'm about to get a dozen offers for this shit, but if you want in on my millions, find me a deal that blows everything else out of the water. You do that, and I might pay you forty percent—because there is no way in hell I'm paying you fifty!"

He called me the minute he received my care package. "Um… Griffin…what in the world did you just send me?"

"Oh, hey, Denny. That's my demo for my solo album. I'm sure it's some sort of conflict of interest for you to represent me as well as the Douchebags, but I'm throwing you a bone. Who knows, you might want to drop them for me. Personally, I think I'll do better. Or maybe you can keep representing them and I'll take Abby." I let out a low laugh, thinking of Denny's wife waiting on me hand and foot. "Yeah…I like that idea."

"Whatever thought you just had about my wife, clear it, before I fly down there and scrub it out of you."

"Whoa, relax, dude. It was just a suggestion. You've been hanging around Matt too much. You're all…uptight and shit."

He sighed. "Things haven't exactly been running smoothly lately. Not that you care, but you sort of left a mess behind when you took off."

Chewing on my lip, I wondered if I wanted to know what he was talking about. Curiosity got the better of me. "Like what?"

"You don't follow entertainment news at all, do you?"

I shrugged, even though he couldn't see me. With people giving me shit about leaving the band, then all the rumors floating around about the TV show—rumors I didn't want to deal with right now—I sort of avoided everything. It was strange for me, since before all this I'd Googled my name daily. "No."

Denny sighed again. "Well, let's just say, between Matt and the fans, finding a replacement bassist has been challenging. At this rate, there might not ever be another album."

Surprise washed over me, followed very closely by an uncomfortable feeling that was akin to having a knife in my gut being twisted around in a circle. I shoved the sensation to the very back of my brain. Their problems weren't mine, and I didn't have time to dwell on them. Hardening my stomach, I told him, "Well, good. You'll have more time to represent me then."

He scoffed at my answer. "That's all you have to say? Good? They're floundering, and you don't care? These guys have been your friends—your *family*—since day one, Griffin."

Matt's words pounded around my brain—*You're dead to me.* "No. We're not like that anymore, and I don't have to give a shit now. Are you gonna represent me or not?"

His answer was quiet but firm. "No...Abby and I won't represent you, Griffin. You're on your own."

"Fine," I said, hanging up the phone. I preferred being on my own anyway.

That evening, Anna and I were in our bedroom getting ready for dinner; my parents were coming over with Chelsey and the girls. Anna was pulling up a pair of lacy tights, while I was still sitting on our bed, naked. How Anna could look at me without jumping me was impressive. I would have caved ages ago.

"So," she said, giving me a coy look. "I don't mean to badger you, but I heard another rumor about the show today...and this time it was from one of the cast members. Cole, I think? Rumor is he's working on a movie right now...I even saw pictures." She twisted her brows in confusion.

My muscles all clenched and my face felt on fire, like someone had just set a torch over me; I got this way whenever Anna brought up the show, when I was reminded of the monumental lie I was nearly drowning in, it was so deep around me. What would she believe? "Oh, yeah, that fucker left a few weeks ago. They killed his character off...that episode is going to blow people's minds." My aptitude at lying was blowing my mind, and sickening my stomach.

But it was just a little longer, and then I could come clean. Once I was firmly on the path to success again, with no chance of failing, then I could tell her absolutely everything.

Pulling the tights over her bright red underwear, she showed me her ass before adjusting her skirt. I instantly felt a little better. *Do that again.* "Huh…that's kind of weird that it's already out there that he's on another job. *Acing It* is still set for January, right?"

The shape of her ass outlined in that flimsy red material replayed through my mind. Anna crossed her arms over her chest and pursed her lips. She must have said something I was supposed to listen to. "What, babe? I was distracted."

She pointed to my growing chub. "Yeah, I see that." With a sigh, she put on a red, clingy top. *Oh yeah, Daddy likey.* "I was just…worrying. I mean, when are they going to pay you?" With apprehension on her face, she looked around our massive bedroom. "I've been checking the bank accounts, and not much has come in recently…but a *lot* is going out. We can't stay here forever like that, Griff. Not until they pay us. Every month our bank account gets so much smaller…"

By her expression, this was something she'd been worrying about for a while. It had crossed my mind a time or two as well, but I always shoved the thought away. Once I had a contract and my album released, I would triple that shit in no time. Acting was never for me…music was my real strength. I knew that now. Denny was an idiot for letting me go. "We've got at least enough for six months, babe, and by then the show will be a smash. No problem."

She snapped her gaze to mine. "No, we won't make it six more months, Griff. Between this house, our place in Seattle, utilities, groceries, all the people you've hired…we'll be broke long before the show airs. Maybe we can hold out until spring, if we start being smart and tighten things up now."

She was overreacting. I wasn't good with money, but I was sure we still had plenty of it. Standing, I walked over to her and grabbed her forearms. Massaging her, I soothingly said, "We'll be fine, but if it will make you feel better, I'll start being more careful with our money. Maybe let some of the staff go."

A weak smile played across her lips, but it died almost instantly. "I've noticed something disturbing." My heart instantly started pounding in my chest. No...I wasn't ready for her to know that I'd been lying yet. I needed a contract before that happened—a shield. That was the only way she'd forgive me. Anna studied my face for a second, then slowly said, "We're not getting any royalties from the band. Nothing. I almost called Denny about it, but...do you know why we've been cut off?"

I scratched my head. Great, I hadn't anticipated her discovering that. How did I answer without her killing me...or calling Denny to verify? Fuck. I had to tell her what I'd done. Goddammit. "Yeah...um...when I signed off with the band...I signed off on *everything*."

Her eyes opened much wider than I thought was humanly possible. Shit, here we go. "Everything...? Griffin? Why the hell would you do that? I mean, doing it on the last album was bad enough, but everything? Are you fucking crazy?"

I knew she was right, I knew it had been a pretty stupid, knee-jerk reaction, but I wasn't about to admit that to her now. Not with Denny's refusal to manage me ringing through my ears. "No, I just don't want anything from them. They're dead to me," I spouted. It felt good to use Matt's words against him, even if he wasn't here to hear it.

Closing her eyes, she inhaled a deep breath. When she re-opened them, she was a little calmer. Not by much though. "For the sake of your family, and those two little girls out there who idolize you...stop fucking around and fix this. Call Denny, call Harold, and start bringing in some fucking cash. Or I fucking will, and you won't like the way I do it."

With that, she grabbed her boots and stormed out of the room.

Jesus. I knew she worried about money and crap, but damn, she should have more faith in me. I was her husband, she should believe in me. Till death do us part and all that shit. A tiny part of my brain told me that she'd have more faith if I'd been more honest, but I yelled at that part of my head to shut up. I didn't need to hear it. I felt bad enough as it was.

Chapter 18

The Price of Awesomeness

Two months later, as the end of the year approached, so did the end of my lie, and the end of my rope. I could almost see it dangling in the distance, taunting me with everything I wanted but couldn't seem to get. No record label would take me. Most wouldn't even talk to me, but the ones who did all said the same thing: *No.* Sometimes, *Hell no.* I wasn't sure what to do next.

Even though I'd been in a band for years, I had no clue how to go about making music. I only had a handful of completed songs under my belt, besides my rapidly produced demo that had no music other than my awesome background noises. My favorite song was entitled *Cocknado.* It was fucking amazing, but at this rate no one was going to get to hear it.

I hounded everyone I could think of, even Justin. "What gives, bro? I thought you were getting me an in with your label?"

There was a long sigh on his end of the line. "I never said that. When you asked, I said I'd give it to them, and I did. It's not my fault they said no. There's only so much I can do, Griffin." The calmness in his voice was clearly forced.

"Well, I guess being friends doesn't go as far as I thought it did in this city." I hung up the phone before he could respond, then I threw the phone against the wall. The cover over the battery pack broke off when it clattered to the floor. Damn it.

A small tap on the doorframe was followed by the words "Griffin? You okay?"

I looked over to see Anna standing there, supporting Onnika on her hip. I made myself smile. God, I hoped she hadn't heard any of that. "Of course. What could possibly be wrong with me? I am the epitome of awesome after all."

She cocked an eyebrow, then glanced at the broken phone. "You sure? Is it the show? Have they given you an airdate yet?"

A spark of hope flashed over her face, followed by confusion. She didn't understand why the studio was keeping me in the dark. And she didn't understand because she didn't know that I was lying my ass off every day; I was even still dying my hair brown to keep her as clueless as possible. It was just to save her stress though. She might have a heart attack if she knew I was unemployed and we were hemorrhaging thousands of dollars every month... Fuck, I needed to fix this. Fast. "Not quite. But soon, I'm sure."

She pursed her lips, and the discouragement and frustration on her face was clear to see, even for someone as boneheaded as me. "Well, keep calling them. They can't just *not* pay you. It isn't right."

I opened my mouth to give her some more unfounded encouragement, but she turned and left before I could. Stepping over to the phone, I threw it against the wall again. Damn it. What the hell was I going to do? If no label would take me and I couldn't get a stream of cash flowing again... Anna and I would be flat-broke in another couple of months. And she'd leave me. She'd leave me for lying, she'd leave me for dragging her down here, she'd leave me for not fulfilling my role as her provider. I'd never see her or the girls again. Fuck.

Desperation washed over me, and for a brief second as I stared at the phone in pieces on the floor, I considered calling the D-Bags. Maybe if I begged hard enough, Matt would let me back. Or maybe if I went to Kellan instead. It was more his band than anyone else's. Yeah. I could go to Kellan and bypass Matt completely.

But just the thought of doing that made my skin crawl. I'd have to endure countless hours of ribbing: *Remember when you tried to do a TV show, but it was a complete and total failure that never even made it on the air? Remember when you tried to make an album, but no one would take you? Remember when you tried to stand on your own two feet like you didn't need us? How ridiculous of you to think you could survive without us. We're the reason you're not a floundering piece of shit, and don't you forget it. Now shine our shoes…*

No thanks. I'd rather flounder than subject myself to that. They could kiss my ass. If no label would take me, then I'd make my own. A spark of excitement burned away my moment of anxiety. Yes, that was exactly what I'd do—make my own label, make my own record.

Turning on my computer, I went through the online Yellow Pages and started finding people in the industry. By the time I'd contacted everyone I thought I might need, I had at least a dozen new people on my payroll. This was going to shrink my bank account so much faster than even Anna had anticipated, but it was a gamble that was going to work. It had to work.

But I would need money to get this started. A lot of money. Looking around my castle, I slowly came to a hard conclusion… Anna was right. It *was* time to downsize. I knew she would be on board with it, but I didn't know how to tell her why I was suddenly agreeing to it. The truth seemed like my only option.

Well, a vague, hazy version of the truth. The longer I could keep her in the dark, the better.

That evening, I approached her after she put the girls to bed. She could tell something was up by the look on my face. "What?" she asked, her voice tentative.

My palms were sweaty, and I kept wiping them on my jeans. Shit, I had no idea how she'd react to this. "I have a confession to make." Fuck. I should just tell her everything. She deserved to know the truth—that she'd married a fucktard who messed everything up. She'd be so pissed though…she'd storm out and I'd never see her again. I couldn't handle that possibility. No, I was in too deep to back out. All I could do was keep plowing forward and hope this album fixed all my fuckups.

Eyes wide, cheeks pale, she sat on the bed and put her hands in her lap. "Okay…what?" She stared at me with fear in her eyes, and

I wondered what she thought I was going to say. Did she suspect the truth? Or did she think it was something as simple as cheating? I almost wished I could tell her I'd done something with another woman. Confessing that would be easier than confessing I was a lying, asshole failure. But no...I wasn't confessing that tonight. I was delaying that information. Again.

"Uh...earlier today...when I tossed the phone across the room...it wasn't nothing." A sigh escaped me and bile started rising up my throat. I didn't deserve her. "The studio called. They pushed the show back again. We're not going on until next fall now..." Fuck. How deep was my hole now? Deep enough to bury myself in, I was sure.

Anna shot up off the bed. "What? Are you serious? Why the fuck would they do that?" She started pacing and wringing her hands together. "They're not going to wait until next fall to pay you, are they? Because we can't go that long, Griffin. We're sinking here."

If she only knew how much. "Yeah...they are. I guess it was in the contract, I just didn't notice it. I don't get the bulk of my pay until the show airs." That sounded believable, like something I would do, and actually, with the full season stipulation in the contract, that was close to what I *had* done. I'd thrown my life away for an illusion. But I was getting it back now. Fuck, this *had* to work.

Anna turned to face me and fire was burning in her eyes. "You didn't notice? How could you not notice getting completely fucked over? This is absolutely ridiculous. Give me the phone, I'm calling Harold." She stuck her hand out, but I ignored the gesture.

"I signed a contract, Anna...it's already done." *The show is already over.* "I'm sorry." *For all the lies I'm telling you right now. For everything.*

Hands balling into fists, her voice trembled when she spoke. "Sorry? You're sorry?" One finger uncurled to point at me; it was trembling in her anger. "You said this would work. You assured me that it would all be okay. I trusted you when you said we weren't throwing away our livelihood for nothing!"

Raising my chin, I looked her in the eye. If I seemed confident, maybe it would convince her that things were still fine. "It wasn't for nothing." I hoped it wasn't for nothing. No, I *prayed* it wasn't for nothing.

The expression on her face shifted between panic, horror, and hope. "This is our future you're playing around with, Griffin. Our future, and our daughters' futures. We have to have a plan. What's our plan?"

Sighing, I felt that weight on my chest grow even heavier. I could have sworn some ribs were cracking under the strain. "I can still make this work, Anna." *I think.* "I just have to get some cash flow going while I wait for the show to start."

"How?" she asked, folding her arms over her chest.

"Well…now that the show is all caught up on episodes and I have more time…" *Lots of fucking time.* "I was thinking about putting together an album." I debated telling her that I was going to fully fund the album myself…tell her the truth in at least one area of my life, but the steel look in her green eyes warned me not to. I had to skirt around the truth, or I was going to lose my fragile hold on her. In as optimistic a voice as I could, I tossed out, "I'll get myself a record contract, so we'll have enough money to keep us in the clear until next fall." *And hopefully by then I'll be a household name and you'll have forgotten all about the show.*

Anna clamped her mouth together so firmly, her lips turned white. It took her a full minute to calm down enough to speak. "So…instead of going back to the D-Bags in the interim, who still don't have a bassist, by the way…you want to form your own band? Are you doing this just to show them up? Are you really that angry at them?"

Her words made a flash of bitter heat run up my spine. Yes, I was. Guess letting go wasn't something I was much good at. "No, this is what I was meant to do. I'm not doing a group thing again. I'm going solo. It'll be just me, rocking the world." Carefully approaching her, I wrapped an arm around her waist. "What do you think of that, babe? You'll be married to the hottest solo artist of all time."

She didn't look as awed by that statement as she should have been. "I don't mean to sound insulting, but…do you even know how to put together an album?"

No, not really. To hide my doubt, I smiled. "This is going to work, and it's going to be great." When she still didn't look convinced, I added, "I'll get help, okay? As much help as I need. In fact, first thing tomorrow, I'll start calling record labels. Everything else will fall into place. You'll see."

Anna cocked an eyebrow at me. I felt like I was still in dangerous territory, so I said the most honest thing I could say. "You were right. Being a rock star has always been my dream. And I think music has been in the back of my mind ever since I left the D-Bags. I miss the stage, miss performing." *I miss the guys.* Shaking off that errant thought, I told her, "Now just seems like the perfect opportunity to do something about it, since I've got time…" She narrowed her eyes, so I quickly changed topics. "I think you were right about the house and about our expenses though. I think we need to scale down."

For the first time since our conversation began, her expression softened. "Well that, I can definitely get on board with." Wrapping her arms around my neck, she looked around our opulent bedroom. "This house is way too big."

Yeah…I was gonna miss it though. But tough times called for tough decisions. Like constantly keeping my wife two steps behind the truth.

A few weeks later, the house was almost packed up, and we were narrowing down where we wanted to rent. I'd already hired the crew who'd be creating my epic solo album masterpiece, and each one of them cost ten times more than I'd expected. I wasn't a whiz at math, but I knew a financial black hole when I saw one. I hated to do it, but it was time to make even harder cuts, which meant…I needed to talk to my wife. Again.

Anna was in the living room with the girls, supervising while they played with dolls. Gibson was pretending that her doll was Onnika. She had her tied up with yarn and lying across a train set. The train was speeding down the tracks, and Gibson was making no move whatsoever to save the replica of her little sister.

Just when I was thinking that maybe I should have another talk with Gibson, Onnika decided to save herself. She waddled over to her distressed miniature and picked her up, right before the train collided with her. It made me feel connected to my youngest daughter. *Exactly, Onnie. When life shits on you, sometimes you have to be your own superhero.*

Gibson didn't feel the same. She shoved Onnika backward, onto her plump diaper. I don't think the fall hurt her, but the sudden movement definitely scared her.

Anna and I snapped at Gibson at the same time. Seeing us both upset made her cry, which made Onnika cry.

Girls. The tiniest things sent them into hysterics.

I held Onnika while Anna had a heart-to-heart with Gibson. With crying children in our arms, it was difficult to talk to my wife. Or maybe it wasn't. She couldn't kill me if she was trying to calm down our daughter. "So...I called a real estate agent today. I was thinking maybe it was time we put the house in Seattle up for sale."

Anna stopped mid-cuddle and stared at me openmouthed. "You...? Really?"

I shrugged. "Yeah, I think we should. It seems like a waste of money, making payments on an empty house. And we're trying to cut back, you know?"

"Oh, well I guess that makes sense," she said, surprised but looking pleased. "Okay, yeah, make it happen." She didn't ask what we should price it at, and I was grateful. From what the agent had said, we were going to lose money on the deal; we'd paid way too much when we'd bought it.

Knowing I had to break the news to her sooner or later, I inhaled a deep breath, then said in a rush, "And actually, I was thinking...it's stupid to waste money on renting a place right now. We should just save as much as we can until the show launches in the fall. I called Mom and Dad, and they said we could move back in with them. So...I told them we'd move in next month."

Anna slowly closed her eyes, then shook her head. "If we'd just gotten something modest in the beginning..." she said. Her voice trembled in her effort to stay calm.

Setting Onnika down, I walked over to her. After scooting Gibson out of the way, I got down on my knees and looked up at her face. Feeling my presence, Anna opened her eyes. The green gems I adored were a little duller than before. That was my fault. The stress of dragging her down here, the stress of lying to her, everything I'd done recently had changed her. Me too. I felt worn from the inside out most days. I just needed *something* to work out like I planned it to.

"I know. I fucked up." *On so many things.* "But the album will get us through until the fall. And then everything will be okay. I promise. I promise this will all work out, Anna." It had to, because there were no more backup plans.

Her eyes widened, and the fear in them was unmistakable. "You don't make promises."

Nodding, I told her, "Exactly. But on this…I am. Just don't give up on me. Okay?" *Please see this through with me.*

She was silent so long that I was sure she was going to tell me my crazy antics were finally too much for her and she was out of here. Jesus, I really hoped she didn't say that. I couldn't handle the sudden uncertainty of my life without her by my side, which was why I was selfishly piecemealing the truth to her. If I told her how fucked we really were, she'd be gone.

Anna studied me for a minute longer, then said, "Okay, Griffin. We can live with your parents. Until the fall."

The sudden relief made me light-headed. Thank God. I at least had until the fall to dig myself out of this gargantuan hole I'd created. Hopefully that was enough time.

It didn't take much to convince Anna that we should purge our household items so we had a safety net until the show took off. We sold most of the big-ticket items—like my fucktastic Hummer and some of Anna's jewelry. Everything else we put into storage. We were going to live simply for a while, which kind of sucked for everyone, but it was only temporary. I'd get everything back, and then some.

We moved into my parents' place with only a week's worth of clothes each and a handful of toys for the girls. All of our stuff fit into four boxes that I stuffed in Dad's minivan, since all of my cars were gone. Most everything of real value was gone. But surprisingly, Alfred was the hardest thing for me to part with. I'd gotten attached to having someone on hand to satisfy my every whim. I'd maybe even grown fond of the quiet, obedient ghost of a man himself, who seemed to appear out of nowhere right when I needed him the most. I teared up when I told him his services were no longer required. His only response was a curt nod goodbye. Damn my bad luck. And bad choices.

After the last of our boxes were shoved into my childhood bedroom, Anna sat on the bed and sighed. While Gibson jumped on the mattress and Onnika took halting steps around the room, I sat on the bed beside Anna. Wrapping my arm around her shoulder, I told her, "It could be worse."

As the kids started fighting over a toy sticking out of a box, Anna tilted her head at me in question. "Really? How so?"

I opened my mouth to answer her, but before I could, Onnika threw up over everything inside the box. *Well, that could happen.*

Or you could find out just how fucked we really are.

Chapter 19

Not That Awesome

Almost every day, someone seemed to ask for more money—my songwriter, my producer, the guy designing my album cover, the recording studio, and even my family. They were all siphoning me dry. The house in Seattle finally sold, but with what I still owed on it, my bank account was hovering in the mid-four-digit mark. That wouldn't last long in this city.

"What do you mean you need another five thousand," I asked my songwriter when he upped his price yet again.

"I had to pay out of pocket for the musical arrangement. I just want to be paid back for expenses that are rightfully yours."

I ran a hand down my face, discouraged. If I paid him five grand, I'd have nothing but pocket change left. "Musical arrangement? I thought I paid *you* for that shit. Why do I have to pay someone else?"

He sighed like he'd explained this to me a dozen times already. I wasn't sure if he had or not. Dude had a tendency to talk like he was Shakespeare or something. "Like I said before, my genius is combining words into flowing art forms that glow with life and pulsate with sound. But I need a partner to make the words take flight. And five grand. Per song."

"Per song? Are you fucking high?" When he didn't respond, I growled, "Fine. I'll get you the fucking money."

Hanging up the phone, I cursed and refrained myself from chucking it against the wall. I couldn't break my dad's handset too. "Well, great. What the fuck do I do now?" I asked Onnika, standing at my feet. She only stared up at me with her dark eyes and gave me a tooth-filled smile. "Being adorable won't help," I told her.

Closing my eyes, I groaned and considered my options. My parents? My brother or sister? The guys? No, none of those were doable. If I was going to get the amount of money I needed, I would have to do something stupid. Because I couldn't let Anna know how screwed we were. The only reason she was still on board with any of this was because of the TV show. The ace in the hole, or so she believed.

Deciding to just do it before I could think too much about it, I called my credit card company and had them raise my limit. Then I called the bank and set up an appointment to get a loan. I had to. I'd never get out of this mess if the album never got finished. And if I didn't finish it, my marriage was over. I just knew it.

Tossing the phone onto the mattress, I reached down for my daughter. The house was oddly quiet for a change; the peace was nice. Onnika was in that busy stage where she didn't really want to be held, she just wanted to be free. As I suddenly felt a collar being shackled around my neck, I understood, and I released her so she could do as she pleased. Scrambling over to the phone on the bed, she picked it up and started punching buttons while saying my name.

"Don't let her fall off the bed, babe." Appearing in the doorway, Anna pointed at Onnika.

Walking over to me, Anna sat herself in my lap. My cock instantly twitched in excitement. Our sex life had dwindled some, since we were sharing a room with the kids. And sneaking off to have sex in the shower, while great, was starting to wear thin. I just wanted to fuck my wife senseless on a king-sized mattress with no child within earshot. God, I missed those days.

Lacing her arms around my neck, Anna asked, "Have you heard back from the producer? Can I hear the first song yet?"

A twinge of guilt ran through me so fast, it instantly killed my arousal. I hadn't wanted to lie about leaving all the time to record the album, so a few days after we'd moved in with my parents, I'd told Anna a half lie—that a record label had picked me up. She'd been excited to hear that, and proud, which had made me feel pretty goddamn shitty. Honestly, it still made me feel shitty. But having hope on the horizon had eased Anna's mood and her mind, so the lie was almost worth the regret. Almost.

The song that she was curious about was the first single. I'd recorded it last week, but the guys I'd hired were still tweaking it. Seemed odd to me that they needed to. Once a D-Bags song had been laid down, it was good to go...no alterations required. But I'd heard the raw cut of the single, and I agreed with my producer. It needed...something.

Frowning, I told her, "No, not yet...it's not good enough."

By the look on Anna's face, it was obvious she was shocked to hear me admit that. I could understand why. Typically, I loved everything I did. But I wasn't all that fond of myself at the moment, and I was under a lot of pressure. This album needed to be *perfect*. "Not good enough? You always think everything is...well, amazing."

Yeah, but I have so much more riding on this than I usually do. My entire world is wrapped up in that CD...you just don't know that. Smiling, I shrugged. "Oh, don't get me wrong, it's spectacular, but it's just not quite the right level of awesome yet." I pinched her butt. "You just have to wait."

Giggling, she squirmed on my lap, lightening my mood and making my dick harden back up. Then Onnika laughed and I completely lost it. Goddammit. If we didn't get out of here, I might not ever have sex again.

Anna let out a long sigh as she threaded her fingers through my hair. It was wistful, and I couldn't help but wonder if she missed having sex with me too. Rubbing her back, I murmured, "Maybe Mom and Dad can watch the kids tonight, and we can borrow the car? Take a drive somewhere nice and quiet...get freaky in the backseat?" I wriggled my eyebrows at her and she smirked.

"You want to borrow your parents' car and make out at a lookout point." Closing her eyes, she shook her head. "It's like I'm fifteen again."

Ignoring the humor in her tone, I said, "Just an idea. You seemed like you wanted to do me, that's all."

She made another wistful sigh. "No…that's not what I was thinking about." When I gave her a funny look, she smiled and amended her statement. "Yes, I do want to do you, and not just hidden away in the pantry, but…" She sighed again. "Kiera called this morning. She's pregnant…"

By the way she said it, and the way she stared at Onnika beating the phone against the mattress, it was clear she wanted to be pregnant again too. "You want to try for another one, babe? 'Cause we can put Onnie down for a nap, find Gibson, and…" Peering over Anna's shoulder, I listened for my eldest daughter. "Where is Gibson anyway?"

Anna shook her head and answered my first question. "We can't afford another baby right now, Griffin. Not until the show starts." By the way she said it, she was holding on to that possibility like it was a lifeline. Like she was hoping the album did well, but the show was her true salvation. A horrible feeling welled within me—it was corrosive, like battery acid, and for the millionth time, I thought I should just tell her the truth. I opened my mouth to do it right as Gibson ran into the room holding a foot-long snake.

"Look, Mommy! It's squirmy!"

Gibson laughed. Anna screamed. And the truth never made it past my lips.

Thanks to loans and credit cards, I was able to pay all the people I owed money to and was able to finish my album. It took two more very long months to do it, but I eventually had a full, finished record. And even though the album was the best thing I'd ever heard while I'd been recording it, I was nervous to hear the final product, scared even. It was a strange feeling for me. I was never nervous. For anything. Maybe it was the stress of living with my parents. Maybe it was the fact that I owed a shitload of money that I wouldn't be able to repay if this album wasn't a hit. Maybe it was because I had a ton of pressure on me now, like never before. Or maybe it was just the fact that I was doing this alone, without Anna

100 percent beside me, because she didn't know the whole story. I hated it. In many ways, life had been so much easier when I was with the D-Bags.

On the night the album went live for preordering, I brought a copy home for everyone to listen to. Mom invited the family over for dinner and made a batch of her world-famous lasagna. I almost wished she hadn't, since I was kind of freaking out about this CD— literally everything I had was riding on this album—but I supposed it was only appropriate to have the people I cared about most there for the unveiling. It better be good. I couldn't afford for it to be anything less than amazing.

While dinner cooked, I sat everyone down in the living room. My palms were sweating, I was so tense. Damn it, I hated clammy hands. This was my moment of glory. I should be flying high, so full of confidence it bordered on arrogance. And any other time I would have been, but this flimsy little disc was either going to make me or break me. Fuck.

Grabbing the plain CD case, I showed it to my family. "This is going to blow your mind." I hoped they bought the assurance, since I didn't really feel it.

Liam, leaning forward, asked, "Who is Figfrin Hancock?"

Wondering what the hell Liam was talking about, I looked at the CD case. Sure as shit, written in bold Sharpie across the CD were the words "Figfrin Hancock Promo Copy." What the fuck? "The idiot producer spelled it wrong, is all."

Liam snorted. "Wow, if he can't even get your name right, I can't wait to hear this."

Drilling holes into him with my eyes, I opened the case and popped out the CD. My stomach felt like I'd eaten a questionable taco from an even more questionable food truck. If I had antacids, I'd be downing them like candy. It made me wish I had a drink in my hand. Or several. *Please let this be good.*

The CD started to play, but oddly, what was coming out of the stereo wasn't music. It was me complaining to the producer. "Is it going? I can't hear the music. Should I be able to hear the music? Or am I supposed to fucking guess where we're at in the song. Oh, wait…here we go. I hear it now. Let's do this shit!" Then a hard-driving beat started. Weird that he'd kept that in, but oh well, I guess it worked. What didn't work was the fact that I came in late. Even I could hear that I was a beat behind the rhythm. Chelsey and Mom had their eyebrows bunched, like they knew something was off. What the hell? I thought maybe it would correct when it got to the rapping section, but it didn't. If anything, it was even more off.

Liam went into a fit of laughter during my rap montage. "Wait…are you rapping about deli meats? Oh my God, you are."

Annoyed, I pressed the skip button. The next song was a ballad. Those were popular and impossible to mess up, so I felt better about the odds of it being good. Until I heard my voice. "What the fuck is wrong with this piece of junk?" I asked, examining the stereo for some lever that was adjusted wrong. My voice sounded like I was a robot singing through a tin can who couldn't hold a note to save his life.

"Um, babe," Anna's quiet voice said, "I don't think it's the stereo. I think that's how it was recorded."

"Damn it," I muttered, hitting skip again. But every song just got worse and worse.

When it was over, the room was silent. Even the kids were staring, speechless. Chelsey cleared her throat. "Griffin, they weren't all bad…maybe a few could be cleaned up or rerecorded…"

I ran my hands through my hair as icy panic flooded my veins. *No.* This was supposed to be epic. It was supposed to fix everything…not make everything worse. "I can't. They've already gone to distribution. This is the final product, and I don't have any money left to fix it anyway. I spent every dime I had on this, maxed out every credit card. I'm fucking broke! I'd have to take out another bank loan just to buy the matches to burn this shit!" I threw the empty CD case against the floor, cracking the frame and breaking the hinge.

Anna stood from her spot on the couch; her face was ghostly white. "What are you talking about, Griffin? What do you mean you spent every dime? You said you got a record deal."

Feeling my heart start to pound, my head start to swim, I tried to swallow the icy lump of shame in my throat. It wouldn't budge. There was no way she would be okay with what I'd done. Not now, when I had nothing good to show for it. I was fucked. We were fucked. And it was all my fault...

"I tried, Anna. I did everything I could think to do, but no label would take me. The only way I could do the album was to make it myself. And it was so goddamn expensive, so much more than I ever thought it would be, but I had to find money somewhere. I *had* to. I couldn't leave it unfinished." *Because this was the only chance I had. And now it's gone.*

Anna started breathing heavier; she looked like she was on the verge of hyperventilating. I wanted to comfort her, but I knew touching her right now would not be a good idea. Behind her, Gibson was watching us with wide, scared eyes. Goddammit, I was hurting two of the people I cared about most. I wanted to run, but there was nowhere to go.

"You lied...again. You went behind my back...again. Why? Why would you do that? We're supposed to be honest, Griffin! We're supposed to talk things out!" Tears were welling in Anna's eyes; the pain in them was killing me. I was such a fucking idiot. "You're supposed to want to include me. You're supposed to care." The tears fell to her cheeks. Each one that dropped felt like a sledgehammer across my chest.

Gibson was crying now; Mom silently swept her from the room. "I do...I do care." My voice came out weak and warbled. I hated it. I'd done all this for her...she just didn't know that. "I didn't have a choice, Anna. The album was the only way..." I paused to scrub my eyes; they were stinging so much I could barely see. "Everything was riding on this, and now...we're so fucked."

Swiping her cheeks dry, Anna asked, "How much do we owe, Griffin? How in debt are we?"

"Fifty," I whispered. At least, that was where it was at the last time I looked.

Anna looked confused. "Fifty...dollars?"

Guilt, remorse, and fear welled up in me, making it impossible for me to look her in the eye. I should have told her. I should have talked with her. I shouldn't have fucked this all up. I should have been honest from the start. Avoiding her gaze, I stared at the shattered case on the ground. Broken. Just like every single one of my dreams. "Fifty thousand," I finally admitted.

The room erupted in gasps of disbelief. When I looked up, I saw Anna standing there with her mouth wide open. Her cheeks were flushed with anger, and she was cracking her knuckles like she wanted to hit something. Wanted to hit *me*.

"Why the fuck would you get us fifty thousand dollars in debt for an album when you've got a show…" And just like that, the light flicked on. She brought her hands to her mouth, then slowly lowered them. "There is no show…is there?"

I felt like my chest was going to explode as I took a step toward her. "Anna…" *Please understand, I did this for you, for the girls, for our future.* Fuck. No, I didn't. I did it for me.

She put a hand up to stop my pathetic attempt to placate her. "All this time, the facts were right in front of me, but I didn't want to believe them, because I didn't want to believe that you would lie to my face, day in, day out." She started trembling in her rage. "Is that what happened? Have you been lying to me? For months!"

I felt like all the oxygen was being sucked out of the room. I didn't know how to explain myself, didn't know how to tell her how freaked out I'd been, how goddamn miserable it had made me to keep her in the dark, how alone I've felt trying to fix something that wasn't fixable. But breaking her heart…losing her faith and support…Lying had been a way to avoid doing that, and like the lazy, self-absorbed asshole I was, I'd taken the easy option. "I'm so sorry. I wanted to tell you, but I didn't know how. The show got canceled and I panicked…I didn't want to let you down." *Please understand*, I silently begged. *You're always so understanding. That's why we work.*

All the color drained from her cheeks but flared in her eyes. "Jesus…how long have you been lying to me? How long have I been in the dark?"

My heart was pounding. I was such a fucking idiot. Maybe in

the beginning I could have convinced her, but there was no way she'd understand and support me now. None. The sham was over. "The show was canceled... right after the VMAs."

Her eyes widened in shock again, and she opened and closed her mouth, but no words came out. With glistening eyes, she looked around the silent room, then she turned and stormed off to the bedroom. I followed as quickly in her wake as I dared. When she got to our room, she slammed the door. It felt like the wind from the motion slapped my face. "Anna?" I knocked again when she didn't answer. "Anna? You're gonna have to talk to me some-time. It might as well be now." *Please don't shut me out.*

The door flew open so fast I again felt the breeze. "Talk to you? Why should I talk to you? You don't have the decency to talk to me. Or even tell me the truth! You make all these plans behind my back, then you fill me in on them when it's too late to change them!" She slugged me in the arm. "You lied to me for months? And you lost everything we had! What the hell were you thinking?"

I tried to step into the room and close the door so I could put at least a small buffer between us and everyone listening, but with Anna not letting me inside, it was difficult. I finally managed to step in and edge the door shut behind me though. "I'll fix this, Anna. I swear." How, I had no fucking clue.

Anna echoed my thoughts. "How the fuck are you going to fix this, Griffin? We have nothing, and we're fifty *thousand* dollars in debt with no possibility of paying it back with income from your sure-to-be-a-hit show. I should have known it was crap the second you told me they weren't paying you until it aired. God, I am such an idiot."

She obsessively started smoothing back her hair while she paced, like she was frantically trying to calm down. I could tell from her expression that it wasn't working. Her eyes were watery with pain, but her cheeks were red with anger. All the torment I'd been trying to keep from her was hitting her all at once. Watching the struggle was choking me up, but anticipating the outcome was making me sick.

"No, you're not," I said in a hoarse whisper. *I am*. Defeat settled around me like a toxic cloud, choking every last remnant of hope I had. "It wasn't supposed to turn out like this. The album was supposed to fix everything. It was supposed to be amazing…"

"Well, it's an amazing piece of shit." I snapped my eyes to hers and she shrugged. "I can't sugarcoat this one, Griffin. It's not well-produced, it's not well-written, it's not well-anything. It's terrible, and you're going to be a laughingstock when it releases."

I was so shocked by her brutal honesty, I didn't know what to say. What I did say was probably something I should have said months ago. "Okay…so what do you suggest I do now?"

Anna crossed her arms over her chest. "You call the guys and beg for your job back."

Bitter heat temporarily blanketed the mountain of guilt that had been suffocating me. Lifting my chin, I firmly stated, "No." Begging was not an option.

Anna narrowed her eyes as she nodded. "Of course that's your answer," she sneered, her voice shaky with rage and pain. "You and your goddamn pride."

Stopping right in front of me, she stared me down. There were flecks of gold in her green eyes, and they flared at me as brightly as the sun. "I'm sick of this. I'm sick of the people, the city, the *I'm better than you* attitude. I'm even sick of the weather, and I'm not even sure how that's possible." She lifted her hands in frustration, then dropped them with a long exhale. "And it's weird, because L.A. never bothered me before. Honestly, I think the real reason I hate it here is because it's not where we're supposed to be. We should be home…in Seattle."

Like all of her strength was gone, Anna collapsed onto the bed. "Do you know why leaving Seattle was so hard for me?"

I shrugged. I wasn't sure I knew anything at this point. "Your sister?"

With a wistful sigh, Anna nodded. "In part. But it was so much more than that. For the first time ever, I finally loved every aspect of my life. I was completely happy with where I was and with who I was, and I didn't crave more. I was just…content. And then you ripped me away from everything I'd grown to love, and I felt like I would never get that feeling of being completely satisfied back. But I tried to be a loving, supportive wife anyway, because I felt like that was what I was supposed to do...but what thanks did I get for my loyalty?" She shot up off the bed and thrust her finger into my chest. "You lied to me! Over and over! Just so you could keep doing what you wanted. Well, I can't do this anymore, and I don't want to be here anymore. This isn't home to me. Seattle is home. The *D-Bags* are home." She said their name slowly and deliberately, like she wanted that to sink in.

Hating this conversation, hating that she was unhappy, and hating that she was telling me what I already knew—that this was all my fault—I defiantly crossed my arms over my chest and let the darkness inside me shift my shame into a shield. "Because we were loaded when I was with them? Is that why you were so 'content'?" I wanted to slap myself for saying it. Anna wasn't a gold digger, and I knew that, but I was humiliated and scared, and being defensive was easier than being kicked while I was down.

Her lips flattened into a hard, thin line while her eyes narrowed into daggers. I knew that look. It meant I was so far off the mark, I was about to get verbally slapped back on target. "No, you know it's not about the money," she started, her voice icy. "Even when I lived in a crappy apartment and worked at Hooters, it was better than being in that fancy mansion, waited on hand and foot. I would have returned to that life in an instant if you'd asked me to. But instead of admitting defeat and returning to Washington, you lied to me. You *pretended* to go to work, just so you could keep living your fantasy. Don't you see how fucked up that is?"

She stood taller, prouder, and even though she was smaller than me, I suddenly felt dwarfed by her presence. "I didn't want any of this. I tried to make the best of it to keep our family together, but I just can't anymore. Our entire family *isn't* together, and being here has brought us nothing but misery. I want to go back to Seattle." She put a hand on my arm. "Call the guys, Griffin. Tell them your situation. Apologize."

Rage and betrayal waged war within me, and I jerked my arm

away from her. "Apologize? What the fuck for? I didn't do anything to those assholes." I pointed toward Washington, the last place I wanted to return to. "They're the ones who fucked me over. They're the ones who should apologize. They're the ones who should be begging! Not me!" *They cast me aside. I can't go back.*

Her eyes started watering again, and her hands curled into frustrated fists. "You always say the guys were the ones holding you down, but you are so goddamn blind."

"What's that supposed to mean?" I challenged. I didn't want to lash out at her, not after everything I'd done, but the guys *weren't* an option. That bridge was burned long ago.

Face firm, she told me, "*You* hold you down. Your pride, your ego, your refusal to dig deeper and do the hard labor. That's what holds you down. The only person you can blame here, Griffin, is you. And I'm not going to let you drag down this family any further. I'm taking the reins before you plunge us right off the cliff... if you haven't already."

She pointed at the space between our feet, marking a line in the sand, so to speak. "I'm captain of this team now. And as captain, I say we're making the right decision for once, and we're moving back to Seattle. I'll get my old job back, and I'll provide for the girls... alone, if I need to. Now... are you coming with us or staying here to drown?" She extended her hands, clearly offering me a chance to back down and accept her will... or cross over the line.

Something painful in my chest started expanding outward. It hurt so bad, I wished I could take a baseball bat and have her thwack me across the rib cage with it a few times. That would feel infinitely better. Breathing was hard. Standing was hard. Being in this room was hard. Fuck. This was exactly why I didn't do relationships. 'Cause feeling this vise closing around me fucking sucked. *What do I do?*

Clearing my mind, I said the first thing that came to me. "I'm not done... I can't leave." *I can't be done.*

Anna sighed, but she didn't look surprised. "No... you *won't* leave. Your pride will be the end of you, Griffin."

She started to move around me to get to the door. A surge of panic swept through me, and I grabbed her arms. "Dad's got a Ping-Pong set in the garage. Let's play to win. Let's negotiate."

Calmly, Anna removed my fingers from her arms. "This isn't a game, Griffin. And I'm not negotiating this time. You lied to me, you kept me in the dark. You disrespected me and our relationship, and I'm done. I'm going home. End of discussion."

She put her hand on the doorknob, and I put my palm against the door. "Anna...come on."

When she looked up at me, I saw the tired defeat in her eyes. She really was done with this...done with me. The swell of panic shifted to terror. *She couldn't leave me.* She and the girls were my entire world. Her hand came up to my cheek; the softness of her skin only made the hollow feeling in my gut worse. No fucking way she was really saying goodbye. Not to me. *We were a team...*

"I hope it works out for you, Griffin. I really do." A tear fell from her eye and splashed onto her cheek.

My throat tightened, my eyes stung, and a wave of pain was rolling around my stomach so hard, I felt like I was going to throw up. I hated feeling shit like this. I *avoided* feeling shit like this. Shoving down the agony rising within me, I hardened my face, hardened my heart, and hardened my soul.

Stepping away from the door, I put on my armor of indifference. *You can't hurt me.* "Fine. Leave. Whatever. You know you'll be running back in a week anyway." I grabbed my junk. "I mean, who else is gonna fuck you as well as me?"

Anna's expression turned to ice as she wiped the tear trail off her cheek. "Thank you," she said, her voice cold. "You just made this so much easier."

Opening the door, she slammed it shut behind her. Now that a panel of dark wood was separating us, I screamed, "You won't actually leave me, Anna! I know you won't!"

When she didn't respond, I started hyperventilating. *Fuck... she was leaving me...and I was letting her go. What the fuck was I doing?*

There was hustling, bustling, and a flurry of conversations in the house, but I did my best to ignore them. It got hard to do when

I heard Gibson calling my name and Anna shushing her. Sitting on the bed, I rocked back and forth with my hands covering my ears. My only defense against the onslaught of agony battling its way through me was to repeat, *It doesn't matter, it doesn't matter, it doesn't matter. None of this matters.*

What felt like hours later, when my body was purged of all emotion, good or bad, I finally opened the bedroom door. With robotic steps, I made my way toward the kitchen. I needed a drink. Hopefully one strong enough to make me forget everything about my life.

Mom and Dad were whispering together. They silenced the minute I entered the room. Cigarette in hand, Mom asked, "How… are you?"

"Great. What do we have to drink around here?" My voice was coming out so monotone, I didn't sound like me. I wondered if that was permanent. Maybe I'd forever sound like a lifeless corpse. I was fine with that. That was what I felt like.

Puffing out a long stream of white smoke, Mom told Dad, "Get him the good stuff."

Dad immediately started rummaging through a cupboard that had always been locked when I was a kid. It wasn't anymore. Good thing too. I'd probably break it open if it were. He started pouring scotch into a glass half-full of ice.

After he handed it to me, I thanked him and started shuffling into the living room. Mom and Dad cast each other worried glances, then followed me; Dad was still holding the scotch bottle.

"Son…you want to talk about…anything?" Dad's voice was hesitant. Like most of the men in my family, he didn't do "talks" or "feelings" or any of that girly shit. He wouldn't have even asked me if Mom hadn't rapped him on the shoulder. But I didn't need to talk. I needed scotch, so he'd already done all he could for me.

"Nothing to talk about," I stated.

I sipped my drink as I looked at them. Wanting them to stop looking at me like I was some fucked-up science experiment, I calmly asked, "What? Do I have something on my face?"

Mom directed me toward an open chair. "Why don't you have

a seat? I'm going to make a salad for the lasagna. It's been done for a while now…" She started to leave once she forced me to sit. The sight of another woman turning her back on me made a flicker of something dark start to squirm its way to the surface. I buried it with a long gulp of scotch.

Before she left the room, Mom turned back to me. "In case you were wondering, Anna and the girls are staying with Chelsey. Dustin is still gone, so she's got room…"

I wanted to tell her to shut the fuck up, that I didn't care what the hell Anna did or didn't do, but she was my mom, and I couldn't say that to her. Plus, acknowledging the fuck-fest that was my life was something I didn't want to do at the moment. Numbness was all I wanted. I raised my glass in answer. *I hear you and I understand, so stop talking.*

She left the room without another word. Dad refilled my scotch while he and Liam glanced at each other. They were making go-ahead motions, like they were volunteering each other for a task neither of them wanted.

Face mournful, like someone had died, Liam finally said, "Sorry, man."

I waited for an add-on to his comment, something insulting like, *I knew you weren't good enough for her,* or *Guess I won the pool on that one,* or *Mind if I date her, now that you're through?* That last thought made my fingers tighten so hard around my glass, I was positive it was going to shatter. If anyone fucking touched my wife, I would kill them—brother or not.

"That it? No snarky joke? No witty comment? Not even a put-down to go with it?"

With my tone, which was no longer dull and lifeless, I thought Liam might get ruffled, but he only shook his head. "No, just… sorry."

My throat constricted so tight I could feel it in the back of my skull. As I nodded at him, I wished he'd made some jackass comment. His sincerity was painful.

It doesn't matter, it doesn't matter, it doesn't matter. None of this matters.

Wanting to be alone, I yanked the scotch away from Dad and trounced back to my room. Once I was inside, I slammed the door shut and started taking long pulls directly from the bottle. The room still smelled like Anna, and her things were everywhere—a shirt here, a bra there. Tiny reminders of my monumental loss. Or *her* loss. She was the one throwing in the towel and giving up. She was the quitter here, not me.

I ripped down everything of hers and the girls that I could find and shoved it all under the bed, where it couldn't haunt me. Out of sight, out of mind. Gibson's doll was the last thing I put away. Before I shoved it into the darkness, I studied its opaque eyes. They were as lifeless as I felt.

As the night wore on and my bottle of alcohol dwindled, the room began to spin. Any second now I'd be puking or passing out. Either end was fine with me, so long as I could stop thinking.

While I studied the swirling ceiling and concentrated on my breathing, my cell phone rang. When I saw Chelsey's name displayed on the screen, I considered letting it go to voicemail. Curiosity, or maybe alcohol, compelled me to pick it up though. "What?" I gruffed.

"Hey…how are you doing?" Chelsey's voice was soft, sweet… and grating.

"My wife walked out on me, how the fuck do you think I'm doing?"

She sighed. "You're not mad that I took her in, are you? Because she didn't have anywhere else to go…except maybe Liam's, and I thought you'd like it better if I took her than him."

My hand clenched around my phone. No, I'd never get through the night thinking Liam was the one comforting Anna. If she even needed comforting. "No, I'm not mad. I'm not anything. Except drunk. That, I definitely am. In spades." After Chelsey sighed again, I quietly asked, "How is…? How are my kids?"

Chelsey seemed to know what I'd originally meant to ask, and her answer covered a lot of ground. "Everyone is doing okay. Not great, but okay."

I made a grunting noise into the phone. Anna was "okay" with leaving me. *Awesome.*

Chelsey cleared her throat. "Look, Griffin, I wanted to let you know... Anna booked a flight for tomorrow morning, and I'm taking her and the girls to the airport. If you want to see her... that's your last chance."

In answer, I hung up the phone. She abandoned me. Fuck if I was going to see her off.

Chapter 20

Now What?

I'm not sure what time I passed out, but it was late afternoon when I woke up. My head throbbed, but that was nothing compared to the ripping sensation going on in my chest. *She was gone. They were all gone.* They were probably back in Seattle by now. Maybe they'd gone to Kellan's? It made sense that Anna would have called Kiera for help. But she could have just as easily called Jenny or Rachel, or one of her friends from Hooters. She could be anywhere. The only thing I knew for certain was that she was no longer here. I was alone.

I considered texting her. It was something we did a lot whenever I was touring without her. I'd text her, *Good morning, sweet ass, I woke up with a boner thinking about you.* She'd text me back, *Good morning, hot stuff, if you were here, I'd take care of that for you.* Then she'd go on to describe exactly what she'd do to me.

More often than not, her words would get me all hot and bothered, and I'd send her a picture of me jacking off. Sometimes video. That would get her all worked up, and we'd share a moment, even though we were thousands of miles apart. I was getting a chubby just thinking about the steamy things we used to send each other... but things were different now, and if I sexted her today, she wouldn't respond. I was sure of it. It was just one more thing in a long list of things that I'd never get to do again.

This fucking sucked.

Sitting up on the bed made the throbbing in my head feel like someone was jackhammering my skull, but lying here thinking about my wife wasn't helping anything. Fuck. Was she still my wife? Or were we separated and on the fast track to divorce? I had no fucking clue, and that scared the shit out of me.

My future had always seemed so clear to me, like I was swimming through tropical waters. I could see every pebble of possibility, every coral of comfort, every fish of fame that was going to come my way. Now though, the water was so murky, I couldn't see my hand in front of my face. And it was iced over. And covered in concrete. The treasure buried deep beneath the waves was so unobtainable to me now, it seemed ridiculous that I'd once had my fingers buried deep in the gold. I'd had it all, and now...I had nothing.

Well fuck that. I wasn't about to just sit here wallowing in woe-is-me crap while my world turned to shit. I had time to fix this, so that was exactly what I was going to do.

Grabbing my jacket off the floor, I strutted out of my room. I was going to get what I deserved, then get my wife and kids back. Anna's smile flashed through my brain, followed quickly by Gibson's laugh and Onnika's curls. Goddammit, I already missed them so much, it was hard to function. I had a job to do though.

I decided I had to make do with the best of a bad situation. Yes, the album sucked...but no one outside of my family knew that. If I could somehow convince the world that it was awesomeness dipped in awesomeness, then maybe I could collect enough preorders to make a dent in my debt. A small part of my brain warned me that preorders could be returned later, but I ignored that part. I had to *try* to make the album successful. I had to *try* to earn some of my cash back. It was the only option I had left.

Over the next month, I did everything I knew how to do as a promoter. I hit every TV show, radio station, club, and newspaper in town, begging all of them to showcase me. But no one was biting. I tried to keep my thoughts off Anna and the girls while I scrambled for attention, but it was impossible to do; they were on my mind twenty-four/seven. Eventually I broke down and called Anna. My hands were slick with sweat when I dialed her number, and my fingers were shaking when I brought the phone to my ear. I'd never been more nervous to talk to my wife, not even in the beginning, when she was just a hot chick I wanted to bang. But now…there was so much between us, and so much at stake that I could lose, if I hadn't lost it already. I was a wreck, and she hadn't even picked up yet.

Her voice was cool and distant when she did answer the phone. "I was beginning to think you weren't ever going to call," she stated, her voice flat and lifeless.

Instead of telling her how much I missed her, how nervous I was to talk to her, how scared I was about my future, about *our* future, I let the shell surrounding me harden; it was the only way I could get the words out. "I wanted to check on the girls. Are they all right? Where are you guys staying?"

A long, controlled exhale met my ear, like she was fighting her own emotional battle. I wasn't sure if she was going to respond, but after a while, she finally did. "We're staying at Kellan and Kiera's for now. Gibson…asks for you every day, but she's fine, I think."

That damn lump in my throat returned. I hated the thought of my little girl being denied something she wanted. She should have everything, wrapped in a pretty pink bow. God, I missed her. "Is she nearby? Can I talk to her?" My voice came out scratchy, like I'd swallowed sandpaper.

"Of course," Anna whispered. Her voice was rough too. The line was silent a minute, then a sweet, familiar voice came on. "Daddy? Where are you? When you come home?"

A surge of something so strong went through me that I had to bite down on my knuckle to hold it together. "Soon, baby. Soon." My throat closed, I couldn't speak. Luckily, Gibson had lots to tell me, so I didn't need to.

"Onnika hit me! And Ryder broke my toy! And I found a kitty, and Mommy let me keep it. Her name is Kitty Sunshine…"

She went on and on with all the details of her life that I was missing out on. The pain in my throat eased with each sentence, but the ache in my chest grew larger. I should be there. I should head home on my hands and knees, admit all my failings, and beg Anna to take me back. I should be a better husband, a better father...put all of their needs above my own...since they were all I truly lived for anyway. But still, I couldn't leave yet. I couldn't admit defeat. I needed to see this album through, on the off chance it might save me, and in turn, save my family. If that was even still possible. Fuck, I hoped it was. I couldn't stomach this being the end of Anna's and my story. She was everything I wanted, everything I needed.

So why the fuck did I let her go?

On the morning of the album's release, I paced the living room. Chelsey had one eye on me, one eye on her laptop screen. "Any reviews yet?" I asked her for the umpteenth time.

She hit refresh, then shook her head. "No. But we didn't give out advanced copies, so that's to be expected."

I nodded but kept pacing. I'd done everything I could think to do to advertise the album. I'd even gone on a public TV game show called *Guess My Claim to Fame*. I'd hated every second of it; the producers had decided that my claim to fame was leaving the hottest band on the planet at the height of their popularity. I'd sat there with a smile plastered on my face and let them insult, mock, and ridicule my life choices. Whatever I had to do to get people to buy the album. And today was the day I found out if anything I'd done was worth it. Fuck, it had to be worth it. I'd given up everything for this. Literally everything. If the album didn't pay off, if I couldn't climb out of debt and show Anna my worth...I didn't know what I would do to win her back. And living a life without her just seemed...pointless.

"Now?" I asked Chelsey. I just wanted one review to pop up so I could know what to expect from the rest. But honestly, I knew what to expect. The album was shit, and I was fucked.

Chelsey sighed, then closed her laptop. "Maybe we should go do something...see a movie?"

"No…but thanks." I gave her a half smile in appreciation. Then I pointed at her computer. "Can you check again?"

Finally, a review came in. It was one star, and the headline read, "I WISH I COULD GIVE THIS NEGATIVE STARS!!" The reviews seemed to pour in after that, and none of them were good. "Worst album ever made!" "I could do better with my keyboard!" "My ears are bleeding!" "I want two hours of my life back." "I think my IQ just went down after listening to this." "It's obvious the D-Bags are better off without him!" The only slightly positive review, and the one with the highest rating—three whole stars—said, "This made me laugh so hard I peed! Best comedy album I've heard in a while."

I fell onto the couch while Chelsey softly closed her computer. I didn't ask her to check again. I didn't need to. The facts were clear. I was a joke.

Chelsey put a hand on my knee. "I'm so sorry, Griffin. I know you tried…"

Staring at nothing, I shook my head. "Not hard enough. I'm starting to think I don't try anything hard enough…"

I stood, left my sister on the couch, and went to my room. I wanted to be alone, and fittingly enough, that was exactly what I was now. Completely alone.

The next morning, my dad put a hand on my shoulder. "Chelsey tells me the album flopped. Sorry, son."

I looked up at him with a cringe. *Thanks for breaking it to me gently, Dad.* "Yeah, well, I can still…" My voice trailed off. I had no idea what I could still do. I was haunted by my failed TV show, hounded by critics for that joke of an album, I had no money, a massive debt that I couldn't repay, and a wife who needed me to help raise our two daughters. But my bank account was overdrawn, and all I had left was the change in my pocket. I was so far beyond fucked, I wasn't even sure what the proper term for it was.

I stared at my fingers curled around my coffee cup instead. Because that seemed like something I could do.

Dad sat down beside me. "Look, I get that you aren't where you thought you would be, but that's life, son. You get pummeled and punched, then you stand up and say fuck you, life, and keep trudging on...until you finally keel over."

I lifted my eyes to his. "Wow...that sounds awesome. Can't wait for that to start."

He patted my shoulder. "I'd say it already has. But how you deal with the disappointment is still your choice. You can immerse yourself in sex, you can immerse yourself in work, barely coming up for air, you can belittle everyone who's better off than you, trying to make yourself look better, or you can drink yourself into oblivion every night." Dad shrugged. "Or, you could make the best of your situation, pull your head out of the clouds, be responsible and reliable, put your nose to the grindstone, and provide for those who need it. And while you're doing it, you try to remember *why* you're doing it, so you can attempt to get through each day with as much of your sanity intact as possible."

"And how do I do that?"

He smiled. "I'm so glad you asked. The place I retired from, the place I worked my ass off for twenty-eight years, is hiring. I talked to the foreman, and he's willing to give you a shot. It's an entry-level position, grunt work, and it will be hard, but you'll make a somewhat decent living. You'll get by."

Up until his retirement a couple of years ago, Dad had worked in one factory or another for the majority of his life. When the plant he'd been at in Kansas closed and our family had moved to L.A. to live with Uncle Billy, Dad had gotten a job at a place that made machines that made other machines. It was the sort of repetitious, mind-numbing work that made my skin crawl. But Dad was right, he'd made a decent income, enough that Mom had been able to stay home with us kids. Problem was, I didn't want a "decent" life. I wanted more.

Sighing, I told him, "Thanks, Dad, but I don't want to work where you worked. That place sucked the life out of you. And I don't want to get by...I want to *live*. I want to rock the world with my best friends. I want the woman of my dreams...my best friend...to be by my side again. I want...everything I gave up."

Standing, Dad shrugged. "You gave it up for a reason, Griffin. But even so, it doesn't matter. Your options aren't what they used to be, and it's time for you to grow up. I told Tyler you'd be there Monday morning, seven a.m. sharp."

A groan escaped me as I sank my head to the table. Seven a.m. was too fucking early to do anything productive. But again, Dad was right. It was time for me to grow up.

I was still sitting there with my head on the table, my coffee long cold, contemplating my future of perpetual monotony, when my sister, Chelsey, came over to visit. She bounded into the kitchen, and even though I wasn't looking at her, I could feel her radiant energy. Mom was washing the dishes, and she stopped when Chelsey exclaimed, "Great news! I talked to Dustin last night. He's coming home Monday! For sure this time!"

She squealed, and I contained a groan. Her life was getting back on track Monday, while mine was falling further behind. How the fuck did this happen to me? I was on top of the world...now I was nothing. A joke. Laughed at, then discarded.

I made a moaning sound, and I heard Chelsey ask Mom, "Is he...okay?"

Mom took a puff on the cigarette in her mouth. "He's been like that all morning. Dad got him a job. He's...absorbing."

I groaned again. I was in the biggest band in the world, barely doing anything that constituted real work, and now I was going to be tightening bolts for ten hours a day, six days a week, fifty-one weeks a year. More, if I didn't take any vacation time.

Fuck. My. Life.

Feeling Chelsey sitting beside me, I lifted my head; it felt like it weighed a thousand pounds, and I was pretty sure I had a flat spot from the table. "Hey," I muttered.

Her smile was bright and her eyes were twinkling, but I could tell she was trying to rein in her joy. "Hey, yourself. How's it going?"

"Like Mom said, I've got a job now...so it's going fantastic..." She made a scrunched, I'm-sorry-but-too-giddy-to-frown expression. "Dustin's coming home, huh?" I asked.

A supernova smile erupted on her face, and she nodded so hard a blond curl fell from a clip in her hair. "Monday."

"That's great, sis. You deserve your happy ending." One of us should have one.

Like she could hear my silent sullenness, she put a hand on my arm. "You do too, Griff. You're not such a bad guy, you know? A little self-absorbed, maybe, but we all are, to some extent."

Even though I nodded in agreement, I didn't quite agree with her assessment. She was the most selfless person I'd ever met. And me... I'd rather take a mundane job that I knew I was going to hate than go home and face the guys. And my wife. I was a fucking coward, too proud to throw in the towel. But at least if I stayed here and took this job, I'd be able to help my family. That was one bright spot, I supposed.

Tilting her head, Chelsey regarded me with appraising eyes. "Did you learn anything?"

That my ideas were shit and I should never take my own advice? Yeah, I think that one had finally sunk in. With a half smile, I told her, "Yeah, never hire someone off the Internet."

Chelsey laughed, but then stopped. It wasn't really funny. I'd spent everything I'd had on that worthless album. Staring at the table, I sighed. "I think I finally get what you were talking about..."

She squeezed my arm. "What do you mean?"

Looking over at her, I felt my chest compress tighter. Maybe I was having a heart attack. Or maybe this was just what despair felt like. "The dog and the steak. I think I get what you were saying. And you were right... I understand too late. The steak is already gone..."

Switching my gaze to my mom, I thought about her relationship with Dad. They'd been together forever, since Mom was eighteen and Dad was twenty-eight. They'd gone through so many ups and downs in their marriage, but they were still a team. United. Where had I gone so wrong? Why had my team fallen apart? I knew the answer to that though. Anna and I fell apart because I stopped acting like we were a team. I kept her in the dark, made all the choices, and then lied my fucking ass off. The only surprise here was that she hadn't left me sooner.

"She was my best friend," I whispered. "They all were...and I tossed them aside for something I thought I needed more. I'm such a fucking moron." When I looked back at my sister, her eyes were watery; mine felt the same. "What do I do now, Chelse?"

She stared at me so long, I started getting uncomfortable. I felt like I'd just pried open my chest and exposed my innards, and I was going to bleed out if she didn't say something. Just when I was about to repeat my question, because the silence was killing me, she spoke. "You forget about what you never had...and you go after what you lost...even if you have to crawl through the mud to do it."

She made it sound so easy, but I knew it wasn't. Just the thought of picking up the phone and telling the guys I was wrong...about everything...made me feel sick. And Anna...I didn't even know where to begin with her. How could I do this? I wasn't even sure I had the necessary skills to be all repentant and shit. "How do I do that?" I murmured, feeling defeated. I was really beginning to hate feeling that way.

I'd moved my head so I wasn't looking into her eyes anymore, but she moved hers until I had no choice but to meet her gaze. "You take that pride that you hold on to so hard, and you shove it down a deep, dark hole. You show them something real. Be human. Be fallible. Be flexible. Be humble."

None of that sounded easy. Or like me. I tended to be the opposite of all those things. It was simpler to be an awesome god who could do no wrong. Because...admitting I was wrong...was complete and utter torture. I didn't think I could do it. "So...you want me to be lame, is what you're saying?"

Smiling, she clapped me on the back. "That's entirely optional, but it might help."

A small chuckle escaped me, and it felt good to release it. I felt like I hadn't laughed in years. And, if I were honest, it had been a while. I don't think I'd let out an honest laugh since I'd parted ways with the band. That's when everything had gone downhill for me, and now I was so far down, it was hard to see my way back up.

"Thank you," I told her. "For everything. I think you're the only one who gives a shit."

Chelsey rubbed my back. "No, more people care about you than you think. But... it's like your ego is a force field... it pushes people back, instead of letting them in. You'd see the world differently if you opened yourself up to the possibility that..."

She bit her lip while she stared at me, and I saw a grin growing in the gesture. "That what?" I asked, knowing whatever her answer was, it was going to be smart-assed.

She released her lip and the smile broke free. "That you're an imperfect person... just like the rest of us."

Six months ago I would have wholeheartedly denied that, but now... "Yeah... I know. Brat." I bumped her shoulder, and laughing, she wrapped her arms around me and squeezed.

"I love you, Griffin, and I know everything is going to be okay."

Closing my eyes, I prayed she was right.

Chapter 21

Reality

I was woken up Monday morning by a buzzer going off in my ear, and I decided right then and there that that was not a dignified way for a human being to be roused from sleep. If I ever had the opportunity, I would hunt down the sick son of a bitch who had invented the damn thing and drive a couple of spikes through his forehead. *How does that feel, fucker?*

Shucking off my covers, I painstakingly rose to my feet. God, I hated mornings. There was no good reason for them. My body felt tight, my head was throbbing, and my knees cracked when I stood up. Man, I was getting old. Either that or my body was rebelling against the time. The time, and the task that I was about to do.

I was starting at Dad's old factory today. Yippee. The money would help me make payments to the bank though, and at the moment, that was more important than the potential suckage of this monotonous job.

Nobody was awake when I stumbled into the kitchen. I thought my parents would be up to see me off, but no, I could hear Dad snoring in his room. In the kitchen, I found a note attached to a small paper bag, the kind I'd used as a kid to take my lunch to school. The note said, "Good luck," and inside was a ham sandwich, a bag of chips, an apple, and two chocolate chip cookies. Damn. Now I felt like I was eight again.

"Thanks, Mom," I muttered, grabbing one of the cookies. I popped it in my mouth while I debated adding a beer to my lunch. It was a factory, surely adult pop was allowed if you were on break.

Thinking better of it, I closed up the bag and looked around for my dad's car keys. He'd told me I could take the minivan to work until I could afford a car of my own. That was a good thing, since biking that far every day would have seriously sucked. It also filled me with an empty hollowness to think of how long I was going to have to be there to afford a car, get my own place…get my shit together. And before I could even think of doing any of that, I needed to make sure Anna and the girls were being taken care of. It was all so surreal. Not that long ago, the money was flowing in so fast, I never even had to think about it. Now I cherished every dime. How had so much changed in such a short amount of time?

When I went outside to start the car, it was still sort of dark; even the sun wasn't fully up yet. Awesome. As I listened to some animal chirping away in the distance, I considered getting in the car and driving back to Seattle. Would that be running away or running home? I had no idea, but I knew it wouldn't solve my immediate money problems, so I scrapped the idea.

When I got to work, I instantly realized I wouldn't get through this with any of my dignity still intact. "Okay, grunt, you listening, 'cause I don't want to have to explain this twice." I nodded so my "instructor" would get on with the mindless orientation. "You take this wrench, and when this piece comes down your line, you insert ten bolts in these ten holes, then tighten them. You send that piece on its merry way, then start on the next one. Sound like something you can handle, newbie?"

I gave him a blank stare. "Putting in ten bolts and tightening them? Yeah, I think I can manage that."

He clapped me on the back so hard, I stumbled forward a little. "Great. Don't mess up the rest of production by being a slow ass. Break is at eleven sharp. Try not to nod off."

With that, he left me to my menial task. I'll admit, the first piece was a challenge, and I let out some sailor-worthy curses, especially when I pinched my finger and started bleeding, but by my seven millionth bolt, I could have done it with my eyes closed.

My mind wandered while I worked. I pictured myself onstage at Pete's, the guys beside me and a horde of adoring fans in front of me. Remembering that time made an ache expand inside my chest. It was painful, and I wanted to think of something else to get rid of it, but I apparently wasn't done torturing myself, because my mind wouldn't let go of the memory of hopping offstage.

Matt squeezed my shoulder and told me I'd done awesome. Evan gave me a thumbs-up before wrapping Jenny in a hug, and Kellan gave me a bright smile and asked if I wanted a beer. It felt like a million years ago, and yet, at the same time, it seemed like only yesterday.

With nothing to do with my mind during work, I had daydream upon daydream during my shift. A lot of them were centered on the band, but even more were about my wife. Her eyes filled my mind, her laugh filled my ears, and her body...well, let's just say it was a good thing the work table was hiding everything below my waist.

I kept picturing moments we'd had together. Our first kiss, dancing in the middle of my old living room. Then pulling her into my bedroom and stripping her bare. Her body had blown my mind. She was everything I loved in a woman, wrapped up in one perfect person. And she was just as dirty as me. She was game for anything I wanted to try, anything I wanted to do. She was exactly what I'd wanted in a partner...and I'd let her leave. As the day wore on, it got harder and harder to remember just why I'd done that. Anna was the right girl for me. She was the *only* girl for me. *Then why are you still here?*

By the end of my shift, I wasn't sure what hurt worse, my head or my hands. They were so raw, it was hard to hold the steering wheel on the drive home; even my blisters had blisters. After the noise from the factory all day, the anticipation of the chaos waiting for me at my parents' busy house was almost intolerable. Dustin was finally home, and we were all celebrating. I was happy for my sister, but I really wasn't in a partying mood. My feet felt like lead weights, my arms felt like rubber, and my heart... well, that was just fucked.

When I stepped into the house, I cringed at the noise. Kids were running, screaming, and banging pots and pans together. Adults were laughing, barking at the kids, and telling stories at about five times the necessary volume. The chaos of my family used to never bother me, but at the moment, it was hell. Pure, life-sucking hell. It made me miss my quiet foursome all the more.

I was dirty, smelly, and mentally drained, so I darted to my room before anyone could stop me.

My mom bellowed at me when dinner was done, and I knew by her tone that I had better sit down with the family. Hiding out the entire night in my room was *not* an option. Used to large gatherings, Mom had the longest table known to man in her dining room. It still wasn't big enough for all of us though, and a couple of folding tables were set up for the kids. It was like Thanksgiving on crack.

After helping Mom set the table, because not helping wasn't an option either, I took a spot next to Dustin and mumbled a polite greeting. Chelsey was on his other side, beaming up at him like he was the center of her universe, and maybe he was. She certainly hadn't looked this at peace while he'd been gone. It made me think of my own universe and how a huge piece of it was missing.

Mom set down heaping bowls of cut tomatoes, avocados, olives, onions, and lettuce. Then she brought out about five pounds of ground beef and enough tortillas to tile the entire house... and I didn't want any of it. Eating sounded about as appealing as licking the toilet seat. After Liam had used it.

I made a plate, 'cause I knew Mom would flip a lid if I didn't, but as the rest of my family dug into their tacos, I only nibbled on a piece of lettuce. Everyone asked Dustin about his time away, which allowed me to sit and stew in silence. I didn't want them to ask about my first day. I didn't want to think about my first day. Or my second, third, fourth...

Luck wasn't with me though. As soon as Dustin had a break in recounting his heroics, he asked me, "So, Griffin, Chelsey tells me you changed jobs, and today was your first day. How was it? Anybody recognize you from the band? Ask for a signature?"

By the look on his face, I knew he sincerely meant that. He didn't realize the way people saw me now. The way the general public saw me. I didn't want to tell him either. It was embarrassing to admit that I *had* been recognized...and laughed at.

Admitting the truth wasn't an option, but my lie kind of sucked too, just for a different reason. "No...nobody recognized me."

Dustin seemed as disheartened to hear that as I was to say it. "Oh, well...that's probably for the best anyway." He gave me an award-worthy smile. "Knowing a celebrity was in their midst would be distracting."

My smile was brief. Yeah...distracting.

Dustin seemed about to ask me more, but luckily Liam asked him a technical question about fighter jets. Dustin hadn't worked on or around planes, but I guess Liam just assumed he'd be an expert on them since he was in the military. Jackass.

While Dustin told him the tidbits he did know, I zoned out. My gaze returned to Chelsey as she watched her husband and ate her taco. She looked so satisfied just staring at him. It made me wonder if all Anna and I'd had was physical. Was Anna happy with me when it came to the nonsexual side of our relationship? I wanted to believe she was, but I really wasn't sure. She must not have been if she left. *And you must not have been if you let her leave.*

Pushing that nagging thought from my brain, I rewound to a simpler time...a time when we'd been happy, with no cares in the world. It had been back when we were just fooling around—fuck buddies. The best of both worlds. Not really, but that was what I'd been telling myself at the time.

We'd just left a restaurant in Seattle and were walking back to the car. When I'd parked us down by the pier, we hadn't been sure where we wanted to eat, and we'd wandered almost a dozen blocks to find this little hole-in-the-wall Irish pub with great beer and awesome food.

Stuff like that happened a lot with Anna. We'd play it by ear, go where the wind took us, and wind up having an amazing night. But after leaving the pub, we were both too stuffed to make the long trip back to my car. We hadn't been sure what to do when I'd suddenly spotted the answer.

"Let's take a horse carriage ride." I pointed in front of us to where a white stallion was hooked up to a carriage lined with red roses. It was a pretty romantic setup, but at the time, I'd just wanted to get off my feet for a while.

"But that won't get us any closer to the car. It goes in a circle."

Nodding, I started pulling her toward the carriage. "Yeah, it will get us a little closer if we bail halfway through...and if we don't, we'll at least get to work on these food babies." I grabbed my stomach with my free hand and Anna laughed. God, I loved that sound.

"Sounds good. Let's do it!" Her eyes had shone in that adventurous way she had, and I'd known right then and there that this girl would be my undoing. Gorgeous, sexy, horny, and ready to have a good time at the drop of a hat...she was pretty much me with boobs.

When the carriage driver told me how much the ride was, I'd almost reconsidered, but Anna had been cooing at the horse and making kissy faces; I paid him without a second thought. Holding a hand out for her, I helped her into the carriage. It smelled, but Anna was smiling so much, I hadn't cared. We could have been sitting in the middle of a sewage treatment plant and I would have been happy. And turned on. The curve of her sultry lips went straight to my libido.

The driver flicked the reins, and the horse began its pointless journey. With the distinctive clip-clop of its hooves against the road as our background music, Anna and I leaned back in the seat and relaxed. Pulling her tight to my side, I'd tried to ignore the emotion swelling in my chest. It was just a by-product of the surroundings. I wasn't developing feelings for her. She was a great lay—no, an *amazing* lay—one I wanted to experience over and over again, one who made every other girl seem like a floundering virgin...but that was all she was to me. Sex.

God, I'd been such a fucking idiot.

Looking back on the moment now, it was easy to label the emotion that had begun to bubble that night. I'd been falling in love with her, and I would have done anything to avoid admitting that. It was so cliché, overused, and... mainstream. I hated the word on principle. Even now, I never...

I stared at my plate as empty realization hit me. *I never tell her I love her.* She'd even called me on it, and I hadn't changed my pattern. Why was it so hard for me to say that word? To her. To my kids. To my family. To my band... Was I rebelling against something that didn't need to be rebelled against? Maybe the word was overused... but maybe that was because it was the only word that accurately described how important someone was. Not saying it was like trying to pretend the sun didn't exist by staying indoors all the time—ridiculous and futile. Even without acknowledging it, I'd still experienced it that night, and if I were honest, I'd experienced it every night after. I was experiencing it now, only now the feeling was laced with pain, because the girl of my dreams wasn't sitting beside me in that carriage anymore. She was completely out of reach.

We'd ended up staying in the carriage for the entire loop, and somewhere around the halfway point we'd started kissing. No girl I'd ever kissed before had felt like Anna. She had the softest lips... But I had kissed girls with soft lips before. With Anna, it was more than that. It was like her lips had been specifically molded for mine. Like we were yin and yang, broken apart and separated by thousands of miles. But we'd found each other again, and when our bodies met... it was fireworks.

That night had been warm, her fingers stroking my stomach under my shirt had been invigorating, and the threads of her hair blowing across my face had been intoxicating. The night had been perfect. And when we'd finally made it back to my car, I'd driven her to her apartment and we'd fucked like bunnies. It had been just one of the many incredible evenings I'd had... with my best friend. My soul mate, if such a thing existed. And now...

"You okay, Griffin? You haven't eaten anything, and from what I remember of having meals with you, you were always the first one done. You were usually the one digging into dessert while everyone else was only halfway through." Dustin laughed, then smiled at me.

I couldn't even fake a smile in return, not after that memory. "Yeah…guess I'm just not hungry. Long day." Pushing my plate away, I stood from the table. "Thanks for the meal, Mom. I just can't eat."

After she nodded at me, I trudged to my room, closed the door, then sat on the bed.

I'd never felt this defeated and depressed before, and I really didn't have anyone to share it with. Chelsey was the one I felt most comfortable talking to, but now that Dustin was back…They'd been apart so long, I didn't want to keep them apart even longer, not for my pathetic shit. And Chelsey wasn't the one I really wanted to be talking to anyway. No, who I really wanted was my best friend.

Pulling out my cell phone, I stared at it for twenty minutes. I'd really had a crap day, and hearing Anna's voice right now sounded like a great reprieve. Assuming she had anything nice to say to me, that was. Eventually we had to talk about…us…right? Might as well get it over with. But what if her solution to this was to end it? What if she was happier without me? Or what if she just wanted some space, and me bugging her drove her over the edge? I had no fucking clue what I was supposed to do and what I wasn't supposed to do. I was in completely foreign waters, and I was drowning.

"Fuck it," I muttered. Finding her number, I hit the send button. Restraint was never one of my strong points anyway.

When she answered my call, I opened my mouth to speak. I shut it instantly when I recognized her voicemail prompt. I debated leaving a message, but then decided not to. If she was ignoring me, then she wouldn't get to listen to what I had to say. Stubborn, sure, but she'd have to answer if she wanted to hear me.

Thinking I could get around her security system, I called Kellan's house instead. It didn't even dawn on me that Kellan might answer until the phone picked up. A flash of panic hit me while I waited for a greeting. What the hell would I say to him?

For once, luck was with me, and a feminine voice answered. "Hello?"

"Oh…hey…it's Griffin. This Kiera?"

There was a pause, and I wondered if I'd just gotten my wife's voice wrong. It happened on occasion; she and Kiera sounded a lot alike. But then the voice said, "Oh…hey…yeah, it's Kiera."

"Oh…awesome…is Anna there? Can I…talk to her?" I wasn't sure why the words were haltingly coming from my mouth. I usually just asked for what I wanted without hesitation. It was like my entire world had flipped upside down recently, and I was a shadow of who I used to be.

"Anna actually went out…"

My throat constricted. With a guy? I wanted to ask, but if Kiera said yes, I'd be on the next plane north. And after I found whoever the son of a bitch was who thought he could date my wife, I'd pummel him into unrecognizable goo. Then I'd go to jail, and I'd never see my girls again. The threat of jail time was the only reason I stayed silent.

Sensing the awkwardness, Kiera cleared her throat. "I'm watching the kids for her…do you want to talk to them?"

A calm warmth passed over me at the thought of hearing those sweet voices. "Yes." My speech came out in an unmanly squeak, and I had to clear my throat before I could try again. "Yes…please."

The pleading in my answer must have moved Kiera. Her voice was thick with compassion when she told me she'd go get them. "Wait," I said, stopping her. "Before you go…is Anna…is she…okay?"

Kiera let out a long sigh. "She's getting by. What about you? Are you okay, Griffin?"

Her words hit me right in the gut. Okay? I had no idea anymore. "Yeah, I'm…" My voice trailed off as the desolation of my empty room struck me over the head. My empty room, my empty life. "No…my life is shit without them…" I had no idea if I meant Anna, my girls, or my band. I think I meant exactly what the word "them" implied. They *all* had a piece of me, and with all of them removed, I was dying inside, little by little, day by day.

With a sniff, I gruffed out, "Can you put Gibson on the line please?"

I'd died enough for one day, and I didn't need to let Kiera see any more of my pain.

Chapter 22

Hardship

Three weeks went by at my soul-sucking job, and I eventually did get used to the work. My hands were no longer raw and bleeding by the end of the day; I had some super sweet calluses built up. They felt awesome when I was jacking off. Not. It was just another thing that made me miss Anna.

I yawned six times in a row on the drive to work. I hadn't adjusted to the godforsaken hour, and I never would. No one should be awake at this time unless they were still up partying from the night before. My partying days were pretty much over though. I stopped by a bar after work for an hour or two, just to unwind before heading home to the chaos that was my parents' house, and then I came home and crashed so I could do it all over again.

I hadn't even been taking advantage of my one day off a week to go out and do anything. The desire just wasn't in me. I wanted to get through the day, that was all I cared about now. Sometimes just getting through the hour was a struggle. *Just keep going... tomorrow will surely be better.* It never was though.

I'd always been able to make the best of situations, go with the flow, find joy in the oddest stuff, but now...the only bright spot in my day was thinking about Anna and the girls. While I went about my menial task of tightening bolt after bolt, I daydreamed about them.

The memory most often tangling my mind was when Anna and I had decided to move in together. Well, we hadn't really decided it, we'd just sort of done it. It had made sense though, since we were already married. And had a kid. It was after the D-Bags tour with Sienna Sexton, when we'd all trudged back home after Kellan had gotten hurt. I'd been living with Matt up until then, but it seemed weird to go back there and leave Gibson and Anna all alone at her apartment. No, it had seemed more than weird, it had seemed wrong. She was my wife, and I wanted to be with her.

So we'd gone to her place together. Anna had carried Gibson, while I'd carried the rest of our bags. I'd been huffing and puffing by the time we'd reached her door; between the three of us, we'd had a ton of crap, even after we'd shipped a bunch of shit home.

"Here's your new home, baby girl," Anna had cooed as she'd gently swung the car seat from left to right, showing Gibson her new spread.

Anna's apartment had been fine when we'd been rolling around in it, but all of a sudden it had felt cramped. "We should get a bigger place, somewhere Gibby can run and play. Somewhere with a pool." The bags fell off my shoulders and thumped to the floor in a pile. I massaged my sore shoulders. "And a hot tub."

With a seductive giggle, Anna swung her eyes my way. "I don't know, I like how cozy we are here."

Pulling the car seat from Anna's hand, I gently set Gibson on the floor. Wrapping my arms around Anna's waist, I'd told her, "Yeah, but what about the others? We'll feel like we live in a box when they arrive."

Anna had scrunched her brows in confusion. I don't know why, but the expression had turned me on. Okay, I knew exactly why—everything she did turned me on. "What others?" she'd asked.

Leaning in, I'd sucked her bottom lip into my mouth. "The other kids we're gonna have."

She'd let out an erotic groan that was way too sensual for our daughter's young ears. I was instantly hard. "Mmmm...you want more kids?" she asked, her voice throaty.

Pressing my eager body into her hip, I growled, "Yes...let's start now..."

Anna laughed as my lips attached to her neck, then she gently pushed me back. Green eyes serious, she again asked, "You really want more kids?"

I'd glanced down at my daughter—my perfect, beautiful angel of a daughter—and a peaceful smile had spread across my lips. "I do. I want more mini versions of you. A dozen at least...and maybe one or two of me." I'd given her my studliest smile, and she'd returned it, but her eyes were wetter than before.

"You want a dozen versions of me?"

Cupping her cheeks, I'd nodded. "Anything less than that would be a crime against humanity. You're perfect...your DNA should be replicated over and over and over..."

She'd kissed me then, hard, and we'd quickly put Gibson down for a nap in her room so we could get to work on giving her a brother or sister in our room. And it wasn't much longer after that that we'd moved into the mammoth house by the lake. My dream home, with my dream girl. But now the dream was over.

When my shift ended, I didn't feel like going home. Honestly, I didn't feel like doing anything. Staying at the factory overnight wasn't an option though, so, dirty and sore, I plodded out to the parking lot. Maybe I'd head to the local bar and drown my sorrows in whiskey. It wouldn't solve anything, but maybe it would temporarily remove the cloud of despair around me; I didn't even feel like myself anymore. I barely looked like myself either. There were bags under my eyes, holes in my clothes, blisters on every finger, and grime, grease, and sweat in every nook and cranny. Chelsey had helped me get my blond hair back after Anna left, since the grow-out had been driving her crazy, but like the rest of me, it was dull and lackluster, and I swear to God, it was turning gray.

As I dragged my feet across the concrete, I thought maybe I'd just go home and lose myself in an hour-long shower. That was when the skies opened and the heavens puked heavy raindrops on me. Shaking my head, I looked up at the sudden downpour that was slowly washing away my will to live. *Fuck you, universe, that's not what I meant.*

Coworkers were trudging through the rainstorm with me, slowly ambling to their cars at a robotic pace. Above the noise of the water pelting the earth, I heard one of them shout, "Hey, Cocknado...that your girl?"

Used to being teased at work, the nickname slid right off my shoulders. My heartbeat started racing as the words hit me. Holy crap. Was Anna here? Had she forgiven me? I snapped my gaze to where the coworker was looking, and for second, my vision hazed and I thought I might pass out. It *was* her. She was here...to save me from this hell. Thank God...

I was just about to shout out Anna's name when my tired, aching eyes realized that I was mistaken. My heart fell to the bottom of my weary feet...it wasn't Anna. It was Kiera. What the hell was Kiera doing here?

I had no clue what the answer to that question was. She was standing at the back of my dad's minivan, holding a gigantic black umbrella, and shivering, like she was cold or nervous. She looked like she wasn't entirely sure what she was doing here either, but she brightened when she spotted me. For a second, anyway. Once my appearance became clearer, her cheeriness dimmed. Damn it. I really didn't want her to see me like this. I didn't want anyone to see me like this. Broken. Hopeless. Defeated. A pale specter of who I once was.

I felt nauseated as I walked over to Kiera. She lifted her hand in greeting, and I feebly returned the gesture. I tried to walk as casually as possible, but curiosity was starting to eat at me. What was she doing here?

She was biting her lip as she studied me, and as soon as we were close enough, she asked, "Are you okay?" Her eyes were shiny, like she was about to cry...for me. That was almost as shocking as her being here.

Instead of answering her question, I asked one of my own. "What are you doing here? Come to gloat? See how low I've fallen?" I indicated the dirty, dusty factory drowning in the deluge behind me. If only the rain would completely sweep the hellish place away. But sadly, no…I needed it too much.

Kiera's expression turned incredulous. "No, of course not. I was worried about you. I just needed to know you were okay. And now…I'm not so sure you are." Her eyes scanning my face, she stepped forward so we were both covered by her mammoth umbrella; someone sheltering me felt oddly nice. It choked me up a little.

Swallowing the lump in my throat, I waved off her concern. "I'm fine." I smiled, and it hurt. I was anything but fine. Studying Kiera, I asked, "Why are *you* checking on me? You hate me."

A flush of guilt crept over Kiera's features. "I don't hate you, Griffin. I may not always *like* you…but I don't hate you." She sighed. "But my sister loves you, and that's why I'm here. She's miserable without you, Griffin. They all are…Anna, the girls…the guys." She shrugged as her gaze fell to the concrete.

I felt like she'd just grabbed a slab of that stone and cracked me over the head with it. They were *all* miserable? Without *me*? I wanted to believe that…but they weren't exactly knocking down my door asking me to come back. Any of them…

"Nobody's miserable without me. Nobody even cares that I'm gone. I've been living here for over a year now, and you're the only one of them who has come down to see me." I wanted to cross my arms over my chest and stand there in proud defiance, but I couldn't. I had no pride left.

Frowning, Kiera nodded at my car. "Can we go somewhere quiet and talk? Preferably somewhere dry?" She looked up at the underside of her umbrella. "Your mom told me it was going to rain when I asked her where I could find you. I didn't believe her at the time, but yeah…she's a smart woman." Her eyes returned to mine, and I could see the compliment in them.

I shook my head. "Yeah, she is. But apparently, her smarts wasn't something she passed down to her kids. Not all of them, at least."

Kiera's eyes widened in surprise; she'd probably never heard me put myself down before. Not wanting to hear her say it wasn't true when we both knew it was, I pulled out my car keys. "There's a diner nearby. Are you hungry?"

I couldn't eat, my mouth felt like ash, but Kiera had just traveled hours to get here, and...as I just remembered...she was pregnant. I made myself smile. "You're pregnant, of course you're hungry. Congratulations...I bet Kellan's stoked." Seeing Kiera's glow reminded me that Anna had wanted another baby. God I missed her.

Kiera giggled as she rubbed her belly under her jacket. "Thanks, yeah, we both are. I'm due in November, a girl this time. Anna's been going crazy, helping me shop for her..." Her voice trailed off, like she knew that hearing about my wife would hurt me. And like a knife to the gut, it did. Fuck, would it ever stop hurting?

Wanting away from this waterlogged misery, I opened my car door and helped Kiera inside. I drove us to a quaint diner a mile away, and we settled into a booth near the back. Kiera ordered a meal while I ordered coffee; until I knew what she wanted, I couldn't eat. While we waited for the food to arrive, Kiera started in on her speech.

She smiled at me, then frowned. "First off, I want to clarify something you said in the parking lot. The guys *do* care about you, Griffin. It's just...everyone has been really busy lately...and, well, they're just as prideful and stubborn as you are. You hurt them when you left. No, more than that...you crushed them."

A smart retort started to bubble in my brain, but I let it fade away and continued sitting there with my head hanging. Yes, I *had* hurt them, I knew that. Kiera put a hand on my arm and I looked up at her. "There's still hope here, don't give up."

Shaking my head, I indicated my grimy exterior, the run-down diner that was the best I could afford. "Look at me, Kiera. I lost everything I owned, I'm living with my parents, I'm so deep in debt that even my piss is red, I'm doing a job I hate just to get by, and...I lost my wife, my best friends, and my children. What hope? How can I possibly fix all of that?"

Her face was firm but sympathetic. "That's why I'm here. Things have been really hard on the D-Bags since you left. Denny told me he mentioned some of it, but probably not all of it. Have you been following the news?"

With a sigh, I shook my head again. "No, once the TV show fizzled, I tuned out. Even before that actually. Once I left the band…I didn't want to hear about them. It kind of hurt, you know?" I felt weird admitting something so personal to Kiera, but she only nodded.

"Yeah, I know. Kellan and the guys kind of felt the same way about you. But they had to move on to keep the group going." She let out a long exhale. "And it hasn't been easy. There was a huge backlash when you left. Fans were hurt, confused…angry."

Remembering some of them heckling me at Pete's, I nodded. "Yeah, I know."

Kiera shook her head. "No, I don't think you do. A lot of people were mad at you for leaving, but there's this group of Griffin hardcores…and they're making life hell for the rest of the guys."

That shocked the shit out of me. "I have hardcores?"

Grimacing, Kiera nodded. "Yes. And they're very vocal and very loyal. They started harassing the guys for pushing you away." She closed her eyes for a second as she shook her head. "It got so bad with some of them, Kellan, Evan, and Matt had to get restraining orders." She couldn't have surprised me more if she'd said my TV show had been resurrected from the dead.

"Restraining orders? They…they okay?"

Her eyes opened slowly, like she was dead tired. "They're fine. It was just pretty intense for a while. But this group, they've spread, and now every event the guys play at has protesters. Protesting what the band did to you. There were even some at the VMAs."

I tried to think back to that night, if I recalled anything weird, but I'd been pretty wasted when I'd arrived, so I couldn't remember seeing anything like that. "Wow" was all I could say.

Kiera gave me a half smile. "Yeah. And when the band finally did find someone to replace you, the protesters gave the new guy such a hard time…he quit." With a sigh, she shrugged. "Thanks to your fanatics, every single person the band has hired to replace you has quit. The band can't move forward. They can't tour, can't record another album…it's been hell."

I stared into my coffee cup as guilt churned inside me. "I had no idea they were struggling." *Why hadn't they called me?* I knew the answer to that the instant after I thought it. Because they didn't want to admit defeat either. We were all drowning in our fucking pride.

Kiera sighed and I looked up at her. "Sales have dropped across the board, the band is floundering. Kellan has even mentioned disbanding...everyone going their separate ways..."

My eyes grew so wide my face started hurting. No, this wasn't what I wanted. "They're disbanding? Kellan can probably go solo, but Matt...Evan...what are they gonna do?" I was so worried for them, my heart started pounding harder.

Kiera's peaceful smile made me feel a little better. So did her next words. "Denny convinced Kellan to try one more thing to replace you, so the band isn't disbanding yet."

Her words were bittersweet. I didn't want the band to break apart, I really didn't, but I wasn't thrilled that their mission was to replace me. Feeling sullen, I asked her, "Yeah? And what's that one thing Denny dreamed up?"

Surprising me, she laughed a little. "Ironically enough, it's a TV show. Or a TV special, I guess I should say." My expression must have been complete confusion, because she kept explaining. "Denny thinks that if we have a televised contest to replace you, where the fans get to vote, get to have a say, then your hardcores will be more accepting of the new person."

My brain felt like Jell-O as I processed this new development. They were going to replace me on national TV. Kind of fitting, since that was how they lost me...

While I processed the information, Kiera softly said, "They've been having auditions all over the country...I'm a little surprised you haven't heard about it."

With a sniff, I told her, "I've been preoccupied." Yeah, trying to keep my head above water was a full-time job on its own.

Kiera gave me a sympathetic smile. "Their last stop is here in Los Angeles...two weeks from now." With a raised eyebrow, she added, "Tryouts are open to anyone. All a person has to do is show up and they'll be given a chance."

By the look on her face, it was clear she meant me. I could show up. I could audition. I could face the guys as a contestant looking for a job. I could start over. If I was brave enough. A conversation with my sister flashed through my tired brain.

What do I do now, Chelse?

You go after what you lost... even if you have to crawl through the mud to do it.

Since I felt like I'd been wallowing in mud ever since Anna left, crawling through it sounded easy.

I smiled at Kiera in appreciation, then gave her a small nod so she would know I understood what she was saying. "Thank you. Thank you for coming all the way down here to check on me and to tell me that. You don't know how much I appreciate it." Kindness and compassion of any sort was a rare commodity, something to be cherished. I understood that now.

As she looked me over, her expression turned sad. I must sound really pathetic, like a completely different person. I supposed I was. In a soft, compassionate voice, she said, "I'm sure you and Anna can fix this. She's crazy about you."

And I'm crazy about her. "I hope so," I told her, looking away. Something occurred to me, and I returned my eyes to her. "Do the guys know you're here? Telling me this?" *Did they want me to audition?*

Kiera shrugged. "Kellan knows. He's the one who booked my ticket." She winked, then she sighed. "I don't think he's telling the others though. He doesn't want to put any pressure on you."

I nodded. That was nice of him. Not surprising... Kellan was a good guy. "Thanks. Does... does Anna know you're here?"

Kiera paused, then shook her head. "No. I didn't tell her. She's living on her own now, did you know that?" When I shook my head, she sighed. "Yeah, she got an apartment for her and the girls, and she got her old job back at Hooters. I told her she could stay with us for as long as she needed, but she wants to make it on her own. She's stubborn like that." She laughed.

I smiled. "Yeah... we have that in common."

The waitress arrived with Kiera's food, and she grinned as she looked down at her bacon and eggs. She was a couple of forkfuls into it before the waitress even left. Her appetite made me grin, even though it painfully reminded me of Anna's pregnancy cravings.

"Hey, Kiera," I said, swirling a spoon in my untouched coffee. When she looked up at me, I cringed. "Please don't tell Anna about this." I indicated my dirty, scrubby, beat-up look. Kiera seemed about to protest, but I cut her off. "I'm serious. I don't want her worrying about me."

Kiera thought about that for a minute, then nodded. To ease her mind, I added, "I'm gonna be fine, Kiera, no need to worry." And for the first time in a long time, I actually believed that.

Chapter 23

What to Do?

When Kiera and I got back home, I offered her my bedroom for the night. With lips curled in distaste, she started to say no, but then she looked around my room with wide, disbelieving eyes. Almost instantly, they started to water, and it wasn't long before she was wiping tears off her cheeks. I didn't comment on it, but I was pretty sure I knew why she was starting to get so emotional. Being here kind of did that to me too.

Some time ago, I'd turned the room into a shrine of my family. I'd ransacked the house for every photo Mom had of Anna and the girls. She had quite a few, and now every wall was covered in four-by-six glossies of the moments in time Mom had captured. There were some of Anna and me before the kids, when we'd visited my parents while I'd been in L.A. recording the band's very first album. That was the first time Anna and my parents had officially met, although they had already known about her, since I had talked about her all the damn time. Anna had been pregnant with Gibson in those photos, and there was such an aura of contentment around her that she almost glowed in every shot. Damn. My wife was so fucking beautiful.

There were pictures from the party my parents had had for us after we'd eloped. Gibson was a tiny little thing in those shots. Anna was in a fancy dress; she looked like a princess. A sultry, seductive, smoking-hot princess. There was one of Anna looking down at Gibson on her lap that choked me up every time I looked at it. I tried to avoid staring at that one for too long.

Pictures of the three of us from summer barbeques, both here and at my place in Seattle, dotted the wall, along with images from Christmas and Thanksgiving holidays, and the occasional birthday party. Then the visual timeline progressed to photos of Anna holding Gibson's hand while she was pregnant with Onnika. If she glowed while being pregnant with Gibson, then she radiated while being pregnant with Onnie. There were photos of right after Onnika was born, when Anna was happy on life and feeling no pain. Then there were pictures of the baptism, moments I hadn't really noticed while they were happening—Anna laughing with her sister, Dad twirling Gibson, and Mom cuddling Onnika. And then some breathtaking shots of the ceremony itself. I'd been so focused on other crap that I'd practically missed the entire thing. That was time I couldn't get back, memories I couldn't re-create. That fact really ticked me off. *How could I have been so stupid?*

Melancholy came over me as Kiera's wide eyes took in my room. Aside from the massive assortment of photos, I'd tacked up every memento and keepsake I could find—Gibson's favorite candy bar, a wrapper from a wine Anna loved, one of Onnika's rattles…one of Anna's bras. My room was one gigantic fucking scrapbook. I wasn't sure if that was sweet, psychotic, or pathetic. Maybe it was a mixture of all three.

Like she was seeing a different side of me, Kiera looked my way and consented to staying in my room. Clearing my throat, I shrugged, nodded, and acted like everything she'd just seen in my room was no big deal. It was weird, but after Kiera closed the door, I wanted to take my offer back. I wanted my bedroom back. I'd grown used to being surrounded by my wife and kids every night. They were my support system, even when they weren't anywhere near me, and even in this weird way, it was painful to be apart.

I grabbed a blanket and made my bed on the couch. Sleep was

impossible. Too much crap was running around my head. Giving up on the rest I wasn't getting, I found some paper in my mom's desk and then lay back down.

The first words were easy. *Dear Anna…* The rest of the words were exceedingly hard. I'd never laid out my heart before, not even when I'd finally admitted to Anna that I loved her. Anna and I tended to gloss over sappy shit like that. But I couldn't avoid it anymore. In her absence, all of my emotions were backing up, and the dam was going to burst soon. It was going to burst *now*.

Let me start off by telling you what I should have told you months ago. What I should have told you every morning when we woke up, and every night before we went to bed—I love you. I love you so fucking much…

The tears were streaming long before I finished the damn thing.

The next morning, I woke up extra early so I could give Kiera a ride to the airport. She was taking the earliest flight so she could get back to Ryder as soon as possible. She said she'd just take a cab, since I couldn't drop her off and get to work on time, but that didn't sit right with me. I felt like it was my duty to drive her back, to make sure she was safe and sound, since she'd gone above and beyond to check up on me.

Since I already woke up at the crack of dawn for work, waking up even earlier made me feel like I'd rewound time and it was still last night. Kiera was struggling with the early hour too, but she was more alert after I poured her some coffee. Decaf, since she was preggers. "I'm surprised you can function this early in the morning," she mused.

With a smile, I told her, "I'm kind of used to it now…not that it doesn't suck donkey balls, 'cause it definitely does."

Kiera laughed, then yawned. "Yeah, it does."

Feeling closer to her than I possibly ever had before, I again thanked her for coming out to see me. "It means a lot that you took the time to…check on me. Thank you for that."

Smiling, she told me, "You'd do the same for Kellan." Her grin turned to a frown. "I think."

Even though her words had a note of truth to them—I could be pretty self-absorbed at times—her expression made me laugh. Pursing her lips, Kiera quietly asked, "So…are you…? Are you going to show up at the auditions?"

As I stared at her, I thought about that. Was I? "I don't know. I just…don't know."

Kiera nodded, but she looked sad. "Are you going to come back to Seattle at least? Work things out with Anna?"

I sighed. "I wish I could, but I'm up to my eyeballs here. I *need* this job." She had no idea just how true that was. Like it or not, I was stuck.

Kiera opened her mouth, and I could tell she was thinking—*your old job paid better*—but then she closed her mouth and left the words unspoken. I wondered if she'd considered what I'd already considered. Showing up at the auditions didn't mean I'd get to be a D-Bag again. It didn't guarantee me anything. And besides, that was a couple of weeks away, and I had bills to pay. I couldn't go anywhere.

We drove to the airport in comfortable silence. When we got there, Kiera thanked me as she opened her door to get out. I stopped her when she was half in, half out of the car. "Wait…" Reaching into my jacket, I pulled out the note I'd written last night. Thinking I should tear it into a thousand tiny pieces, I handed it to her. "Will you give this to Anna for me? Please?"

I could see the curiosity in Kiera's eyes, but the letter was sealed inside an envelope. She wouldn't be able to read it until Anna did. Fuck. Did I want Anna to read it? Kiera nodded and took the letter from me, and that was when I realized that I did want Anna to read it. Sure, it was lame, sappy, and something that would typically make me gag…but I wanted Anna to know how I felt. How I *really* felt.

When Kiera closed the door with a small wave, my body was lighter, my head clearer. Maybe a letter wasn't enough, but I finally felt like I was doing something productive, something positive, and something…unselfish.

I watched Kiera until she safely disappeared inside the airport, then I took off so I could get to work on time. Or almost on time.

My supervisor gave me a stern scolding about punctuality when I was late, telling me my time wasn't my own, and I was basically stealing from the company. He'd said he'd fire me if I made a habit of it. Sanctimonious asshole. But all I could think of while he was yelling at me was Kiera's news about the audition. I didn't know what to do.

As much as I would love to take the time off work to try out for a gig I'd already had once, I knew in my heart I couldn't. I couldn't take yet another financial risk that might cost me everything, and I wasn't lying when I told Kiera I needed this job. If I lost it and the contest didn't pan out like I hoped—a distinct possibility given the outcome was determined by viewers—then I would be completely screwed; there would be no hope left for me. As much as I wanted to, I couldn't risk leaving this job to audition for the band.

Realizing that made me moodier than usual during my shift. God, my life sucked. I could barely remember back to when I'd thought I couldn't lose, and I'd gambled with everything in my possession, even my marriage. And now I was being offered another chance, a real one this time, and I couldn't afford to take it. I was damn near catatonic with depression when I shuffled off to lunch.

I studied my coworkers while I scraped the bottom of my pudding cup. Watching and listening to them was like being given a glimpse into my future, and from all I could tell, it wasn't going to be good. Most of the guys here were struggling to make ends meet. A lot of them were drinking away their problems every night and on their second or third marriage. I loathed the idea of *that* being my future.

But could I take another risk? Assuming the guys invited me on the show…and that was a big assumption since most of them didn't like me at the moment…the winner was voted on by the fans. They *did* hate me. They hated the way I left, they hated what I did to the guys, and…I didn't blame them. I was a selfish asshole who hadn't appreciated a single fucking thing I'd had. I didn't deserve to be in the band again. I didn't deserve to be with Anna again. I wasn't good enough for anything I'd once had...

Kiera's words wouldn't leave me alone though. *They're miserable without you... They do care...*

Pushing away the rest of the lunch I couldn't eat, I closed my eyes and tried to think what Anna would want me to do. Where would I end up if I stayed at this job? I instantly knew the answer to that. I'd wind up with the same miseries I saw around me on a daily basis. I'd lose Anna, I'd lose the girls... I'd lose my family, and probably my mind.

Mentally, I shifted my focus to the other path in this crossroads before me. Where would I end up if I auditioned? Like I was waking from being numb, just the thought made tiny pinpricks of hope start to tingle my nerves. I could end up a D-Bag again, if fate was with me. But what if it wasn't? What if I quit my job and lost the contest? How would I pay off my debts and support my girls? Then again, without Anna and the girls with me... what was the point of any of this? I'd rather scrape by with pennies in my pockets, or even beg for cash on the street corner, than spend the rest of my life without them. If I lost, I could start over. Somehow. But if by some miracle I won...

Opening my eyes, I suddenly knew exactly what I had to do. My future was with Anna, and with the D-Bags, with my *family*...if they'd have me.

Feeling the burn of hope in my chest starting to expand outward, I smiled. It was painful, but I welcomed the ache. *Okay, Kiera. I'll go to the audition.*

Trying to be smart for once, I didn't completely quit my job. Instead, I put in a conditional notice. If I made it through the auditions and onto the show, then my job would be lost, but if I didn't make it that far, I would have something to fall back on. It made me a little proud of myself that I'd thought out a plan before rashly jumping off the cliff. *See, Anna, I'm learning.*

I was still scared though. If I made it on the show and lost, I'd have to completely start over. My job gave new meaning to the word "suck," but it paid well, and I knew I'd never make that kind of money right off the bat again. I'd have to work three times as hard just to barely scrape by. But no, I couldn't think that way. I needed to be positive...like I used to be. I could own this contest. I mean, it was *my* position I was fighting for; I'd been preparing for this my entire adult life.

When I got home that night, there was an unusual spring in my step. I now saw a small light at the end of my very dark tunnel. It was just a pinpoint at the moment, but it was there, and I was going to hold on to it for as long as I could.

Mom noticed it instantly, and Dad seemed to spot it as soon as Mom pointed it out. "You're more chipper than usual. Something up? Did you talk to Anna?"

My enthusiasm died a little as Mom mentioned my wife's name. Had Kiera given her the note? Would she read it? Or would she just throw it away, throw us away? Would she be moved if she did read it, or was she already set on us going our separate ways? I wouldn't know until I talked to her, and maybe it was chickenshit of me, but I didn't want to talk to her just yet. I wanted to cling to this tiny thread of possibility that I'd been given.

"No...I quit my job."

Dad dropped the newspaper he'd been reading. Mom dropped her cigarette. Almost. She caught it at the last minute and stuck it back in her mouth. She sadly shook her head while Dad sighed. "Griffin, I had to pull a lot of strings to get you that job. Your resume isn't really...well, it's not the best for that industry."

I nodded. "I know, but it isn't what I want."

Both parents seemed confused. Sitting down at the kitchen table, I explained. "The D-Bags are having auditions to replace me."

Dad put a hand on my shoulder and patted me a couple of times. "Sorry to hear that, son."

I brushed off his concern. "No, they're having open auditions... so I'm going to audition."

Mom still looked confused. "You're going to audition for your band...to be *your* replacement?"

My smile was wider than it had been in a really long time. I felt like flakes of rust were cracking off me and drifting to the floor, exposing a shiny surface underneath. "Yes. I'm going to audition for my old spot and work my ass off until I have it." I hoped.

Mom gave me a half smile, like she supported me, even though she didn't fully understand the situation. Dad frowned. "Okay... well, why did you have to quit? Couldn't you do both? Didn't you like it there?"

I could tell from the look on his face that he was hoping I'd stay at his old job. Maybe he wanted just one son to follow in his footsteps, and he'd been hoping that would be me. I felt bad for crushing that desire, but this was my dream, and I had to go for it.

"No, I can't, Dad. The D-Bags are a full-time commitment, and they're what I want. Everything I'd once had...is everything I want." Why couldn't I have realized that sooner? Before I'd lost it all. Because I hadn't seen what I'd had until I lost it all. *The steak in the water had looked so much bigger than the one in my mouth, but it hadn't been real.*

God, I hoped Kiera gave Anna that letter...

"What's going on?"

I turned around to see Liam entering the kitchen. He dropped by a lot for dinner. Dad said it was because he hated cooking, but I think he just didn't like to eat alone. Liam didn't have the widest circle of friends.

Dad sighed as he indicated me. "Your brother quit the job I worked so hard to get him."

Liam didn't seem surprised to hear that. I gave Dad a withering look, before facing my brother again. "I'm auditioning for the D-Bags contest to replace me. If I get on the show, *then* I'll quit my job." I gave my dad a so-there smile.

Liam got really quiet, then he muttered, "Oh..."

His voice was so odd, I turned back to look at him. He had an expression that was both miffed and horrified. "What?" I cautiously asked.

Liam looked at my parents before looking back at me. "Well... it's an open audition, and I've been looking for some exposure, so I thought it would be a good idea..."

"A good idea to do what?" I asked, my voice firm.

Liam raised his chin. "I'm auditioning too."

My first instinct was outrage. This was *my* audition, *my* job, but then I remembered...it wasn't. I'd given it up, and now it was open for anyone to pursue. I stood from the table and Liam backed up a step, like he was sure I would deck him. I didn't though. I was trying to be a better, more mature person. I was trying to grow up. And a part of doing that was learning to be gracious and supportive. I wanted the best for Liam, I really did.

Holding out my hand, I told him, "I hope you get on the show."

Liam seemed shocked by my admission, but I meant it. Even if he didn't win the contest, the show would rev up his career in a way that nothing else would, and I wanted that for him. Finally seeing that I was serious, he clasped my hand. "Thank you," he told me.

Nothing but sincerity was in his voice, and I smiled at hearing it. "You're welcome."

The next two weeks flew by. I barely had time to think, there was so much to do. Practicing was at the top of my list. If I wasn't at work, I was in my parents' garage, busting out beats on either a bass guitar or a lead. I'd had to rent them, since I'd sold mine in "the purge." Well, technically Liam was the one renting them, since I didn't have the money. Liam practiced on one while I practiced on the other, then we'd swap.

Liam had played a bit as a kid, but he hadn't touched an instrument in recent years; he was even rustier than I was. I helped him get caught up, giving him refreshers on chords and notes, and teaching him every single one of the D-Bags' songs. The ones I could remember, at any rate. More than a few had slipped from my memory, a by-product of barely paying attention for years. God, I was a lazy jackass sometimes.

Mom was ear-to-ear smiles whenever she watched us rehearsing. She loved seeing her kids getting along. Chelsey and her girls watched us sometimes too, and sometimes the kids would bang on pots and pans and sing whatever lyrics came to mind. That was sort of annoying, but I ignored it and focused on the music. If I could keep my concentration during their ruckus, then I could keep it through anything.

Before I knew it, auditions were upon me. When we arrived at the crack of dawn, there was already a line around the block. People must have camped out for this. My heart was thudding in my chest as I took my spot at the end of the line. From behind me, I heard Liam say, "I'm gonna be sick, and we're not even inside yet."

Turning around, I put a steadying hand on his shoulder. "You're gonna be great. You had inside help on learning all the songs. That gives you a huge advantage over everyone else here."

Liam swallowed, then smiled. "Everyone but you."

I wished I could believe that, but I had too much baggage in my way. For me, my experience was a handicap. "I may know the songs, but I don't think it will help me. I need all three guys to say yes to the next round...and as far as I know, hell hasn't frozen over yet."

Pissiness started seeping into me, but I pushed it back. The only way this was going to work was if I tore down my pride. And begged. I figured I had lots of that in front of me. But that was okay. Whatever I had to do to get my life back.

It took forever for the line to move. Liam and I entertained ourselves by chatting with the other contestants. There were a surprising number of girls in the line. I figured they just wanted a glimpse of Kellan, but...maybe not. All the ones I talked to knew their shit. In fact, most of them knew more technical crap about music than I did. I could have used their expertise when I'd been putting together that godforsaken album.

Liam had helped disguise me, so no one around knew who they were actually talking to. My brother seemed to think I'd be best un-recognized as a ginger. He said it was because I'd been blond when the band first got big, then brunette when I'd quit on live TV, so a redhead was my only remaining choice. Personally, I think he'd just wanted to torture me. He'd borrowed some supplies from a recent commercial he'd filmed—a red wig in a cut so short, I had to crop my hair again...and just when it had been almost to my chin too; a red fake goatee; green contacts; and red paint for fucking freckles. I had been afraid I was going to end up looking like Raggedy Andy, but Liam knew what he was doing, and when he was finished, I looked like a completely natural redhead.

There was excitement in the line as it inched closer and closer to the front doors. People had come from all over for this, and some of them had waded through a lot of crap to get here. Hearing their stories only added to my regret. I'd been handed fame on a platter and hadn't appreciated it until it was too late. Story of my life.

As I trudged along that sea of hope and possibility, it became increasingly clear to me that Matt had been right all along. I *had* ridden the guys' coattails, and *I* was the one who owed them, not the other way around. They'd all put so much effort into making the band what it was, and me? I'd enjoyed the spoils, but I hadn't really contributed to earning them. Well, if I won this, that would all change.

Not wanting any distractions, I'd left my cell phone at my parents' place. I was regretting that now, as thoughts of Anna clouded my mind. I wished she was here, cheering for me, supporting and encouraging me, even if it was over the phone. She hadn't called yet, and I hadn't had the guts, or time, to call her either, so I had no idea if Kiera had given her my note or not. If she had, Anna's silence didn't bode well for our future. Like the D-Bags, that was completely up in the air. To be determined. God, I hated those words.

When Liam and I finally got inside, we were herded to one of many registration tables. As I watched people filling out paperwork, Liam asked me, "Are you going to stay in disguise or let them know it's you?"

I watched as people handed over their IDs to the people behind the table, and sighed. "I didn't bring a fake ID along with me, so it looks like I'll be telling the truth."

Liam gave me a squeeze on the shoulder, then sighed. "Hey, before we do this, I just wanted to let you know…I'm sorry for all the jerk comments. I was just…really jealous about everything you had, but it was stupid and petty, and I'm sorry." Dropping his hand off my shoulder, he studied the floor. "It's just hard to see some-one you know have everything you've ever wanted, especially when they don't seem to appreciate it." He met my eye again. "But I do care about you, and it was wrong of me to feel that way. Basically, I suck, and I know it, and I'm sorry."

His apology hit close to home, and I smiled. "I know you suck...but thank you. I think I did something similar with the guys...so I get it. We both suck...must be genetic."

Laughing, Liam clapped me on the back. "Definitely."

Chapter 24

Hope

Liam and I were called up to different stations at the same time, but I gave him a good luck clap before we parted ways, not that this part was hard or anything. It was just paperwork. The lady at the table had a number waiting for me when I stepped up to her. I smiled at seeing it—6969—my favorite number.

"Name?" she asked, her fingers hovering over her laptop, ready to record the information.

Clearing my throat, I stated, "Griffin Hancock."

She started to type, then stopped and looked up at me. "Are you messing with me?" she asked, scrutinizing me. Since Liam had done such a good job on my disguise, she was having a hard time seeing the former rock star in the person standing before her.

I sighed, then shook my head. Leaning down, I told her, "I'm Griffin Hancock, former D-Bag. I don't want people to recognize me, that's why I look like this. I just want to try out, like everybody else."

Her eyes were wide, but instead of outright believing me, she asked, "May I see your ID please?"

After I handed it to her, she gasped. "Oh my God, it is you. You realize this is a contest to replace you, don't you?"

"Yeah, I know. Can I fill out the forms?"

"Oh, yes, yes…" She handed them my way. Once I began working on them, she asked, "Can we get a testimonial? Before your audition." When I looked up at her, she said, "Just a little something we can use for the broadcast, to help the audience get to know you. Not that they don't already know you." She could barely contain her enthusiasm. She was either one of my elusive fans or, more likely, she recognized television gold when she saw it.

"Sure. Why not." The more the audience knew me and knew my side of the drama, the better my chances were.

The girl looked over my shoulder and snapped her fingers. When she had someone's attention, she pointed at me and mouthed the words *He's next*. After I handed her my completed paperwork, she handed me my number and gestured to a waiting area. "You'll be called when it's time for your group to enter the auditorium. Until then, wait over there for your testimonial." With a beaming smile, she stuck her hand out. "I'm not supposed to say this, but good luck!"

I clasped her hand with both of mine. "Thanks." I was going to need it.

When the camera was finally thrust in my face, the host of the show said, "So what is your story? How is it that you came to be here today?"

Inhaling a deep breath, I told him, "My name is Griffin Hancock, and I'm here to get my job back."

Frowning, the host looked over at the cameraman. "Cut," he said, making a kill motion with his hand. The red light instantly died on the camera. The host turned back to me, irritated. "Look, this is a serious part of the show, to let the audience get to know your personality. So, just tell the truth okay? What's your name?"

Leaning forward, I said, "Griffin...Hancock. I'm the former bassist of the D-Bags, and I'm here to get my job back."

The host sighed, then spoke into something at his wrist. "Sally, contestant 6969...who is this guy?"

I could see his eyes widening as he listened to her response. "Holy shit..." he muttered, then snapping his fingers at the cameraman, he barked, "Start filming. Now!" When he spoke to me again, his tone of voice was completely different. "Griffin, this is such a surprise. Do the guys know you're auditioning, and why are you wearing a disguise?"

Shrugging, I shook my head. "No, they have no idea I'm here. No one knows I'm here, and for now, I want to keep it that way. I just..." I looked down at my hands, not able to face him anymore. "I've made a lot of boneheaded mistakes lately, but leaving the band was the biggest. I just want to show the guys that I'm serious now." I looked up at him, determination in my voice and my face. "I want this, and I'll do whatever it takes to win my spot back."

"Excellent. Inspiring words for an inspiring moment. We're all rooting for you, Griffin." The host started to motion to the camera guy again, but I interrupted.

"Wait. I want to say one last thing." The host leaned in, instantly intrigued again. Staring directly at the camera, I said, "If my wife is watching, I just want to let her know...Anna, you mean the world to me...and I'm sorry I..."

I couldn't say anymore 'cause my damn throat closed up. I gave the host an *I'm done* signal, and he signed off with flowery words about love and heartache. When the camera died again, he extended his hand and wished me luck, just like the other girl had. I soaked it up like a sponge.

About an hour later, our group was led into the auditorium. The entire room smelled like nerves, and everyone around me was sweating. Even though I knew what I was doing, even though the guys on the judging panel were my best friends, and even though I loved being the center of attention, I felt like I was going to throw up.

Liam and I grabbed some seats in the back of the room so I could observe without being observed. Kellan, Matt, and Evan were set up at a table in front of a stage. They were listening to a guy jamming on a guitar that was provided for the auditioners. They had about ten different types to choose from, along with drums, keyboards, and various other musical equipment. The point of the audition was to showcase a person's best talent, and the guys understood that that might not necessarily be bass guitar.

Matt was bobbing his head to the beat while the guy onstage

shredded it. Evan was casting glances at Kellan and Matt, but by the grin on his face, I could tell Evan liked this guy. I could see why too; he sounded amazing. Fuck. I suddenly felt very inadequate surrounded by so much raw talent. But I was good too, and I knew what I was doing. That had to count for something. Kellan was the only one who seemed unimpressed. Well, maybe he was impressed, he just wasn't showing it. Whenever I got a peek at his face, his expression was completely blank.

When the guy was done, all three guys accepted him into the next round. I hoped it went as smoothly for me. And Liam. As he sat there beside me, sweating and rocking in his chair like he had a mental condition, I could see how badly he wanted this.

Just as I was about to wish him good luck, a group of people in front of us caught my attention. I elbowed Liam. "Look who's here," I said with a smirk.

Liam looked over to where I was pointing, and spotted them instantly. Our entire fucking family was here. Chelsey was giggling as she pointed out Kellan to Mom. Dustin seemed transfixed by the entire production. Surprisingly, it was Dad who turned and spotted Liam and me in the back. He waved, then gave us each a thumbs-up. I didn't know what to do, say, or think. My parents had always been supportive, yes, but it had typically been a backseat kind of support. I don't think they'd ever even seen a D-Bags show. It kind of choked me up that they were here, which was sort of irritating. I was quickly becoming as much of a girlish wuss as Kellan. God-dammit.

When my number was called, I went down to the waiting area. I was next. My nerves spiked as I watched the person before me. He looked awkward onstage, like he was about to shit his pants or puke in the bucket just off camera. I sympathized; I sort of felt the same way. After his lackluster performance, all three judges said no. It felt like bad luck to have a bad review right before I went on. The announcer called my name—my nickname, since they allowed contestants to use them.

"Next up…G-Dog."

There were a few chuckles in the crowd, and a lot of screams.

My family was in on the disguise, and they weren't the subtle type. I raised a hand in acknowledgment, then made my way to one of the guitars on the stage. I kept my head down, and my ball cap low. I wanted the guys to hear my music first, before they realized who I was. I couldn't play that way though. I needed to engage the crowd. Showmanship was just as important as ability; I'd been drilling that into Liam all week long. Playing well was only half the battle. But once I started up with my usual antics, the deception would be over—the guys would recognize me instantly. Nothing to be done about that though.

I'd chosen a D-Bags song, since I knew them better than anything else out there. I picked an old one though, one that had never been officially released. I figured I'd stand out from the crowd better that way, since *everyone* was playing D-Bags songs.

Since this was a music competition, there were no accompanying background rhythms. No drums, no vocals, no nothing. It was just me, and whatever noises came out of my guitar. That was nerve-wracking. It was pretty much the solo from hell.

I chose a lead guitar so the rhythm would shine through. And unlike that dreaded time when I'd fucked up a perfectly good D-Bags song during rehearsal for my parents, I was going to nail it. I silently counted out the rhythm, then started in. The intro was quieter than the chorus, and I kept my head down while I played, stretching out my anonymity for as long as I could. Once I got to the chorus though, I let it rip.

Dropping all of my doubts and fears, I imagined that I was back at a D-Bags concert, rocking out with fifty thousand of my closest friends. The music electrified me as I made eye contact with the crowd. I started singing along to the song I was playing, and making playful faces at the people. They were clapping along, dancing in the seats, and cheering my name. Well, my nickname, at any rate. For a few glorious minutes, I completely forgot that I was fighting for my life; I just had fun. Man...I'd missed this. But then I noticed the judges, and I was suddenly yanked back to reality so quickly, I swore I had whiplash.

I knew in five seconds flat that the guys had recognized me.

Matt was scowling. Evan looked shocked, and Kellan...he was finally smiling. Matt raised his hand to stop me. I played four more
bars before I consented and stopped my fingers; they vibrated
along with the last chord, and the listening crowd cheered and
clapped. I'd rocked the shit out of my audition.

By the look on Matt's face though, you wouldn't think that was
true. "What the hell are you doing here, Griffin?"

I heard murmuring in the crowd as people tried to figure out
what was going on. Knowing the jig was up, I removed my hat,
my wig, and the expertly glued-in-place goatee; that one stung
like a mofo to remove. Without my getup, people started recognizing me, and I heard gasps, then screaming. But mixed in
with the screaming, there was an awful lot of booing. I was not
universally loved.

Matt turned around in his seat to silence the crowd. When he
got them under control, he swiveled back to me. His face was firm;
he wanted an explanation for this. For a lot of things, probably.
"I'm auditioning," I told him. "Just like everybody else."

His eyebrows scrunched together and he shared a look with
Evan and Kellan. "You're auditioning...for your old spot?"

Why did everyone keep asking me to reaffirm that? I was well
aware that it was kind of ironic, but it was the only way I could get
back in. "Yes," I said, as seamlessly as possible.

Evan leaned forward then. "You know that the winner is going
to be determined by the fans, right? We don't have a say."

I nodded. "I know. But the three of you determine who gets
on the show...and all I'm asking for is a chance. Put me through
my paces, like anybody else. Let me prove to you, to everyone,
that I'm good enough to be a part of this band. Let me earn my
right to play with you again...because I don't think I earned it
the first time around, and I definitely didn't appreciate it. I do
now though, and I want this. I want to play with you guys again.
I want to be a D-Bag."

The auditorium was so silent, I could hear myself breathing; it
was much heavier than it usually was. I felt like I'd just run a fifty-
meter dash, and I was waiting on the judge to tell me if I'd won or

not. By the impassive looks around me, I couldn't tell. It could still go either way.

Kellan was the first one to break the silence. "I'm a yes. He should move on."

The crowd cheered in agreement as Kellan's eyes moved over to Matt and Evan. *One down.* Matt's lips were pressed into a firm line. Of all the guys, I'd hurt him the most when I'd left, both physically and emotionally. I'd taken a gigantic dump on our familial bond; he wasn't going to forgive me anytime soon.

With Matt not speaking yet, Evan piped in. "I'm a yes too," he said with a nod toward me. *Two down.* The crowd screamed again, and then all eyes shifted to the last judge. Getting in had to be a unanimous decision, and I silently begged Matt to give me a chance. I even hung my head while I waited. *You have all the power here. I know that, and I accept it. Just don't say no... I've got nothing left.*

Like he could hear me, Matt simply said, "Yes." When the shrieking from the other contestants died down, he added, "You're in, Griffin... but just so you know, it's not going to be easy."

Feeling like my face was going to split apart from smiling so hard, I nodded. "I don't want it to be easy." I wanted to prove to them, to the world... and to myself... that I belonged here.

Liam went on after me. I was nervous as hell watching him with my family; it was even worse than when I'd been up there. People in the stands were watching me more than Liam. I ignored them and focused all my attention on him. Hopefully if I didn't engage them they'd watch him too. And he deserved to have their attention. He was killing it!

When his song was over, I shot to my feet, whistling and shouting at the top of my lungs. All three judges approved Liam going to the next level, and I almost fell into the people in front of me I was jumping around so much. Matt walked onto the stage to give his cousin a quick hug of congratulations, and the crowd cheered at the display. Liam looked like he was going to cry. Fucking pansy. I couldn't have been happier for him.

When he joined us in the audience, I picked him up in a bear hug. And even though he was my oldest sibling, I gave him a noogie like he was my kid brother. After everyone in our group had auditioned, our lot was escorted out so the next set could come in. Mom and Dad wanted to take Liam and me out to celebrate, but there was something I needed to do first. Well, there were several things I needed to do, but there was one thing in particular that couldn't wait.

"You guys go ahead. I need to talk to the band."

Liam looked around the lobby flooded with people who'd just finished auditioning or were waiting for their turn. Now that I wasn't wearing my disguise, people were starting to notice me. I was getting stares, whispers, and curious expressions. *Is that who we think it is?* "Even if you were a part of the band once, bro, they're not going to let you talk to them. You're just a schlub now, like us."

Shaking my head, I told him, "I have to try. I need to clear the air before the chaos starts."

Nodding, he patted my shoulder. "I hope they let you in then."

When it was clear there were no more groups left, I started to get nervous. What if the guys were whisked away by security, slipped out the back so nobody could bother them now that their job for the day was done. It was strange to not be a part of that. Looking at their fame from the other side made them seem larger than life, unapproachable. They weren't though. They were my friends. Or were, once upon a time.

Hoping they were still there, I snuck back into the auditorium. Luckily, they were. All three guys were clustered around the judging table, discussing the auditions. Matt was saying, "I knew we'd find talent in L.A." I hoped he meant me.

Just as I started to approach them, a hand clamped onto my shoulder. "Auditions are over, you need to leave now."

I looked up at the massive bulk blocking my path and was about to tell him who I was, when I realized he already knew. "Sam? Damn, it's good to see you." Giving him a slug in the shoulder, I wondered if he felt the same.

He cracked a small smile. "Griffin…it's been a while."

Taking that small gesture as a positive, I started moving around him. "I need to talk to the guys before they leave."

He moved to block my path. "Auditions are over. The band isn't seeing anyone right now."

My expression was incredulous. "Dude...it's me."

Sam shrugged. "I have my orders. No one is to bother the band once auditions are over, and I hate to have to tell you this, Griff, 'cause I do like you, but...you're not part of the band anymore. I'm sorry, but you need to leave."

He started pushing me back toward the doors. *Unbelievable.* I'd known this guy since he was a glorified bouncer at Pete's. But I guess I couldn't fault him for wanting to keep his job. Maybe if I'd been equally diligent, I'd still have mine. I wasn't about to give up that easily though. "Kellan!" I shouted.

Kellan turned my way after hearing my voice. A wide smile stretched across his lips as he waved me over. "Let him through, Sam. It's okay."

I adjusted my clothes once Sam moved aside to let me pass. "See," I told him. He merely shrugged, and I knew he'd do it again if he thought it was what the guys wanted.

As I trudged past him, I noticed Matt slap Kellan's shoulder in a gesture of *Why did you invite him down here?* Kellan ignored him and kept his eyes on me. When I was close enough, he lifted his hand in greeting. "Griff, it's good to see you. I'm glad you came down." By the twist of his lips, I knew what he really meant was, *I'm glad you listened to my wife.*

Slightly uncomfortable now that I was directly in front of them, I scratched my head. "Yeah...well...I couldn't let this opportunity go by without trying, you know?"

Matt's face darkened. "Opportunity? Do you have any idea how shitty the last year has been? Do you even care?"

Swallowing, I debated how honest I should be. Then I realized the only thing I had left was honesty. "No, I really didn't know how hard it had been on you guys...and no, I really didn't care. All I cared about was getting what I thought I deserved...and I ended up pushing everyone who meant a damn away from me. I was a selfish, self-centered, self-absorbed, diva, asshole, creep, moron… and I'm so sorry."

The guys were all staring at me in shock. I usually never admitted when I was being an idiot. Typically, I wrapped my *I'm awesome* mantra around me like armor. And I knew why…admitting I was flawed fucking sucked. I'd rather be doing just about anything other than telling the guys what I was telling them, but that would only get me stuck in the same dark pit I'd been stuck in for the last few weeks. No, I'd be stuck in an even worse pit, since I'd just kissed my job goodbye by moving forward in the competition. I had nothing to fall back on.

Matt regained his composure before the other two. "Do you think you'll go farther if you butter us up?" he asked, his expression suspicious.

Shaking my head, I told him, "No. I don't expect anything from any of you, I just…I fucked up, and I wanted to apologize for it…even if it is too late to change anything."

I turned, prepared to walk away, but Kellan put a hand on my shoulder. "I accept your apology," he stated. "Good luck in the show."

"Thanks," I said, then I gave him a brief one-armed hug. I'd known that Kellan was the least angry of the three, but I felt a little better after hearing him accept me.

Evan sighed, then extended his hand. "What you did gave new meaning to the word 'jackass'…but I forgive you too. Good luck, man."

I shook his hand, feeling even better. Matt was glaring at me, so I figured I wouldn't get very far with him. I'd been expecting that though, so I just nodded, to let him know I understood why he couldn't say the words.

I was halfway up the aisle leading out of the auditorium when I heard him curse and say my name. "Wait."

Pausing, I watched in surprise as he jogged over to me. When he was in front of me, he shoved his hands in his front pockets and stared at me for a second. "Look, I can't forgive what you did like the others, but…I'm sorry for how I treated you."

My jaw dropped. The last thing I'd expected from him was an apology. He twisted his lips as he took in my expression. "I'll admit, I was a dick when you left. I was just…mad, and hurt. I felt betrayed. The way you left…you may not have needed us, but we needed you, Griffin. You screwed us, big-time, and you didn't even care. And that fucking hurt."

Nodding, I studied my feet. "I know, and I'm sorry." Looking back up, I told him, "I was wrong, about so many things. I do need you guys. Even if I'm not in the band anymore…I need you guys. You're my family…all of you."

Matt silently stared at me for a moment, then clapped my shoulder. "Good luck in the show, Griffin."

My smile was huge as I nodded. "Thanks." He started to turn away to rejoin the guys, and I grabbed his elbow. Matt bristled a little, and I released him. We were slowly mending things, but we weren't entirely on good terms yet. "Have you seen Anna? Is she…is she doing okay?"

Matt opened his mouth, then closed it and looked over at Kellan. With a frown, he returned his eyes to me. "You should call her," was all he said. I had no idea what that might mean, and a spike of fear went up my spine.

"Yeah, okay…thanks."

He clapped my shoulder, then trotted off. I left the theater in a daze, Matt's words ringing through my brain. *You should call her.* And once I got back to my shrine of a bedroom, that was exactly what I did.

Well, that was what I did after I stared at my phone for forty minutes while family members banged on my door wanting to congratulate me. The entire house was in party mode, with loud music, lots of chatter, and enough food to choke a horse. There was so much noise that even with my door closed, I could barely hear myself think. It wasn't exactly the ideal situation to try to reconnect with my wife, but if I waited for the perfect moment, it might not ever happen.

Knowing I just needed to be a man and do it, I dialed her number. Anna had been sporadic on answering her cell phone when I'd called her in the past, but this time, if she didn't, I would leave a message. From here on out, I would always leave a message. She was the girl of my dreams, and I wasn't going to give her up without a fight.

Surprising me, she picked up on the third ring. "Hello?" she sniffled, like she'd been crying. Fuck. Was that because of me?

"Hey...it's me...Griffin."

A small laugh escaped her. "I know it's you. I know your number."

Duh. Right. "I was just calling to see if you were okay. I saw Matt today and he said..." Not knowing where to go with that, my voice trailed off.

Anna was silent for a few seconds, then said, "You saw Matt? Where?"

Smiling, I told her everything about the auditions, from Kiera coming down to tell me about them, to the disguise Liam had cooked up, to how nervous I'd been. "I was sure the guys were gonna say no...but they moved me to the next round. I think I've got a good shot to get on the show...to get my job back."

She let out a small sigh. "That's great, Griffin. I'm really happy for you."

A distance seemed to stand between us as her end of the line went silent. "Anna...I can't do this without you. Even if you're in Seattle, and I'm down here, I need your help, your support. You're my best friend...I need you."

She sniffled again. "You're my best friend too, Griffin. I think that's what makes this so hard..."

I didn't want to know what she meant by "this." Separation...or divorce? Instead of asking her to clarify, I asked, "Did you get my letter?"

There was a long pause, then she quietly said, "Yes...You love me? Just straight-up love me?"

I smiled, remembering back to her complaining that I never told her those words. God, what a stubborn idiot I was. "Yes, I love you. I think I've always loved you, even when it freaked me out to love you."

She laughed. "Yeah." After another pause, she said, "Okay, Griffin. I'll be your support, I'll be your friend. But that doesn't mean we're suddenly fine. You hurt me. You... *betrayed* me. That's not something I can just get over. Understand?"

"Yeah...I understand." *You need time. I'll give you all the time you need, because all I really need is you.*

Chapter 25

A Chance

The next two weeks were brutal, and I called Anna so frequently, she started answering the phone with "Just breathe. You're doing great, you'll get through this. One step at a time." It helped, but only until the next panic attack set in. The show was culling the herd. Massive cuts were happening left and right as the hundreds from across the country who had been allowed to the final round in L.A. were whittled down to the twenty who would make it to the televised broadcast. Those lucky twenty were the ones the fans would vote on to be the next…well, me. And every day I wasn't sure if I was going to be moving forward or going home.

I'd never experienced anxiety at this level before, and I worried that I'd break under the strain. I think this process was a hundred times harder than the actual gig. That fact fortified me. If I could just make it through this, the next step would be easy. Or easier, at any rate. None of this was easy.

The stress was getting to Liam too, and every night when we met back up in our hotel room, he was a bundle of nerves. "They're gonna cut me, I just know it. I'm not good enough for this, they're gonna cut me."

I ended up using Anna's words on my brother each night. "Just breathe. You're doing great, you'll get through this. We both will." Like me, he was calmed by those words. For a time.

My brain was fried though, and my spirit was right behind it. On the evening before the final day and the final round of cuts, I felt like I was teetering on delirium. "I think I overestimated my abilities, Anna. I think I do that a lot..."

She let out a dismissive sound. "I wouldn't have married you if you overestimated your abilities. You're as good as you think you are, Griffin, you just have to believe it."

That made me smile, and for a second, I felt just as awesome as she said I was. But then I remembered the distance between us, and my self-assurance cracked again. "I know everything isn't cool between us, but I'm really glad we can talk like this. I think it's the most we've ever talked." Our relationship before hadn't been *only* physical, but that had been a pretty large chunk of it. Being apart right now but still connected like this was actually bringing us closer. In my mind anyway. I hoped she felt the same, and I told her as much. "Even though you're up there with the girls, I feel even more connected to you. You know?"

Anna laughed, and the sound relaxed me more than her words had. "Yeah, I know. I think the distance is actually helping us right now. And you're able to focus on you while I focus on me. I think it's a good thing."

"Yeah. I'm horny as hell though," I said, grabbing my junk and giving it a good squeeze.

A throaty sound escaped Anna. It instantly took me back to my happy place—buried deep inside her with her arms and legs wrapped around me. "Me too, babe...me too."

Needing to get my mind off how much I wanted to kiss her all over, how soft her skin was and how good she tasted, I said, "We only ever seem to talk about my shit. Tell me what you've been up to. I want to know every little detail."

"Really? You do?" She seemed genuinely surprised that I wanted to hear about her life. Was I that self-absorbed that it was shocking for me to care about anybody else? With a ripple of shame, I realized I was...I don't think I'd ever asked her about her day before.

Sitting back in my chair, I made myself comfortable. "Yes, I want to know everything about you. And then I want to hear everything about the girls. And if I interrupt to start talking about myself, I want you to tell me to shut the hell up so you can finish."

Anna was silent for a moment, then she said, "All right. Well, when I first got here, I lived with Kiera and Kellan, but, they live soooooooo far from town, I couldn't take it." Her assessment made me laugh; I often felt the same way about Kellan's house. With a giggle, she continued. "So I left their place and got an apartment for me and the girls near work…Oh, I got my old job back at Hooters. Actually, I got a better job. I'm the assistant manager."

Pride swelled in me. "That's amazing, babe. Tell me more."

And she did. For the rest of the night, she told me all about her life without me, but instead of it making me sad or mad, like I thought it might, I was thrilled. I felt like I knew my wife better, like I was getting a sneak peek into *her* hopes and dreams. Dreams she'd put on hold to be a mother and a rock star's wife. Hearing her talk just reminded me how much I loved her, and I ended the phone call with a sentiment I never would have used before.

"Have a good day tomorrow, Anna. And remember…I love you."

When she spoke, her voice trembled. "I love you too."

There was a pit of dread in my stomach when I woke up the next morning. Pushing it aside, I texted my wife. *Thank you for last night. It was amazing.* It was weird to be texting something like that when we hadn't done anything even remotely sexual, but it was true. We'd screwed each other in every conceivable way, but I'd never felt closer to her than listening to her talk last night. Her voice was still playing through my mind. And I knew that made me sound like a fucking whipped pansy, but I didn't care. I was in love with my best friend, and once this show was over with, win or lose, I was going up north to be with her. Nothing else mattered.

Anna texted me back while I was getting dressed. *Yes, it was! I saw your audition on TV last night. What you said, it was very touching.*

It made me smile that she'd seen my message to her. Of course,

I'd been too emotional to finish it on air, but I had a feeling that just made it even more powerful. *I'm glad you saw it. It was hard to say.*

I know, she texted back. *Good luck today. I love you.*

A weird feeling went through me, but I immediately shoved it back and texted, *I love you too.* It was still odd for me to say, but I knew Anna needed to hear it, and really, however I could make her happy right now was worth it.

Putting the phone in my pocket, I left my room and made my way downstairs to where the rest of the remaining contestants were gathering.

Everywhere I turned, I was given high fives, brief hugs, and well wishes. Even though we were all in a competition, we supported each other. We'd become a strange sort of family, bound together by one common goal—survive to the next round. Today was going to be brutal though, and as I hugged people back and offered my own words of encouragement, I knew almost everyone around me would be going home today. Hopefully, I wasn't one of them.

There was one final round of cuts this afternoon as the crowd was culled to less than half of what it was now, then the final twenty would be chosen tonight. To say I was nervous would be an understatement.

When Liam came down to join the group, he looked as anxious as I felt. After giving him a hug, I looked him in the eye. "You all right?"

Looking green, he said, "I just threw up on a plant in the hallway. And I don't think I'm done…" He put a hand on his stomach.

Laughing, I told him, "It's okay to be nervous, just don't let it lock you up. Be loose and easy up there, and you'll do fine."

A group nearby had heard me, and they came closer. "You know what they're looking for, since you were one of them for a long time…You got any tips for us?" Their spokesperson was a man named Cruz. He was doing really well from all I'd seen, shredding whatever piece of music they gave him.

"Just keep doing what you've been doing. You're killing it." I smacked his shoulder in encouragement, a little surprised at myself that I was honestly hoping for him. And Liam. If only we could all be D-Bags.

Thinking of something else, I added, "Maybe try engaging the crowd more? Yeah, it's important to get the music right, but being onstage is a performance, you have to invite the audience in, or they'll feel left out."

That was something I'd actually picked up from Kellan. I'd never seen anyone play with the crowd quite like him, and man, it worked. The energy of a D-Bags crowd was about five times as high as other bands I'd seen, and that wasn't just because of Kellan's face. It was because we all interacted with the fans. Well, except for Matt. Even now, he kept his head down and kept playing, but his talent made up for it. Yes, I could admit that now, my cousin was a genius on the guitar. He'd earned his spot, and now it was time to earn mine.

I let that thought repeat throughout my head the entire day, and by the end of it, I was shocked that I was still alive. I'd made it through the last round of cuts. Now I just needed to be included on the show.

As the last hundred contestants gathered in a room to be talked to one on one, Cruz and a couple of his buddies came up to me. Extending his hand, he said, "Thanks, man. I think your tip helped save me."

I shook my head. "Your talent saved you."

He beamed under my praise, then wiped his hands on his pants; they had been a little clammy, but I hadn't said anything. Mine were too. "I suppose you're not nervous at all, huh? Since your spot is all but guaranteed."

Falling into a chair beside Liam, who looked a little better than this morning, I let out a long sigh. "Honestly, I don't think they'll invite me on the show. The guys and I...we have baggage. All of you have a much better chance than I do." It hurt to admit that, but it was the truth. And from some of the harsh critiques the guys had given me the last couple of weeks, it was clear they weren't holding any punches.

Liam patted my knee. "Nah, I've been watching them with you.

Sure, you're not getting any special treatment, but you're not being singled out either. You're just another contestant to them, no better, no worse...so you have as much chance as any of us."

That thought actually perked me up some, and I wrapped my arm around Liam and rubbed my knuckles into his skull. If my odds were as good as everyone else's, I'd take it. "Thanks, little bro."

He shoved me back to get away. "I'm older than you, asswipe."

"Oh yeah," I said, laughing. "I keep forgetting."

As time ticked down, I got more and more anxious. If Liam was right about my chances, then maybe I could actually get on the show. But even still, only twenty of the one hundred people in here were moving on. That meant eighty of us were going home. I wasn't sure what percentage that was, but I knew it wasn't good. My only hope was that the guys thought I was worthy of a second chance.

I called my wife as the chopping block loomed larger and larger in front of me. I felt like I was going to one-up Liam and toss my cookies right there in my seat. My fingers were shaking as I brought the phone to my ear. I needed this so much.

"Hey, you. I was wondering if I was going to get a phone call today. How did you do?" Anna's voice was light and carefree, everything I wasn't feeling.

"I made it through the last cuts, but I'm sitting here in a room with a hundred people, and only twenty of us are moving on. I think I'm gonna be sick."

"Just breathe...you'll be fine."

I inhaled a deep breath, and it did calm me some, but not nearly enough. "I'm gonna need a little extra support today. Can you put Gibby on the line?" Hearing my little girl laugh lightened even my worst moods.

Anna paused. "I can't right now...but I can do something better."

Wondering if we were ready for phone sex, I crooked a smile. "Oh yeah...what?"

"Come to the door at the back of the room."

I looked back, puzzled. The room I was waiting in had two sets of doors. One led to another room, where the judges were waiting to give us our final evaluations, and the other set of doors led out, to the main area of the hotel. I stood and headed back to the doors that led out. Maybe Anna had delivered something to the hotel for me. Hopefully it was a sedative. Or alcohol. Maybe both.

There were camera crews recording our every movement inside the room. The host was also in there, interviewing contestants, getting their hopes and dreams on film, in case they were the lucky ones about to be chosen. A camera had been on me when I'd called my wife, and the guy running it was filming my every step. I was so used to having them around me now that it barely registered as he followed me to the door.

"You send me something?" I asked Anna.

"Kind of," she said with a giggle.

A couple of the staff looked at me as I opened the door, but nobody said anything. Until the final round actually started, we were free to leave. If we didn't make it back here in time though, we were automatically disqualified, which is why no one but me was leaving.

Opening the door, I looked out. I'd been expecting to see a delivery person with balloons or flowers or maybe even pizza, but what I found waiting out there was so much better.

Anna was standing in the hallway, holding our children and smiling at me like she'd been looking forward to this moment all her life.

My breath caught, my heart stopped, and my cell phone slipped out of my hand and crashed to the ground. *I must be dreaming, there's no way this vision before me is real.* But as Anna disconnected her phone and slipped it back into her purse, I knew I was awake, and she really was here with me. It took every ounce of willpower I had to not pull her into my arms, but I didn't know if I could, and not knowing if I could touch Anna was a foreign, unsettling feeling. I just wanted my wife back.

Anna was holding Onnika on her hip, while Gibson stood at her side. Gibson picked up my phone, then tackle-hugged my legs. "Daddy!"

My eyes were stinging as I dropped down to my knees to give my daughter a proper hug. Her familiar smell filled me, an oddly appealing mix of watermelon shampoo and cinnamon graham crackers, and I suddenly felt completely at peace. *God, I have missed this.* As I rubbed her back, I looked up at Anna. A fat tear was dripping down her cheek as she watched us. "What are you doing here?" I finally asked her. "I thought we were going to reconnect from a distance?"

Wiping her tear away, she gave me a breathtaking smile. "We are...but they're not. Your children need you, and you need them."

She bounced Onnika on her hip, making her grin. She was gnawing on a rubber ring, and drool was all down her chin and her shirt, and it was the cutest thing I'd ever seen. As I stood to take Onnika from her, Anna told me, "We'll stay at a different hotel, but the kids want to cheer for you in the audience. *I* want to cheer for you in the audience," she added in a whisper.

Standing close to Anna as I wrapped my arms around Onnika, I shook my head. "I might not make it that far."

Anna's eyes were a deep, calm green as she stared at me. Her lips were so full and luscious, it was physically difficult to not lean down and suck on one. "You will, Griffin. I know you will."

Onnika grabbed my shirt and I kissed her head as I squeezed her tight. She smelled so good, like her mom, but even sweeter. Gibson was still clinging to my leg, refusing to let go, while Anna stared up at me with unabashed longing in her eyes. I couldn't stand it anymore. I needed my family, I needed my wife.

Releasing one hand from Onnika, I wrapped it around Anna. "Come here," I murmured, pulling her into me. Our lips instinctively found each other's, and she breathed a sigh of relief as we connected. I knew this wouldn't fix everything, but I felt like it was a start, and as our mouths softly moved together, I felt the massive hole in my body, a hole that had been growing larger every day she'd been gone, slowly begin to fill.

When we broke apart, I cupped her cheek. "I love you, so much," I told her, surprised at how much easier it was to admit that. Anna's smile was glorious. It made me wish I'd been telling her how much I loved her from the beginning. "You're everything to me," I added, meaning every word. I felt like I'd learned that the hard way, and I also felt like that experience had made the words so much more powerful to me. I'd earned them.

"I love you too," she murmured, her eyes filling again. "Good luck in there. We'll be here when you get out." By the way she said it, I got the feeling she meant, *Regardless of the outcome, we'll be waiting for you.* I still wanted to win, to prove myself to the guys and the world, but if I lost...I'd be okay with it, because I'd still won *her.* And that was worth more than all the rock bands in the world.

When I walked back into the waiting room, I felt invincible. The best people in the world loved me for me, and were supporting me, no matter what. There was power in that knowledge, and I held my head high as I took my seat.

Liam wasn't feeling nearly as confident. Shaking in his chair, he looked over at me with wide eyes. "Dude, I thought you left. I totally thought you gave up and left."

For a second, I wondered if he'd been hoping I had. I pushed the feeling aside immediately after I had it though. Liam wouldn't think that. We were family, we had each other's backs. Feeling completely at ease, I clapped him on the shoulder. "Liam, do you know what you're missing? That final ingredient to being one of the world's biggest rock stars?"

Liam tilted his head as he considered. "A tattoo," he murmured, glancing at some of mine that were visible.

I shook my head. "No. Well...actually, yes, I can't believe you're still a virgin at your age...it's embarrassing, really." He frowned, and I quickly got my motivational speech back on track. "The only thing you're lacking is confidence. You need to realize that you've got talent, and that the world is your playground. You need to own this shit. You're about to be a fucking rock star, after all."

Liam gave me a slow smile, and I felt my own confidence bolstering. How had I forgotten how awesome I was? I was so worried about impressing the guys and getting my job back, but really it was always mine. I just needed to reach out and take it...which was exactly what I was going to do.

Liam nodded, like he was having the same thoughts. Then he frowned. "But what if I don't make the cut."

I smacked him across the back of the head. "Rock stars don't fucking worry about making the cut. Rock stars don't worry about anything. When you're onstage, you're a god and nothing can touch you. Understand me?"

I held his gaze until he nodded and gave me a smile worthy of the name Hancock. Oh yeah, we had this in the bag.

The killer smile on Liam's face faltered some when his name was called. Mine didn't though, I knew he would make it. I gave him a thumbs-up, then helped shove him out of his seat before his nerves made him permanently a part of the chair. He looked like he was about to throw up as he stepped through the doors. I wouldn't know his fate until after my turn. The group waiting wasn't allowed to know who had made the cut and who hadn't. The winners went somewhere else, the losers too. So, when I was the last man standing in the room, I was completely clueless as to whether or not the twenty yeses had already happened, and *my* confident smile faltered some.

As I bounced my knees and picked at a callus on my hand, I ignored my own advice and began to worry. What if the guys were still mad about how I'd left and they held me back out of spite? No, Matt had said they'd give me a fair shake. That meant no advantage over anyone else, but no disadvantage too. And I was good at my job. That much, I'd never doubted.

I shifted my thoughts to Anna and the girls—my rocks. I still couldn't believe they were here. It felt like a dream, knowing they were right in the next room. A part of me wanted to open the door and kiss Anna again, maybe sneak her inside so she could wait with me, but I didn't want to do anything that might disqualify me. I settled on texting her instead. I tried to think of something sweet and flowery, something Kellan would send Kiera. That shit didn't come easy to me though. Mainly, I thought that crap was ridiculous. But I knew Anna would like it, and I wanted to please her, so I did my best.

Hey, babe. Thank you for being here. Seeing you and the girls made my night. I feel like I can lose now, and I'll still win. I was proud of myself when I hit send. *See, I can do sappy,* I thought.

Apparently, Anna could too. Her response was, *You're a star. Always have been, always will be.*

Not able to help myself, I typed back, *Your tits look amazing in that top.*

Proving that she was the exact right woman for me, she texted back, *You should see what they look like without it.*

Jesus. I started getting hard just thinking about it. I hadn't had an orgasm in so long, I almost forgot what they felt like. Hopefully that was something I could rectify soon. But first…

"Griffin Hancock?" I looked over to see a PA standing in the doorway that led to the judges' room. "They're ready for you."

My palms instantly got so clammy, it was like I'd stepped into a sauna. The rest of my body was sticky and sweaty too, and I had an almost uncontrollable urge to hop in a shower before I walked through those doors. There was no time though. This was my now-or-never moment.

My heart was pounding in my ears as I stood up, and all of my words of wisdom to Liam failed me. *What if they say no?* was vibrating through my brain. *What if I don't even make the show?* A voice buried deep inside was screaming at me to listen to it, but my doubts were roaring so loud, the shrill words were hard to hear. It took a lot of self-control, but I silenced the fear so I could listen to the spark of hope trying to break out. And when the rumble of discontent was quieted to a gurgle, I finally heard it.

You are a fucking rock star. Own this shit.

Following the PA, I burst through the double doors like I was greeting the adoring fans back at Pete's. *I am the walrus.*

The hallway to the judges' room was dramatically lit up with giant spotlights shining down on the floor, and a camera guy on the far end was filming every step of my walk toward victory. Keeping my chin up, I ignored the man who was hoping to see me crack. I wasn't going to crack.

The door to the judges' room was opened for me, and I strolled right to the table. When I got in front of Matt, Evan, and Kellan,

I stood with my feet slightly apart and my hands clasped behind my back—a position of confidence, but also a position of respect. I wanted them to see I'd changed.

Kellan was smiling at me. Evan too. Matt's face was blank, and for some reason, it really bothered me to see him that way. I was tired of this ongoing feud between us. We'd always managed to patch things up before, but lately…

Kellan leaned over the table, examining me. "So…Griffin Hancock. You think you have what it takes to be a D-Bag? Think you can handle the workload? It's not all fun and games, you know?"

I smirked at him. I knew better than anyone what the job entailed. I also knew how much of a slacker I'd been before. Like a lazy asshole, I had ridden their fame to the top. Well, not this time. Returning to a neutral expression, I told him, "I will work my ass off for this show, and for this band. I know this is a group effort, and…I want to be on the team. I want to do my part. I *will* do my part…I promise."

I lifted an eyebrow, so they would truly understand me. I didn't make promises, and they knew that. But I was making one now. I would do this, and I would do it to the best of my ability. I couldn't afford to be a slacker anymore.

The three guys shared a long look with each other, and I nervously swallowed as doubt threatened to resurface. *Please say yes, please give me a chance.* Matt was the one who finally turned from the others to look at me. "Griffin…I don't know how to say this…" My heart filled with dread, the sound was a booming gong in my ear. Matt crooked a smile. "You're in. Congratulations."

My relief left me in a shaky exhale. "You fucking assholes," I said with a laugh.

Matt laughed, along with Evan and Kellan, and seeing their humor brightened my spirits more than being allowed on the show. We could fix this. We could fix us. All I had to do was win.

Chapter 26

We Can't All Win

A PA led me from the judges' room to the winners' room. He put a hand on the door to open it and I held my breath. *Please let Liam be in there too.* The door swept opened and a roar of cheer met my ears as I stepped in. People were clapping me on the back, congratulating me, and someone handed me a drink as I scanned the crowd. When I spotted Liam striding my way, I let out another sigh of relief. He'd made it too. Good.

He tackled me in a bear hug when he joined me, almost spilling my beer. "Can you believe it, Griff? We both made it!"

Even though I was buzzing with energy and excitement, I gave him a nonchalant shrug after we pulled apart. "That shouldn't surprise you. I told you we would, and as you know, I'm always right."

He slugged my shoulder and we both started laughing.

While diligent crew members recorded everyone's reactions to making the "team," I noticed something strange near the doors. Sam had just walked in. Looking like an imposing fortress of bone-crushing muscle, he searched the room. When his eyes fell on me and he started heading my way, my stomach leaped into my throat. Was it the guys? Had they changed their mind about me?

I clenched my fingers into fists to stop them from shaking. Emotionless, Sam stepped in front of me and said, "Someone wants to see you outside."

My heart sank. "It's Matt, isn't it? He's still pissed at me, and he changed his mind, didn't he?" Sam didn't respond one way or the other and I sighed. Yep. Matt had changed his mind. Turning to Liam, I told him, "I have a bad feeling about this... If this goes south, and the guys kick me out, it's up to you to represent the Hancock name, okay?"

Liam's mouth dropped open. Speechless, he alternated between gaping at me and Sam. Downing the rest of my drink, I handed Liam my empty cup, then followed Kellan's burly bodyguard outside. As we walked out the doors, I told Sam, "You know, I think I liked you better when you were bouncing at Pete's. At least you smiled back then. And talked. And even occasionally had drinks with us. Now you're all business, all the time. What the hell happened to you? Did Kellan buy your balls as well as your brawn?"

Once the door to the party room was closed, Sam turned to me with a cheesy grin on his face. "Shut the hell up, Griffin," he said, then he grabbed me and hugged me. I was so shocked I couldn't move. And I kind of couldn't breathe either. Sam was fucking strong. "Congratulations, man," he said, setting me down. The D-Bags just haven't been the D-Bags without you."

I gasped for air once I could breathe again. "I haven't won yet, you know."

Sam swished his hand like the rest of this contest was just a formality, and I had it in the bag. Tilting my head, I asked him, "So, it's not Matt who wanted to see me? He's not kicking me out?"

Smiling, Sam shook his head. He pointed down the hallway, and my eyes followed. There, looking like a goddess under the fluorescent lighting, was my wife. She was standing there with her head tilted, staring at me and chewing on her lip. For the second time today, I was taken aback by how fucking gorgeous she was. I smacked Sam on the chest with the back of my hand. "I'm gonna be a minute."

A low rumbling laugh escaped his chest. "Yep, I know."

I started walking her way, and my eyes roved over her body with every step I took. It was warm outside, and she was wearing shorts that were almost illegal they were so tiny. Her trim thighs were a golden honey color, and I knew they'd be smooth as silk to the touch. My dick twitched just thinking about it. Then my eyes wandered up to her chest. She was wearing a tight tank top with thin straps and...fuck me...a built-in bra. Her nipples were poking through the fabric in a way that almost made my legs give out. I walked faster.

When I was almost to her, she started coming my way. We instantly melted together when we met. Her arms went around me, mine went around her, and our lips joined. Goddamn...she tasted so good.

"Congratulations," she murmured between hungry kisses. "I knew you would make it."

My hand ran down her back, and I groaned as I grabbed her ass. Fuck, I wanted her so much. "I'm so glad you're here, Anna." I meant that in every way possible—physically, emotionally, all of it. I didn't know what I would do without her. Well, no, I did know...I'd be miserable, just like I had been the last several weeks.

Even though all I wanted to do was hold her up against the wall and drive into her over and over again, I made myself step away. She was surprised and breathless when we separated. I was struggling to breathe normally too, and I was pretty sure my cock was turning colors. It was definitely screaming at me to keep going. I ignored it though, and held her a foot away from me. "I don't want you to think that everything is back to normal just because you came back here and stuff. I know I fucked us up when I lost everything...when I lied to you. I know I ruined what we had. And I know it will take time to repair us. I'm willing to put in that time."

With a sigh, I smiled. *God, I want to be inside her right now.*

Anna smiled as she studied me. "It wasn't you losing everything that messed us up, Griffin, and it wasn't just the lying. It was you...deciding everything. It was you shutting me out. It was you keeping me in the dark and treating me like I didn't matter, like my opinion didn't matter."

I tilted my head in confusion. I'd never treated her like she didn't matter. Not intentionally, at any rate. Seeing that I wasn't connecting the dots, Anna stepped closer to me. She put her arms around my neck again, and I laced mine around her waist. "I know you don't like to show your emotions, it makes you uncomfortable and stuff...and I get that." She shook her head. "It's hard for me too, and I'm not the kind of girl who needs flowers and sonnets anyway...but the last few weeks, when you've opened up and reached out to me...in the letter, in your phone calls...it's meant the world to me, and I suddenly realized that was what went wrong for me." Smiling, she rested a hand on my cheek. "I think that was what was missing between us. I never felt like you needed me. Yes, you liked having me around, and you definitely liked having sex with me...but you never really needed me, and that made me really...lonely." She frowned and removed her hand from my cheek.

I grabbed it and held on tight. "That's not true. I do need you...you're all I need. All I've ever needed. I was...lost without you."

Anna smiled, and I felt the warmth from it inside the deepest parts of me. She *was* all I needed. "I finally feel like that's true," she told me.

She leaned in for a soft kiss that electrified me, and at the same time, moved me. I felt dazed when we pulled apart. "You're my best friend," I told her. "You're the only one who gets me, and loves me anyway. And I will do anything to keep you. Anything," I repeated, holding her gaze.

Anna closed her eyes, absorbing my words, then a devilish smile spread on her face. "There is one thing you can do for me," she said. Opening her eyes, she shyly asked, "Show me the stage?"

I blinked in surprise. By her expression, I thought she'd request something else.

Her smile turned playful, so I grabbed her hand and started leading her away. She giggled, like we were on an adventure. It reminded me of all the fun times we'd had in our relationship. Before Anna, I'd never met a girl as fun-loving as me. She really was up for anything. I loved that about her.

When I found the door to the stage, I fully expected it to be locked, but it wasn't. Thankful that I didn't have to try my hand at picking a lock, I checked to make sure the coast was clear, then hurried Anna inside. She let out a low whistle as she walked past the rows of empty seats. "It's bigger than I thought it would be." When she got to the stage, she hopped up and looked around with awe on her face.

The room was dark, with only the emergency lights gently illuminating it. I hopped up to join her on the stage, then headed to the back to turn on some lights. I found one that I thought was a spotlight. Luckily, it was, and a glowing circle formed around Anna. She laughed at being in the limelight, and I shook my head at her amusement. As I stepped out on the main part of the stage with her, I took a look around. It wasn't nearly as big as the places I was used to playing with the D-Bags, but it was pretty decently sized. "Yeah, it's all right."

"So this is where you're going to show the world how magnificent you really are for the next six weeks?"

I looked over my shoulder at her. "Yeah. It's my new home away from home." I returned my gaze to the rows and rows of empty chairs. "Where my future will be decided…"

"Well then, I say we spread a little good luck upon it."

Not knowing what she meant, I turned to face her. She grabbed the edge of her tank top and lifted it over her head. Once it was free from her, she kicked off her shoes, unbuttoned her shorts, and slid the rest of her clothes down her legs. Holy crap. Seeing her perfection laid bare before me was almost more than I could handle. Were we ready to jump right into this? Was I capable of turning her down? No. I was as incapable of rejecting her as I was unworthy of her devotion. But for some reason I had it, and I was never letting it go again.

Completely naked under the lone spotlight highlighting the stage, she crooked a finger at me. "Come here."

My breath sped with every step I took toward her. Did she know having sex on a stage was my number one fantasy? Yes, she probably did, and that's why she was doing this. I was the luckiest son of a bitch in the entire world to be able to claim her as mine. What a fucking fool I'd been, and how blessed I was to be given another chance. I didn't deserve her, but I'd make it my life's mission to be a better man. And with her firmly by my side, maybe one day I would be.

When I got close enough to her, I cupped one of her incredible breasts in my hand. The familiar weight made my cock come to life. "You are so gorgeous," I told her, stroking my thumb around her nipple.

She bit her lip as a moan of delight left her. "I have missed you...so much, Griffin. Make love to me, right here, where everyone will be watching you on Monday..."

Bending down, I sucked her nipple into my mouth. She held my head in place as she gasped. My hands slid down her waist to her hips, then my finger ducked between her legs. She was so fucking wet. She cried out as she arched against me, and I couldn't stand it anymore. It had been too long. I needed to know how she tasted...

Sinking to my knees, I replaced my fingers with my mouth. Anna moaned my name, and her fingers cinched in my hair, telling me I'd better not fucking move. It drove me wild. And *goddamn*... she tasted so good.

I lay back on the ground, making her frown at me, but then I motioned for her to join me. She lowered herself so I could taste her again. I watched her body being highlighted by the spotlight on her, watched her fingers massage her breasts, rub her nipples. It was too much for me, it was too much for her.

She moved off me, then immediately got to work on my pants. Once they were free and clear of my body, she took me inside her mouth. Knowing we were center stage almost made me come instantly. I gently pushed her off, then stripped off the rest of my clothes. I didn't want anything between us.

I laid her down on her back, so her head was to the crowd, then I drove into her. Fuck...she felt amazing. Our hands roamed each other's bodies as we moved together, and every second that ticked by I was hyperaware of how exposed we were. We were the only thing in the room with a light shining on us, and it felt *so* right, it made the moment that much sweeter. It was just how I'd hoped it would be.

The excitement brought us to the brink pretty quickly. I knew I was almost there, and by Anna's cries, she was getting close too. Wanting to give her more, I repositioned us so we were at the very edge of the stage. Once Anna realized how I was showcasing us for our imaginary audience, she groaned and dropped her head back over the side. We weren't hiding anything.

Gripping the edge of the stage, I used it as leverage so I could thrust deeper and deeper into her; Anna's throaty cries of ecstasy grew more pronounced with every plunge. Looking up, I gazed at the sea of seats awaiting cheering fans. Fuck, yes... with Anna by my side, I was going to own this stage Monday night.

We were both panting, shaking with need, we were so close. Fuck... she felt so good. It seemed like years had passed since the last time we'd been together, and even then, it had never felt quite like this—like we were completely and totally one, on the same page in every way.

Captivated, I watched the ecstasy on Anna's face building as I moved against her, with her. She was stunning beneath me, made even more so by the spotlights. Being with her, here, now, was the single most erotic thing I'd ever experienced, and I felt unstoppable as my climax started building.

"Oh God, yes, Griffin...yes...there...right there! More, more... oh God..."

Anna's words turned unintelligible as she started coming, and I couldn't take my eyes off the sight. Watching her fall apart, knowing she was letting me do this, letting me take her there, it meant more to me than I could say at the moment. *All I want is for her to be happy.* Anna clutched me tight as she rode out her release, then she pulled my head to hers for a searing kiss. I started coming as our tongues collided. I could only groan in her mouth as bursts of pleasure swept over me. Fuck...yes. God, I'd missed her.

When the intensity was over, I slumped against Anna. Her arms came up to cradle me, and I felt more complete than I had in my entire life. We would have to do the show like this, because I never wanted to let her go. Not wanting to hide from her or ignore the emotional chaos swirling within me, I made myself say how I was feeling.

"You're the only thing that matters to me, Anna. Sure, there's things I want, like winning my job back, but…you're the only thing I *need*. You and the girls." I shifted to her side, so I could more easily look at her. "I got so caught up in myself, I lost you. I lost us. I think I even lost *me*. Because without you, I'm not really anything. Nothing worth a damn, anyway. You're the best part of me. The very best. You're my best friend, and I should have put you first, you and the girls. And I'm so sorry I didn't." With a sigh, I shook my head. Anna opened her mouth to speak, but I stopped her with a kiss. I wasn't done yet. "I love you, and I'll go wherever you want me to go. I'll live wherever you want me to live, I'll do whatever you want me to do…just take me back. I can't be without you anymore. It's killing me."

Her eyes watered as she stared up at me. "Griff…I love you so much, and a huge part of me wants to say sure…come home, and let that be the end of it. But for the sake of our family, for the sake of our girls, I need you to know that what you did—the lying, going behind my back to get what you wanted—that can't *ever* happen again. This is truly your last chance with me…so don't fuck it up." She gave me a sweet smile on the end of that, like she'd just asked me to bring home a gallon of milk.

Laughing, I kissed her again. "Trust me, babe, I would rather stab myself in the testicle than ever hurt you like that again. I just want my best friend back," I said with a sigh. "I want my wife back."

Anna cupped my cheek. "You've got her. Now be quiet and make love to her under the spotlight again, before someone comes in here and kicks both of you out of the hotel."

I was instantly hard again. "You are the sexiest thing on earth, and I am the luckiest son of a bitch there is." I cupped her cheek. "And I won't ever forget it again."

She was nodding, tears in her eyes, when I slid into her again…

Monday evening was the first live show, where we'd be showcasing our talent for the audience, not the judges. I was both excited and nauseated about performing. Sure, I'd done it a million times before, but never with this much pressure on me. My entire career was riding on making the fans like me again, an uphill battle considering how I'd cracked things when I'd left the band. I hoped they could see my repentance onstage, my determination, my drive. I wanted this.

It was a short special, only six weeks, so multiple people would be leaving after each results show. I didn't want to be let go in the first group. Or the second. Or the third. I wanted to make it all the way through. I didn't let that desire turn me against my rivals though, and I helped out wherever I could.

When I wasn't giving the contestants pointers or lifting Liam's spirits, I helped out around the stage. There were crew everywhere, and they always seemed to need a hand with something. It helped me keep my mind off my nerves to stay busy, so I volunteered with as many tasks as they would let me do. They seemed to appreciate it; they even wished me luck on the show, then invited me to play poker with them afterward. Sounded fantastic to me.

Liking how it felt to be a part of something bigger than myself, I offered my services to anyone who needed them. I helped Anna with the girls, helped the host run errands, helped the camera guys with their equipment, and even helped the producers map out shots. All day, I was anywhere and everywhere. Wherever I was needed, that's where I wanted to be.

When it was finally time for the show to begin, I was pumped up and rearing to go. The twenty of us huddled backstage and said a quick prayer for each other. A bunch of the crew joined us too, and I had one arm around Liam and one around the guy who controlled the lighting. I'd never felt so connected to something. After we broke apart, we all went our separate ways to do last-minute preparations for the show.

Finding a quiet corner, I closed my eyes and inhaled and exhaled deep breaths. *I can do this.* That was when I heard a voice full of cheer screech, "Found you, Daddy!"

I opened my eyes to see Gibson running toward me; her long blond pigtails bounced around her shoulders as she bobbed along.

Anna had long ago taken a seat in the crowd with Onnika, but Gibson had refused to leave my side. She'd been running around backstage, charming everyone she came in contact with. She was a lot like her mom that way. Sinking to my knees, I scooped her into a gigantic hug.

"There you are. Where'd you run off to? I thought I'd lost my best girl." Behind her was Sam and one of the camera guys. Gibson had kind of become a backstage correspondent, chitchatting with all the contestants in her own special *I'm almost four and I know everything about life* kind of way.

"I helped Uncle Kellan." She turned to give the camera a cheesy grin. "He loves me bestest. He said I'm gonna win."

With a laugh, I kissed her hair. "I think he's right."

Gibson's adorable face turned to a frown as she turned her attention back to me. "But I want you to win." She stared at me like she was giving me superpowers, then she smiled. "There. I gave my win to you."

She was so sweet, I had to swallow the lump in my throat. The theme music started playing, and knowing I needed to leave soon, I gave her another hug. She didn't want to let go from this one. "Gibby, I need to go, honey. You stay with Sam, okay?"

She was frowning again when I pulled her off me. "When will you come home?" she asked me.

I felt like she'd just impaled me with a foot-long icicle. "Oh…sweetheart…soon, okay? I promise."

She nodded, then, as only a child could, her mood flipped around and she gave me a gargantuan grin. "For my birthday?"

With a laugh, I nodded. "Yes, definitely for your birthday."

She clapped, then squeezed me in a hug. When she pulled away, she pointed at me with such a serious expression, it was hard not to laugh. "Mine though…not Onnika's." Onnika was turning two in a few weeks, while Gibson's fourth was a couple of months away. "Just mine," Gibson reiterated, her face firm.

With a sigh, I grabbed my daughter's shoulders and made her look at me. "Honey, you need to stop being jealous of your sister. Just because I love her doesn't mean I love you any less. I love the both of you…so much. You're both wonderful, beautiful, talented, special little people…" My voice trailed off as I considered my own reoccurring jealousies. Had Gibson picked up on my attitude and felt inadequate next to Onnika because she watched me struggling to let things go? God, I hoped not. I didn't want her to live that way. I cupped her cheeks. "You are the most amazing *you* I know, and you don't need to compare yourself to anybody. There will never be another little girl like you. Ever."

She stared at me a second, then grinned. "Okay."

I kissed her nose, then stood up. It was time for me to be the most amazing *me* I could be. I gave Gibson to Sam, thanked him for keeping an eye on her, then headed toward the stage to take charge of my fate. Time to own this shit.

And I did. When my name was called for introductions, I stepped out onto the stage like I was receiving thunderous, ear-splitting applause, and in my mind, I was. As I stepped right up to the spot where I'd made love to my wife, the thrilling image of driving into her filled me. I would visualize that moment every time I came out here. It would help me get through this.

With a knowing smile on my lips, I kissed my fingers, then found my wife in the crowd and held them out to her. *You're my everything.* Anna was screaming for me as she held Onnika in her arms. Onnika was clapping, and even though I couldn't hear her over the cheering, I could tell she was saying, *Daddy!* Damn. I had the best family ever. How did I almost give them up? Matt was right. I was a fucking idiot.

Liam was announced after me, and I tackled him in a friendly hug around the neck when his moment in the spotlight was over with. He was all smiles as he wrapped his arm around me. It sort of blew me away how close I felt to my family now. I'd always had a bond with them, but now, after everything I'd gone through recently, it was more than that. I'd fight tooth and nail for any one of them.

Spotting my family in the crowd, I waved at them while the rest of the contestants were announced. Mom was hollering for her two sons, Dad was grinning ear to ear, and Chelsey had tears in her eyes. It moved me, made me want to win this for them so they'd be proud of me, although I was pretty sure they already were. Mom had said as much when she'd called me this morning.

After introductions, we were separated into groups to perform as "bands." I was picked to be the lead singer of my group, which made me a bit uneasy, considering the bad reviews from my lack-luster attempt at an album. I put the doubt aside though, and redid a D-Bags song with my own personal flair. Instead of just singing the lyrics, I rapped a part of them. It was a slow, steady rhythm that perfectly matched the classic song we were doing. The crowd went nuts after we were done and, shocking the hell out of me, our group got a standing ovation from the audience…including the judges. Even Matt was beaming as he applauded us.

By the end of the show, I felt exhilarated and energized, and I felt great about my chances of surviving this.

The results show was the next night. My stomach was twisted into knots as I waited to hear if I'd be moving on or not, but I'd kicked ass last night, and I held on to that fact as tightly as I could. They'd liked me. A guest performer was brought in to entertain the crowd, and I was both surprised and not surprised to see who it was…Avoiding Redemption. Justin's band.

I looked around for him backstage, but it was Gibson who found him. "Daddy! Uncle Justin's here!"

Remembering my last words to him, I felt a little stupid when I was face to face with him. "Oh…hey…good to see you, man. How's it been?"

Justin crooked me a smile as he looked me over. Gibson was holding on to his hand so tight, her little knuckles were white; she already had a thing for rock stars. I was not going to make it through her teen years.

"Things are good," Justin answered me.

Running a hand through my hair, which was finally down to my eyes again, I let out a sigh. "Hey, I'm sorry about the stuff I said, about the album. I was being a dick. It wasn't your fault your label didn't want it. And honestly, it was crap."

Justin's eyebrows shot right up his forehead. "Wow. I totally thought you'd just gloss over that incident, pretend it didn't happen."

As I heard the theme music begin to play, I smiled. "The old me would have. But, you know, I'm trying to be more mature and shit."

Gibson nodded. "And shit."

Justin laughed as he looked down at her. "I can tell." When he returned his eyes to me, he extended his hand. "Good luck tonight." As I took it, he admitted, "I voted for you, by the way."

I was surprisingly touched by his admission. "You did? Thanks, man. That means a lot." After we separated, Justin bent down to kiss Gibson's hand, then he handed her to me. For once, she didn't want me. As I struggled to hold her away from him, I asked, "Hey, how's Kate?"

Justin flashed me a grin that made Gibson sigh. I frowned at her while Justin said, "We're great. I asked her to move in with me and she said yes. She's moving to L.A. by the end of the month." He seemed really pleased that I'd asked about Kate for once, and not Brooklyn. I probably should have been more encouraging about his and Kate's relationship.

Clapping him on the shoulder, I tried to make up for all of my inappropriate comments. "That's great. I'm glad you guys have decided to shack up. It's about time."

Justin frowned, then laughed and shook his head. "It's good to see that you're not entirely mature yet. I don't know what I would do if you completely grew up."

I wasn't entirely sure what he meant by that, but with a smirk and a shrug, I let it go.

After introductions and music from Justin's band, it was time to begin hearing the results of last night's voting. I was a wreck while I stood onstage waiting out my fate. They were making the announcements in groups of three. Liam had been in the group right before me, and he'd heard the golden words I was hoping to hear—*You're safe.* I was the last one in my group of three. Both guys before me had been saved. I was happy for them, but at the same time, I knew that their success minutely made my odds worse.

With a straight face, I stared over at Matt, Evan, and Kellan.

The three of them looked nervous as the host stepped up to me. I knew they didn't have a say in my staying or going, but I hoped they were hoping I was continuing on. Breaking eye contact with them, I turned to the host when he said my name.

"Griffin Hancock…you had quite a night last night, but…was it enough?" He gave me a long, hard look before slowly opening the envelope. He took forever fumbling with the paper. I wanted to grab the damn thing out of his hands and see for myself if I was moving on or not, but instead, I made myself calmly stand there. It was the longest fucking ten seconds in my life, but finally, the dude gave me an Oscar-worthy grin. "Yes, it was. Congratulations, you're safe."

The crowd erupted into shrieks and my knees partially gave way. Thank God…for now, I was safe.

Chapter 27

Reconnecting

To give the potential bandmates a feel for what going on the road was like, all the contestants were being sequestered in the hotel… no visitors allowed. It made me miss Anna and the girls like crazy, but it gave Anna and me even more time to reconnect over the phone, which was surprisingly wonderful. And it usually wasn't sexual either, which was sort of weird for us.

"What did you do after that?" I asked her. "Kick her ass? 'Cause that's what I would do, if I heard some chick talking shit about you."

"Well," she hesitated, "I'm technically her boss, so I can't really get physical with her…but I did make her wear a giant drumstick and walk up and down the block all afternoon. It was awesome."

I laughed at her story as I lay back on the bed. I could totally picture Anna getting revenge on a lippy employee that way. Nobody messed with Anna and got away with it. "I also wrote her up and threatened to fire her if she ever called me a silicone-enhanced slut again." She scoffed. "As if I've had implants. These puppies are real."

I groaned as her breasts flashed in my brain. "Yes. Yes, they are. They're perfect…just like you."

She let out a happy sigh. "I'm nowhere near perfect, Griffin."

"You're my kind of perfect, and really, mine is the only opinion that matters." I laughed, then sighed. "Well, mine and the entire nation's…"

Understanding my reference, Anna murmured, "Are you nervous about tomorrow? Picking the final four…that's a big one."

Just her words gave me anxiety. "They're all big ones…and yeah, I'm a little stressed."

"Well, you were amazing tonight," Anna said in encouragement. "I'm certain you'll make it through."

I wasn't so sure. Everyone who was left was good. Really good. Over the past several weeks, the original twenty contestants had been tested, tried, and then, almost cruelly, weeded down. Since there were so few weeks in the contest, the cuts had been drastic. I'd been close to the chopping block a time or two, and positive that I was finished more than once. But somehow, I was still here. There were eight of us left, but after tomorrow…only four. Then next week, only two. Then the week after that was the finale, and only one person would be left standing. God, I hoped it was me.

Changing my focus, I told her, "Thank you for going on this crazy journey with me. I love you with every part of me. You're my best friend, my soul mate, and I'm one lucky fuck for having you in my life." I said something similar to this every time we talked, and the words flowed from me now. It was almost ridiculous that they'd ever been hard to say.

Anna was silent a second, then she said, "You don't have to tell me that all the time, you know? I know you love me, Griff."

"No, I do have to say it. I don't want to be the douche who doesn't let people in. I want those I care about to know I care about 'em. And you and the girls…well, nothing is more important to me than you three."

A throaty laugh escaped her. "I like this new sensitive side to you, babe. It's incredibly hot."

I smiled in the darkness. "If you think that's hot, just wait until this is over with. I'll be so sensitive, you won't know what to do with me."

"I'm sure I'll think of something…Good night, babe. Good luck tomorrow."

"Thanks. Night."

We hung up and I stared at my ceiling for thirty minutes before I finally passed out.

The next morning, I woke up with a very familiar pain in my stomach. It sort of felt like I'd eaten a pile of rocks last night, and they had all merged together into a super-rock that my body was never going to be able to pass without fatally injuring me. I knew the sensation would go away as soon as the results were read though. I was either moving on or not. Simple as that.

As I walked around backstage with Gibson on my shoulders—because even a rule about sequestering couldn't keep my daughter from the stage—I muttered complaints about how the producers should give the contestants a heads-up on the results. "I mean, the polls closed at midnight, so they've known the results for hours. How hard is it to slip notes under our doors, letting us know if we should pack or not?"

"Well, I think it's supposed to be a surprise...otherwise the people who didn't pass would just leave. Kind of anticlimactic for filming."

I looked over at Liam with knitted brows. "I know I asked a question, but I didn't really want an answer. Especially a logical one."

He looked at me blankly for a minute, then nodded. "Yeah, you're right. We're all in the same hotel. It would take them five seconds."

A huge grin erupted on my face. "Exactly!"

I heard the kitschy theme music beginning, and saw Sam coming around the corner to collect my daughter. He always watched her for me when it was my turn to perform. "Time's up, baby girl," I told her.

She whined as I removed her from my shoulders. "I want to go with you!"

I'd heard this before, but the producers had made it quite clear that she couldn't go onstage with me, not even for introductions. They said it would give me an unfair advantage. I had to agree with their assessment. Anyone who laid eyes on my angel's blond curls and sky-blue eyes would vote for me in a heartbeat. The backstage footage of the two of us together was probably the real reason why I'd even made it this far. God, I hoped I passed.

Liam squatted to her level when she began to pout. "Gibby, you've got to stay here and look after Crock for me, remember?" He handed her the stuffed crocodile he'd bought early on as a bribe. Gibson snatched it away from him and hugged it tight. Liam held his arms open. "I need my good luck squeeze." She obliged him, and he laughed as he held her.

Seeing how close they were made me smile, but it faded the minute I heard our cue. "Time to go, bro."

Liam's grin faded as he looked up at me. "Right…"

When it was time for the results to be read, Liam and I were in the same group. I hated it when that happened. It made it even more nerve-wracking. The host doubled up the anxiety by reading our names together. I squeezed Liam's hand as I scanned the crowd for Anna. I found her and Onnika right as the host delivered our fates. "You will both be moving on! Congratulations!"

It took me a minute to register what he'd said. Anna understood first. She started jumping and hollering for me. She was so loud, she startled Onnika, who started to cry. That's when it sunk in for me…*final four*. I'd done it. I was moving on.

The next week's results were just as gut-churning. I swear, by the end of this, I was going to have an ulcer. They had the final four stand onstage together as they announced the final two. I hated that we were all together for this—it meant I had to see the losers' reactions, and if I lost, I'd have the winners consoling me while they were bouncing up and down with excitement. I'd rather be told the news separately so I could take a minute before facing the world. All my dreams were on the line here.

The four of us clenched our hands together as the host walked down the line, saying our names and giving us each meaningful glances. My heart started pounding in my chest. *Just read the fucking card already.*

"Are you guys ready to learn who the final two contestants will be?" The four of us looked at each other, nodded, and squeezed hands tighter. This was going to suck.

"All right," the host said. Our pairing for the final show is…" I closed my eyes and prepared for the worst. "Liam and Griffin!"

My eyes shot open as surprise flooded my body. No fucking way! Liam and I were going to the finale? I'd hoped that would happen, but there were times when my doubt had been so strong that hope had seemed a million miles away.

For the final voting show, we got to play with the D-Bags. Liam went first, while I watched from backstage. The first thing that struck me while I watched him was how natural Liam looked up there with the guys. Matt and Liam joked around while they got ready, Evan gave him a friendly pat on the back, and Kellan helped him breathe. They all looked like they'd been performing together for years. And then, when the camera turned on and they started playing, the sound struck me. They were good together. Seamless. Flawless. The song they'd chosen had a pretty complicated bass line, but Liam was killing it. He sang all his backup vocals on time, and from what I could hear, on pitch. It was a little painful to see how perfectly somebody else could fit in with the D-Bags, and it reminded me of something I should have remembered when I'd ditched them—I needed them more than they needed me. I'd been given a gift when I'd been invited along, and I hadn't appreciated it. I did now.

After Liam's turn, it was mine. I bumped fists with him when he exited the stage, then I gave him a hug and told him what a great job he'd done. He was damn near glowing from his performance high.

Kellan was the first one who approached me when I climbed onstage. He gave me a hug, then said in my ear, "Ready to kill it?" I nodded and he smacked my shoulder. "Just like old times, huh?"

I shook my head. "No, this will be better than the old times."

Kellan scrutinized me for a moment, then nodded. As I strapped on my guitar, Evan held his hand out. "Good luck, man." Grinning, I shook his hand and thanked him.

When he stepped away, Matt approached me. He didn't say anything at first, just looked at me. I started to apologize, since I thought maybe he was still mad, but he held his hand up to stop me. "We're not allowed to vote, but if I could...I'd vote for you. You've been doing amazing, man."

That moved me more than anything I'd heard from anyone else. I had to swallow the lump in my throat before I could speak. "Thank you...cuz."

Matt smiled, then smacked me on the back so hard my skin tingled through my shirt. "Now don't fuck up on camera. You need all the votes you can get." I flipped him off and he started laughing. The familiar ribbing made me feel better than I had in ages. I finally felt like I belonged here again.

On this particular D-Bags song, the bass started first. Even though my heart was racing, I acted as calm and cool as I could. *It's just another show...not the deciding factor of my entire future.* I was a little surprised when I nailed the intro; I usually fucked it up when we played it live. Of course, back in the day, I'd been easily distracted by...well, just about anything. I was focused now though, and I slayed the song. Murdered it in an awesomely gory fashion. It was fucking beautiful.

When the song was over, I raised my fists in the air in victory. The crowd went nuts. Sure, maybe I hadn't won yet, but a little confidence was always appreciated, so long as I didn't go overboard. And I wouldn't. Not anymore.

On the following evening, when Liam and I were backstage waiting for the outcome of our performances from the night before, the surrealism of the moment hit me. Either I was going to win my spot back with the D-Bags, or Liam was. But this was it...it would definitely be one of us.

Seeing the sweat on Liam's brow, I extended a hand to him. "Hey, I want you to know, if you win...I'm okay with that. I think you'd be a good fit with the D-Bags...maybe even better than me."

Liam shook my hand, but he eyed me like I was playing him or something. "Who are you, and what have you done with my little brother?"

I laughed at his question. I supposed I did seem like another person...maybe I was. A lot of shitty stuff had happened to me, and I viewed things differently now. But not completely differently.

"Oh, I'm still in here, asswipe, and if you do steal my job, I'm giving you a wedgie so deep, you'll need a doctor to surgically remove the underwear from your ass crack."

A slow smile spread over Liam's face. "There he is."

Just then, a person I hadn't seen in a while approached us. I stood up to greet him. "Hey, Denny, good to see you, man."

Denny took my hand and shook it, then extended his hand to Liam. "Hi, I'm Denny Harris. My wife and I represent the band." Liam nodded and Denny's dark eyes flickered between the two of us. "I just wanted to congratulate you both on how far you've come, and wish you both good luck tonight."

Liam was giddy as he said, "Thanks." I was more reserved. The last time Denny and I had spoken, I'd been an ass. Seemed to be a pattern with me. "Hey, can I talk to you for a minute," I told him.

He nodded and we stepped away from Liam. I stared at my feet while I prepared my apology. You'd think I'd be an expert at them by now. "I just wanted to say…sorry I was a prick last time we talked." I thought to add more, but there really wasn't any more to add. That pretty much summed it up.

Denny put a hand on my shoulder. "No worries, mate. I've already let that go." When I looked up at him, he smiled. "You seem different," he told me. "In a good way. I think the audience sees it too." He glanced over at Liam before looking back at me. "I'd never tell him this, but…you've nailed it every time you've gone onstage. And you've really rallied the country behind you. No small feat, considering how much of a rift you caused when you left." He patted my arm. "You've worked hard, and the guys and I have noticed. We're all very proud of you."

My nerves evaporated under his praise. "Thank you. I think I needed to hear that."

He clapped my shoulder again. "Good luck tonight."

But after he left, my nerves started creeping back in. This was it…the moment of truth.

When it was time, Liam and I went onstage together. The host gave each of the judges a moment to praise Liam and me for getting this far. Kellan was the last one to speak. He had to wait a solid three minutes for the screaming to die down long enough for him to start. "I just want you both to know, no matter what the outcome is tonight, you're both winners in my eyes. You've both worked hard at earning your right to be in the band. Congratulations."

The crowd started screaming again, so I tilted my head to thank Kellan for his words. I'd always been so jealous of him, and he'd never been anything but gracious to me. I was such a dick.

After each of the judges had said their words of encouragement, the host turned to Liam and me. He smiled and asked us how we were doing. I fought to keep my expression even. If he took his sweet fucking time opening the fucking envelope tonight, a blood vessel was going to burst in my brain. Just end this fucking torture already!

"You've both done so amazing on this show…let's take a moment to recap, shall we?"

I wanted to groan, I wanted to scream. Instead, I scanned the crowd. There were several faces I recognized—all of my family was here, plus some of my ex-coworkers, Justin and his girlfriend, Kate, Denny and his wife, Abby, but the most important face in the crowd was my wife's. While Anna watched the monitors playing my montage, I watched her. When the video got to the section of my audition when I said I was sorry to my wife, a tear dripped down Anna's cheek. She met eyes with me and smiled, then she mouthed the words *I love you.*

Grinning myself, I switched my gaze to my feet. Win or lose, it was okay, because Anna and I had healed something broken between us, and that was more important than any job ever would be. After Liam's video montage ended, the host returned his eyes to us. "Let's not make you boys wait any longer. The winner of *Can You Be a D-Bag?* is…" I closed my eyes and squeezed Liam's hand. Either way, I was fine with this. The host's booming voice echoed around the auditorium as he announced the winner. "Liam Hancock! Congratulations, Liam!"

There was an explosion of light and noise, and confetti streamers started pouring down onto the stage like rain. Opening my eyes, I looked over at Liam. Several things happened to my body simultaneously: joy, pain, elation, sorrow. My brother won! And I lost…

I felt like I couldn't breathe. I'd wanted this so much, and I'd just lost it. Permanently. I felt my vision hazing, my knees buckling, but somehow, I pushed the feeling aside. This contest wasn't mine to lose. I'd had my chance with the D-Bags, and I'd blown it. My time was over; it was Liam's time to shine now. Pushing aside the lingering agony, I squeezed Liam in a gigantic bear hug. This was okay. Liam *deserved* to win. The other eighteen contestants flooded the stage as the host thanked the audience, the viewers, and the numerous sponsors. The cameras eventually stopped recording, the confetti eventually stopped falling, and people eventually started leaving. I stayed on the stage, floored. It was over… and after all of that, I'd lost.

The guys came over to congratulate Liam. They were instantly surrounded by fans who'd stayed for autographs. Some even asked Liam for his, which astonished him by the look on his face. Evan, Matt, and Kellan each gave me shocked, sympathetic expressions. It made me feel better to see them surprised; they'd all thought I'd win. Denny and Abby joined their circle, and I watched from the outside as the *new* D-Bags began forming.

While I stared at them, Anna and the girls approached me. Gibson wrapped her arms around my waist, while Onnika held her hands out and asked for me. I picked up the miniature version of my wife and squeezed her tight. *This is what matters.* Anna tenderly laid her fingers on my shoulder. "I'm sorry, Griffin. I know how badly you wanted this."

Opening my eyes, I shook my head. "I wanted *this* more." I squeezed Onnika and wrapped an arm around Gibson for emphasis. Anna crooked a smile. Wondering just what she thought of our future now, I set Onnika down; she immediately started playing with the half foot of confetti piled on the stage. Facing Anna, I grabbed her hands. "I didn't win, I'm not a D-Bag anymore."

She shrugged. "You'll always be a D-Bag to me."

With a sigh, I looked down. "Do you still want to be with me if I'm not in a band, if I have a regular, crap-paying job?"

Removing her hand from mine, Anna lifted my chin so I'd look at her. "Griffin, it was never about the band, it was never about the money. It was about us being a team, us being honest...that was what mattered to me. Feeling like I was important to you was what mattered to me. And I finally feel that way. So yes, crap job or not, I still want to be with you." She laced our fingers together and stepped forward until we were touching. "Always."

Grinning, I gave her a soft kiss. "At least the sequestering part is over with. We can do a lot more than just talk now."

She laughed as she returned my kisses. "But I like the talking," she said, her voice husky.

"I do too, but I'm ready to go home." My tone started out playful, but ended up serious. I'd missed her. So much.

"Go home...where?" she tentatively asked.

Pulling back, I looked her in the eye. "Wherever you are, that's my home."

Smiling, she leaned in to kiss me again. After several long moments, our kids wanted our attention again. Gibson was practically crawling up my pant leg, so I picked her up, then skillfully, I picked up Onnika too. I half expected them to start fighting in my arms, but maybe having taken my "be nice" message to heart, Gibson handed Onnika some confetti. Onnika smiled and told her, "Tank you."

As the four of us started walking off the stage, Anna sighed. "You know...I'll kind of miss this stage. It was...fun." She looked back at me with a playful gleam, and I knew she wasn't talking about the show.

My grin was devilish. "Yeah, it was. We might have to crash a D-Bags show so we can spread some 'luck' on their stage."

Anna laughed. Oh yeah...we were *so* going to christen their tour. I had no doubt in my mind. I set the kids down as we approached the steps. They were heavier than I remembered. Anna held Gibson's hand while I held Onnika's. As I helped Onnie down the stairs, Anna tossed out, "Oh, before I forget... something happened on that stage that I haven't had a chance to tell you about yet."

I looked back at her, curious. "Oh yeah, what? Were we filmed?" I smiled, hoping she said yes—that would be one fucking hot sex tape.

Anna grinned but shook her head. "No...but you kind of, sort of knocked me up. I'm due in May."

I stumbled off the last step and nearly knocked Onnika over. "You...we...what?"

Laughing, Anna let go of Gibson and slung her arms around my neck. "We're going to have another baby," she told me. A glowing happiness was in her eyes when she said it.

Still thrown off by the multiple recent shocks, I felt like I wasn't understanding her words. "We made a baby onstage?" When she smiled and nodded, I looked around and shouted, "We made a baby onstage!"

Fans and crew members were still milling about, along with Liam and the guys, and the rest of my family was still in the audience, waiting to console me and congratulate Liam. They all looked my way after hearing my exclamation. I saw more than a few puzzled expressions, then my mom screamed, "I'm gonna be a grandma again!" and I knew they understood.

Exhilaration lifted me. I didn't know what Anna and I were going to do, and I still had money problems to deal with, but I felt more hopeful than I had in a long time. I had Anna, and she had me, and our family was about to get bigger and better. I couldn't wait to see what happened next.

Liam left L.A. the same day I did, a few days after the contest ended. I'd wanted to leave earlier to be with Anna, who'd had to return to her job as soon as she could, but I'd also wanted to say goodbye to my family here. I wouldn't be returning. Not to live, at any rate. My home was in Seattle, with my wife and children.

Mom and Dad drove Liam and me to the airport. Mom went on and on about how proud she was of both of us. She started almost every sentence with "Now, I know you didn't win, Griffin, but..." I wished she'd stop prefacing everything with those words. I was fine with the way everything had gone down. Liam was out of his freaking mind with cheer. He practically bounced off the walls in the car.

"We're gonna start working on a new album right away. The guys want to get me out there, get me accepted. Then there will be tours, promotional stuff, TV gigs...ugh! This is all so awesome!"

His excitement made me laugh. It reminded me of how I'd felt when the D-Bags had first gone on Justin's tour. It was a high, that was for sure...but it was nothing compared to knowing that Anna would be home, waiting for me when I got there. Just thinking of the upcoming alone time with my wife was giving me a boner. How long was this fucking flight?

Once we got to the airport, Mom and Dad gave us goodbye hugs, wished us well, and begged for updates. Liam and I attracted attention as we walked through the halls, and quite a few people stopped to congratulate us. By the way they said it, you'd think we'd both won. Liam was gracious and at ease with his newfound fans. He was a natural at being a star. I knew he would be; it ran in the family.

Once we were boarded and resting in first class, compliments of the show, Liam closed his eyes. "I'm already exhausted," he told me.

Shaking my head, I answered, "Better get used to it. It's just going to get crazier."

I texted Anna that I was on my way. She texted me back a picture of her chest. Jesus. This was going to be a long ass flight. As I debated quickly sending her a photo of my hard-on, I got a text from Chelsey. Reading it made me smile. *Don't forget...the dog may have lost everything, but that doesn't mean he didn't get it back. And remembering his loss made the next steak he ate ten times as savory. That's the beauty of second chances.* Don't I know it.

Three hours later, I was walking into my new apartment. A modest two-bedroom place with the backside of a building as its only view. It was small. Pitifully small. But with Chelsey's words ringing through my head, it felt massive. It felt like the largest, warmest, most wonderful place on earth…because my family was here.

Anna had given me a key before she'd left, and I let myself in. Hoping to surprise her, I tried to be as quiet as possible. Being stealthy had never been one of my specialties though, and I bumped and banged a few times as I ran into things. Anna didn't come out to greet me, so I tiptoed down the hallway. Walking past the girls' bedroom made me pause, and I peeked into their room to check on them. They were fast asleep in their beds. Onnika was holding a doll while she sucked on her thumb, and Gibson had Crock tight to her chest as she lightly snored. Like a trail of bread crumb clues, evidence of everything they'd played with today covered their floor; there were dolls, teacups, books, stuffed animals, and building blocks everywhere. A pang went through me as I stared at the chaos. I'd missed a chunk of their childhood. Maybe it had been a small chunk, but I'd still missed it. Never again. I wouldn't miss a second of my new baby's life.

"I thought that was you I heard banging stuff."

My surprise blown, I looked over at my wife as I shut my daughters' door. She'd just come out of our bedroom…and she was wearing her work uniform. My jaw dropped as I took in the tight, bright orange shorty shorts, and the tank top that was just opaque enough that I could have seen her bra underneath it…if she'd been wearing one.

"Oh…holy…fuck…" I muttered.

Anna grinned as she played with a long lock of her hair. "Yeah, I figured you've missed this outfit." She put her hands on her hips, turned to show me her ass, then slightly bent over in a *Come fuck me* pose. Goddamn…

I pointed to the room she'd just stepped out of. "I need to be inside you, right now." Unzipping my pants, I started heading her way. She giggled, then took off into our room. I had my shoes kicked off and my pants around my ankles by the time I got to the door. When I stepped inside, I closed the door, flung my jeans away and ripped off my shirt.

Anna was lying on the bed, her hair fanned out around her. Her back was arched, her nipples were hard, and her legs were ceaselessly rubbing together; she had an ache just as profound as mine.

Giving my cock long, teasing strokes as I approached her, I murmured, "The Hulk will see you now..."

Chapter 28

Winners and Losers

Early in the morning, a couple of days later, I was tackled by two energetic little girls. Luckily I'd put some underwear on before falling asleep the night before. Anna and I had been making good use of our daughters' early bedtime by reconnecting between the sheets. I'd almost forgotten how horny being pregnant made my wife.

I let out a groaning laugh as Gibson jumped on me and Onnika crawled up my legs. Gibson's cat, Kitty Sunshine, crawled up near my head and sat down with her ass almost in my face. "Good morning, Daddy!" Gibson exclaimed, way too chipper for the early hour. Was the sun even up yet?

"Good morning, babe," I grumbled. Reaching down, I started tickling her. Her laughter woke me up better than coffee. I'd missed this. I pulled Gibson into my arms then pulled Onnika up. Rotating my head back and forth, I gave each girl a tender kiss.

Anna was leaning against the doorframe, watching us. She was wearing casual lounge pants and the Douchebags band shirt I'd given to her the first time I'd met her. She'd blown me away that night with her beauty, her fun-loving spirit, her flirty nature…her amazing rack. There were so many things I loved about her that it was almost weird to me that I hadn't been able to properly express it. Until now.

Gazing at her as I held my daughters close, I said, "I love these girls with all my heart, but you're the best thing in my life. I'd be lost without you." Thinking of the weeks we were apart, I frowned. "I *was* lost without you. Let's never do that again, okay? Sink or swim, we make our fate together."

The smile Anna gave me was so warm, I felt the heat from it all the way to my toes. "I like that plan. Us being together, being a team, it's all I've ever wanted." Walking over to us, she sat down on the bed and put a hand on my chest. "You're my best friend."

Loving those words almost as much as the filthy phrases she'd groaned in my ear last night, I grinned. "You're my best friend too." My smile slipped as I remembered something important that I needed to talk to her about. I sat up on the bed and leaned my back against the wall. Gibson mimicked me while Onnika crawled into my lap. "There's something we should probably talk about…"

Hearing the seriousness in my tone made Anna frown. "What?"

With a sigh, I let it all out. "I'm overdrawn, up to my eyeballs in debt, and now, I'm unemployed. Financially, I'm pretty much fuc…" Glancing at Gibson and Onnika, I changed what I was about to say. "I'm in a corner."

My attempt to consciously not swear around my children made Anna smile. "You mean *we're* in a corner. Teammates, remember?" With a smile, I nodded, but Anna frowned. "What are we going to do?" she asked.

I shrugged. "I don't know. I'm so far behind on payments…I don't know how to catch up, even if I did get another good-paying job, but that seems unlikely, since Dad hooked me up with that last one. I'll have to start at the bottom…"

Anna nodded; her face was a mixture of annoyance and resignation. There were long-term consequences to my actions that we were all going to have to deal with. When the moment of silence stretched long enough, Gibson filled up the quiet with tales about her dolls' lives. After listening to her daughter for a while, Anna sighed. "Well, Griff, I only see one solution. You're not going to like it, but I don't see another way."

Having a tiny idea what she was going to say made me cringe. I wanted to argue before she even said it, but instead I made myself ask, "What's your idea?"

"We go to the guys and beg for a loan." An inadvertent groan escaped me. Yep. There wasn't one word in that sentence I liked, and there were several I hated—like "beg." Maybe expecting an argument from me, Anna raised a finger in the air. When I didn't say anything, she added, "And I think it's only right if we pay them back double what we borrow."

I knew she in part wanted to repay them that much to teach me a lesson, so I shut my mouth and nodded. She was right anyway. I'd feel a lot better borrowing from the band if they made a profit from it. Of course, it was going to take me six hundred years to pay them back. "Okay. I'll ask them today. Liam asked me to come listen to their first real rehearsal. Moral support." I shrugged and acted like it didn't bother me, but it did. Watching Liam take over my spot was going to suck on so many levels, but he was my brother, and he'd asked me to be there, and I couldn't say no to him.

Nodding, Anna cupped my face in sympathy. She knew I was hurting, but she also knew I'd get through this. Not being in a band anymore wasn't going to kill me. Los Angeles had taught me that. I was tougher than I thought, and with Anna by my side, there wasn't anything I couldn't do.

The guys were meeting in the late afternoon. Anna had the day off, so she and the girls went with me. We drove Anna's car, a clunky ancient Ford Escort hatchback that a coworker had sold to her for nine hundred dollars. We used to spend that much on coffee in a month, but now Anna had to make payments to her friend to swing it. I wasn't sure which reality felt more surreal to me, the one I used to have or the one I had now.

Being back in Washington was so refreshing that I actually enjoyed the drive to Kellan's place. The seasons were changing, and it was cold, wet, windy, and gloomy, but I loved it. Even though I'd spent most of my life in California, Washington felt like home. I supposed that was because of the people though. Anna and the guys…they made the place feel complete.

When we arrived at Kellan's gate, I lowered the window and pressed the call button. Kellan had a camera on the gate, so he knew it was me when he answered. "Hey, Griff. How's it going, man? What brings you to my neck of the woods?"

It was only then that I realized I probably should have cleared my arrival with the rest of the guys before just showing up. "Oh, uh, Liam asked me to be here today. That okay?"

Kellan's tinny voice laughed. Me asking permission for anything was not something he was used to. "Of course. You're always welcome here, Griffin."

Even as he said it, the gate started swinging open. I only told him, "Thank you," but in my head I doubted his words. I was positive that there had been quite a bit of time right after I'd abandoned the guys where they wouldn't have let me anywhere near them, let alone inside their houses.

When I got to the parking lot at the base of the hill Kellan's house sat on, I started laughing. Kellan had done something about my many complaints about the number of steps that led up to his front door. There was a ski lift gondola resting on a track next to the countless steps. Eager to try it out, I grabbed Onnika while Anna let Gibson out of the car. The four of us easily fit inside the gondola. Gibson spotted the up button and pressed it before I could get to it. Something clicked on the machine, and it slowly started rising. "Now this is more like it," I said to Anna, as I relaxed back on the railing and let the car do all the heavy lifting.

The car stopped in a space cut out of the front porch, so we didn't even have to walk up the porch steps. Kellan was waiting near the front door with an amused expression on his face. I gave him my seal of approval. "That's freaking awesome, man. Good job."

He laughed as he clapped my back. "I thought you'd appreciate that."

I laughed, then told him, "I want to take the buggy back down though."

Gibson heard me and her hand shot into the air. "Me too, me too!"

Kellan grinned at her, then tilted his head inside the house. "Come on, the guys are waiting."

My heart started hammering as we walked through Kellan's place. I needed to ask the guys a huge favor, but I didn't feel like I deserved for them to say yes. I mean, I'd bailed on them, why should they do anything for me? But I'd tried to make amends by helping make their show to replace me a national sensation, although I'd done that more for me than for them, so again, I didn't really deserve their help.

When we walked into the living room, Anna asked Kellan where Kiera and Ryder were. "The girls and I will hang out with them so you boys have time to do your thing."

Kellan gave her a smooth grin. "It's okay. They're actually in the rehearsal room."

That surprised me some, but then I figured they were just having a welcome-to-the-family party for Liam. I bit back the sudden pain of loss and focused on the task at hand. *Be there for Liam, ask the guys for help, then go about getting a job.* That was my to-do list today.

Walking out of the living room, we headed out back to where the rehearsal room was on the other side of the pool. When we got there, I saw about three dozen balloons in bright colors on either side of the doors. Gibson made a beeline for them, and Onnika struggled to get down. I kept a firm hold on her though. Over the door was a banner proclaiming *Congratulations!*, and the door itself was covered in multicolored streamers.

Glancing over at Kellan, I nonchalantly said, "Abby is here, isn't she?" Denny's wife had a thing for celebrations, no matter if they were big or small.

With a laugh, Kellan nodded. "Yeah, Denny too."

Great. So getting on my knees and begging for some financial scraps was going to be even more humiliating. I supposed that was appropriate though.

It took some effort, but we finally got Gibson and Onnika into the rehearsal room. Gibson was mad about leaving the balloons outside, until she noticed that there were dozens more inside. I set Onnika down, then watched in awe as Gibson handed her a squishy balloon from the floor. It had taken a while, but Gibson was finally letting her sister in.

Looking around, I saw more streamers, more balloons, confetti over everything, including the instruments, and a gigantic cake in the shape of a guitar resting on a table placed where Kellan usually stood for practice. Damn. Guess rehearsal was going to have to wait until later.

Denny and Abby were talking with Kiera, Rachel, and Jenny. Kiera was in the last stage of her pregnancy, and she was huge. Not that I would tell her that. She was sitting in a folding chair, but she waved when she saw us. Ryder was running a toy truck through the confetti next to Kiera, and Gibson immediately joined him. She stole his truck, but then she gave it to Onnika, so I didn't scold her for it. It was sort of Robin Hoodish of her—stealing from the rich to give to the poor.

Liam was talking to Matt and Evan, so I headed their way. Liam was staying here at Chateau Kyle for the time being, since Kellan had a much bigger place than me, and it made meeting for rehearsals more convenient for Liam, who didn't have a car yet. Spotting me as I approached, Liam stopped his conversation. He pulled me into a hug when I got close enough. "Isn't this amazing?" he asked when we broke apart. "Abby did it as a surprise. I totally thought we were starting today." He frowned. "Maybe I should have called you and had you come in tomorrow..." He looked really guilty, like he'd suddenly just realized this might be awkward for me.

I clapped him on the shoulder. "Don't worry about it, bro. I'm glad to be here, you deserve this." Liam wrapped his arm around my shoulders, and I couldn't help but smile at the joy on his face. He'd finally gotten the dream job he'd always wanted, and even though it was *my* dream job, I was happy for him.

"You're just in time for the toast," Kellan told me, indicating a tray of glasses and a bottle of champagne. Oddly enough, there was a glass for me and Anna. Even though he'd acted surprised, Liam must have told Kellan we were coming.

Evan popped the cork, luckily without hitting anyone, and then began pouring the champagne into glasses. Matt started handing them out, and I thanked him when he gave me mine. With a warm smile, he nodded. While everyone crowded around Liam, I raised my glass to toast my brother. "To the newest D-Bag. May the music be mighty, may the women be plenty."

Liam's cheeks flushed with color, which made me laugh. Liam and I were a lot alike in some ways, but in others, we were completely different. "Cheers," the guys said clinking glasses with me, and then with Liam.

Anna clinked glasses with everyone, but like Kiera, she set the glass down without drinking from it. That seemed to clue Kiera in that something was up with her sister. "Oh my gosh, are you pregnant, Anna?"

Anna laughed, then shrugged. "Guess the guys didn't tell you, huh? Yeah, I'm knocked up again."

Kiera glanced at Kellan, then smacked him in the thigh. Kellan laughed. "I didn't want to spoil the surprise. We thought Anna should tell you. Besides, the way Griffin announced it...we weren't really sure what she was." He laughed again and I laughed with him.

Over her annoyance, Kiera squealed, along with Jenny and Rachel, and then all three wrapped Anna in a massive hug. When they were done, Denny and Abby took turns squeezing my wife. When Abby hugged her, she exclaimed, "I wish they'd told me, I would have added some rattles and pastel balloons to the mix."

While Anna was attacked by even more people, and my back was pounded in congratulations, I figured it was as good a time as any to make my request. Turning to Matt, Evan, and Kellan, I cleared my throat. "Hey, I know it's not really appropriate of me, and I'm probably going to open up a wound by doing this, but...I have a favor to ask." I sighed, then polished off the champagne in my glass.

Matt and Evan exchanged a glance with Kellan, then Matt asked, "What favor?" He peered over my shoulder at Liam, like he was positive I was going to ask for them to kick him out and let me in. I wasn't though. Liam had won. He'd earned the right to play with them, and I respected that.

Tuning out the silence that suddenly blanketed the room as everyone stopped to listen, I focused all of my energy on my former bandmates. "Well, Anna and I are expecting, as you know...and I'm going to start looking for work, but in the meantime...I've got a really big monkey on my back. I sort of overextended our credit, and I'm so far in the hole, I can't see the sky anymore." I put my hands up to stop the objections I felt coming. "I'm not asking for a handout, but I'd appreciate a loan. I'll make payments, I'll pay you double what I need to borrow. Triple, if necessary. I just...I want to start over."

From the heat on my face, I could tell my cheeks were redder than Liam's. Asking for help like this, in front of everyone I'd wronged, was really hard. I wanted to crawl inside a deep, dark hole, or hang my head in shame, or chop off my nuts and hand them to the band. But I didn't. I stood there and took the embarrassment with as much grace as I could muster. I'd done this. I'd fucked up everything. So I was the only one who could repair the damage.

The three guys looked at each other but didn't speak. Liam put a hand on my back and his eyes drifted to the floor. I was sure he wanted to help, but he hadn't made any money yet. That wouldn't come until after the album was finished.

It was so silent, all I could hear was Onnika making truck noises and Ryder asking her for a turn while Gibson told him, "Not yet." Matt was the first adult to break the stillness. "How much do you need?" he asked.

Crossing my fingers, I told him, "Sixty grand...to start." Thanks to interest and penalties, my debt was increasing daily.

Evan sighed while Kellan frowned. Matt shook his head, then looked over at the guys. He sighed when he returned his eyes to me. "Look, Griff, we'd love to give you the money, but...this is really a bill you should pay on your own."

I swallowed, then studied my shoes. Disappointment flooded over me so fast, it made my eyes sting. I really thought they'd help me. Kellan's hand touched my shoulder and I looked up at him. "You should be able to do that easily enough once the album releases though. Can you stick it out for a couple more months?"

I furrowed my eyebrows, not understanding. "Why would you give me a cut of the new album?"

Evan glanced at Matt and Kellan, then smiled. "Because you deserve compensation for the work you put into it."

"But... I'm not putting any work into it, so why...?" I still had no idea what they were talking about. Matt laughed at my confused expression.

"Griff, this party is for you. You worked so hard to win that contest. But you were humble, and you helped everyone else along the way. We've seen all the behind-the-scenes footage, and... you shocked us, cuz. Shocked us and impressed us, and we want you to come back." He put his hand on my shoulder. "We want you to come home."

I heard Anna gasp, then sniffle. *They want me back?* My confusion shifted to surprise, then excitement, then concern... then anger. "No, you can't do that." Everyone seemed shocked by my statement. I looked over to my brother as I clarified. "Liam won fair and square. You can't kick him out like that."

Liam's face was ghostly white as he looked around the room in horror. I felt so bad for him, and as much as I wanted what they were offering, I couldn't steal Liam's dream from him. No, I *wouldn't* steal his dream. I'd rather walk away. Again.

Matt shook his head. "That's not what we're saying." Shifting his gaze to Liam, he clapped his arm. "You won because you're crazy talented and the fans love you. You're in." His gaze shifted back to me. "But you proved you've always belonged with the D-Bags and you always will belong with us, so you're in too. The D-Bags are expanding to five members." His eyes shifted between Liam and me as a slow smile spread across his mouth.

It took me damn near thirty seconds to understand what he was saying. Needless to say, Liam figured it out first. "We're both in? We both get to stay?" When Matt nodded, Liam snapped his gaze to me. "We're both D-Bags, bro!"

I was so stunned, all I could think to say was, "Well, yeah, I could have told you that."

Anna ran up to me from behind and wrapped her arms around my stomach. She was laughing, crying, and screeching, all at the same time. I was still in shock, but once it finally sunk in, I twisted to hold her. "Anna, I did it! I'm in!" Laughing, Anna nodded. A thought occurred to me and I twisted back to Matt. "Am I bass? Or is Liam?"

Liam stopped jumping up and down once he heard my question. Eyes curious, he twisted to hear Matt's answer. Matt pointed at him. "Liam's on bass." A corner of Matt's lip curled up. "We were thinking about adding a second lead guitar."

Smiling wide, Evan nodded. "And extra vocals."

Already stunned with today's turn of events, I couldn't believe what I was hearing. Second lead? Holy shit! But...vocals? I wasn't sure what he meant by that. "Extra vocals? What's that mean?"

Kellan finished his champagne and set his glass on the tray. "That thing you did with our songs...adding the rap segments... that was seriously amazing. We're thinking about incorporating it into our sound."

Was I dreaming? I had to be...real life didn't map out this perfectly. Just in case I wasn't, I asked for clarification. "You want me to rap? On stage? To D-Bags songs? And play second lead?"

All three guys nodded after every question I asked. I was speechless. I was choked up with emotion. I was humbled and gracious. I was ecstatic. I was...relieved. Finally, when I could manage a few words, I spat out, "Thank you." Even though it was nowhere near enough, it was the only thing I could think to say.

Kellan clasped me in a hug, and then Evan and Matt. Then Liam, Jenny, and even Rachel. I felt numb as I patted each of them on the back. I'd gone so high then I'd sunk so low...I'd never expected to wind up with everything I'd always wanted. But the way I'd gotten it felt cleaner than how I'd attempted to go about getting it before. Back then, I'd been a selfish, spoiled brat who'd basically demanded a bunch of crap I hadn't earned, then I'd thrown a tantrum when I hadn't gotten it. But now, well, I wasn't sure I deserved it, but it was being offered to me, and I was graciously going to accept it.

I was handed back to my wife after all the well-wishers had given me their congratulations. I clamped on to her like she was fresh air and I couldn't breathe. "Can you believe this, Anna? We're gonna be okay."

She ran her fingers through my hair while she held me. It calmed me. "I knew we would be, baby. I always knew we would be." I didn't see how she could have possibly held on to that belief during all of this, but I didn't call her on it. Pulling back, Anna stared deep into my eyes. I could have gotten lost in the brilliant jade of hers. "I told you you could do it, Griff. I told you they'd recognize your talent, that they'd give you your chance. You just had to be patient."

I let out a steadying exhale. She'd been right all along. "Have I told you how amazing you are today? How lucky I am to have you in my life?"

Biting her lip, she nodded. "Yes, once this morning and once on the way here."

"Good," I said with a smile. "I don't want you to ever forget how much you mean to me."

Anna was silent as we locked gazes with each other, then she leaned down to kiss me. Just as our lips met, I felt a tug on my pant leg. Looking down, I saw Gibson standing with Onnika. While Onnika seemed happy as a clam with a balloon in each hand, Gibson looked confused. "What's the party for, Daddy?" Her expression brightened. "My birthday?"

Since her birthday was still a ways off, I shook my head. "No. This is for Uncle Liam's new job...and mine." I squatted down to her level. "Daddy's getting his old job back. I'm going to be in a band again. Tour the world with Uncle Liam, Uncle Matt, Uncle Evan, and Uncle Kellan. That cool with you?"

Gibson's lips pressed into a look of concentration, until finally, she nodded. "Yes. That's okay. Can Onnie and I come too?" She looked between Anna and me with hope in her eyes.

I glanced up at Anna before returning my eyes to Gibson. "We'll see, honey. It depends on how Mommy feels. She's going to have another baby soon. Did you know that?"

Gibson's face fell. "*Another* baby? But you just had one." Her voice was both whiny and incredulous. I laughed at her statement. Onnika wasn't exactly a baby anymore.

Anna smiled as she looked down at us. "Well, there's another one coming, so you better start preparing yourself."

Gibson groaned as she sat down on the confetti-strewn floor. "Goddammit," she muttered.

I brought my fingers to her chin and made her look up at me. "You're too young to talk like that. I don't want to hear any more swearing from you, understand?"

She pursed her lips in annoyance, but she nodded. Anna beamed at me, and I suddenly realized just how much the swearing had bugged her. I made a mental note to try to hold my tongue around little ears more often. Whatever I could do to make Anna happy. She deserved that…and so much more.

Epilogue

Awesome Returns

The first thing the guys and I did was decide the best way to incorporate the new sound. Matt and Evan wanted to focus on new material, but Kellan and I wanted to remix a couple of the most popular D-Bags songs. Liam's vote ended up being the deciding factor, which instantly made me appreciate having an odd number of members; no more stalemates.

Once we decided on the music, we started practicing it. We met every day, and for once, I didn't mind. In fact, I would have met twice a day if the guys had asked me to. I was ecstatic for the new album to be out—people were going to flip when they heard it! Plus, the sooner we released it, the sooner I could pay off my debt. Then maybe Anna and I could eat something other than macaroni and cheese or Top Ramen for dinner. I was rapidly getting sick of pasta.

Maybe seeing that I was starting to lose weight, since I generally only ate once a day, Kellan approached me one afternoon when we were done rehearsing for the day. "Can I talk to you for a minute?"

"Sure," I said, carefully setting my new guitar on its stand. "Is this about Bella's gift? 'Cause I know I said I'd get her something when she was born, and I will, it's just things are a little tight right now. We spent the last of Anna's paycheck on Gibson's birthday... but we are so thrilled for you and Kiera." I elbowed him in the ribs. "Little girls are awesome. You're gonna love it."

Kellan gave me one of those smiles that only new dads could create. It was a mixture of pride and exhaustion. Kiera had given birth to their daughter last week, and the entire house was still adjusting to the new addition, but it was a happy adjustment.

Kellan shook his head and clapped my arm. "No, no, don't even worry about that. Kiera and I don't care if you get her anything, and honestly, Bella has more stuff than five newborns need." He pursed his lips as I laughed.

"Get used to it. From my experience, girls accumulate a lot of shit."

He smiled, then looked around to see if we were alone. "I know things are tight, and I want to help."

I immediately rejected his offer. "No. Things are the way they are because I was an idiot. I don't need a bailout for my own stupidity." Not anymore, not since hope was on the horizon. I just had to suck it up a little longer.

Kellan didn't back down. "You made amends, you deserve a fresh start." I could tell by the look in his eye and the way that he was studying my ragged appearance that there was going to be money in my account tomorrow, whether I asked for it or not.

As guilty as I felt about Kellan spending his money on me, I was touched by his offer, and I felt a bond being strengthened. A brotherly bond as tight as family. Putting my hand on his shoulder, I sucked up my pride and told him, "Thank you, it's been…hard. I'll pay you back, of course. Double, triple, you name it."

Kellan's smile was soft when I pulled my hand away. "You only need to pay me back what you borrowed, Griffin. Family doesn't charge interest."

I felt like I could breathe freely after that. Sure, even with that monkey off my back, things were still tight living on just one income, but it felt good to know we were making it. And it felt even better to know there was a light at the end of the tunnel. The fact that our lives would change when the album released helped tremendously. Although I didn't mind our modest life. Quite the opposite. I loved every minute of it.

The album was releasing in April. There was a lot of hype behind it, thanks to the show, and to the announcement that the band had made early on—that the four original members were re-uniting, but Liam was still in. We were expanding, in every way possible. That had everyone talking about us, and about the new album. It was quite easily the most anticipated album of the year. And because it was so different from the rest of our stuff, I was a nervous wreck. Oddly, I was the only one who was nervous.

Matt, Evan, and Kellan were as calm as could be. Liam was just giddy. He wanted to start playing live. He wanted to go on tour. He wanted his rock star life to start. And about four weeks before the album dropped, he got his wish. The five of us headed out on a massive promotional tour.

The first stop of the tour was back in L.A. Mom and Dad came down to the radio station with Matt's parents to listen to their kids perform. Because I thought it would be fun for them to see behind the scenes of the radio station, I got them passes to join us inside the conference room where we were playing.

I texted Anna for support a few minutes before we played the first single off the new album. Anna had stayed in Seattle with the girls. Promotional tours were even more chaotic than regular tours, and with her about to pop in a couple of months, I felt it was best for her to stay home. Anna was fine with it, she had a job that she loved to keep her busy. Gibson was pissed though. I'd never seen a true tantrum from her until the day I'd told her she couldn't go on tour with me. Needless to say, I'd given my word that she could come on the regular tour with us when it started this summer.

Anna texted me back the encouragement I'd needed to hear, and just seeing her words made me feel calmer. *You have nothing to worry about. The song kicks ass! It's the best song the band has ever done…and it's all because of you.* I wasn't sure about that last part, but it felt good to hear it.

Before we played the new single, the DJs asked us some questions. Surprisingly, most of them were directed at me. "So, why did you leave the band and what made you return?"

It seemed like that should be an easy question, but it really wasn't. There were so many factors. I decided to simplify it though.

"I left because I was an effing idiot. I came back because I... well, I think I grew up."

The DJs laughed while Matt nodded like he agreed with me. Then one of the DJs said, "You technically didn't win the right to join the band. How did it feel to lose to your brother?"

Again, a complicated question. Again, I answered as simply as possible. "I'd never expected to win, and my brother kicked ass during the competition, so I had no regrets over him winning. He earned it."

Liam grinned at me and I fist-bumped him. The DJs shifted their questions to the guys after that. "What made you guys decide to take him back and expand the band?"

Matt, Evan, and Kellan all looked at each other, then Kellan pointed at Matt. "Go ahead. You take this one."

Matt looked down, then up at me. "We saw Griffin's growth and his potential." He smiled at me, then shifted his eyes to the DJs. "We could have gone on without him, but it would have felt incomplete." Smirking, he added, "The D-Bags just aren't the same without their biggest D."

The DJs laughed again, then we set up to play our new song. I was so nervous, I was shaking. But as soon as the intro started, the familiarity of playing hit me and all my nerves evaporated. It was just like we were back at rehearsal—no pressure, no one but us listening, nothing but good times and good music.

Our new song was extra special to me; I'd helped Kellan write it. We'd been talking one night about everything I'd gone through, all the ups and downs, and he'd said my story, my struggles, would make an awesome song. It was about having it all, then losing it, and trying to work your way back. It was probably the first D-Bags song that actually meant something to me... plus, I got to rap in it, which was freaking awesome.

Evan and Liam started us off with a mellow intro, then Kellan came in real quiet. But just one line. After that, I started my rhythmic rap. The DJs clearly weren't expecting that, and seeing that I'd caught them off guard almost made me smile. I would have, if I wasn't concentrating so hard. This beginning part was all me;

in essence, Kellan was just singing backup. As the song started building to the first chorus, I swear I could feel the entire world listening. It was intense. Kellan killed it on the chorus, and all of us played full bore. Then it quieted down to another mellower rapping section, where I poured out my heart, my fear, and my sins. It was odd to be singing about something so personal, but it made me feel cleansed too, and I suddenly began to wonder if all the songs the D-Bags sang were personal for someone in the band. Probably.

After the second chorus, the instruments mellowed again, but instead of me rapping, Kellan came in with a smooth solo. Listening to him made me appreciate his talent. He really was incredibly fucking good at this. The instruments kicked in again and Kellan took his voice up a notch—it gave me goose bumps. We rode out the song on a high note, and when it was over, all I wanted to do was play it again.

Everyone in the room clapped when we were done, and Mom even wiped some tears from her eyes. The texts and messages the station received were all positive, but I really wasn't sure what the fans thought of the song until we stepped outside. The crowd had been listening to the radio station's outdoor speakers, and the screams and cheers they let out when they saw us was damn near deafening. I immediately texted Anna. *They loved it!*

Her response was instant. *Of course they did! I'm so proud of you, baby.* She included a kissy face after that, and I suddenly wished I was home with her and the girls. All of this meant nothing without them.

We went back home after the promotional tour ended. The tour was a mammoth success, and the album debuted at number one. I was excited that the fans were eager for our new bigger and better sound, but I was even happier to be home in Anna's arms again.

Denny and Abby threw a private party for the band at Pete's the following week. It was a huge event, and anyone who had ever supported the band was there—Holeshot, Avoiding Redemption, Poetic Bliss, my family, Matt's family, Evan's family, and even Kellan's family. Plus all of our friends and all the current and former staff of Pete's were there.

It was a party for the record books, and even though it felt good to have my banishment lifted from my favorite bar, I spent most of the night attached to Anna's side, rubbing her lower back. Just as she murmured that she was ready for me to start rubbing other parts of her body, Denny approached us. Smiling wide, he extended his hand to me. "Congratulations, Griffin. The album is well on its way to being the best D-Bags album yet. The reviews everywhere have been outstanding. Fans and critics agree, which is rare. And they're all saying the same thing: You're amazing."

I shook his hand, but his compliment made me uncomfortable. "It's a group effort. I'm only one part, a small part really."

Denny blinked at me, then laughed. "It still blows me away that you're capable of being modest."

Crooking a smile, I shrugged. If there was one thing I'd learned through all of this, it was that I couldn't do it on my own. My success depended on others, and vice versa. We were a team, and I was learning how to be a helpful, supportive member of that team. I wasn't perfect, and I still had the occasional slipup, but I was getting better.

Anna wrapped an arm around me, squeezing me tight. "He's capable of many things." From the suggestive way she wriggled her eyebrows, it was obvious just what she meant by that. I laughed as I squeezed her tight. Gotta love my horny girl.

My family approached me after Denny went off to dance with Abby. Liam was beside himself. "Number one...the album is number one!"

With a nod, I told him, "I know. I got the call too."

Awe on his face, he shook his head. "It's the top-selling album...in the world."

"Yeah...that's what number one means."

Turning from me, he faced Mom and Dad. "The album is number one..."

I shook my head as he got into a conversation with them about it. Liam just couldn't wrap his mind around the sudden success. Well, sudden to him. His reaction reminded me of when the D-Bags first hit it big with Sienna Sexton. I'd probably reacted the same way. No...I'd probably acted like I'd expected nothing less, but inside I'd been freaking out.

Chelsey and Dustin were dancing the night away in the center of the bar, and it was surprisingly good to see my sister dancing again. I hoped Dustin took her out as often as he could, and knowing him and his character, I was sure he did. When their song was over, Chelsey twirled my way. "Hey, little brother, care to dance with your big sister?"

With a huge grin, I told her, "Sure."

Even though it was a slow song, I spun her around and dipped her like a madman. She adjusted to everything I did though. Chelsey was a natural on her feet. Around halfway through the song, I stopped goofing off and danced with her normally. Arms around my neck, she gave me a grin full of sisterly pride. "I'm so happy for you, Griffin. And I knew you could do it."

My eyes shifted to the ground before returning to her face. "You knew I could impress the guys enough that they'd take me back?"

Chelsey shook her head. "The band was never the steak, Griffin." She pointedly looked over my shoulder and I followed her gaze. Anna was talking with Dustin; she shot me a wave when she noticed us staring at her.

I was nodding when I shifted back to Chelsey. "Yeah, you're right. You're always right. It's fucking annoying." Chelsey laughed and I joined in. It felt so good to be on the other side of our grief.

When Anna and I took the girls back to our tiny apartment at the end of the night, I felt complete. Nothing in my life could get any better.

But I was wrong.

Three weeks later, my wife gave birth to our newest child, and my life became even more perfect. We'd wanted the sex to be a surprise, and I was definitely surprised. I'd fully expected to be adding another girl to the family, but instead, my wife gave me a boy. A beautiful boy, with the palest blond hair and eyes that already had a hint of green to them.

As I held him in my arms, I asked Anna, "You still want that name we decided on?"

With a tired smile, she nodded, "It seems only fitting, since he was conceived on a stage. I like it spelled with an *E* though...so it's a little different than the band he's named after."

I thought that was a great idea, so when the guys and my family came in to meet him, I proudly introduced them to the newest Hancock. "Everybody, I want you to meet my son...Linken. Linken, I want you to meet...everybody."

It was hard to give him up to pass him around, and I almost felt more protective of him than my girls. Maybe that was because he was so tiny, and they were getting so big. I think I even told Kellan to watch his head, which was ridiculous, considering he'd just gone through the newborn stage with Bella. What could I say, I was an anxious dad. Besides my wife, nothing meant more to me than my kids.

Matt looked nervous when it was his turn to hold Linken. The look in his eye made me not want to hand my son over. Matt had butterfingers written all over him. "Dude, you don't have to take a turn if you don't want to...if you're scared."

Matt twisted his lips at me. "I'm not scared of a baby. I'm more scared of the fact that you've replicated yourself. There are two Griffins in the world now. I'm not sure the world is ready." He slowly shook his head, like he was already seeing the upcoming apocalypse. Or should I say, Griffinocalypse.

Tossing on a smile, I told him, "Are you kidding me? The world has been waiting for my mini me for a long ass time. And Link is only the first of many. I plan on putting several mini cocks on this planet." As many as my wife would let me.

Matt shook his head again. "And so it begins..."

Frowning, I turned to Evan and Jenny. "He just lost his turn. Which one of you wants him?"

I extended Linken in their general direction, and Jenny immediately scooped him up. "Oh my God! He's so cute! Evan, look how sweet he is."

She cooed in Linken's face while Evan smiled at her. "Yeah, for being part Hancock, he *is* pretty adorable."

Liam, Matt, and I reacted at the exact same time with "Hey!"

Shaking my head, I added, "Not cool, dude. Hancocks are awe-some." Liam, Matt, and I bumped fists together in a show of family unity. While the band's Hancock to non-Hancock ratio had been fifty-fifty before, it wasn't anymore; the band was cock-heavy now, as it should be.

"Damn straight," Liam said.

I indicated Jenny cuddling with my son. "Evan just forfeited his turn. Give him to Liam when you're done, Jenny." I patted Liam on the back. "You're next, bro."

Liam's eyes widened, like I'd just told him his nonexistent girl-friend was expecting. Matt laughed while I shook my head. I was surrounded by a bunch of newborn-fearing pansies. Wusses.

When Linken was ready to come home, we took him to our new place. We'd recently moved from Anna's tiny apartment. Now that the cash was flowing again, and we'd paid off the money we'd borrowed from Kellan, we could have bought just about any house we wanted, but we'd decided on a modest four-bedroom rambler in a quiet neighborhood that was close to some good schools. Anna and I wanted to live a simpler life, less opulence, less extravagance. We just wanted to concentrate on us, and on the kids, and we wanted to be smarter with our money. Plan better, just in case it ever did dry up again. And we wanted to give back.

One thing I'd learned throughout this whole mess was that I'd been given a gift that first go-round, and most people weren't so lucky. Listening to the other contestants on that show, watching them struggle to make something of themselves...it had moved me, and I wanted to help them. I wanted to keep the dream alive, give people a reason to keep going, even when the obstacles seemed too high, the odds too big. I wanted to give people hope for their future.

At first, I'd had no idea how to do that. The task seemed too big, the different ways to go about it too vast, the overall idea too vague. But then Anna suggested I focus in on one aspect of my vision, and then, when I had it, that I start out small. Made sense to me, so I decided to start with the youngest dreamers and my favorite occupation. Anna and I were in the beginning stages of creating our charity—Strength Through Sound. Our goal was to enrich, encourage, and empower children through music. Our hope was to expand band and choir in schools, and offer activity centers where kids could go to express themselves in healthy ways. Even I could admit our plan was an ambitious one, but it meant something to me, so I felt like it was worth it. No, I felt like I was *meant* to do it.

Once Kellan heard our plan, he was 100 percent on board. Music had shaped his childhood, same as it had mine. The other guys quickly asked to be a part of it once they heard us talking, and pretty soon, Strength Through Sound was officially being sponsored by the D-Bags. Our first center was opening next year.

I could have happily stayed at home, planning my new charity while holding my new baby and playing with my girls, but the D-Bags had a job to do, and before I knew it, our summer tour was starting. When I asked Anna what she wanted to do, I fully expected her to say she wanted to stay home with Linken. I was shocked when she said she wanted to come with. "Are you sure? I mean, I know we've done it with a newborn before, but we only had one kid at the time."

Anna gave me an unworried smile. "It will be fine. Linken's a dream baby. He's already sleeping through the night. And I'm already on maternity leave with work, so now is really the perfect time for me to go."

Grinning, I gave her a quick kiss. "I'm glad you said that, because I really wasn't looking forward to not seeing you guys for three months." With a sigh, I placed a kiss on Linken's forehead. "I don't want to miss that much time with them. I don't want to miss *any* time with them."

Anna cupped my cheek. "You don't have to. We'll find a way to make this work, just like we do with everything else. And we'll do it together."

I nodded. "'Cause we're a team."

"Exactly." She gave me a deep, lingering kiss then, and we put Linken down for a nap in his room, so we could benefit from one of the many perks of being partners.

Kiera and her kids ended up coming on the tour too, and so did Jenny and Rachel, so there were no shortages of people to help with the kids. And maybe it was my changed attitude, or my new position with the band, or quite possibly my brother's overabundance of excitement, but that tour was by far the best one we'd ever done. We adjusted some of the classic D-Bags songs for me, adding a second line for my guitar, or just having Matt and I play together. There were ramps on the stage set up in an X pattern that let us run up and down, back and forth, burning off adrenaline and engaging the crowd. We even had pyrotechnics for one of our songs. It was fucking amazing, and when the tour finally wrapped up at the end of the summer, I was sad that it was over with.

And then, once the tour was done and the album was a monstrous smash and all the expected babies had been born, the D-Bags had wedding after wedding after wedding after fucking wedding. Okay, it wasn't that many, but it felt like it.

Matt and Rachel started it off by renewing their vows. It seemed unnecessary to me, since they hadn't been married all that long, but after talking to each of them, I got the feeling they were doing it just so Anna and I could see the ceremony. That moved me, and I didn't even give him crap about the fact that his tuxedo had tails. Who the hell wears tails anymore? Jackass. I made a mental note to get him a cane and a monocle for Christmas. I might not tease him on his "special day," but the other 364 were fair game.

Matt and Rachel had the ceremony at the restaurant inside the Space Needle, which was pretty awesome. They bought out the entire place for the night, and after their brief vows—both whispered to each other with bright red, embarrassed cheeks—we spent the night eating, drinking, and watching the city below us slowly revolve into view.

It was a great night, and as I slow danced with Anna, I asked her if she'd like to do something similar. "Do you think we should renew our vows and shit? We never really had a party." No, we'd pretty much taken the leap, then continued on with life: had a baby and finished up the D-Bags tour.

Anna bit her lip while she thought. "I don't really need the ceremony part, but we could have a barbeque to celebrate? Cook some burgers, drink some beer. That would be great!"

I wrapped both arms around her, giving her a tight squeeze. "I fucking love you."

She laughed as she squeezed me back. "I fucking love you too."

While we made plans for our shindig, Evan and Jenny finally took the plunge. They got married at their house—the old auto body shop with the loft on top. They did it a week before Christmas...and they let Abby decorate. Her outlandish design put every Santa's Village to shame; it gave new meaning to the words "Winter Wonderland." Shimmering snowflakes were hanging from the ceiling, fake snow lined every flat space in sight, and bright red roses were mixed with holly and mistletoe to create one-of-a-kind flower arrangements that had everybody kissing. Once the dorkiness of it wore off...I kind of dug it.

Kellan was Evan's best man, while Matt, Liam, and I were his groomsmen. Jenny had Kiera as her maid of honor, with Anna, Rachel, and Kate as her bridesmaids. Matt was spacey the morning of the event, like he was hungover or something. I had to snap my fingers in front of his face three times to get his attention. "Dude, what's up with you? You look like you're gonna hurl."

Matt ran a hand down his face. "I think I might." Face grim, he looked between Evan, Kellan, Liam, and me. "Rachel's pregnant...she just told me before we came out here. I'm gonna have a kid. I'm completely freaking out." His skin paled so much, I was sure he was about to pass out.

Reaching inside my jacket, I handed him a flask of whiskey. He took a long draw off it, not even questioning the fact that I was carrying it. Kellan slapped him on his back once he swallowed. "That's awesome, man! Congratulations!"

"Awesome...?" Matt whispered, taking another swig.

"Yeah," Liam said. "Kids are...cool." His expression was as awkward as his words. Aside from visiting numerous nieces and nephews, he had zero experience with kids. I smacked him across the chest.

"Kids are awesome, and you'll do great, cuz, just don't overthink it." Matt raised his eyebrows and I understood. He over-thought everything. I smiled and shrugged. Kids were a just-go-with-it kind of deal, and I excelled at that. Matt...not so much.

Evan laughed when Matt took another drink. "Don't worry about it, Matt. We'll figure parenting out together."

All of us swung our heads Evan's way. "Jenny's...pregnant?" Kellan asked.

Evan shrugged, like Kellan had asked him if she'd gotten a pedicure. "Yeah, we just found out last night." He didn't look worried at all, but that didn't surprise me. It took a lot to ruffle Evan.

Matt offered him the flask. "Want a swig?"

Grinning, Evan shook his head. "Keep it. I think you need it more than I do."

Matt raised the flask in a toast, then took another drink.

He seemed calmer during the ceremony, but that was probably because he was half-lit. By the reception, he was full-on blitzed and feeling no pain. And he finally seemed to be excited about his upcoming child. From the middle of the dance floor, he shouted above the music, "I'm gonna be a dad!"

Naturally, everyone started cheering. I booed, just to be an ass to Matt. He didn't hear me though, he was too busy sucking Rachel's face. Anna thwacked my chest, then asked me if I knew about Evan and Jenny's good news. "Yeah, he spilled the beans right before the ceremony."

Anna nodded, not surprised. She had her hair pinned up, away from her neck, and all I wanted to do was suck on her exposed skin. And because I could, I did. Anna purred when my tongue brushed against the vein in her neck. Her voice a little throaty, she murmured, "Did Evan happen to mention that twins run in Jenny's family?"

I pulled back to stare at her; her green eyes were lusty and amused. Grinning, I turned to look at Evan and Jenny slow dancing near the center of the room. "Well, that might finally ruffle him." I started laughing, and just because I was having such a damn good day, I couldn't stop.

By the time Anna and I threw our reproclamation celebration

the next May, the results were in—Jenny was preggers with twins. Matt had been damn near constipated while he'd waited to see if he was sharing Evan's fate, but, unfortunately, no, he wasn't. Rachel was only having one. Damn shame if you asked me. I would have given anything to see Matt fumbling with two screaming babies. God…that would have been awesome.

Evan was a little pale at the party, but he always looked that way now. The closer it got to Jenny's birth, the more of a jittery, nervous wreck he became. One of my favorite things to do now was silently sneak up behind him and scare the shit out of him. He always jumped and screamed like a little girl. It never got old.

I gave him a beer to unwind, then I gave him another one. I had a feeling it was best if he two-fisted it all night. Having someone more nervous than him put Matt in a really good mood all night. When we weren't picking on Liam, who'd had his first successful groupie mating on St. Patrick's Day, we were planning our next tour. "We're gonna wrap this one up a little early, you know, because of the babies and stuff." Matt looked over at Evan. "End of August, man. You ready? Got your duplicate car seats, cribs, bassinets, swings, bouncers? All that shit?" Evan cringed, then took a drink from both beer bottles at the same time. Matt chuckled. "At least there's one thing he can handle two of."

With a snort, I mimicked a pair of breasts. "I'm sure there's one more thing he can handle in duplicate." While the guys laughed at my comment, I reached down to grab my junk. "All this talk of boobs and babies is turning me on. I need to go find my wife and spread my seed again."

Kellan grimaced. "I will give you my entire cut from the band next year if you never say 'spread my seed' again."

I flashed him a smile. "Aw, Kell, I don't need your money. And not only am I going to say it again, but I'm including it as a lyric in the next album. No, actually, I'm making it the title of the next album." I raised my eyebrows and Kellan tossed a beer cap at me.

Laughing, I dodged his halfhearted throw and left the guys to go find Anna. She was having an in-depth conversation with Jenny when I approached her. Unlike Evan, Jenny was excited to be having twins. I think she underestimated how much work came with newborns. Or so I'd heard. My kids were nothing but awesome.

Walking up to Anna, I grabbed her elbow. When she looked over at me and smiled, I told her, "Kumquat."

She looked at me blankly for a second, then turned to Jenny. "We need to . . . we'll be back in a minute."

Jenny rolled her eyes. "If you guys are going to pick a code word for sex, you should really pick something a little less obvious."

Giving Jenny a mischievous smile, I said, "Where's the fun in that?"

Anna and I were laughing as we darted away into the night. "Where do you want to go?" she asked me.

I looked up. There was a section of our roof that was secluded from view by a big tree in the front yard. We'd have an awesome view of the stars from up there, and if we were close enough to the peak, we'd also have a view of our guests. That was kind of hot to me. "This way," I told her, pulling her toward the garage.

It took some preparation time as we wrestled the ladder into place, but we eventually had a blanket spread down on the roof shingles. Lying down on it, we began the process of stripping off our clothes. "Thank God all the kids are asleep," she whispered as she stripped her shirt off.

Her breasts were calling me, so I only answered with a grunt. Unsnapping her bra, I took a nipple into my mouth. Fuck. Heaven. She let out a shuddering moan that was loud to me, but no one below us seemed to notice.

Getting all of our clothes off without rolling off the roof was challenging, and I thanked myself for going easy on the beer; I was sure I couldn't do this if I were drunk. Once we were bare, the slight wind giving us both goose bumps, I braced my feet against the shingles. Anna clung to my body as I pressed against her. From my vantage point near the top of the roof, I could see the partygoers chatting and drinking in the backyard. Knowing none of my guests could see me but I could see them made me even harder.

Anna squirmed beneath me as her hands ran up and down my body. "I want you," she breathed.

Looking down at her, my breath caught. She was gorgeous in the moonlight, like a freaking mythical goddess. And she was somehow mine. All mine. "You're amazing," I told her. My fingers came up to run down her cheek. "So amazing…"

As I leaned down to kiss her, I adjusted our bodies so I slipped inside her. We both gasped when we were finally one. No matter how many times I did this with her, how good we felt together shocked me. And it was even better when we started to move. "Oh God, Griffin," she murmured. "Yes…"

I absolutely agreed, and a low groan escaped me as I rested my head against her neck. Nothing on earth felt this good. As our bodies rocked together the euphoria increased. Anna became a constrained wild animal beneath me, gasping, groaning, squirming, and moaning. Every move she made electrified me, drove me even closer to my own release. "You're so fucking hot," I groaned in her ear.

She ran her nails down my back, then she grabbed my hips and begged, "More."

I knew she needed that final drive to push her over the edge. Fuck, I needed it too. I grabbed the very top of the roof and used it as leverage as I shifted the angle, so I was rubbing against her in just the right spot. Anna's eyes rolled back in her head as she gasped. Then she started panting and murmuring, "Yes, right there…don't stop…yes…"

I wasn't about to stop, because I was getting fucking close too. Anna exploded first, and she let out a cry that I was sure somebody would hear. I lifted my gaze to the party, and just as I did, I hit my peak. As the glory of releasing all that built-up tension sent shockwaves of pleasure through me, my eyes drifted over the oblivious crowd. Awe…some.

When my gaze drifted back down to my wife, she was tenderly smiling at me. Cupping my cheek, she told me, "It's always so amazing with you. Every time blows my mind."

Moving to her side, I thanked the slight chill in the air; it cooled off my heated skin. "Every fucking time," I agreed, closing my eyes. It was right about then that I heard an odd sound, like shoes dragging across the dirt.

I opened my eyes just in time to see my pants slip from the peak of the roof. Sitting up, I leaned over the edge and tried to catch them, but I missed. Weighted down by my belt and the massive amount of crap in my pockets, my pants continued tumbling down the side of the roof, landing on the patio, right behind Kellan.

"Hey, Kell," I whispered.

Looking around, Kellan seemed confused about where my voice was coming from. "Griff? Where are you?"

"Behind you, dude. Up here."

Turning, he glanced up at me, peeking over the edge of the roof peak. "What the hell are you doing...? Oh... never mind. Hey, Anna."

Turning over onto her stomach, Anna leaned over the edge and wriggled her fingers at him. "Hey, Kellan."

I pointed to my pants on the ground. "Wanna toss those up here?"

Kellan got a devilish look on his face. "What if I say no?"

Balancing myself on the slanted roof, I shrugged and stood up. "Then I'll just hop down and get them myself."

Kellan shielded his eyes with both hands. He needed both of them too... I was an impressive fucker. "Goddammit, Griff. Okay, hold on." He chucked my pants at me, and leaning out, I caught them.

As I laughed at Kellan turning away from me in disgust, I picked up a foot to put my pants on; knowing I might get lucky later, I'd decided to go commando tonight. Before I could slip them on though, Anna grabbed them from me. "Not so fast. First you need to kiss me and tell me you'll love me forever."

Smiling, I knelt down on the blanket she was lying on. "Mrs. Anna Hancock... you are my best friend, my partner in crime, my reason for living, and the only thing that really matters to me. Forever only scratches the surface of how long I'll love you."

I wanted to stab myself in the throat for how sappy I sounded, but I meant every word, and I wanted Anna to hear them. She teared up as she whispered, "I love you too. So much…I never thought I could love anyone this much."

I leaned down to kiss her. Our lips moved together softly, but the intensity quickly began to build and my body instantly sprang to life. Grabbing my pants out of Anna's hands, I tossed them over the side of the roof again. We didn't need them.

I heard about three people cursing my name, but I ignored them all. Anna was the only thing that mattered to me. She was *always* the only thing that really mattered, and I was never letting her go again.